MCCREERY • GLASS • NESTERENKO

THE LAST WITCH™

Published by

BOOM! BOX™

BOOM! BOX™

THE LAST WITCH, September 2021. Published by BOOM! Box, a division of Boom Entertainment, Inc. The Last Witch is ™ & © 2021 Conor McCreery. Originally published in single magazine form as THE LAST WITCH No. 1-5. ™ & © 2021 Conor McCreery. All rights reserved. BOOM! Box™ and the BOOM! Box logo are trademarks of Boom Entertainment, Inc., registered in various countries and categories. All characters, events, and institutions depicted herein are fictional. Any similarity between any of the names, characters, persons, events, and/or institutions in this publication to actual names, characters, and persons, whether living or dead, events, and/or institutions is unintended and purely coincidental. BOOM! Studios does not read or accept unsolicited submissions of ideas, stories, or artwork.

BOOM! Studios, 5670 Wilshire Boulevard, Suite 400, Los Angeles, CA 90036-5679. Printed in China. First Printing.

ISBN: 978-1-68415-621-4, eISBN: 978-1-64668-033-7

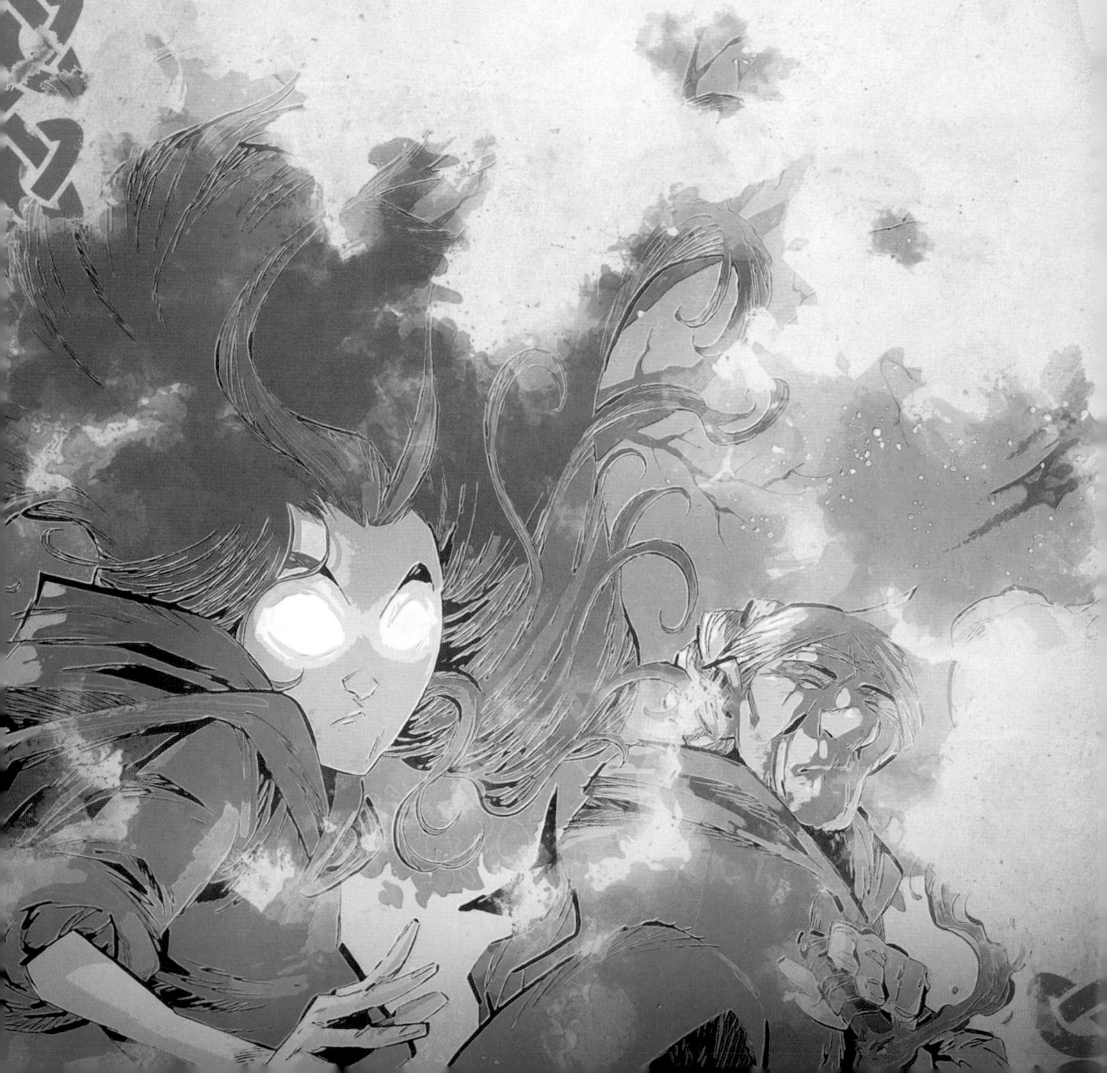

THE LAST WITCH

WRITTEN BY
CONOR McCREERY

ILLUSTRATED BY
V.V. GLASS

COLORED BY
NATALIA NESTERENKO

LETTERED BY
JIM CAMPBELL

COVER BY
V.V. GLASS

LOGO DESIGNER
MARIE KRUPINA

SERIES DESIGNER
GRACE PARK

COLLECTION DESIGNER
CHELSEA ROBERTS

ASSISTANT EDITOR
KENZIE RZONCA

EDITOR
SHANNON WATTERS

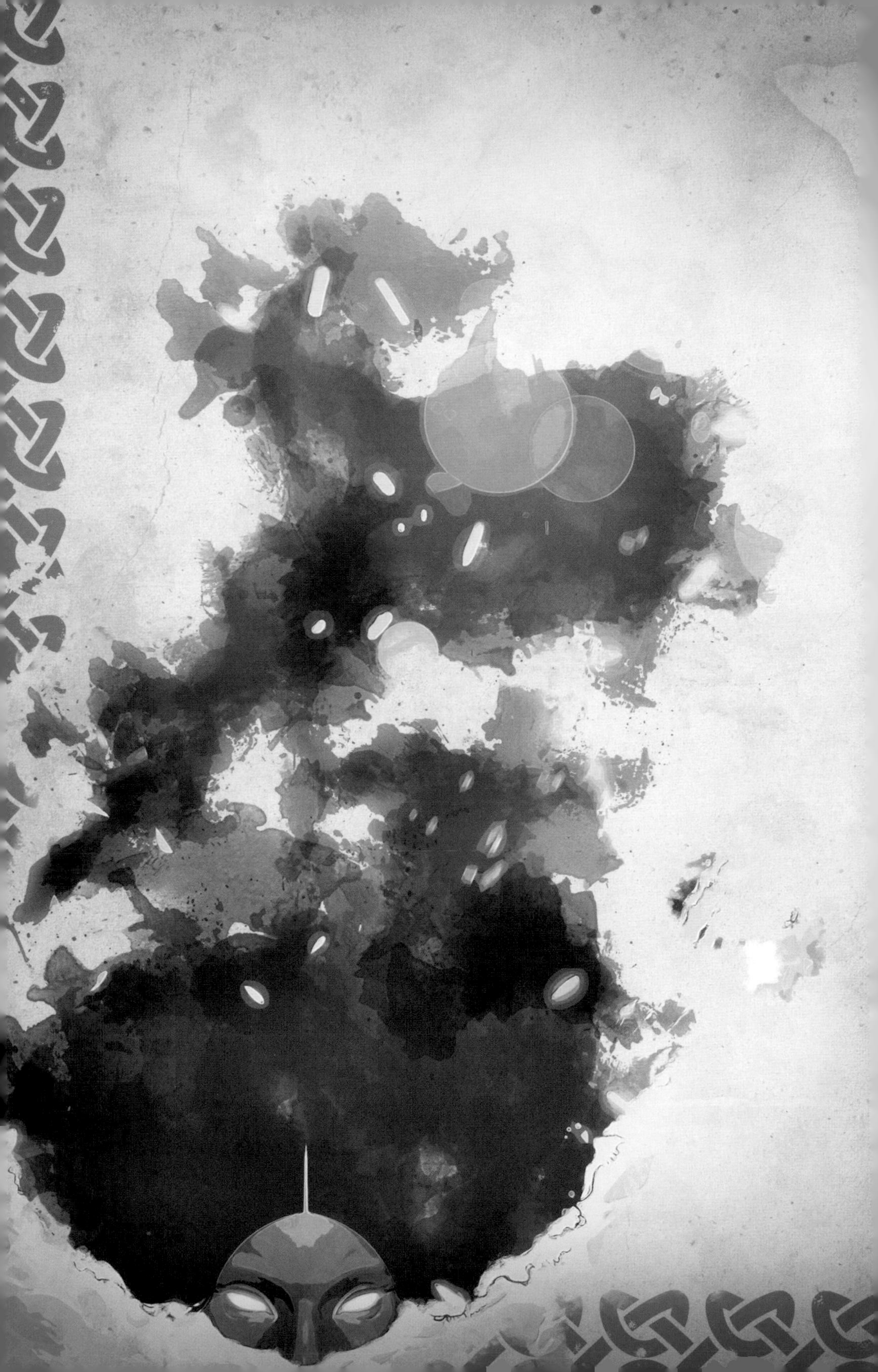

CHAPTER ONE

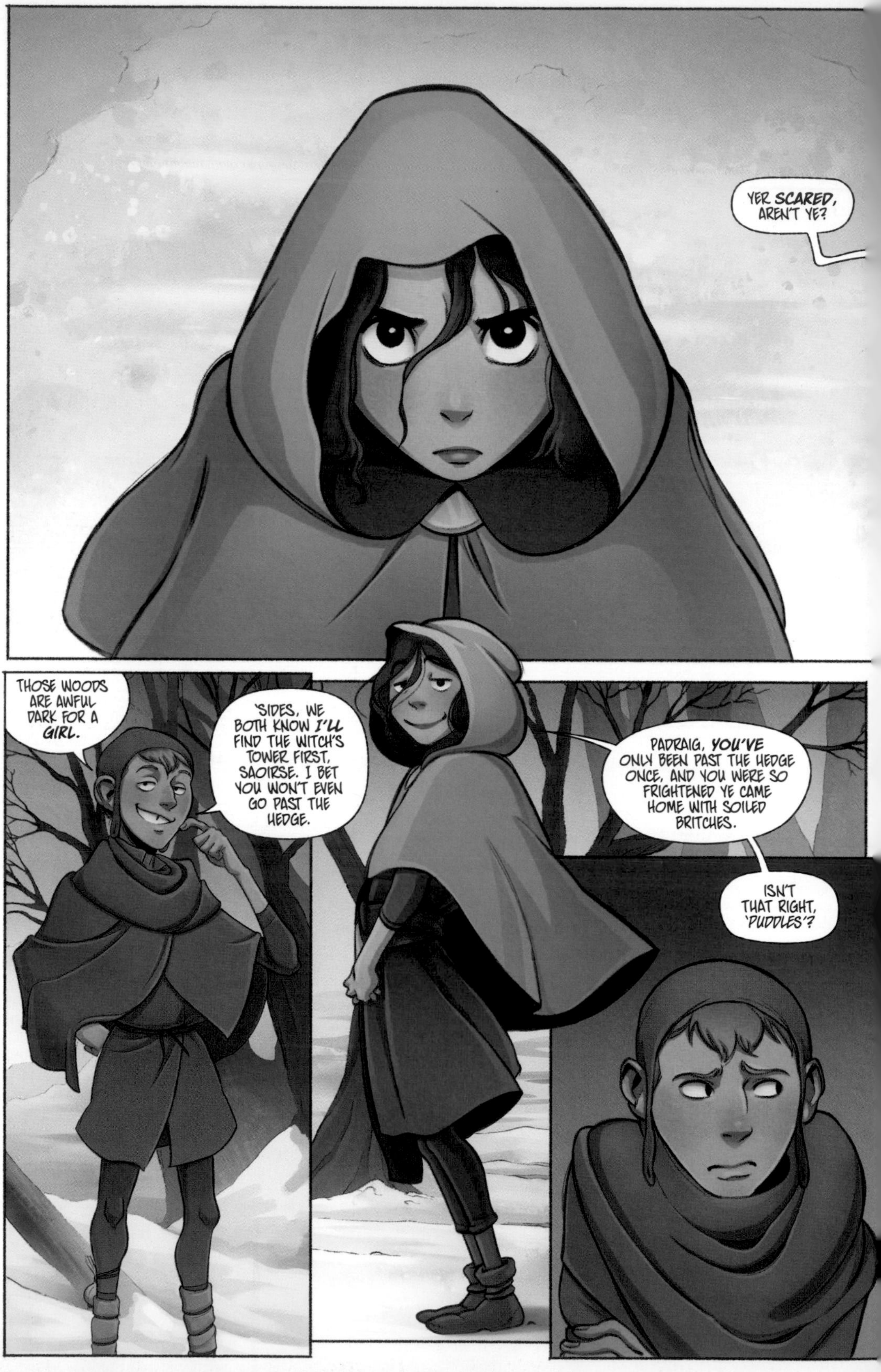
YER SCARED, AREN'T YE?
THOSE WOODS ARE AWFUL DARK FOR A GIRL.
'SIDES, WE BOTH KNOW I'LL FIND THE WITCH'S TOWER FIRST, SAOIRSE. I BET YOU WON'T EVEN GO PAST THE HEDGE.
PADRAIG, YOU'VE ONLY BEEN PAST THE HEDGE ONCE, AND YOU WERE SO FRIGHTENED YE CAME HOME WITH SOILED BRITCHES.
ISN'T THAT RIGHT, 'PUDDLES'?

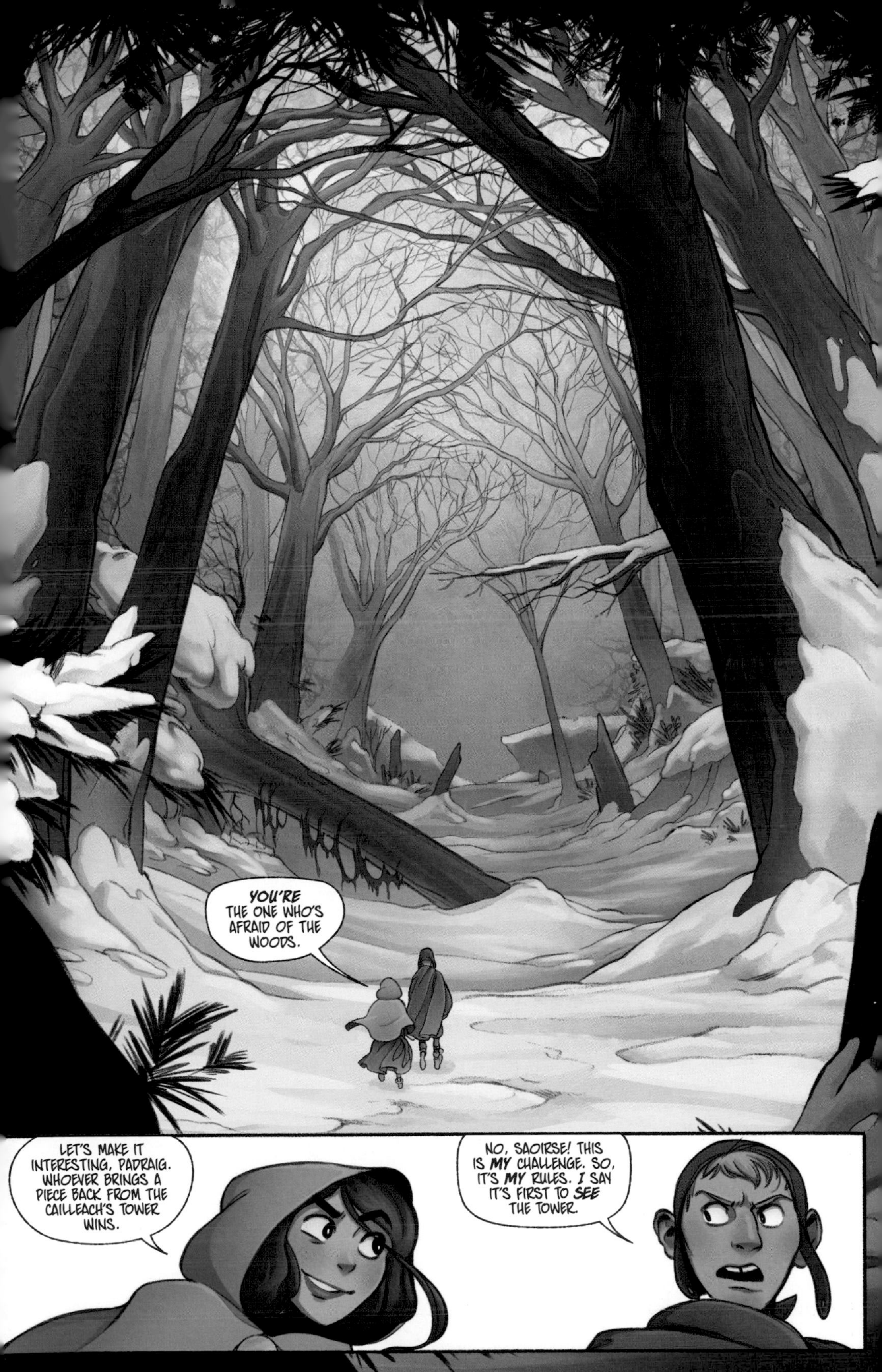
YOU'RE THE ONE WHO'S AFRAID OF THE WOODS.
LET'S MAKE IT INTERESTING, PADRAIG. WHOEVER BRINGS A PIECE BACK FROM THE CAILLEACH'S TOWER WINS.
NO, SAOIRSE! THIS IS *MY* CHALLENGE. SO, IT'S *MY* RULES. *I* SAY IT'S FIRST TO *SEE* THE TOWER.

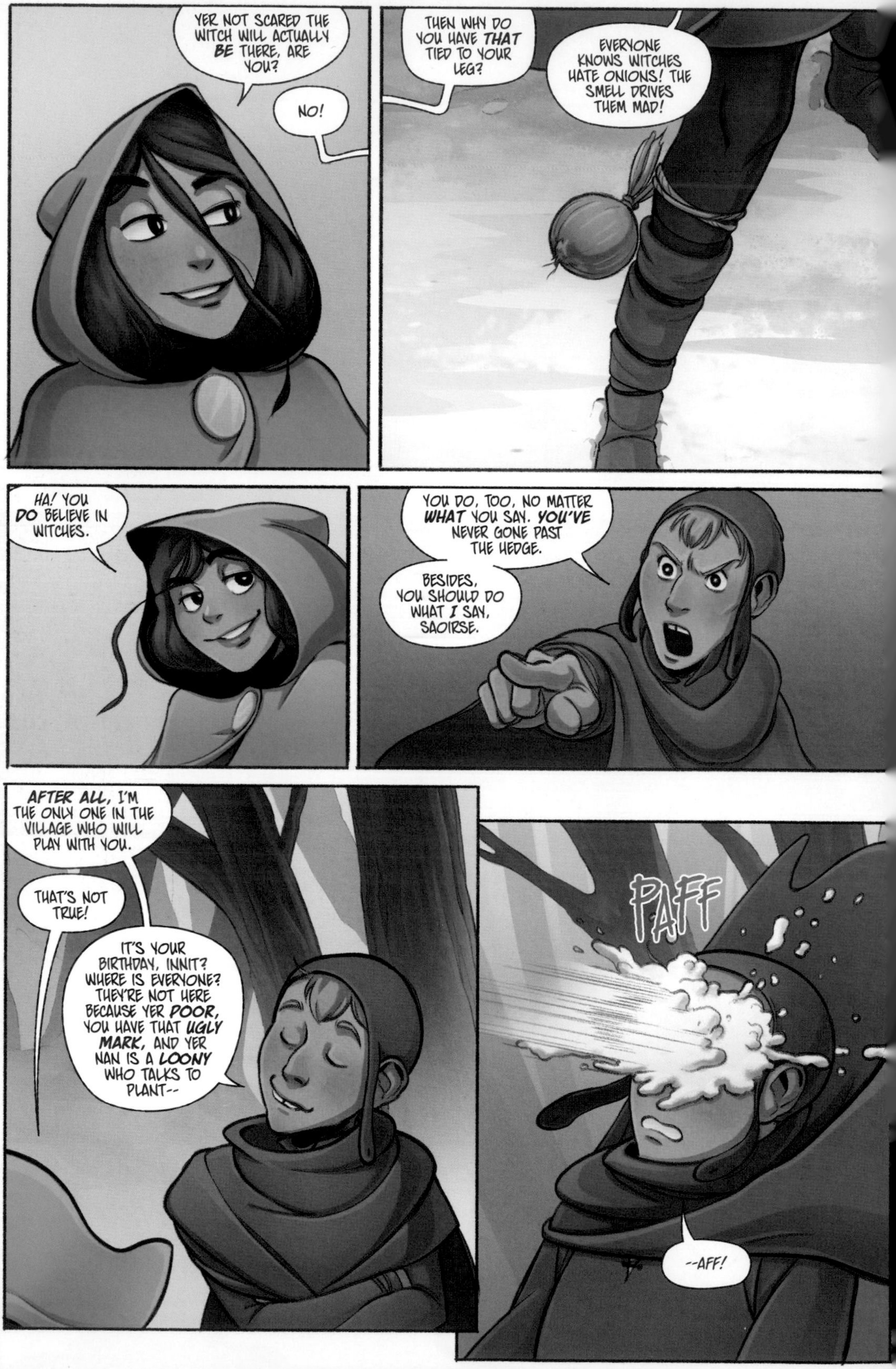
YER NOT SCARED THE WITCH WILL ACTUALLY BE THERE, ARE YOU?
NO!
THEN WHY DO YOU HAVE THAT TIED TO YOUR LEG?
EVERYONE KNOWS WITCHES HATE ONIONS! THE SMELL DRIVES THEM MAD!
HA! YOU DO BELIEVE IN WITCHES.
YOU DO, TOO, NO MATTER WHAT YOU SAY. YOU'VE NEVER GONE PAST THE HEDGE.
BESIDES, YOU SHOULD DO WHAT I SAY, SAOIRSE.
AFTER ALL, I'M THE ONLY ONE IN THE VILLAGE WHO WILL PLAY WITH YOU.
THAT'S NOT TRUE!
IT'S YOUR BIRTHDAY, INNIT? WHERE IS EVERYONE? THEY'RE NOT HERE BECAUSE YER POOR, YOU HAVE THAT UGLY MARK, AND YER NAN IS A LOONY WHO TALKS TO PLANT--
PAFF
--AFF!

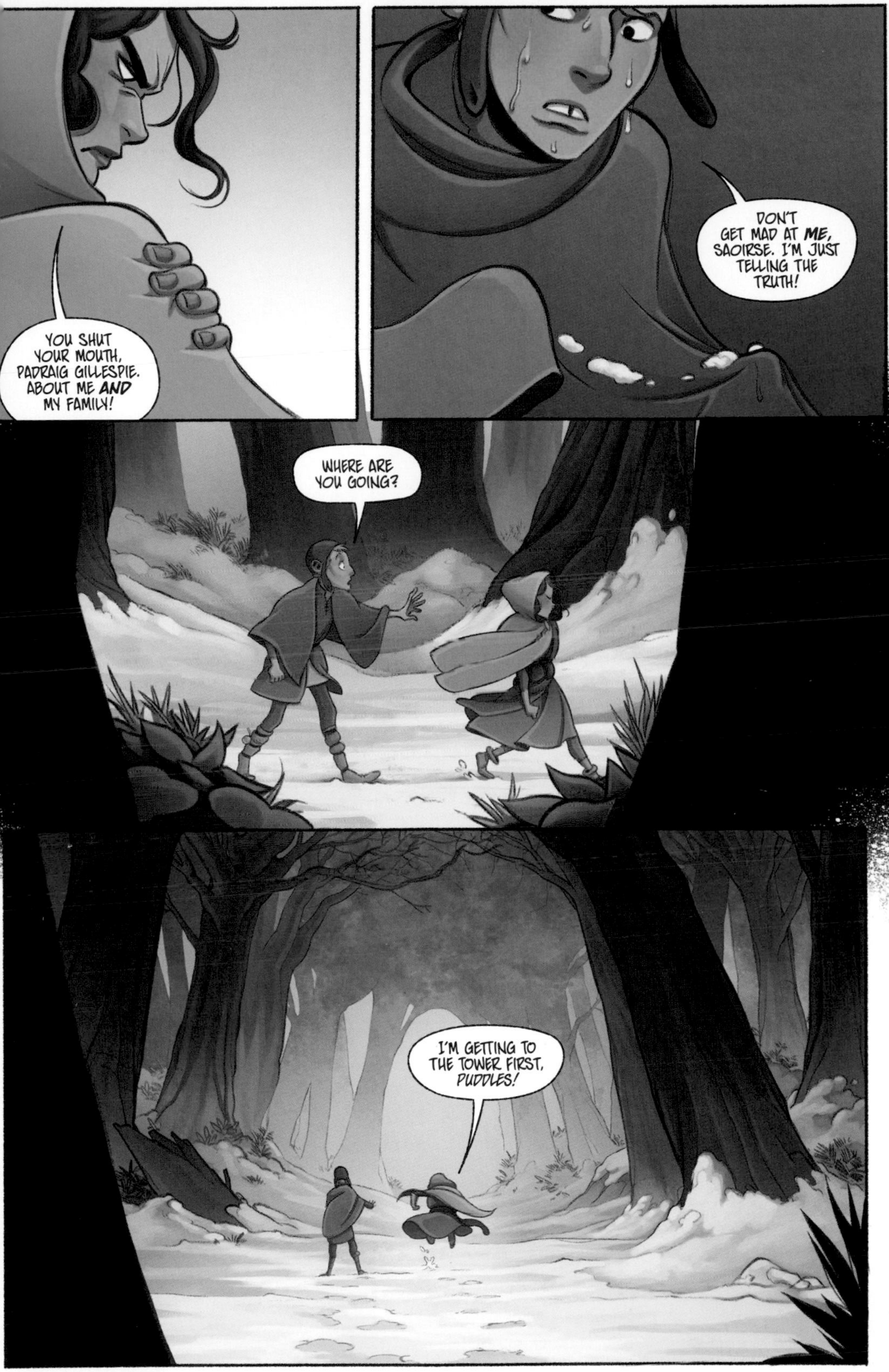
YOU SHUT YOUR MOUTH, PADRAIG GILLESPIE. ABOUT ME **AND** MY FAMILY!
DON'T GET MAD AT **ME**, SAOIRSE. I'M JUST TELLING THE TRUTH!
WHERE ARE YOU GOING?
I'M GETTING TO THE TOWER FIRST, PUDDLES!

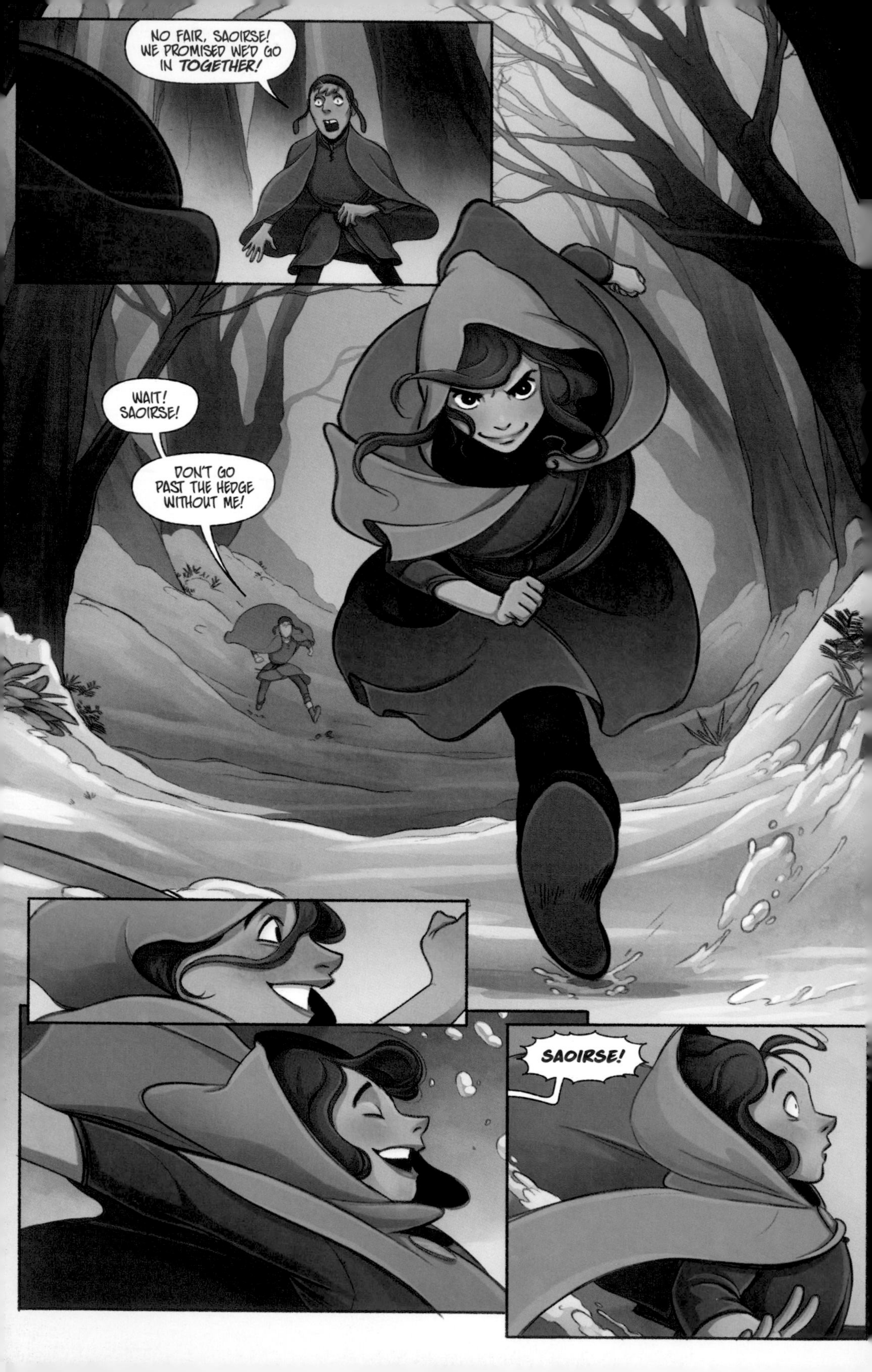
NO FAIR, SAOIRSE! WE PROMISED WE'D GO IN *TOGETHER!*
WAIT! SAOIRSE!
DON'T GO PAST THE HEDGE WITHOUT ME!
SAOIRSE!

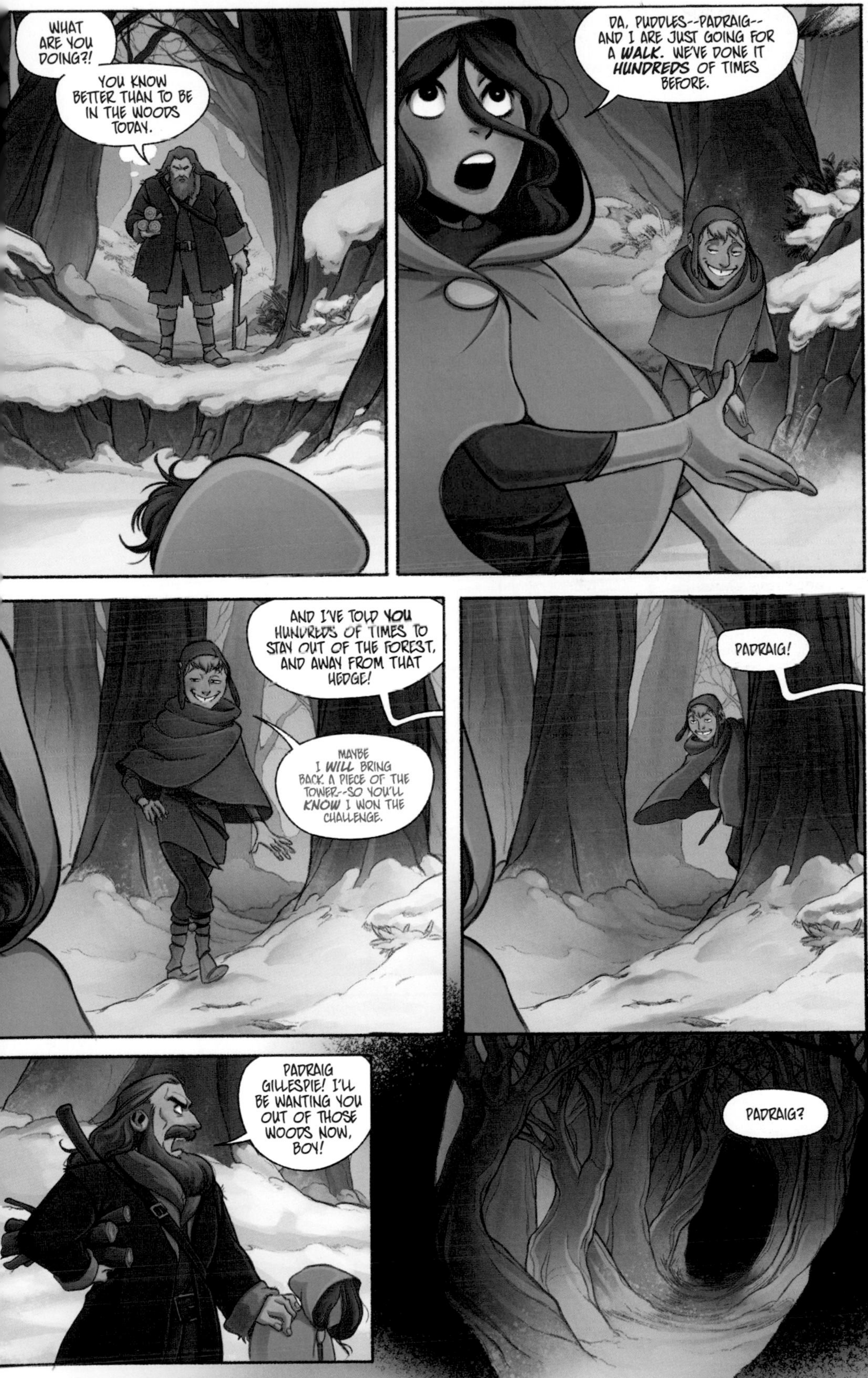
WHAT ARE YOU DOING?!
YOU KNOW BETTER THAN TO BE IN THE WOODS TODAY.
DA, PUDDLES--PADRAIG--AND I ARE JUST GOING FOR A WALK. WE'VE DONE IT HUNDREDS OF TIMES BEFORE.
AND I'VE TOLD YOU HUNDREDS OF TIMES TO STAY OUT OF THE FOREST, AND AWAY FROM THAT HEDGE!
MAYBE I WILL BRING BACK A PIECE OF THE TOWER--SO YOU'LL KNOW I WON THE CHALLENGE.
PADRAIG!
PADRAIG GILLESPIE! I'LL BE WANTING YOU OUT OF THOSE WOODS NOW, BOY!
PADRAIG?

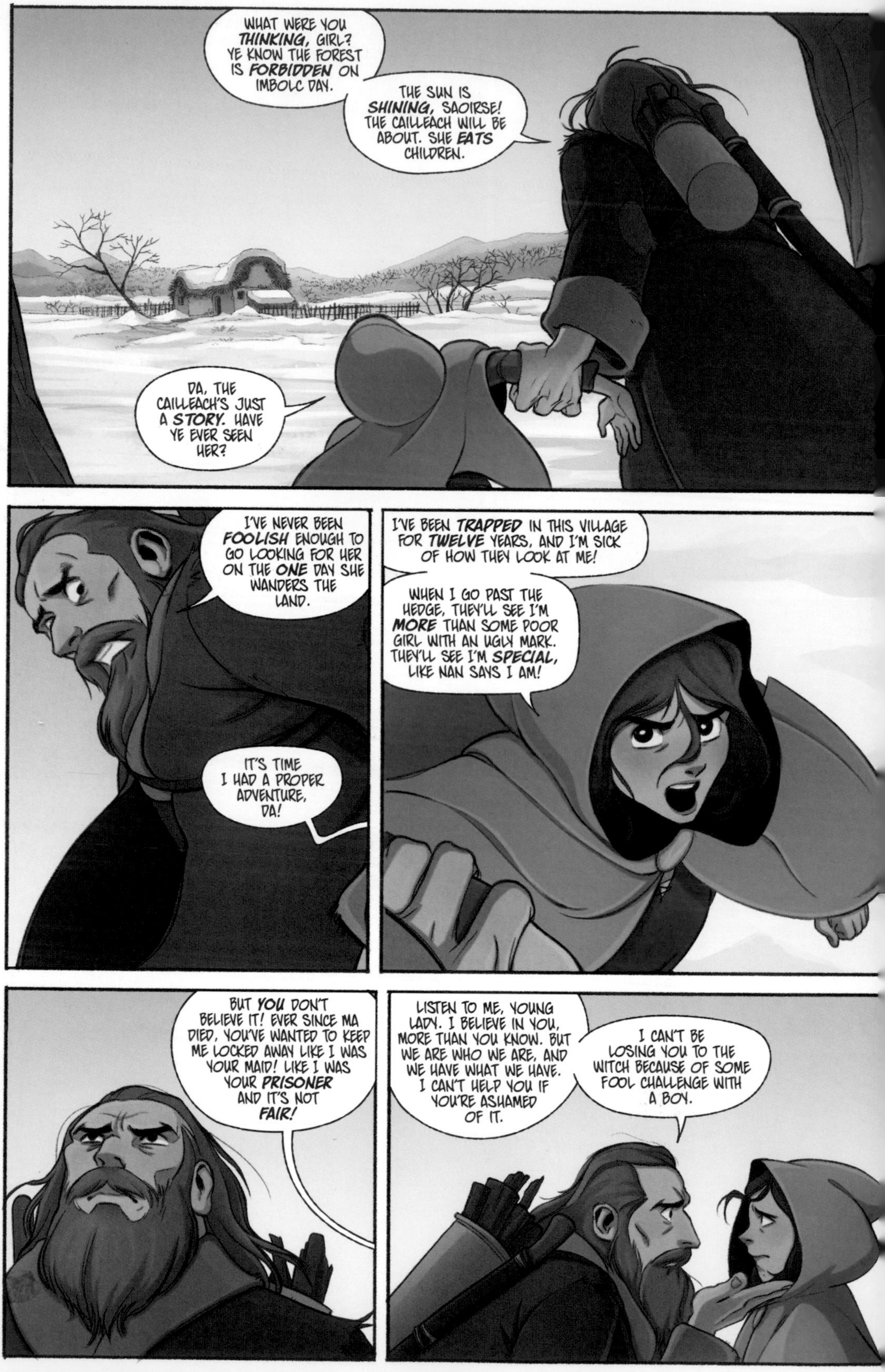
WHAT WERE YOU THINKING, GIRL? YE KNOW THE FOREST IS FORBIDDEN ON IMBOLC DAY.
THE SUN IS SHINING, SAOIRSE! THE CAILLEACH WILL BE ABOUT. SHE EATS CHILDREN.
DA, THE CAILLEACH'S JUST A STORY. HAVE YE EVER SEEN HER?
I'VE NEVER BEEN FOOLISH ENOUGH TO GO LOOKING FOR HER ON THE ONE DAY SHE WANDERS THE LAND.
IT'S TIME I HAD A PROPER ADVENTURE, DA!
I'VE BEEN TRAPPED IN THIS VILLAGE FOR TWELVE YEARS, AND I'M SICK OF HOW THEY LOOK AT ME!
WHEN I GO PAST THE HEDGE, THEY'LL SEE I'M MORE THAN SOME POOR GIRL WITH AN UGLY MARK. THEY'LL SEE I'M SPECIAL, LIKE NAN SAYS I AM!
BUT YOU DON'T BELIEVE IT! EVER SINCE MA DIED, YOU'VE WANTED TO KEEP ME LOCKED AWAY LIKE I WAS YOUR MAID! LIKE I WAS YOUR PRISONER AND IT'S NOT FAIR!
LISTEN TO ME, YOUNG LADY. I BELIEVE IN YOU, MORE THAN YOU KNOW. BUT WE ARE WHO WE ARE, AND WE HAVE WHAT WE HAVE. I CAN'T HELP YOU IF YOU'RE ASHAMED OF IT.
I CAN'T BE LOSING YOU TO THE WITCH BECAUSE OF SOME FOOL CHALLENGE WITH A BOY.

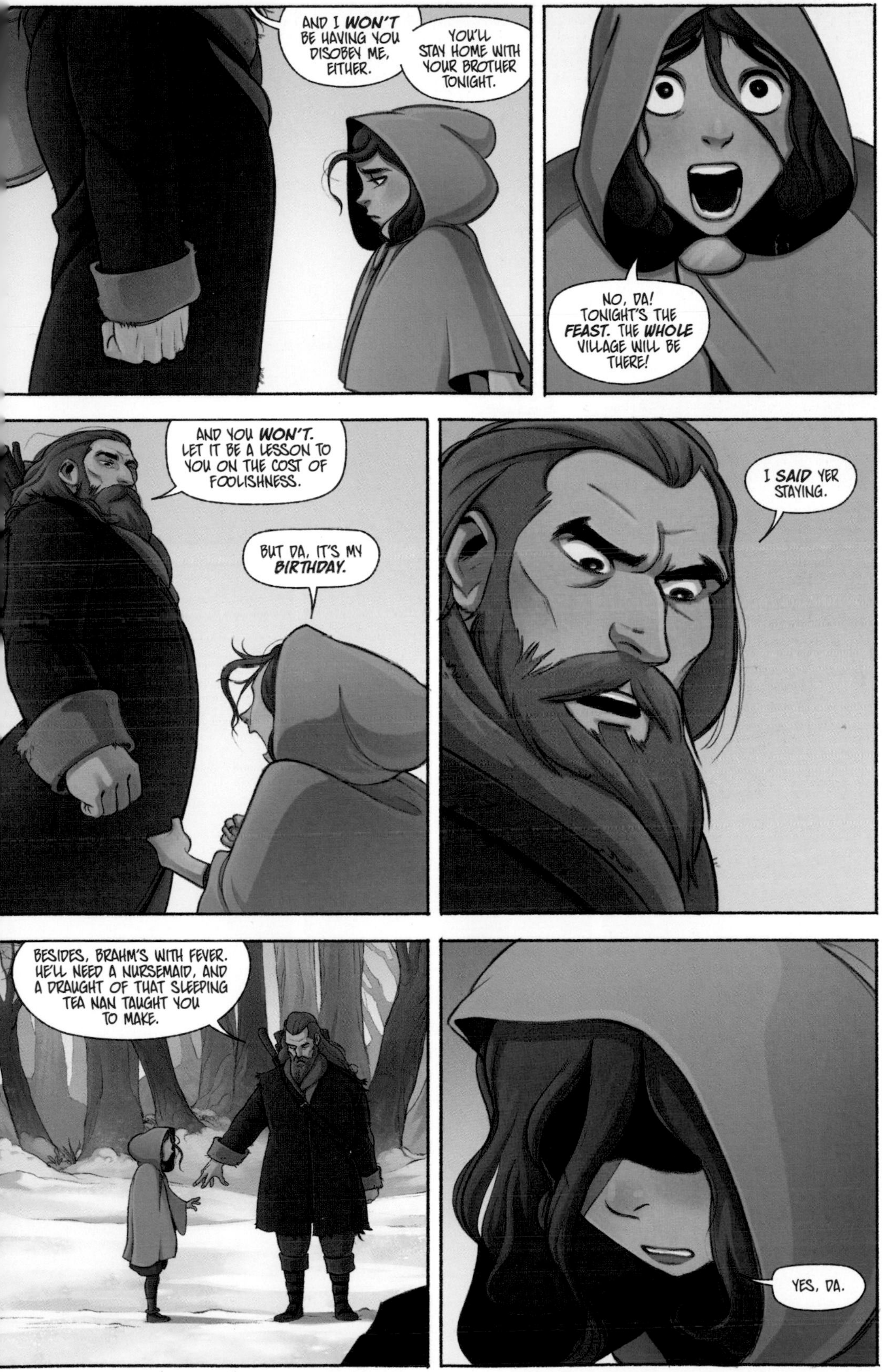
AND I WON'T BE HAVING YOU DISOBEY ME, EITHER.
YOU'LL STAY HOME WITH YOUR BROTHER TONIGHT.
NO, DA! TONIGHT'S THE FEAST. THE WHOLE VILLAGE WILL BE THERE!
AND YOU WON'T. LET IT BE A LESSON TO YOU ON THE COST OF FOOLISHNESS.
BUT DA, IT'S MY BIRTHDAY.
I SAID YER STAYING.
BESIDES, BRAHM'S WITH FEVER. HE'LL NEED A NURSEMAID, AND A DRAUGHT OF THAT SLEEPING TEA NAN TAUGHT YOU TO MAKE.
YES, DA.

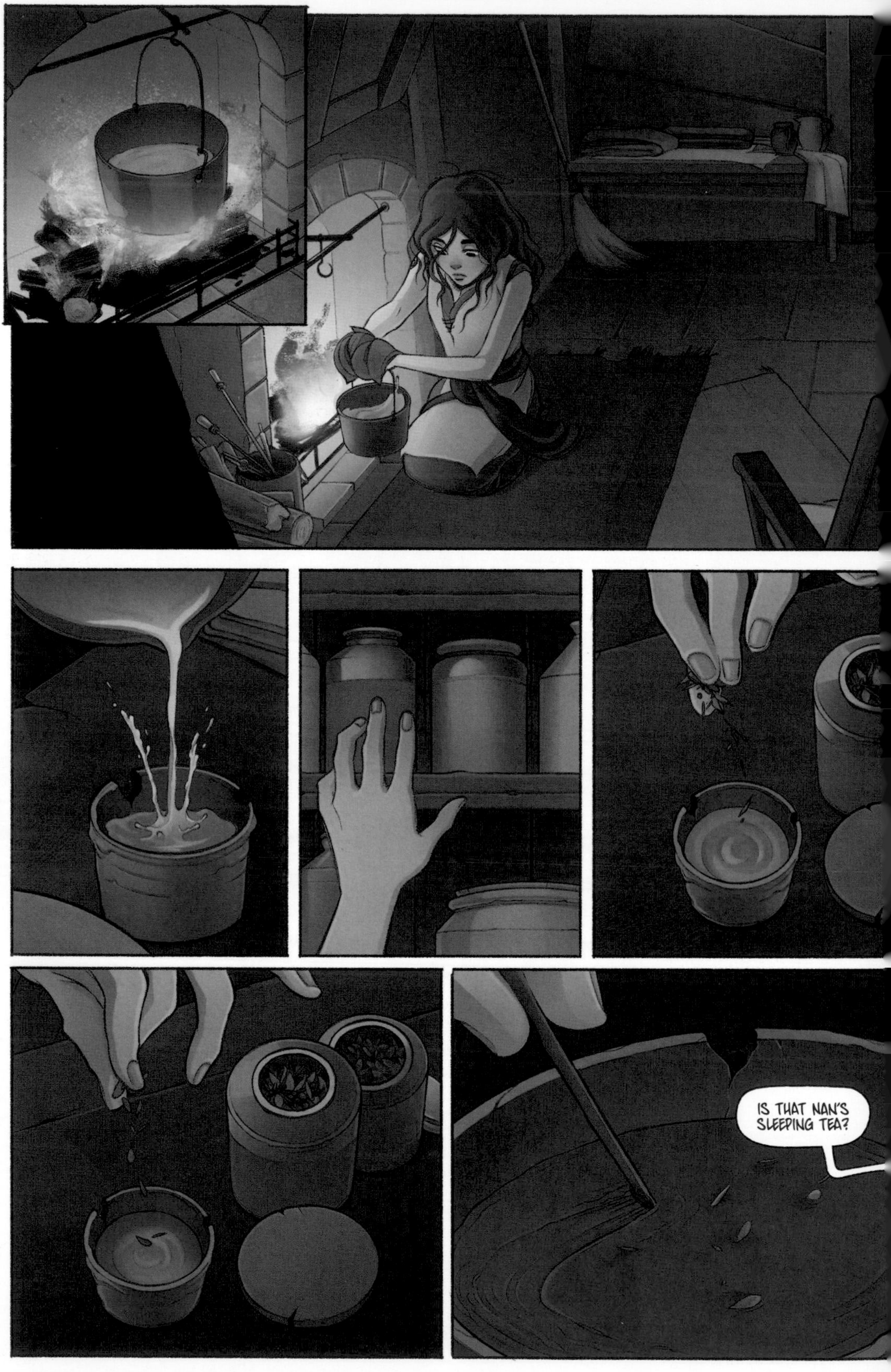
IS THAT NAN'S
SLEEPING TEA?

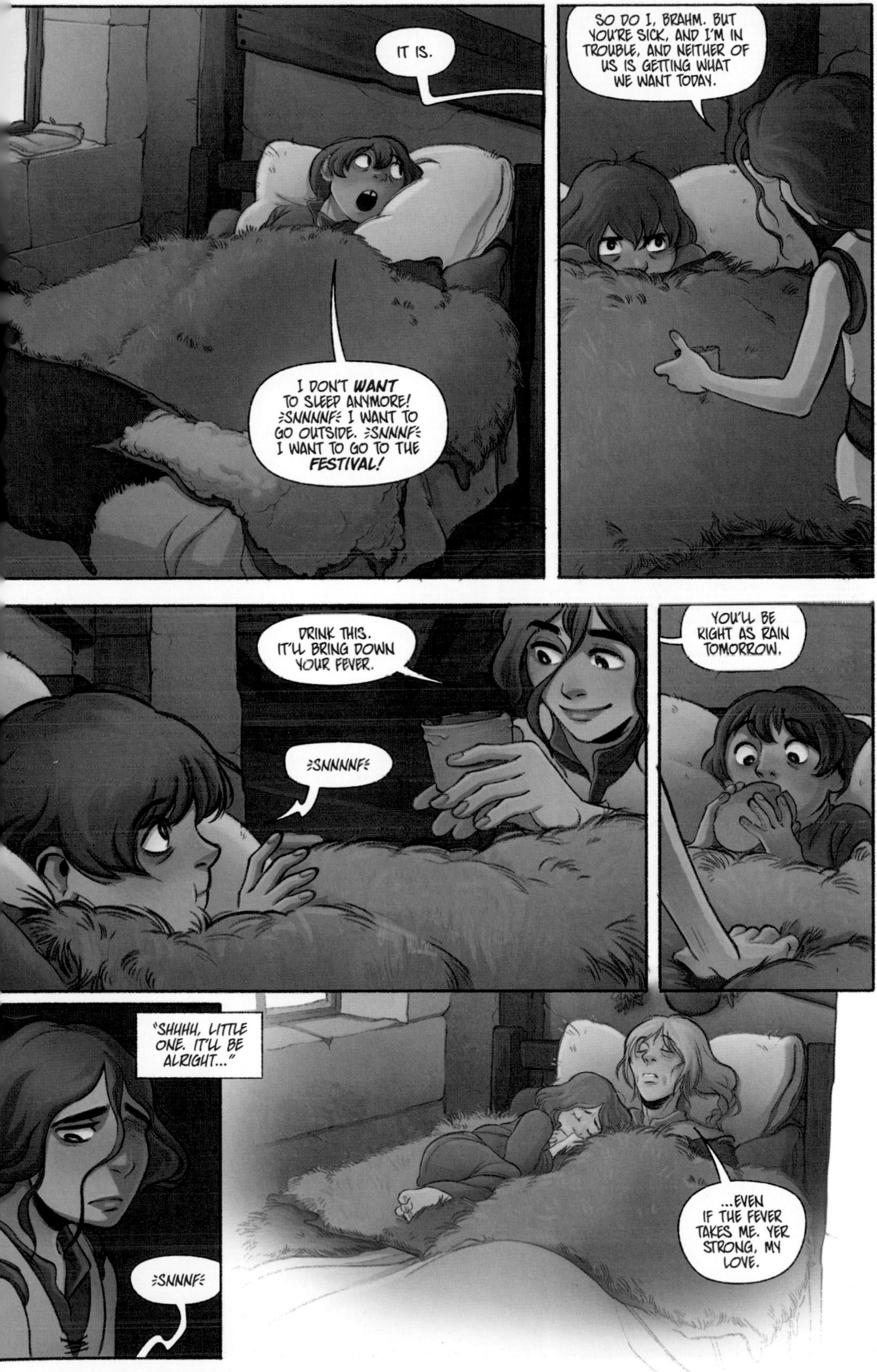
IT IS.
I DON'T **WANT** TO SLEEP ANYMORE! ≈SNNNF≈ I WANT TO GO OUTSIDE. ≈SNNNF≈ I WANT TO GO TO THE **FESTIVAL!**
SO DO I, BRAHM. BUT YOU'RE SICK, AND I'M IN TROUBLE, AND NEITHER OF US IS GETTING WHAT WE WANT TODAY.
DRINK THIS. IT'LL BRING DOWN YOUR FEVER.
≈SNNNNF≈
YOU'LL BE RIGHT AS RAIN TOMORROW.
"SHUHH, LITTLE ONE. IT'LL BE ALRIGHT..."
≈SNNNF≈
...EVEN IF THE FEVER TAKES ME. YER STRONG, MY LOVE.

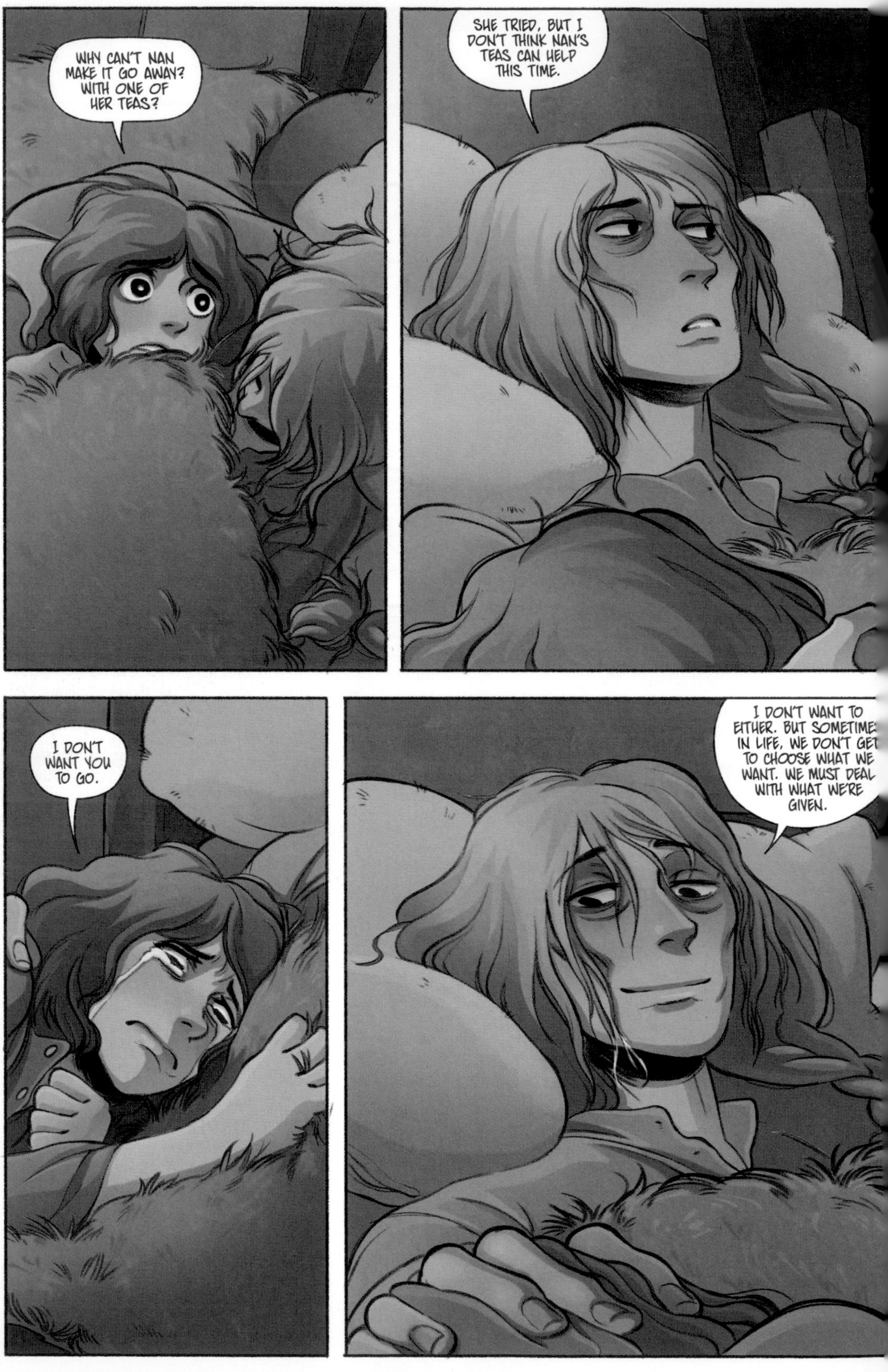
WHY CAN'T NAN MAKE IT GO AWAY? WITH ONE OF HER TEAS?
SHE TRIED, BUT I DON'T THINK NAN'S TEAS CAN HELP THIS TIME.
I DON'T WANT YOU TO GO.
I DON'T WANT TO EITHER. BUT SOMETIMES IN LIFE, WE DON'T GET TO CHOOSE WHAT WE WANT. WE MUST DEAL WITH WHAT WE'RE GIVEN.

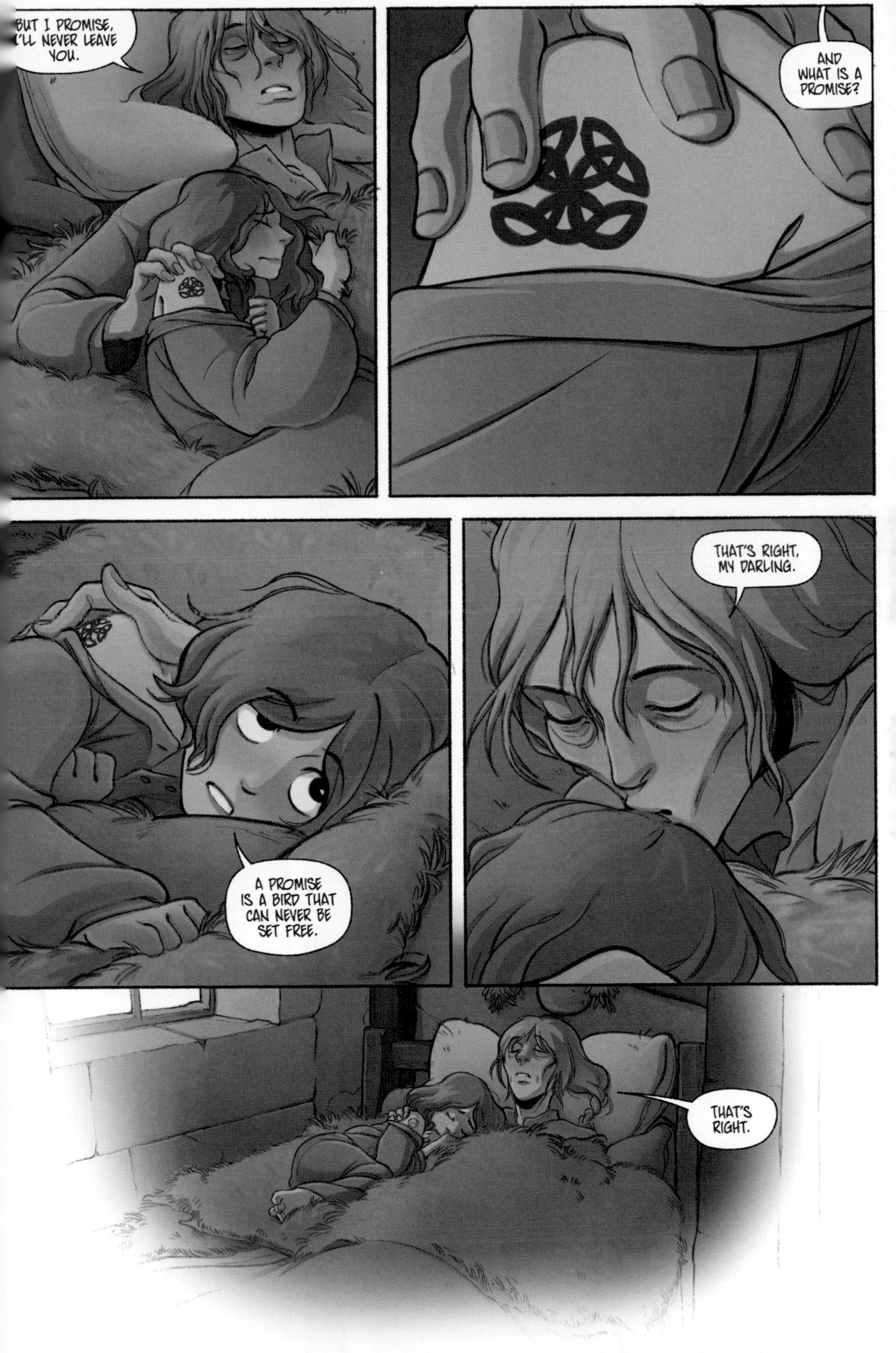
BUT I PROMISE, I'LL NEVER LEAVE YOU.
AND WHAT IS A PROMISE?
A PROMISE IS A BIRD THAT CAN NEVER BE SET FREE.
THAT'S RIGHT, MY DARLING.
THAT'S RIGHT.

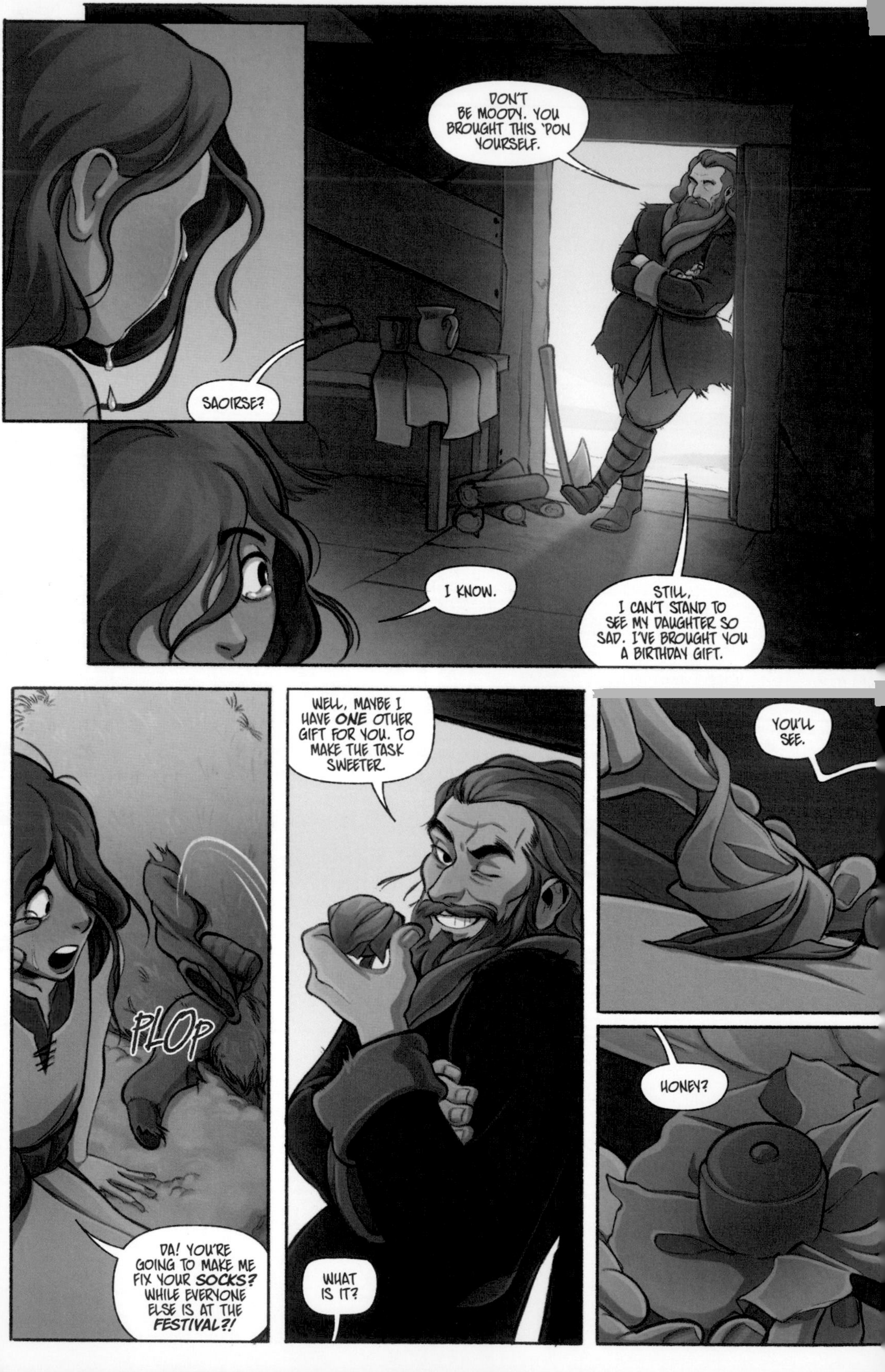
DON'T BE MOODY. YOU BROUGHT THIS 'PON YOURSELF.
SAOIRSE?
I KNOW.
STILL, I CAN'T STAND TO SEE MY DAUGHTER SO SAD. I'VE BROUGHT YOU A BIRTHDAY GIFT.
PLOP
DA! YOU'RE GOING TO MAKE ME FIX YOUR **SOCKS?** WHILE EVERYONE ELSE IS AT THE ***FESTIVAL?!***
WELL, MAYBE I HAVE **ONE** OTHER GIFT FOR YOU. TO MAKE THE TASK SWEETER.
WHAT IS IT?
YOU'LL SEE.
HONEY?

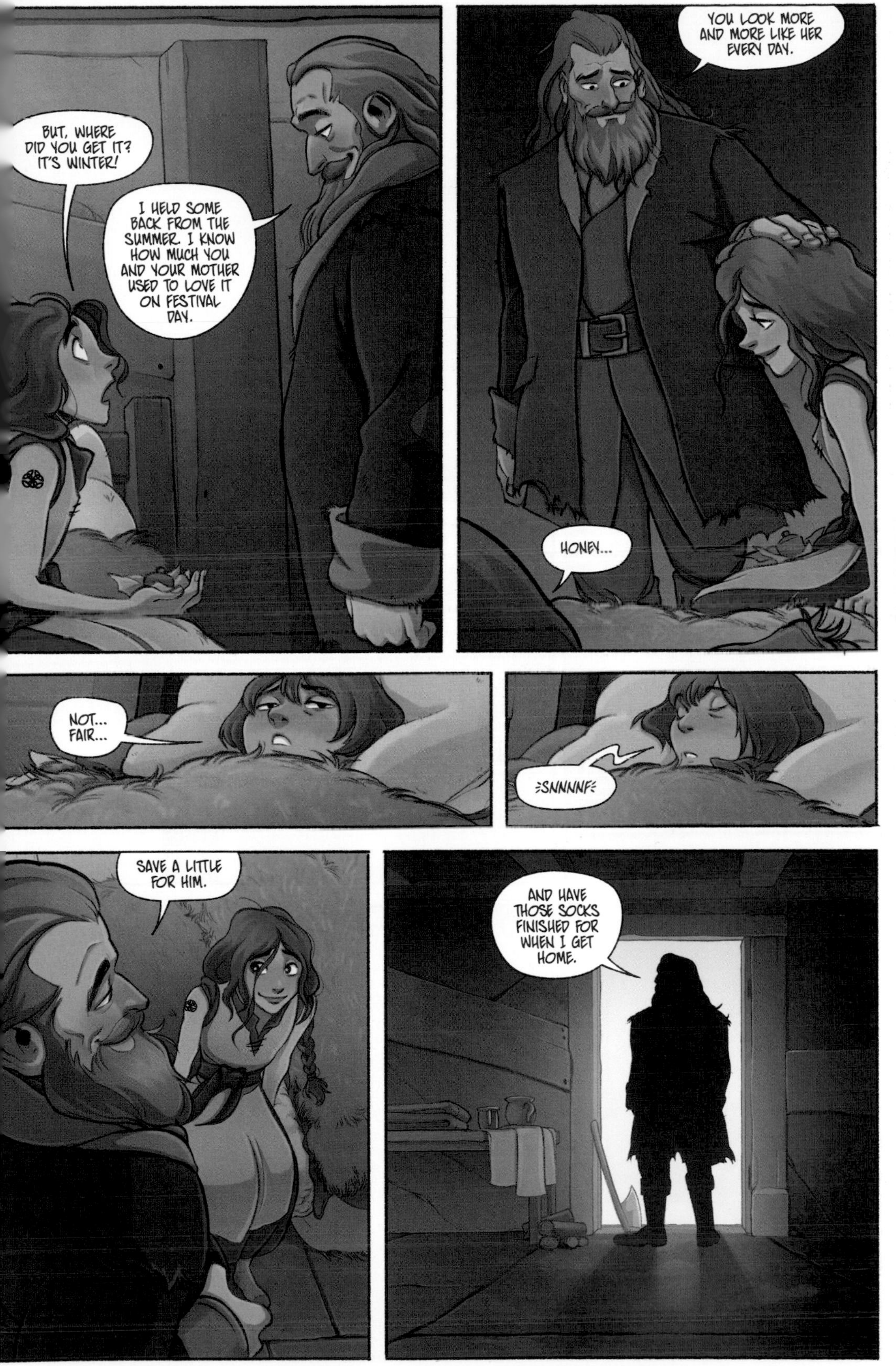
BUT, WHERE DID YOU GET IT? IT'S WINTER!
I HELD SOME BACK FROM THE SUMMER. I KNOW HOW MUCH YOU AND YOUR MOTHER USED TO LOVE IT ON FESTIVAL DAY.
YOU LOOK MORE AND MORE LIKE HER EVERY DAY.
HONEY...
NOT... FAIR...
SNNNNF
SAVE A LITTLE FOR HIM.
AND HAVE THOSE SOCKS FINISHED FOR WHEN I GET HOME.

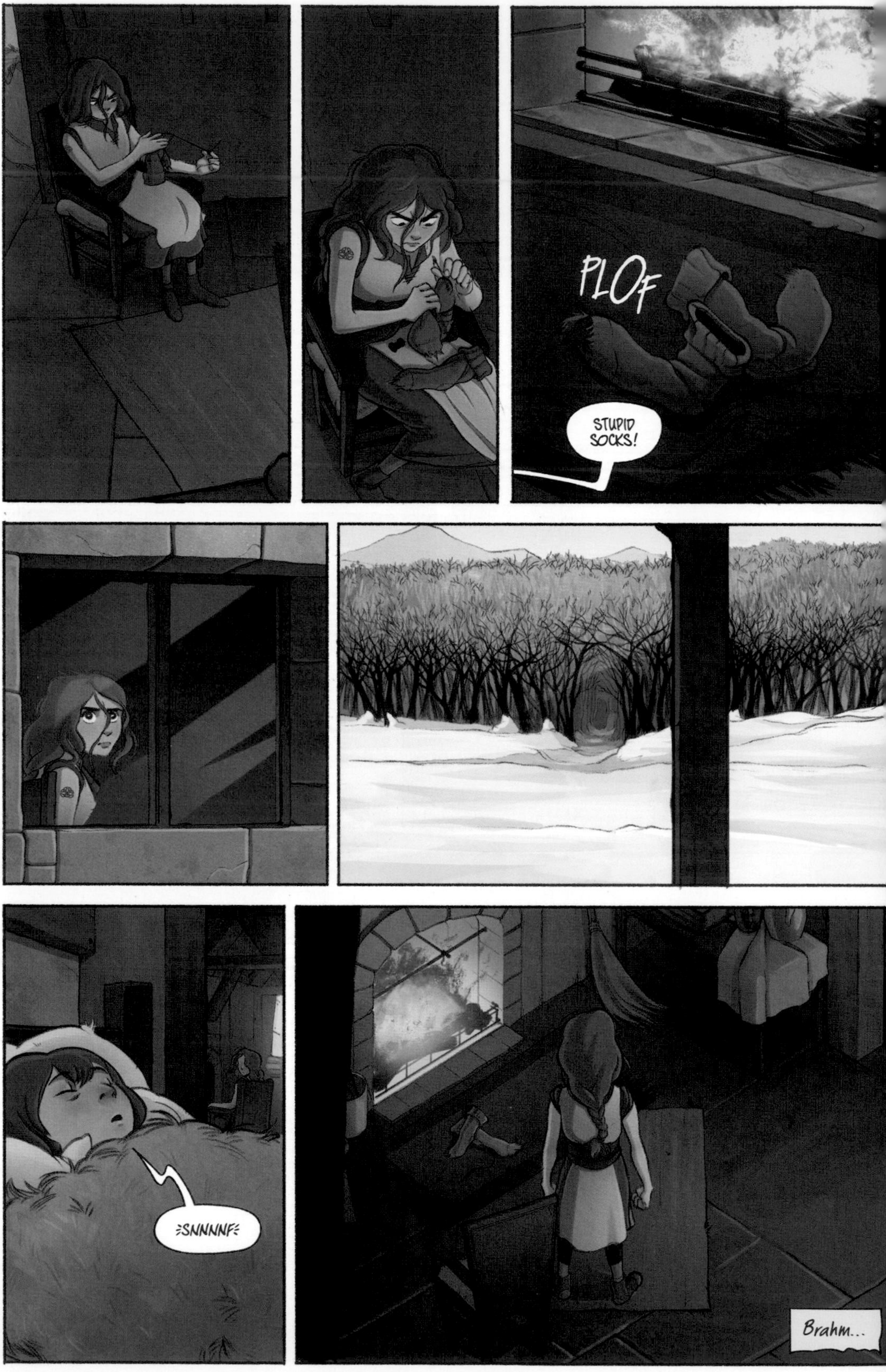
PLOF
STUPID SOCKS!
SNNNNF
Brahm...

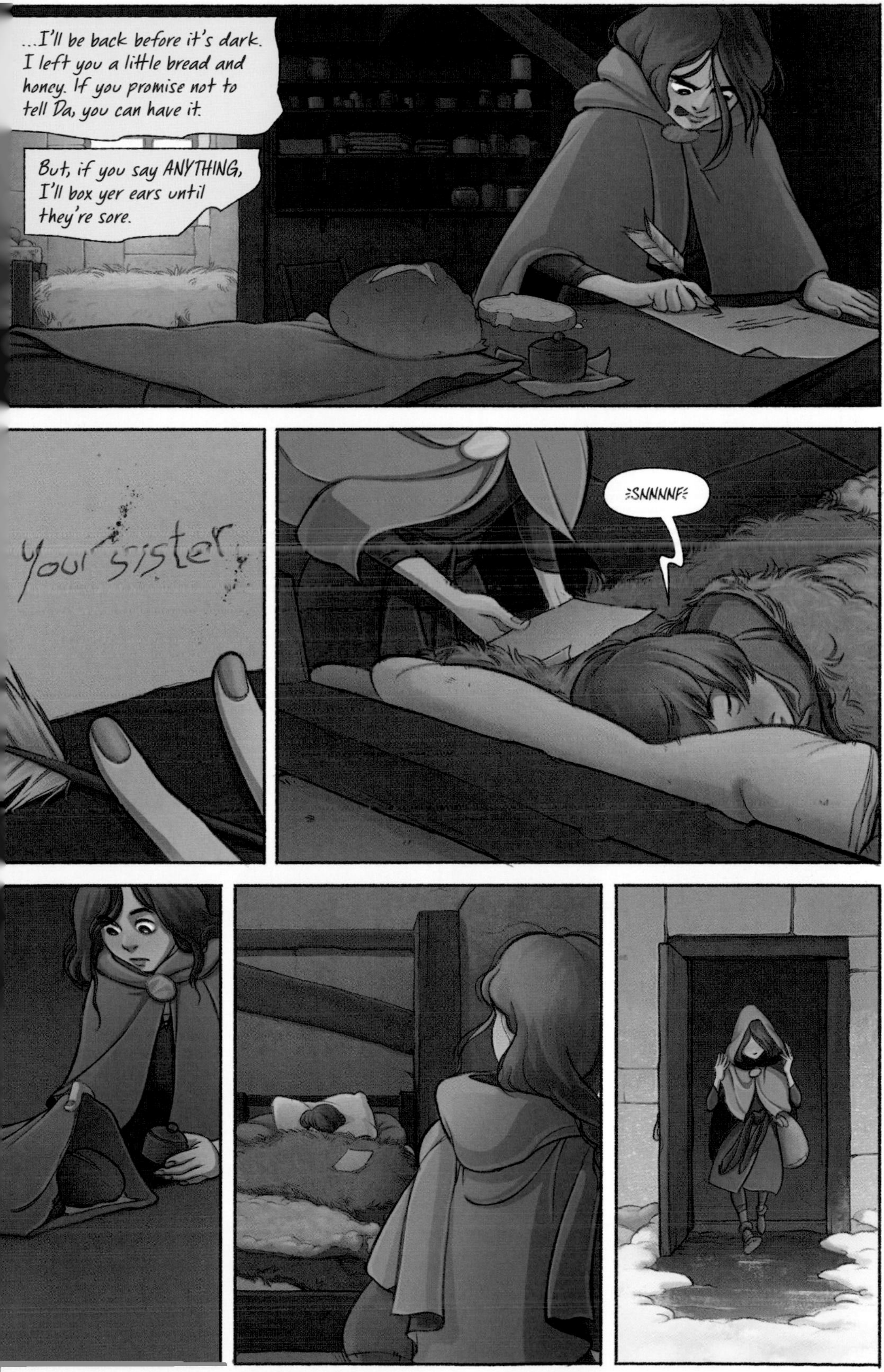
...I'll be back before it's dark. I left you a little bread and honey. If you promise not to tell Da, you can have it.
But, if you say ANYTHING, I'll box yer ears until they're sore.
your sister
SNNNNF

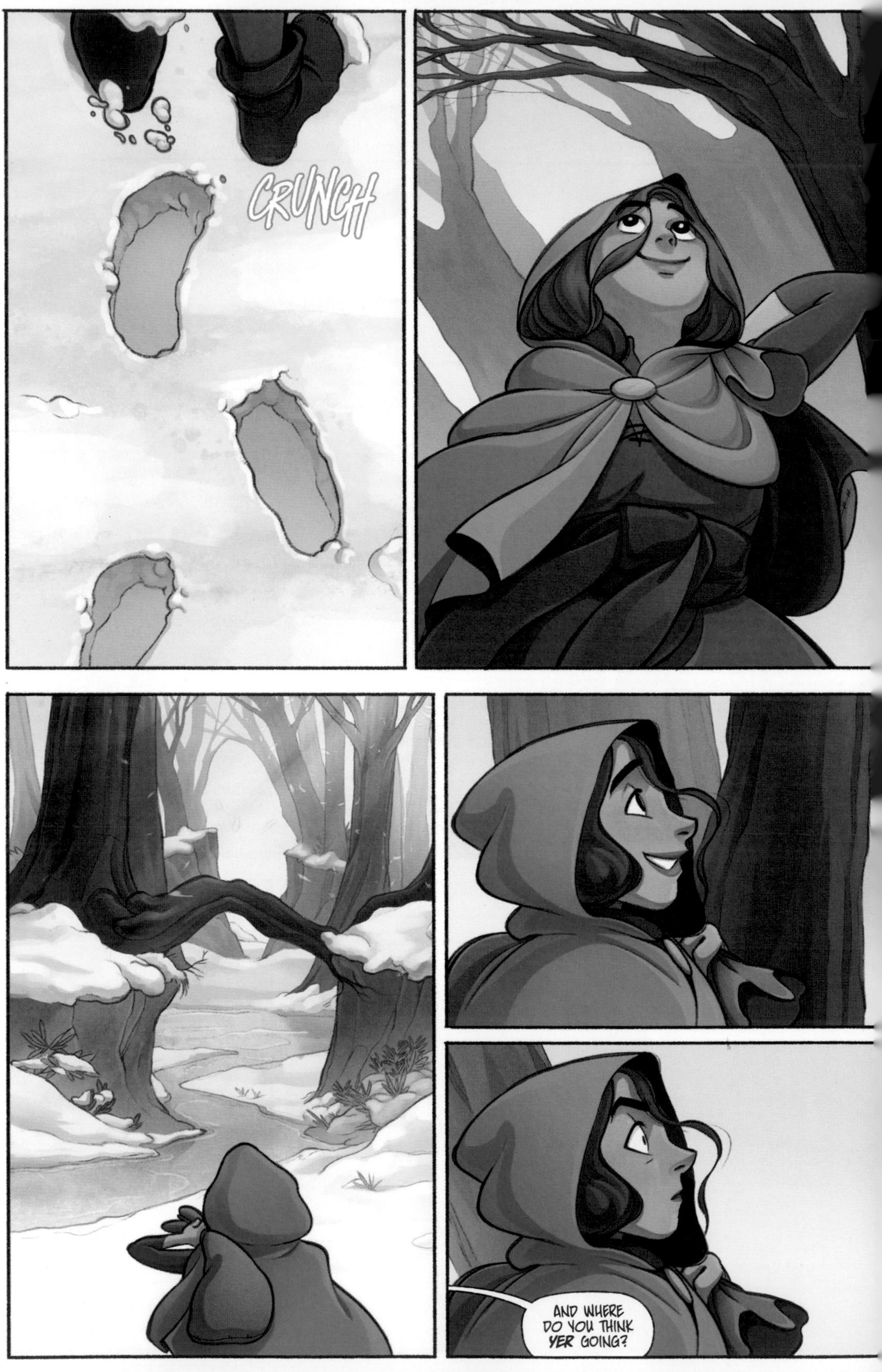
CRUNCH
AND WHERE DO YOU THINK YER GOING?

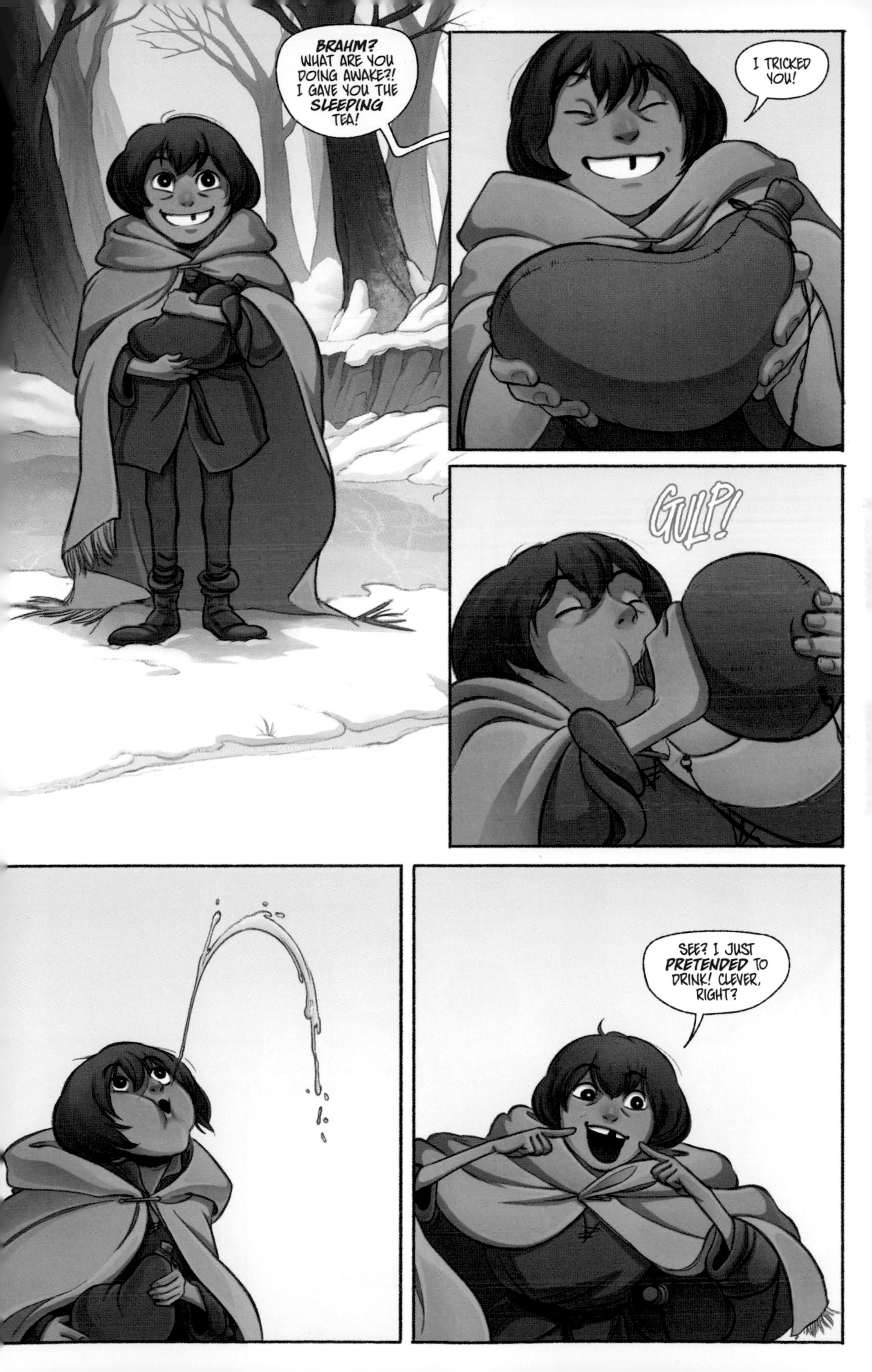
BRAHM? WHAT ARE YOU DOING AWAKE?! I GAVE YOU THE SLEEPING TEA!
I TRICKED YOU!
GULP!
SEE? I JUST PRETENDED TO DRINK! CLEVER, RIGHT?

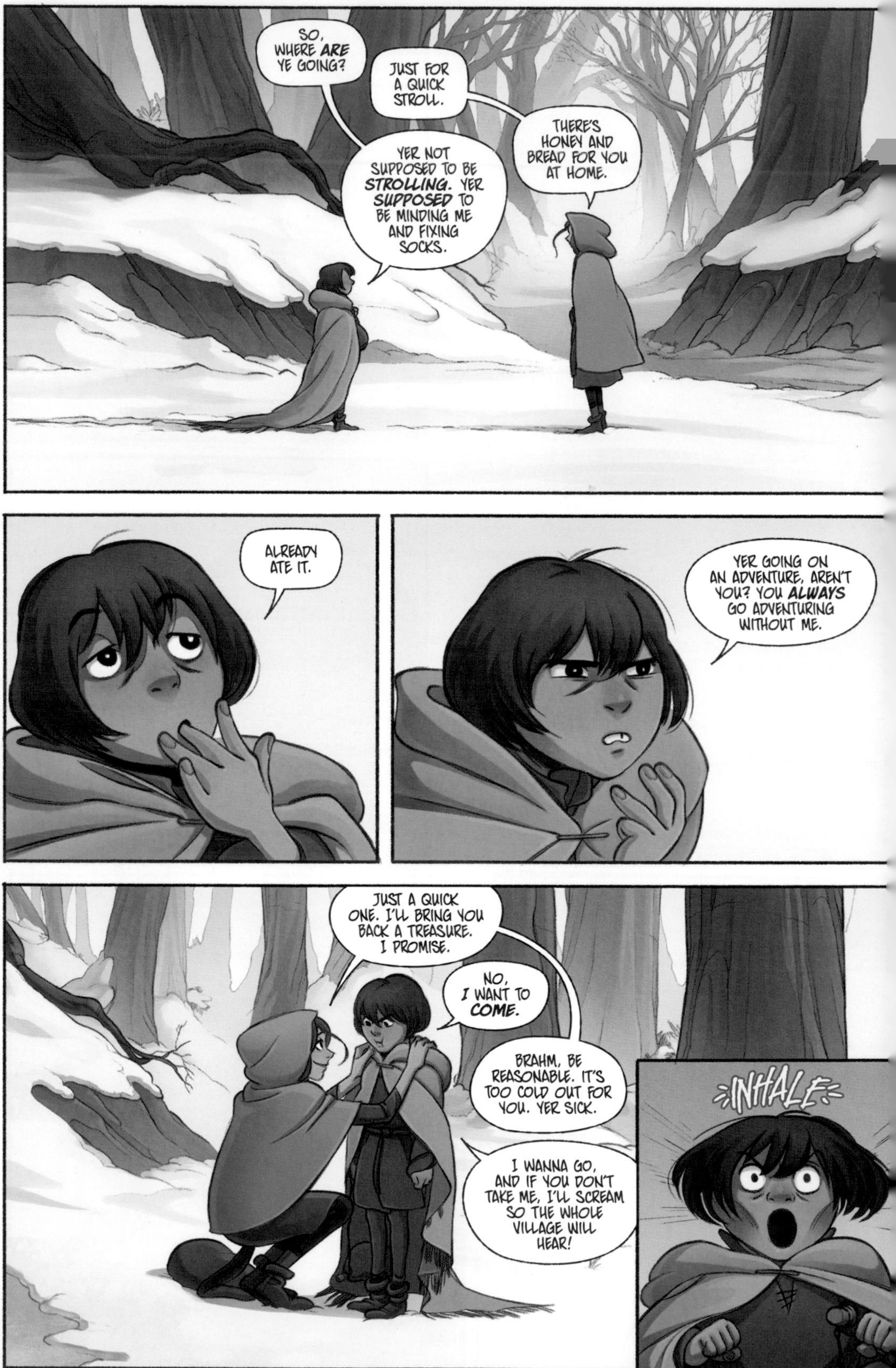

SO, WHERE **ARE** YE GOING?
JUST FOR A QUICK STROLL.
THERE'S HONEY AND BREAD FOR YOU AT HOME.
YER NOT SUPPOSED TO BE **STROLLING.** YER **SUPPOSED** TO BE MINDING ME AND FIXING SOCKS.
ALREADY ATE IT.
YER GOING ON AN ADVENTURE, AREN'T YOU? YOU **ALWAYS** GO ADVENTURING WITHOUT ME.
JUST A QUICK ONE. I'LL BRING YOU BACK A TREASURE. I PROMISE.
NO, *I WANT TO* **COME.**
BRAHM, BE REASONABLE. IT'S TOO COLD OUT FOR YOU. YER SICK.
I WANNA GO, AND IF YOU DON'T TAKE ME, I'LL SCREAM SO THE WHOLE VILLAGE WILL HEAR!
INHALE

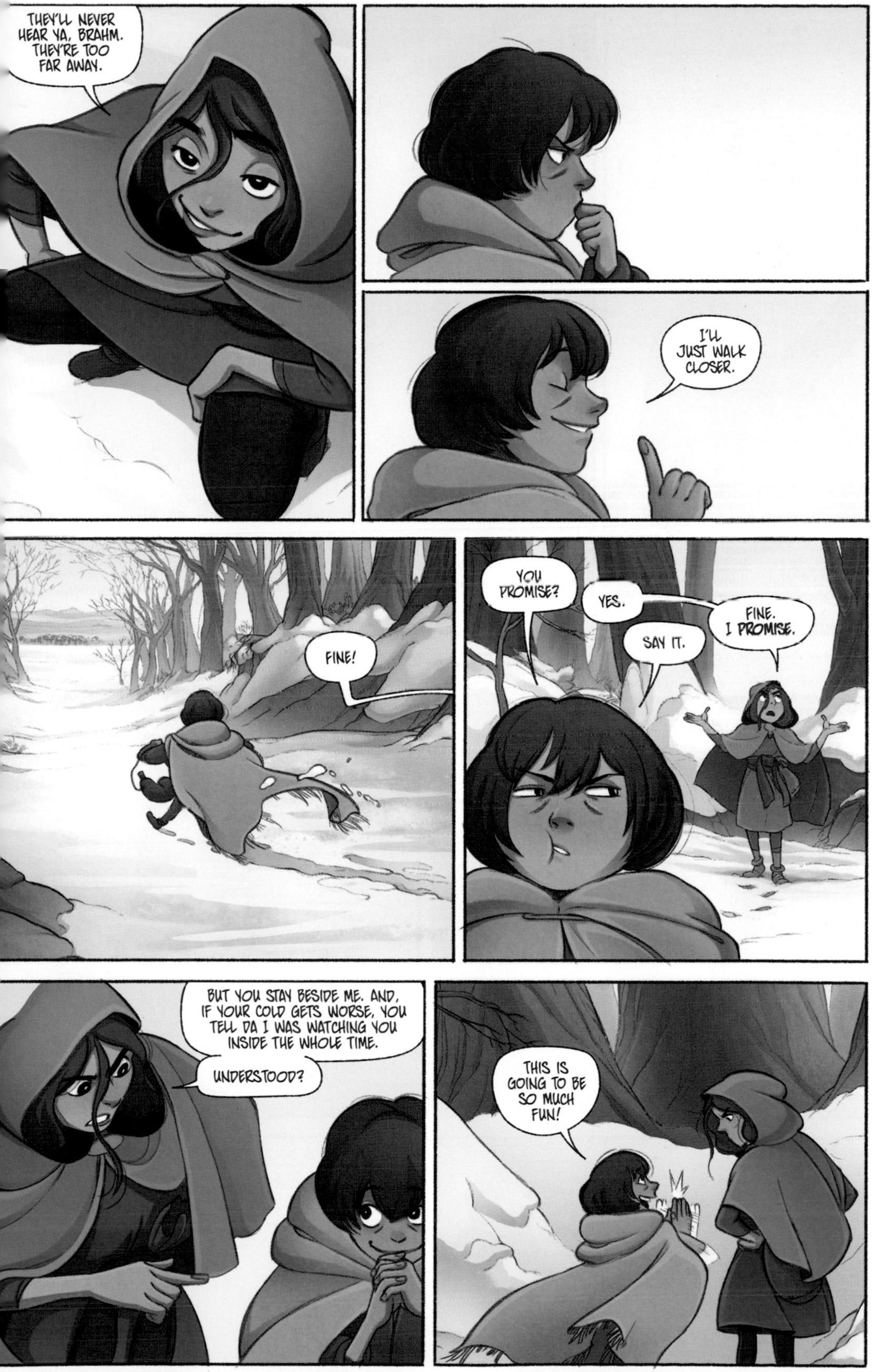
THEY'LL NEVER HEAR YA, BRAHM. THEY'RE TOO FAR AWAY.
I'LL JUST WALK CLOSER.
FINE!
YOU PROMISE?
YES.
SAY IT.
FINE. I PROMISE.
BUT YOU STAY BESIDE ME. AND, IF YOUR COLD GETS WORSE, YOU TELL DA I WAS WATCHING YOU INSIDE THE WHOLE TIME.
UNDERSTOOD?
THIS IS GOING TO BE SO MUCH FUN!

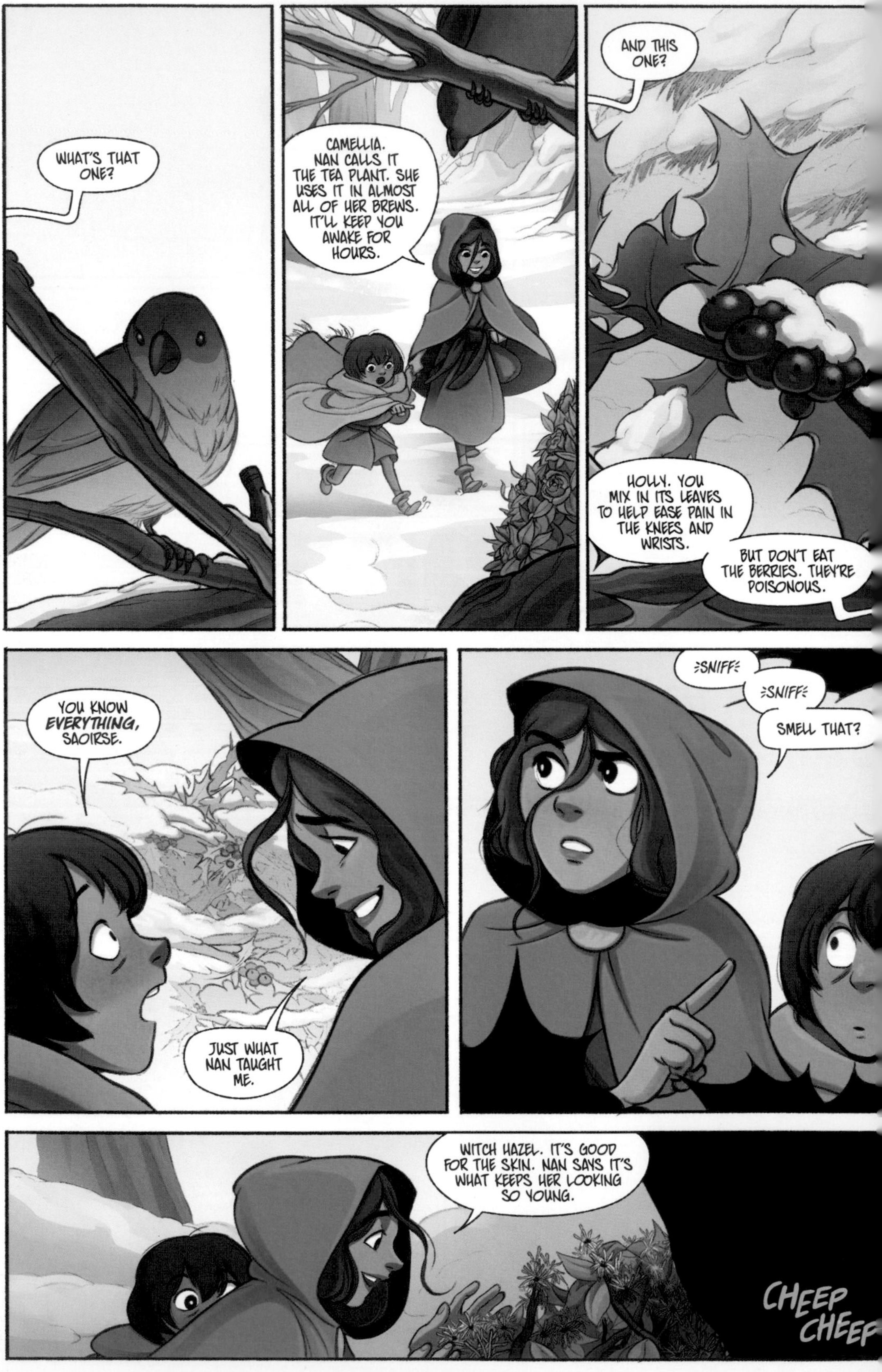
WHAT'S THAT ONE?
CAMELLIA. NAN CALLS IT THE TEA PLANT. SHE USES IT IN ALMOST ALL OF HER BREWS. IT'LL KEEP YOU AWAKE FOR HOURS.
AND THIS ONE?
HOLLY. YOU MIX IN ITS LEAVES TO HELP EASE PAIN IN THE KNEES AND WRISTS.
BUT DON'T EAT THE BERRIES. THEY'RE POISONOUS.
YOU KNOW *EVERYTHING*, SAOIRSE.
JUST WHAT NAN TAUGHT ME.
SNIFF
SNIFF
SMELL THAT?
WITCH HAZEL. IT'S GOOD FOR THE SKIN. NAN SAYS IT'S WHAT KEEPS HER LOOKING SO YOUNG.
CHEEP CHEEP

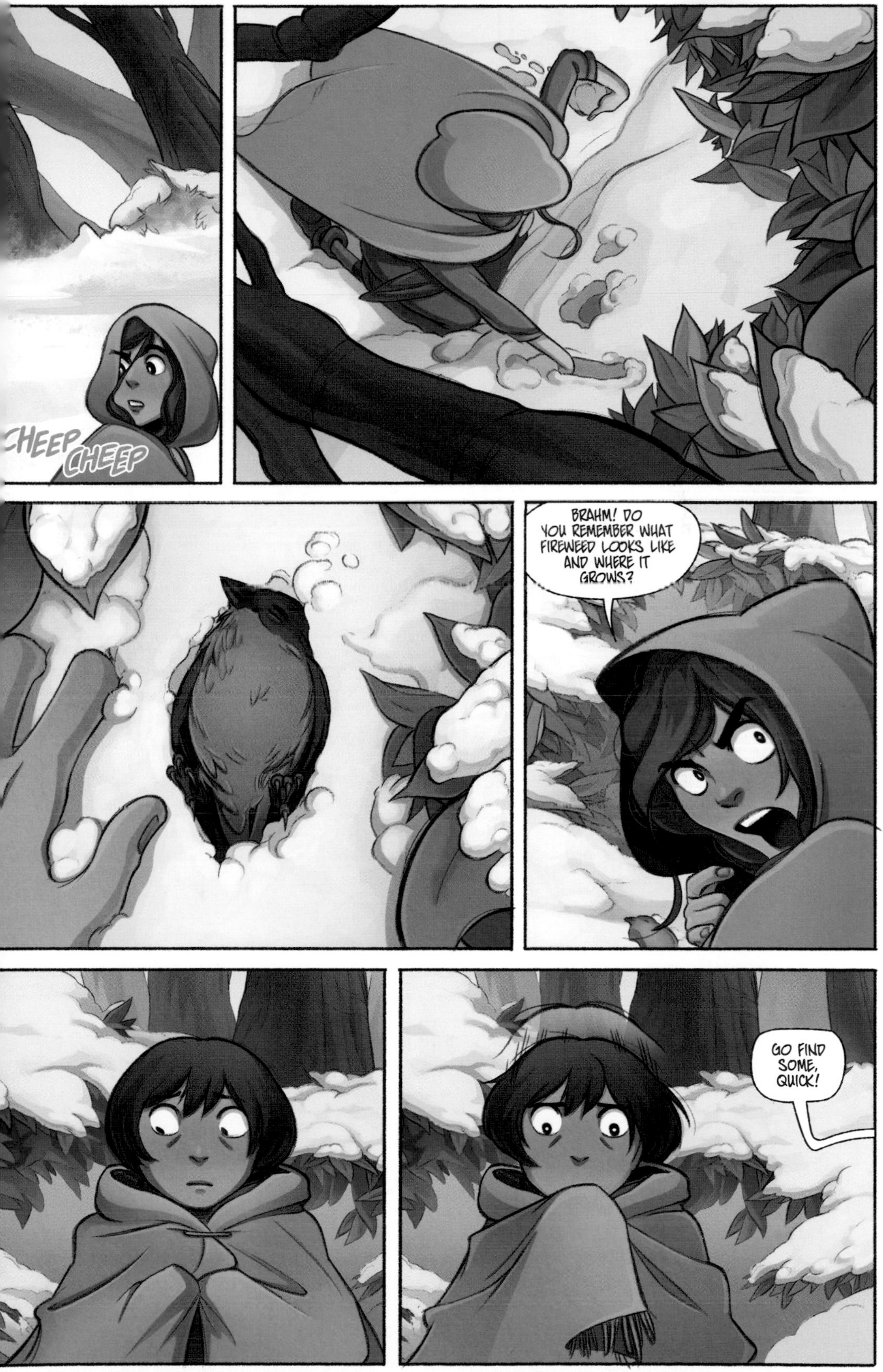
CHEEP CHEEP
BRAHM! DO YOU REMEMBER WHAT FIREWEED LOOKS LIKE AND WHERE IT GROWS?
GO FIND SOME, QUICK!

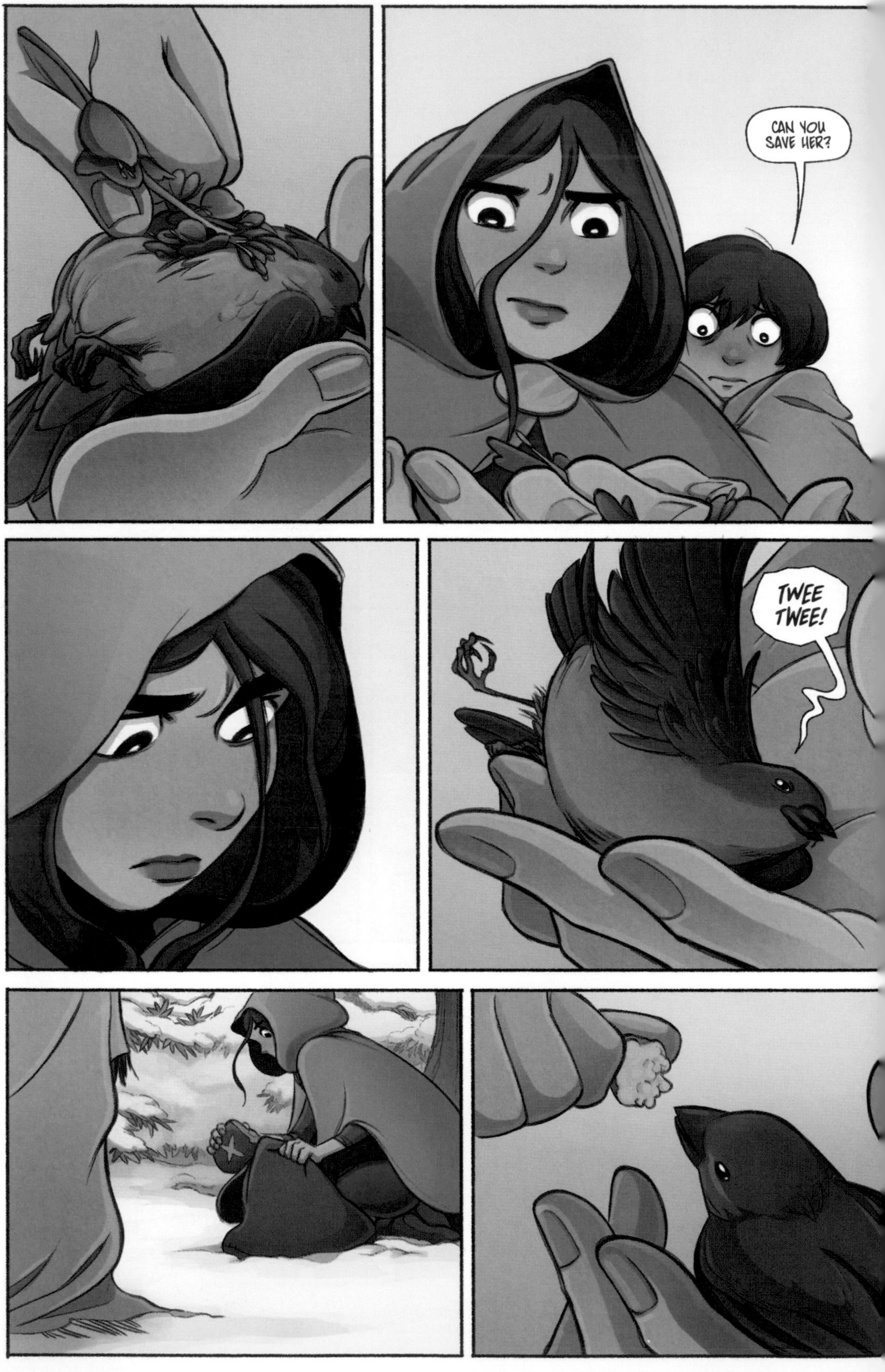
CAN YOU SAVE HER?
TWEE TWEE!

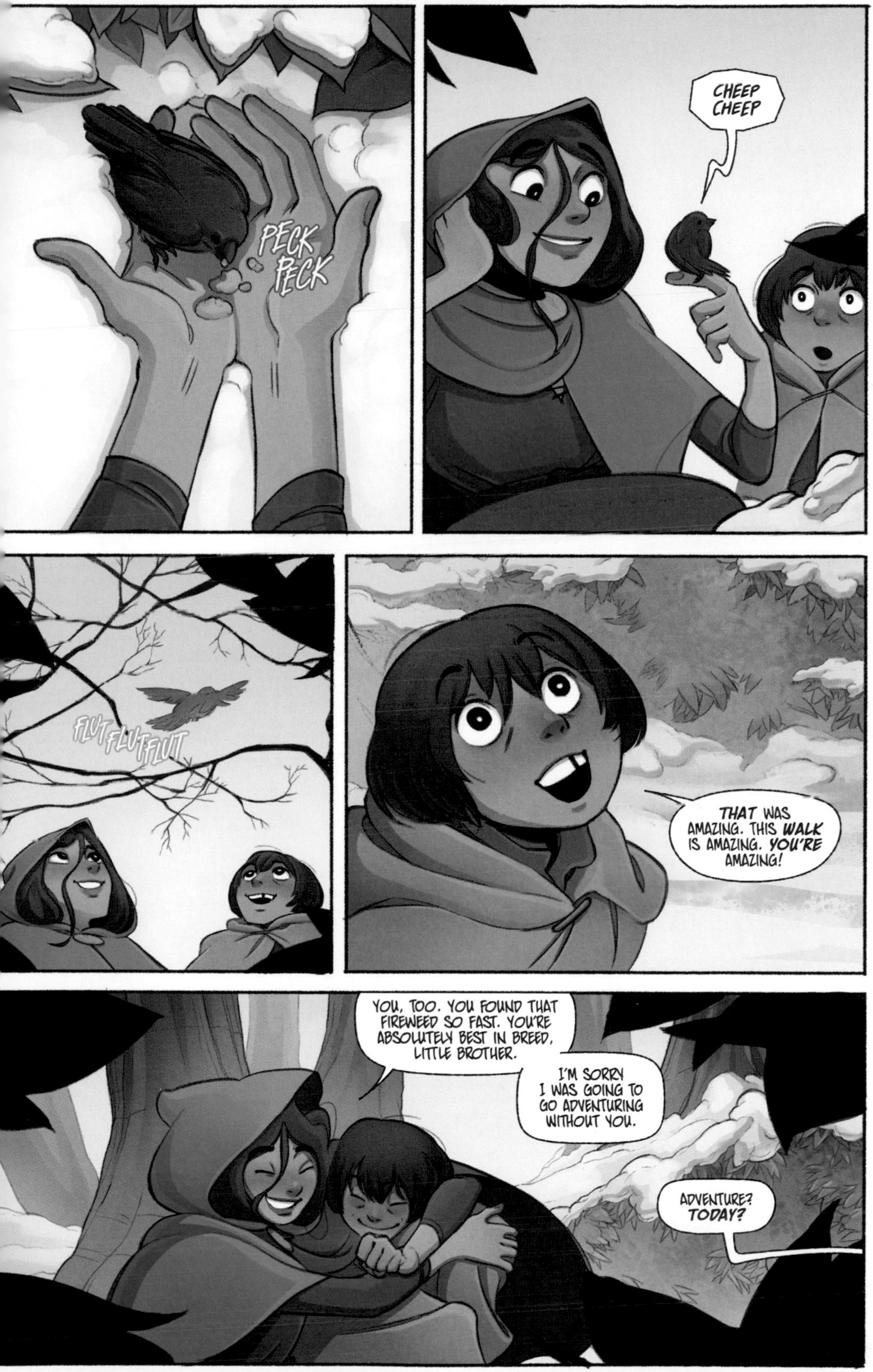
PECK PECK
CHEEP CHEEP
FLUT FLUT FLUT
THAT WAS AMAZING. THIS WALK IS AMAZING. YOU'RE AMAZING!
YOU, TOO. YOU FOUND THAT FIREWEED SO FAST. YOU'RE ABSOLUTELY BEST IN BREED, LITTLE BROTHER.
I'M SORRY I WAS GOING TO GO ADVENTURING WITHOUT YOU.
ADVENTURE? TODAY?

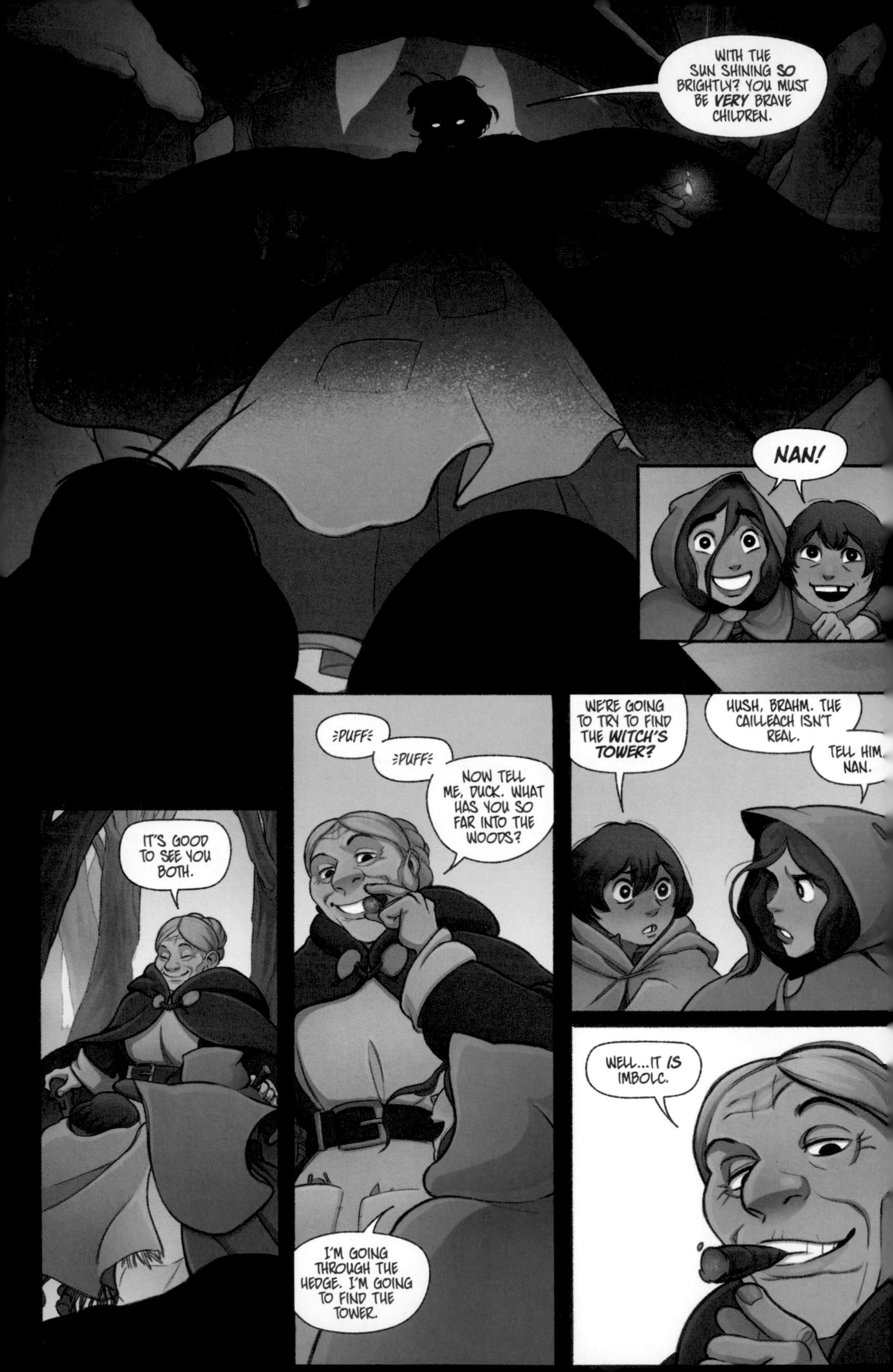

WITH THE SUN SHINING SO BRIGHTLY? YOU MUST BE VERY BRAVE CHILDREN.
NAN!
IT'S GOOD TO SEE YOU BOTH.
PUFF
PUFF
NOW TELL ME, DUCK. WHAT HAS YOU SO FAR INTO THE WOODS?
I'M GOING THROUGH THE HEDGE. I'M GOING TO FIND THE TOWER.
WE'RE GOING TO TRY TO FIND THE WITCH'S TOWER?
HUSH, BRAHM. THE CAILLEACH ISN'T REAL.
TELL HIM, NAN.
WELL...IT IS IMBOLC.

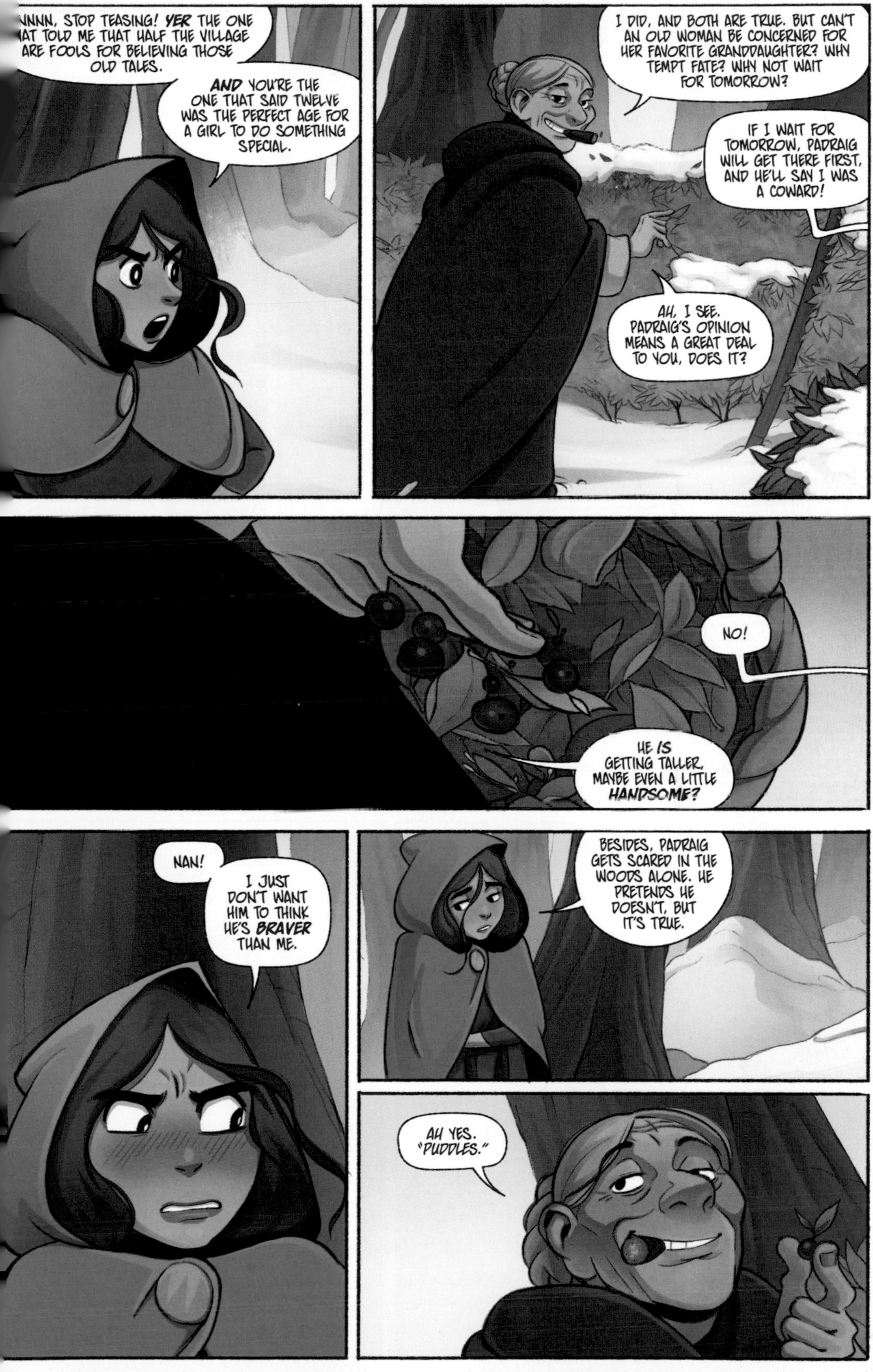
NNNN, STOP TEASING! YER THE ONE THAT TOLD ME THAT HALF THE VILLAGE ARE FOOLS FOR BELIEVING THOSE OLD TALES.
AND YOU'RE THE ONE THAT SAID TWELVE WAS THE PERFECT AGE FOR A GIRL TO DO SOMETHING SPECIAL.
I DID, AND BOTH ARE TRUE. BUT CAN'T AN OLD WOMAN BE CONCERNED FOR HER FAVORITE GRANDDAUGHTER? WHY TEMPT FATE? WHY NOT WAIT FOR TOMORROW?
IF I WAIT FOR TOMORROW, PADRAIG WILL GET THERE FIRST, AND HE'LL SAY I WAS A COWARD!
AH, I SEE. PADRAIG'S OPINION MEANS A GREAT DEAL TO YOU, DOES IT?
NO!
HE IS GETTING TALLER, MAYBE EVEN A LITTLE HANDSOME?
NAN!
I JUST DON'T WANT HIM TO THINK HE'S BRAVER THAN ME.
BESIDES, PADRAIG GETS SCARED IN THE WOODS ALONE. HE PRETENDS HE DOESN'T, BUT IT'S TRUE.
AH YES. "PUDDLES."

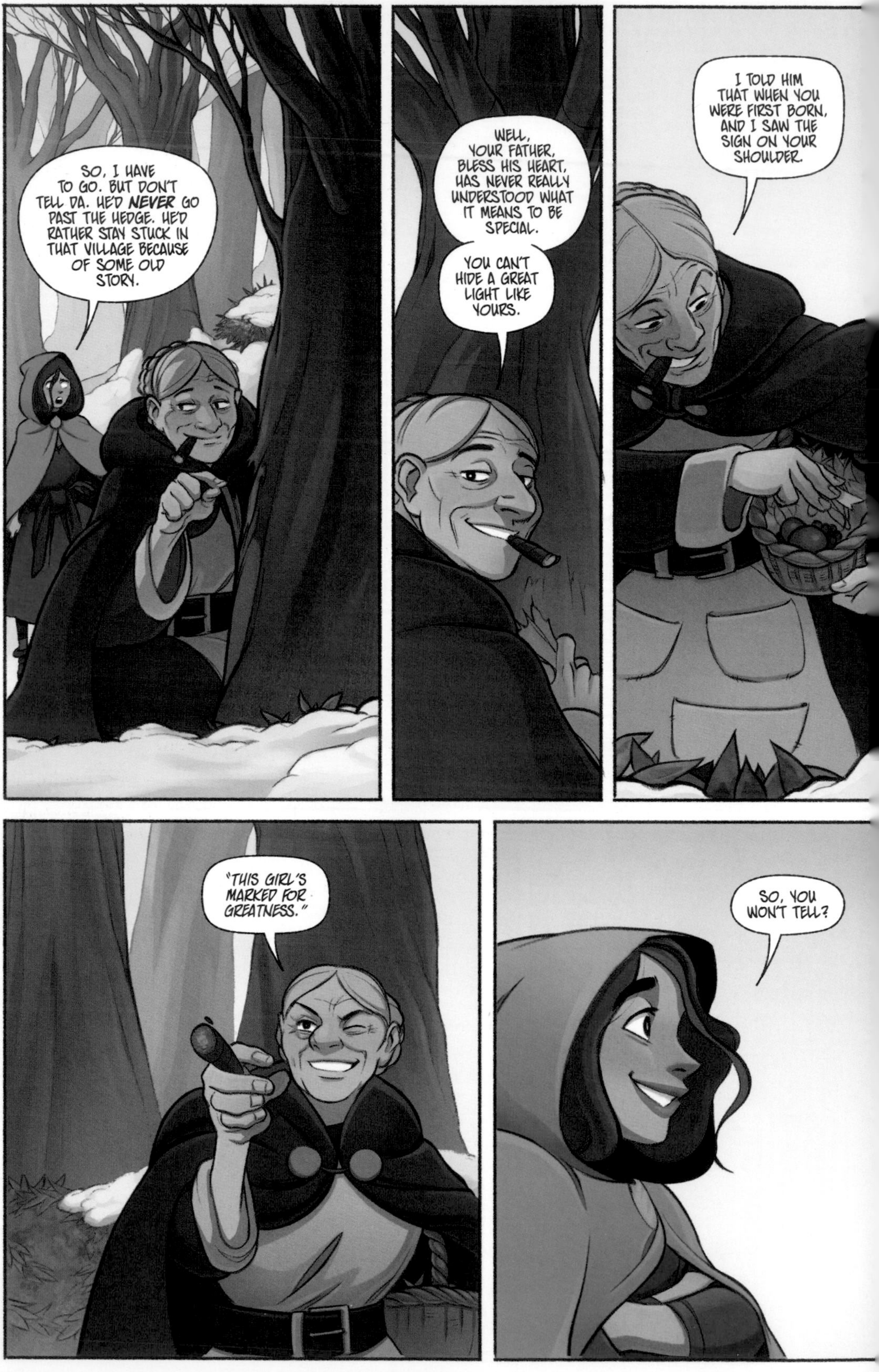
SO, I HAVE TO GO. BUT DON'T TELL DA. HE'D **NEVER** GO PAST THE HEDGE. HE'D RATHER STAY STUCK IN THAT VILLAGE BECAUSE OF SOME OLD STORY.
WELL, YOUR FATHER, BLESS HIS HEART, HAS NEVER REALLY UNDERSTOOD WHAT IT MEANS TO BE SPECIAL.
YOU CAN'T HIDE A GREAT LIGHT LIKE YOURS.
I TOLD HIM THAT WHEN YOU WERE FIRST BORN, AND I SAW THE SIGN ON YOUR SHOULDER.
"THIS GIRL'S MARKED FOR GREATNESS."
SO, YOU WON'T TELL?

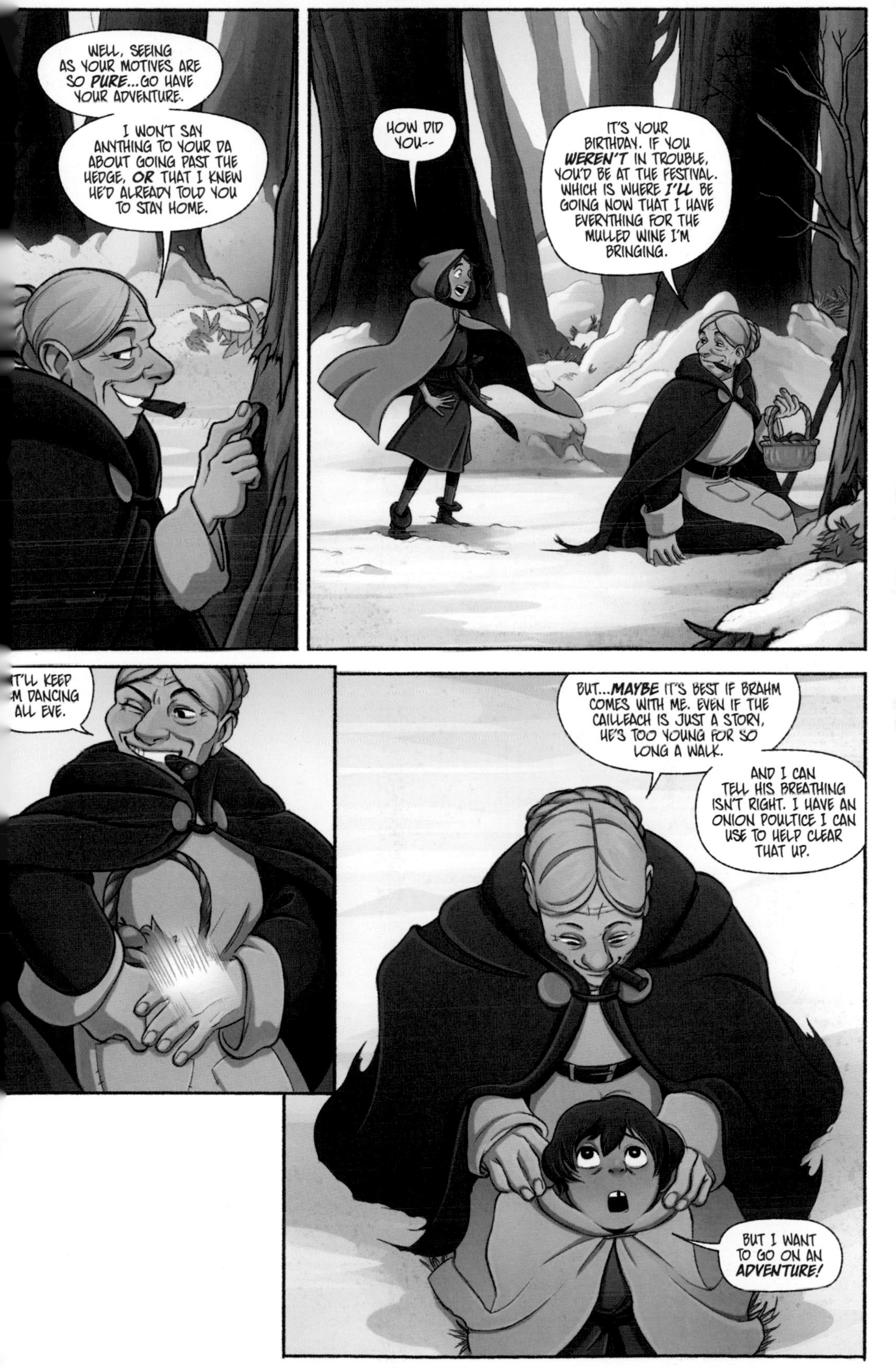
WELL, SEEING AS YOUR MOTIVES ARE SO PURE...GO HAVE YOUR ADVENTURE.
I WON'T SAY ANYTHING TO YOUR DA ABOUT GOING PAST THE HEDGE, OR THAT I KNEW HE'D ALREADY TOLD YOU TO STAY HOME.
HOW DID YOU--
IT'S YOUR BIRTHDAY. IF YOU WEREN'T IN TROUBLE, YOU'D BE AT THE FESTIVAL. WHICH IS WHERE I'LL BE GOING NOW THAT I HAVE EVERYTHING FOR THE MULLED WINE I'M BRINGING.
IT'LL KEEP 'EM DANCING ALL EVE.
BUT...MAYBE IT'S BEST IF BRAHM COMES WITH ME. EVEN IF THE CAILLEACH IS JUST A STORY, HE'S TOO YOUNG FOR SO LONG A WALK.
AND I CAN TELL HIS BREATHING ISN'T RIGHT. I HAVE AN ONION POULTICE I CAN USE TO HELP CLEAR THAT UP.
BUT I WANT TO GO ON AN ADVENTURE!

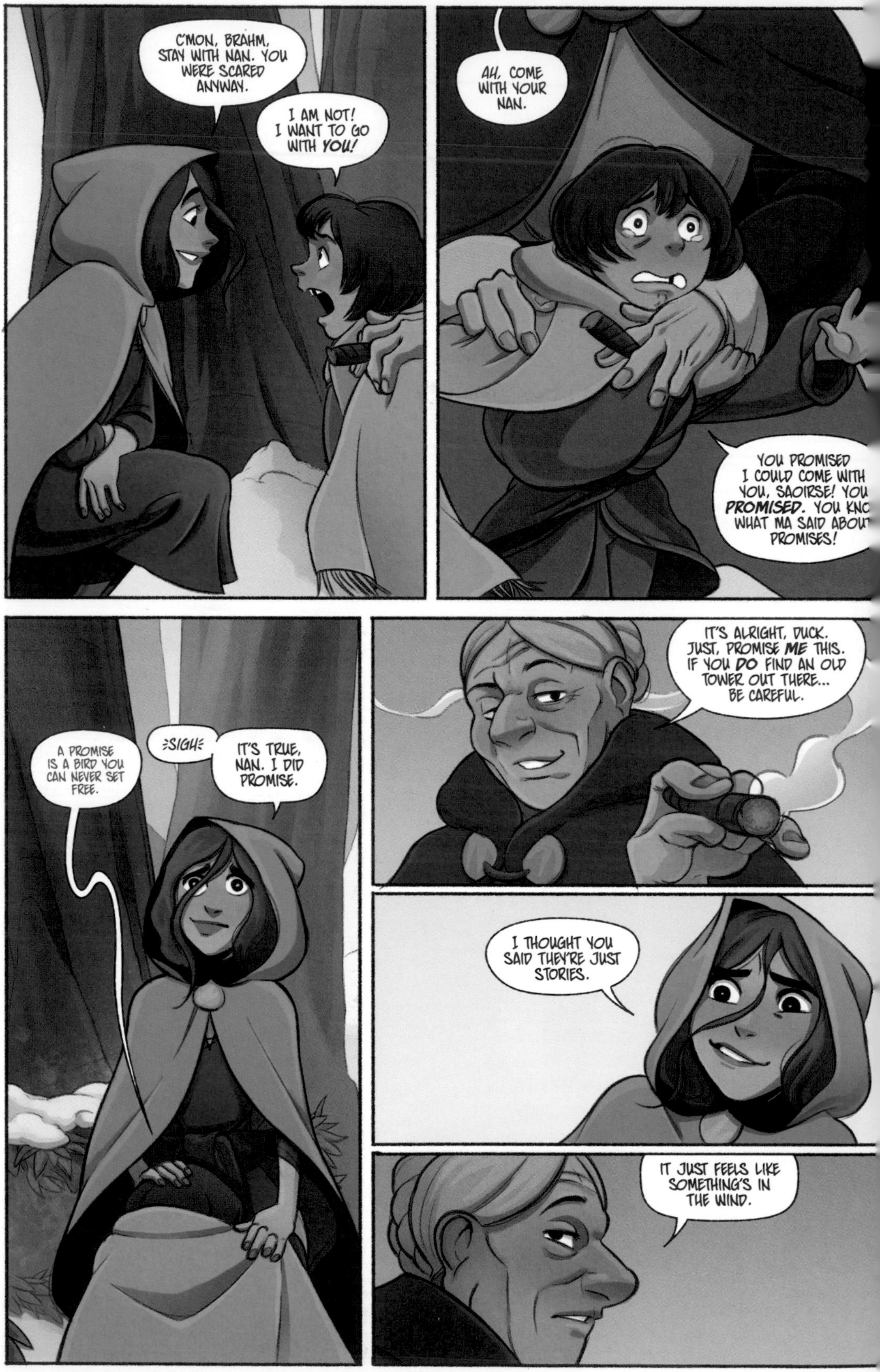
C'MON, BRAHM, STAY WITH NAN. YOU WERE SCARED ANYWAY.
I AM NOT! I WANT TO GO WITH *YOU!*
AH, COME WITH YOUR NAN.
YOU PROMISED I COULD COME WITH YOU, SAOIRSE! YOU *PROMISED.* YOU KNO WHAT MA SAID ABOUT PROMISES!
A PROMISE IS A BIRD YOU CAN NEVER SET FREE.
SIGH
IT'S TRUE, NAN. I DID PROMISE.
IT'S ALRIGHT, DUCK. JUST, PROMISE *ME* THIS. IF YOU *DO* FIND AN OLD TOWER OUT THERE... BE CAREFUL.
I THOUGHT YOU SAID THEY'RE JUST STORIES.
IT JUST FEELS LIKE SOMETHING'S IN THE WIND.

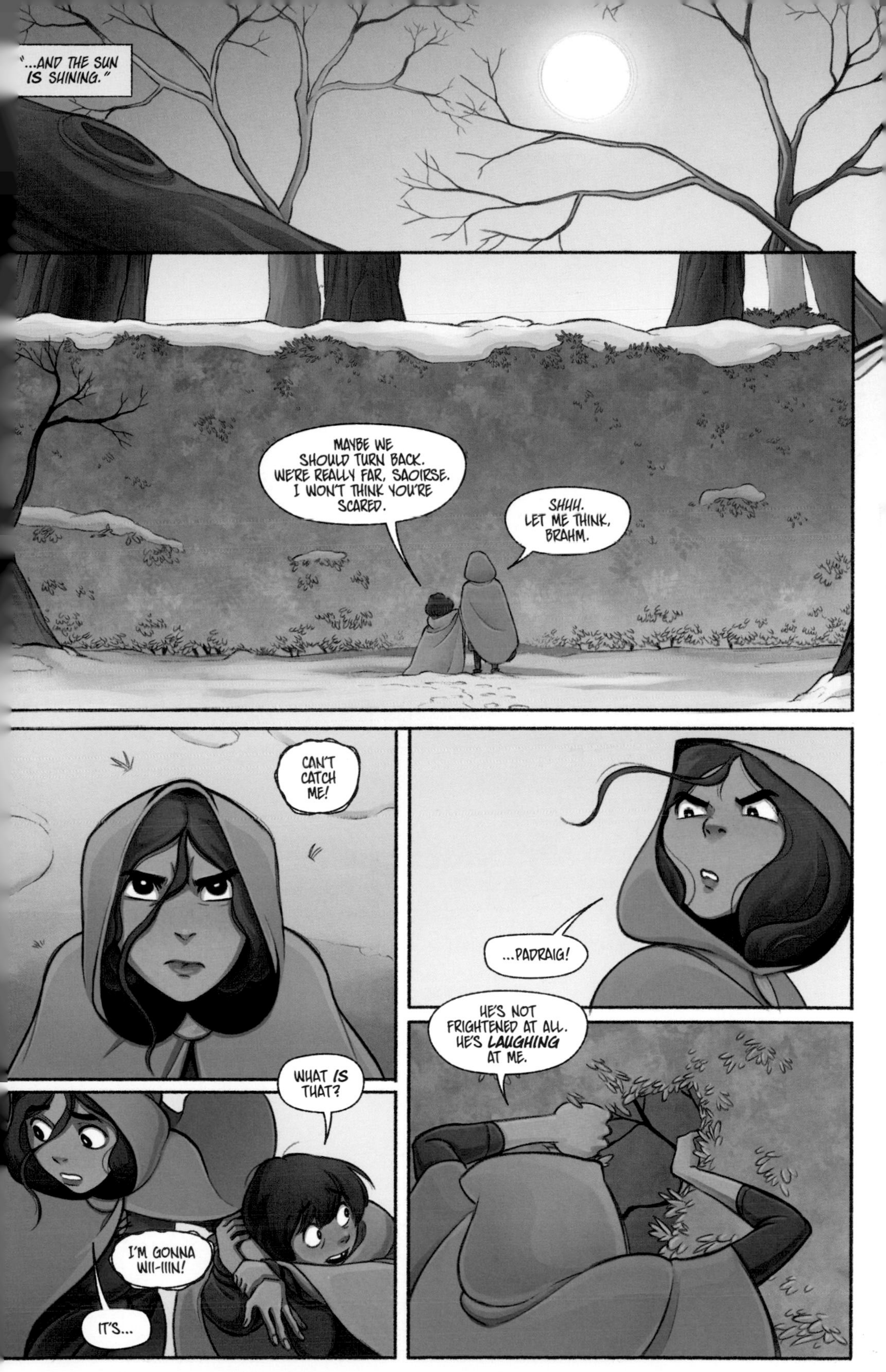
"...AND THE SUN IS SHINING."
MAYBE WE SHOULD TURN BACK. WE'RE REALLY FAR, SAOIRSE. I WON'T THINK YOU'RE SCARED.
SHHH. LET ME THINK, BRAHM.
CAN'T CATCH ME!
...PADRAIG!
WHAT IS THAT?
I'M GONNA WII-IIIN!
IT'S...
HE'S NOT FRIGHTENED AT ALL. HE'S LAUGHING AT ME.

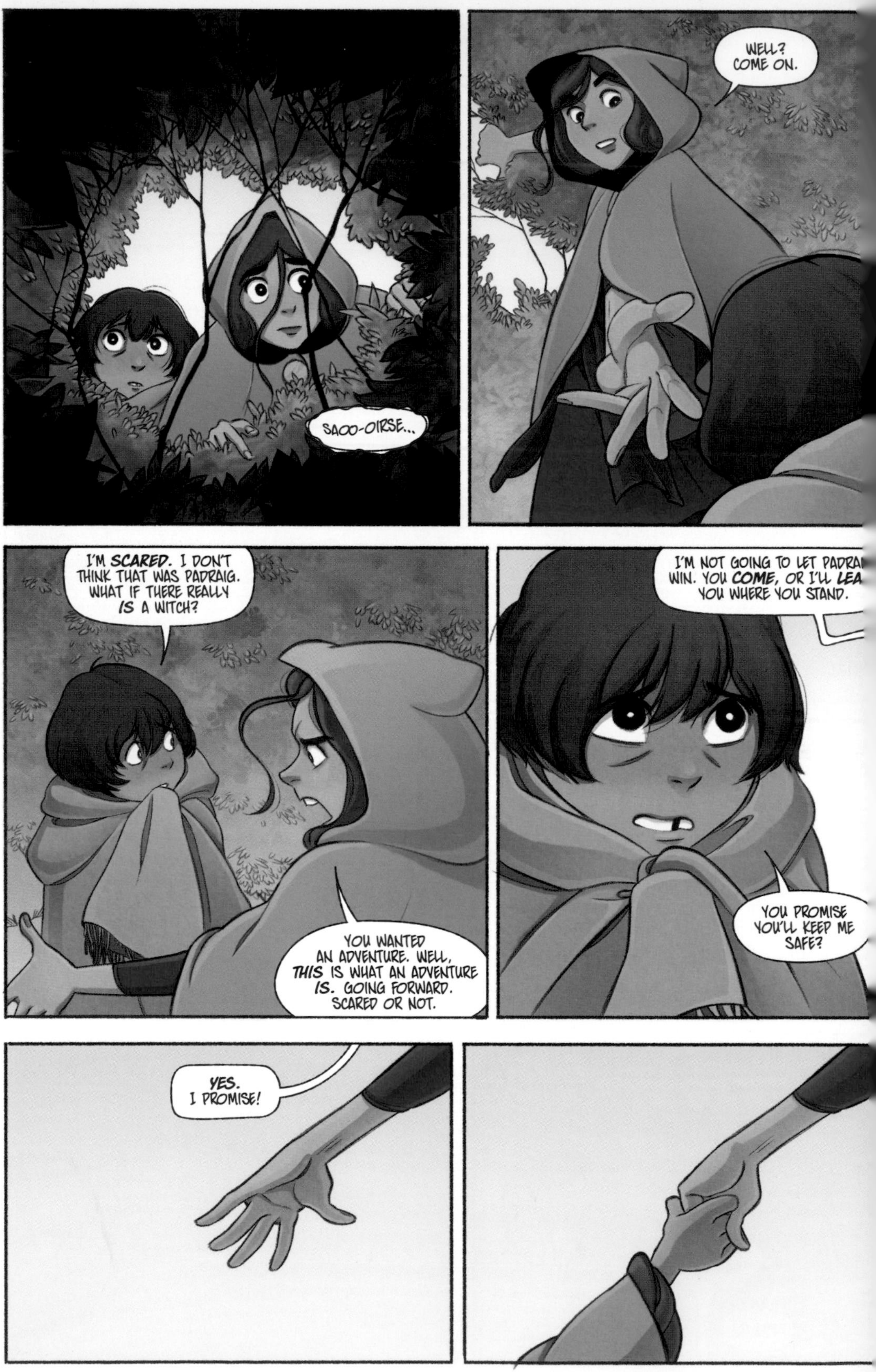
SAOO-OIRSE...
WELL? COME ON.
I'M **SCARED**. I DON'T THINK THAT WAS PADRAIG. WHAT IF THERE REALLY ***IS*** A WITCH?
YOU WANTED AN ADVENTURE. WELL, ***THIS*** IS WHAT AN ADVENTURE ***IS***. GOING FORWARD. SCARED OR NOT.
I'M NOT GOING TO LET PADRAI WIN. YOU **COME**, OR I'LL **LEA** YOU WHERE YOU STAND.
YOU PROMISE YOU'LL KEEP ME SAFE?
YES. I PROMISE!

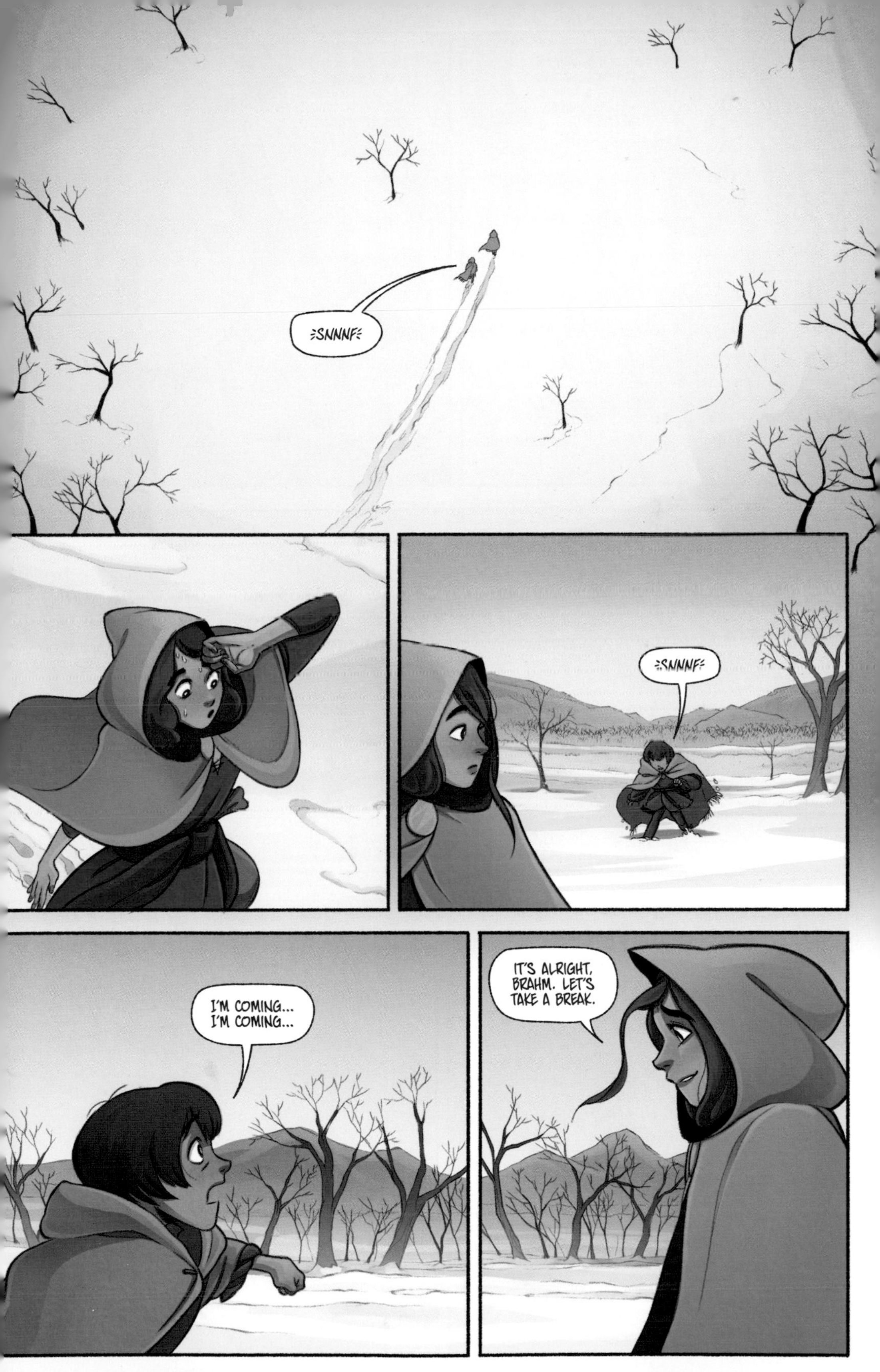
SNNNF
SNNNF
I'M COMING... I'M COMING...
IT'S ALRIGHT, BRAHM. LET'S TAKE A BREAK.

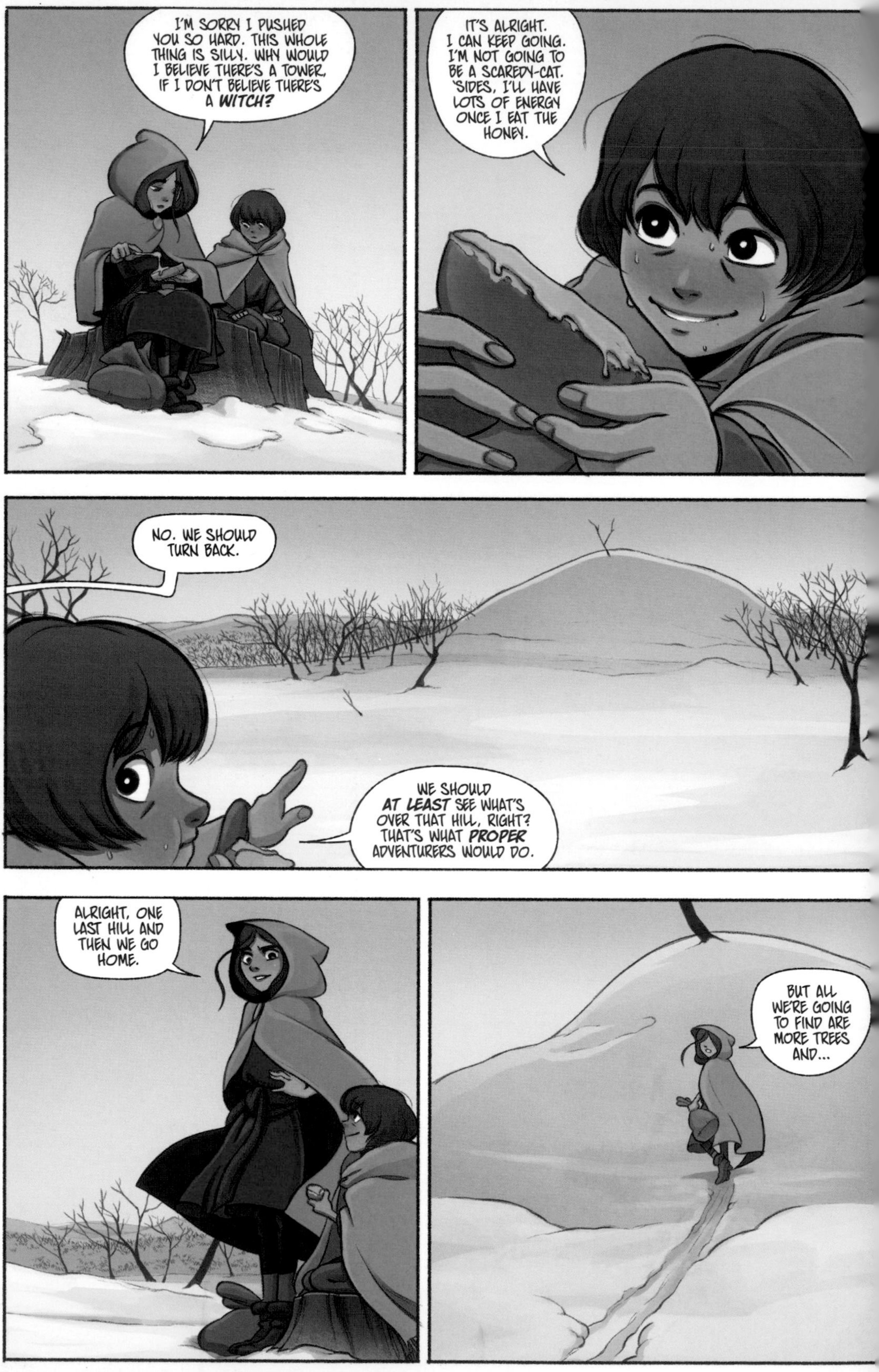
I'M SORRY I PUSHED YOU SO HARD. THIS WHOLE THING IS SILLY. WHY WOULD I BELIEVE THERE'S A TOWER, IF I DON'T BELIEVE THERE'S A **WITCH?**
IT'S ALRIGHT. I CAN KEEP GOING. I'M NOT GOING TO BE A SCAREDY-CAT. 'SIDES, I'LL HAVE LOTS OF ENERGY ONCE I EAT THE HONEY.
NO. WE SHOULD TURN BACK.
WE SHOULD **AT LEAST** SEE WHAT'S OVER THAT HILL, RIGHT? THAT'S WHAT **PROPER** ADVENTURERS WOULD DO.
ALRIGHT, ONE LAST HILL AND THEN WE GO HOME.
BUT ALL WE'RE GOING TO FIND ARE MORE TREES AND...

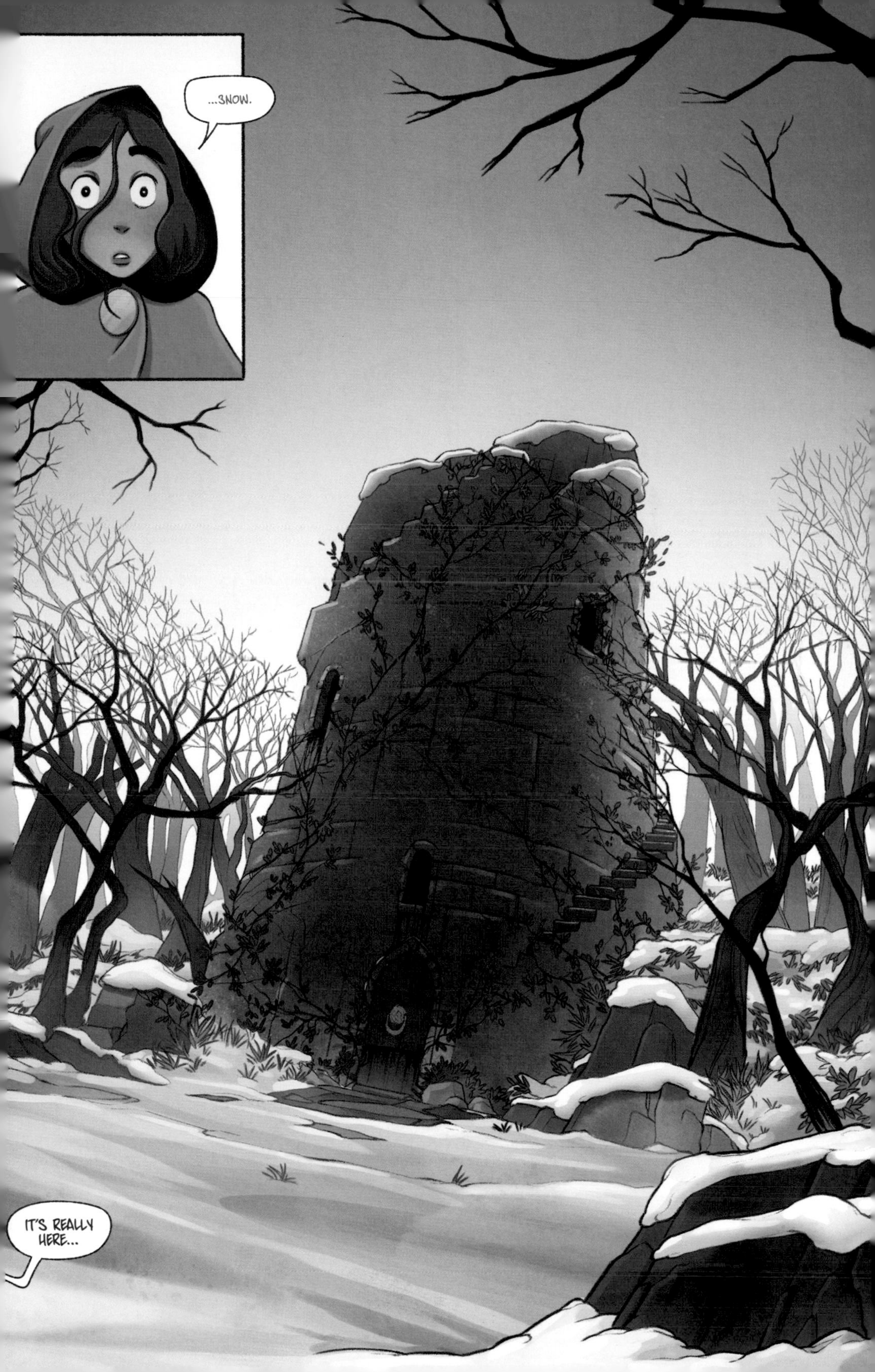
...SNOW.
IT'S REALLY HERE...

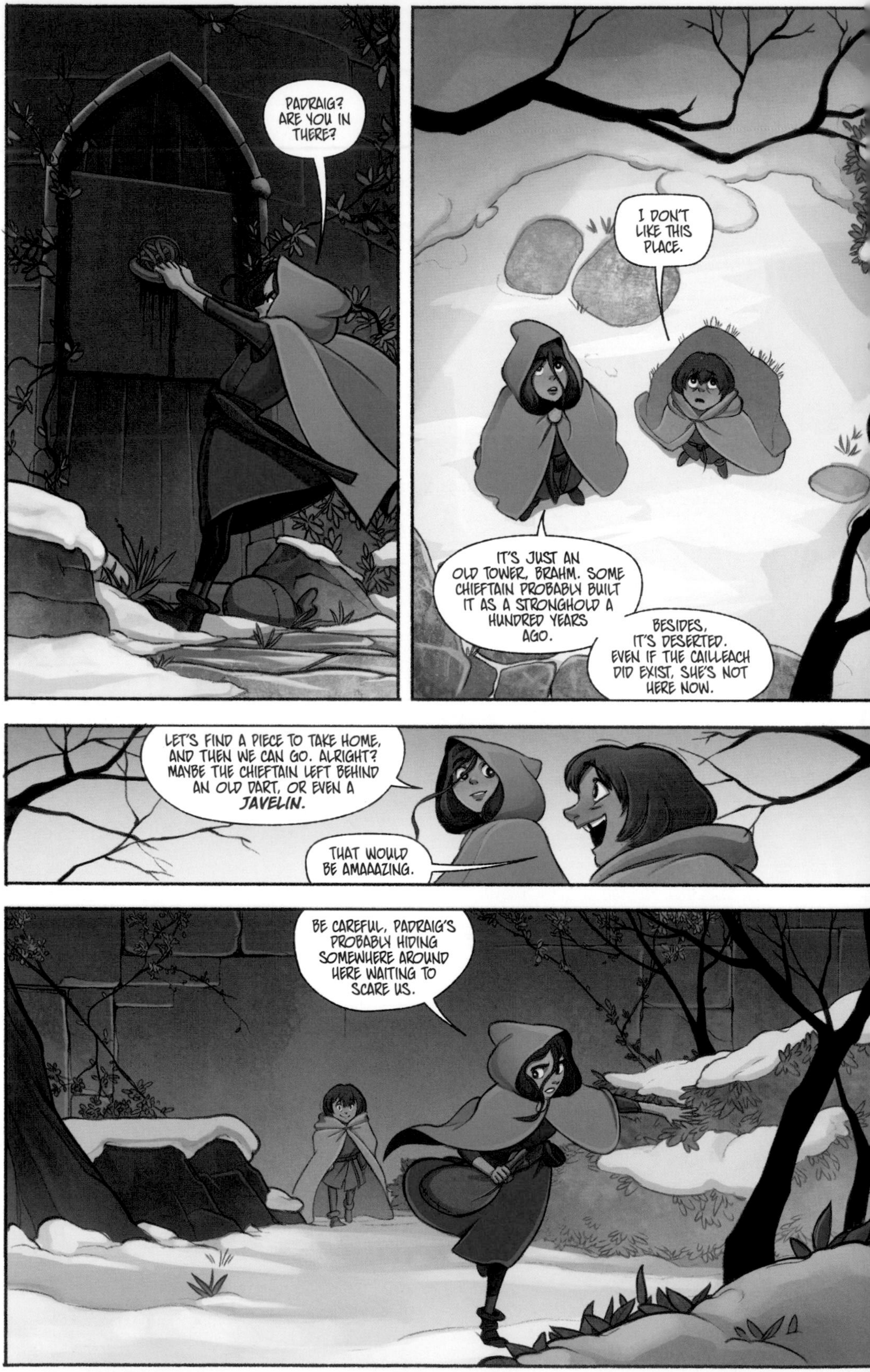
PADRAIG? ARE YOU IN THERE?
I DON'T LIKE THIS PLACE.
IT'S JUST AN OLD TOWER, BRAHM. SOME CHIEFTAIN PROBABLY BUILT IT AS A STRONGHOLD A HUNDRED YEARS AGO.
BESIDES, IT'S DESERTED. EVEN IF THE CAILLEACH DID EXIST, SHE'S NOT HERE NOW.
LET'S FIND A PIECE TO TAKE HOME, AND THEN WE CAN GO. ALRIGHT? MAYBE THE CHIEFTAIN LEFT BEHIND AN OLD DART, OR EVEN A JAVELIN.
THAT WOULD BE AMAAAZING.
BE CAREFUL, PADRAIG'S PROBABLY HIDING SOMEWHERE AROUND HERE WAITING TO SCARE US.

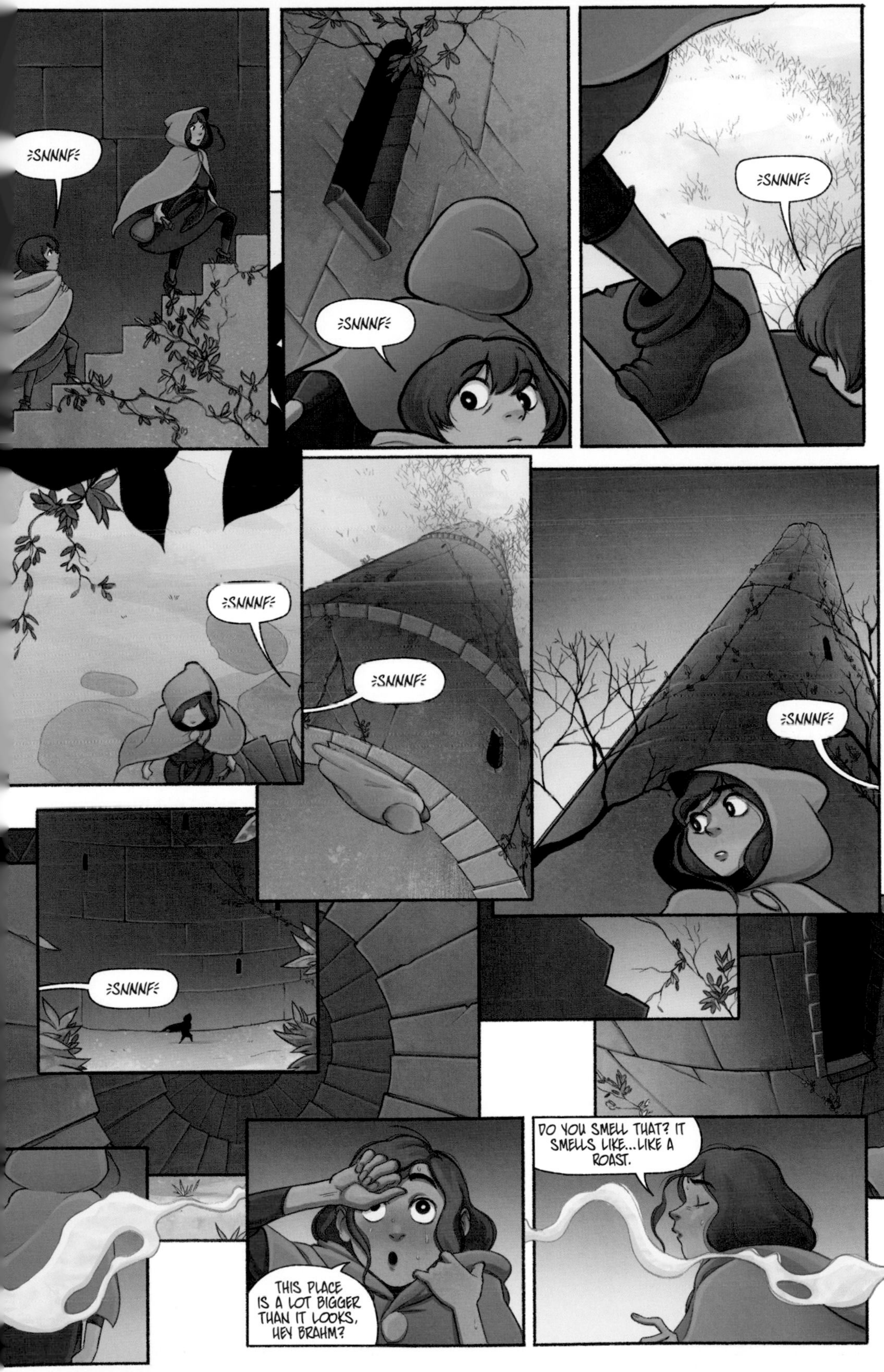

≈SNNNF≈
≈SNNNF≈
≈SNNNF≈
≈SNNNF≈
≈SNNNF≈
≈SNNNF≈
≈SNNNF≈
THIS PLACE IS A LOT BIGGER THAN IT LOOKS, HEY BRAHM?
DO YOU SMELL THAT? IT SMELLS LIKE...LIKE A ROAST.

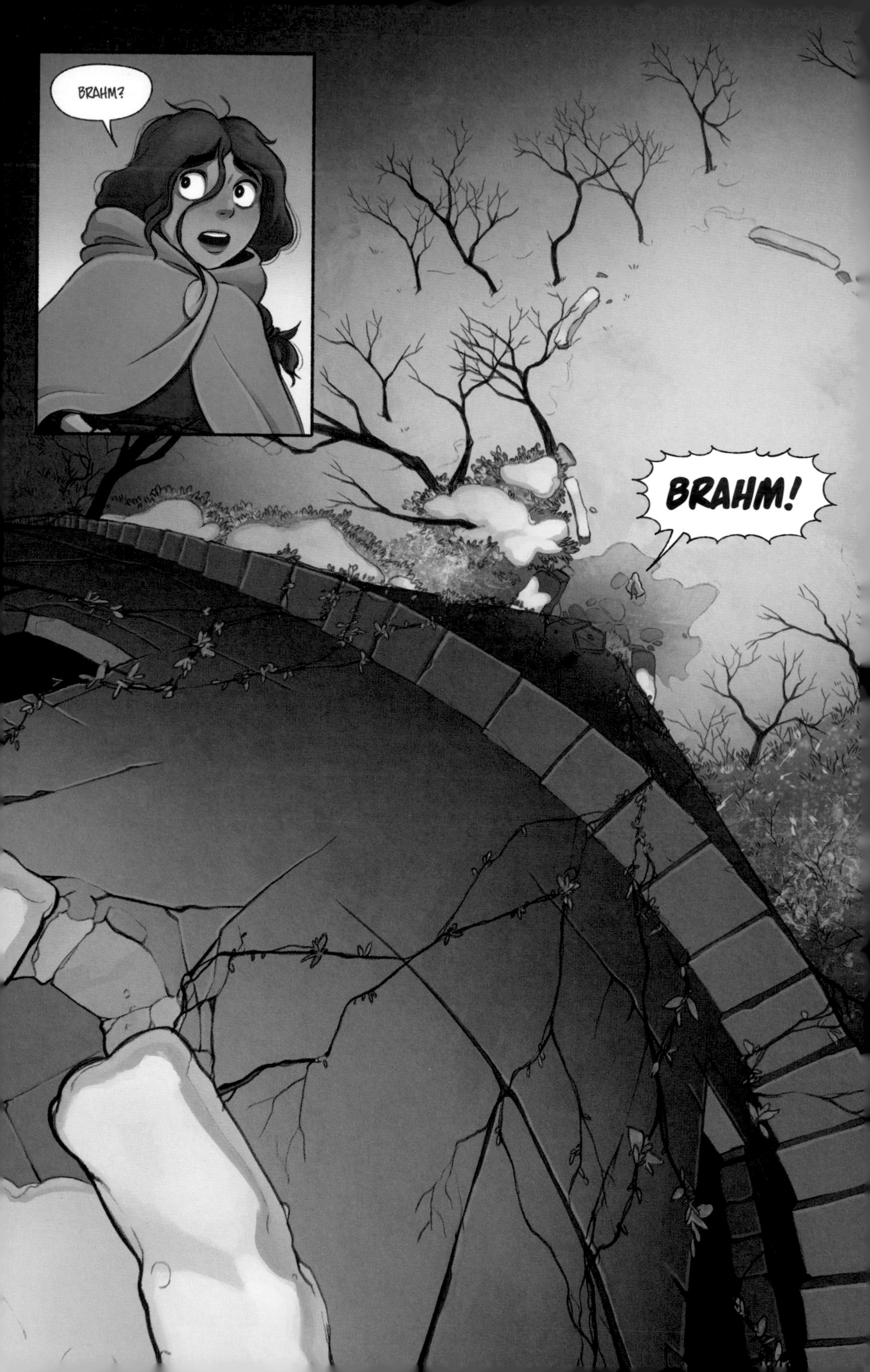
BRAHM?
BRAHM!

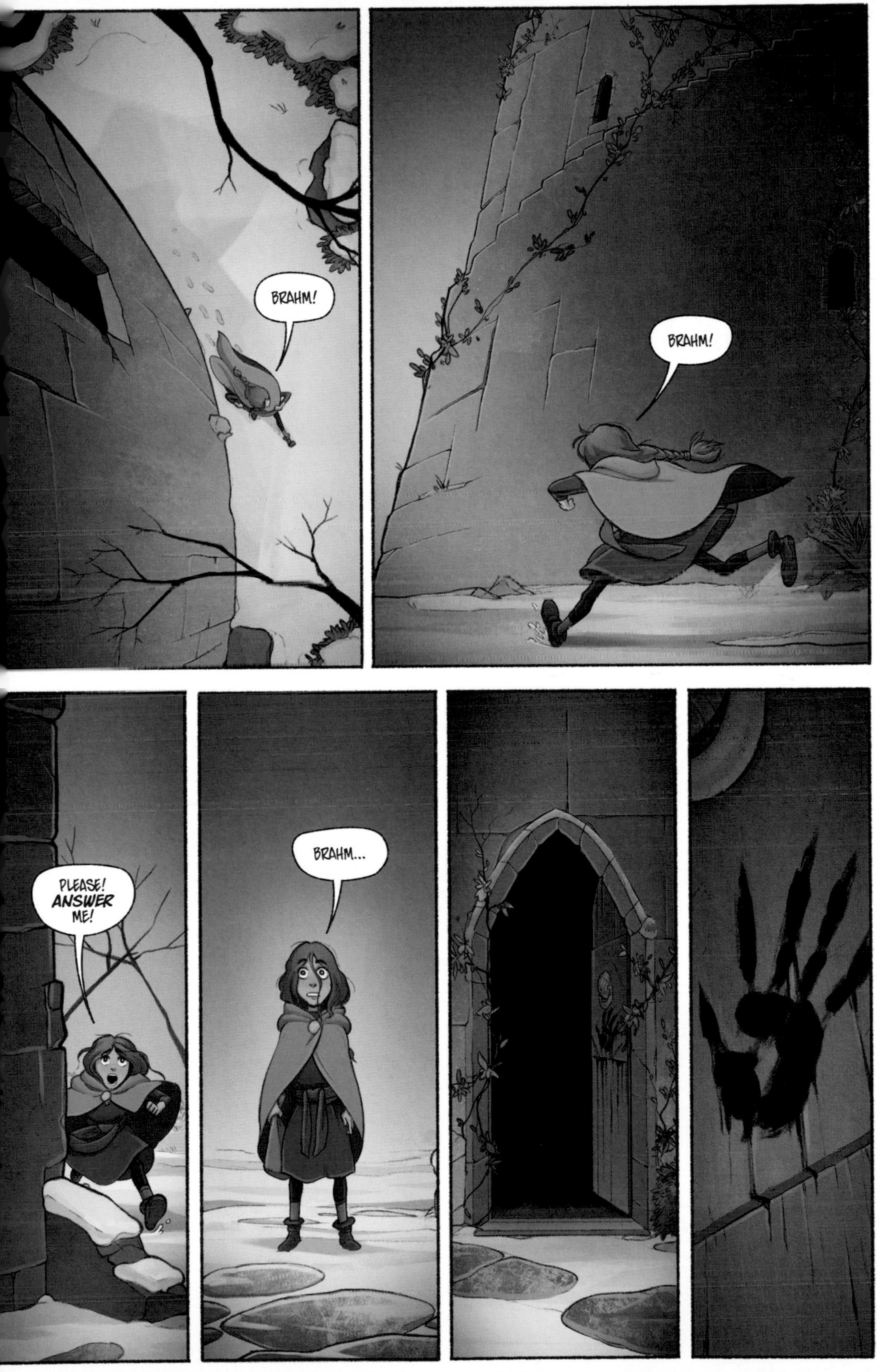
BRAHM!
BRAHM!
PLEASE! **ANSWER** ME!
BRAHM...

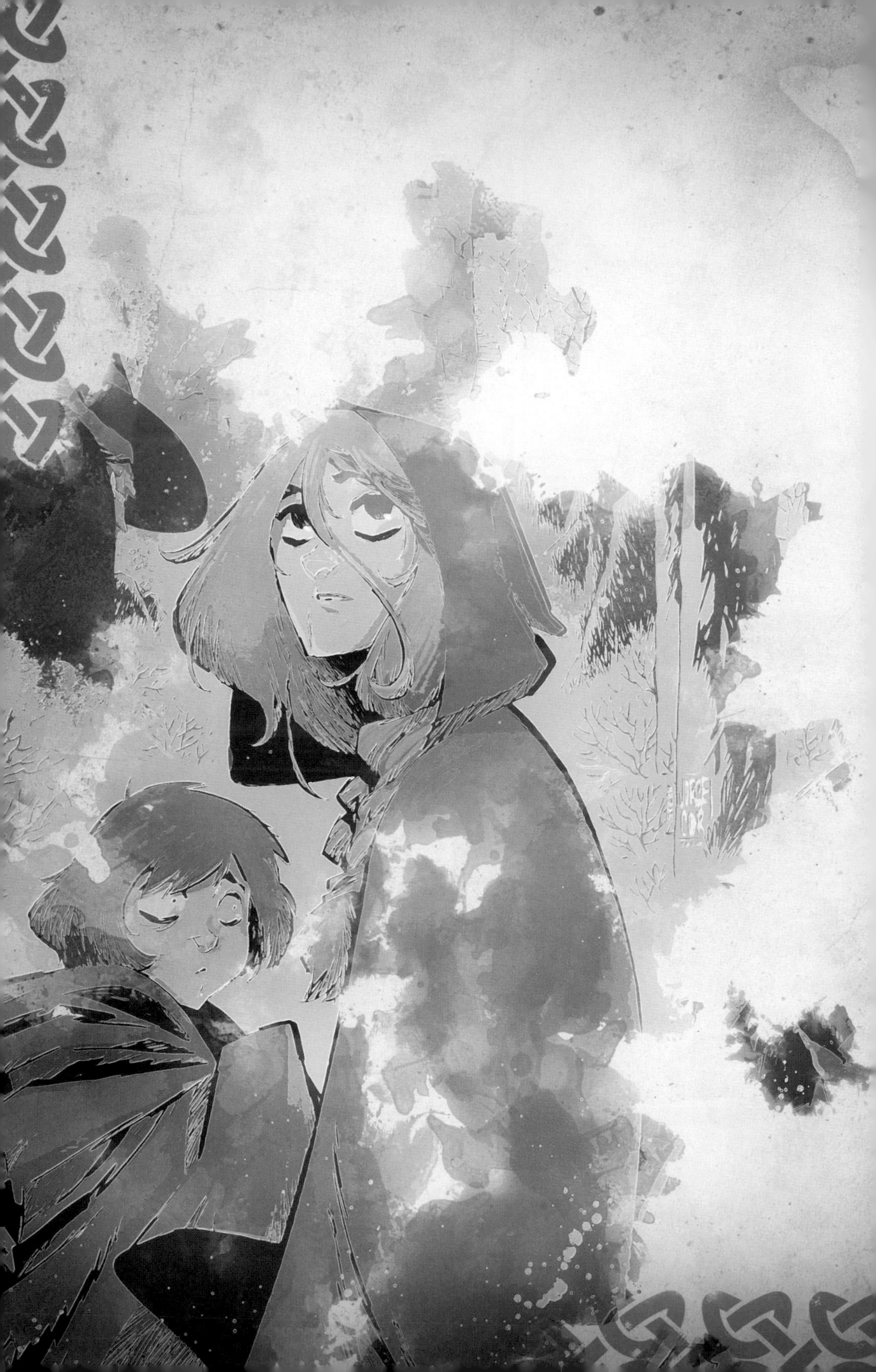

CHAPTER
TWO

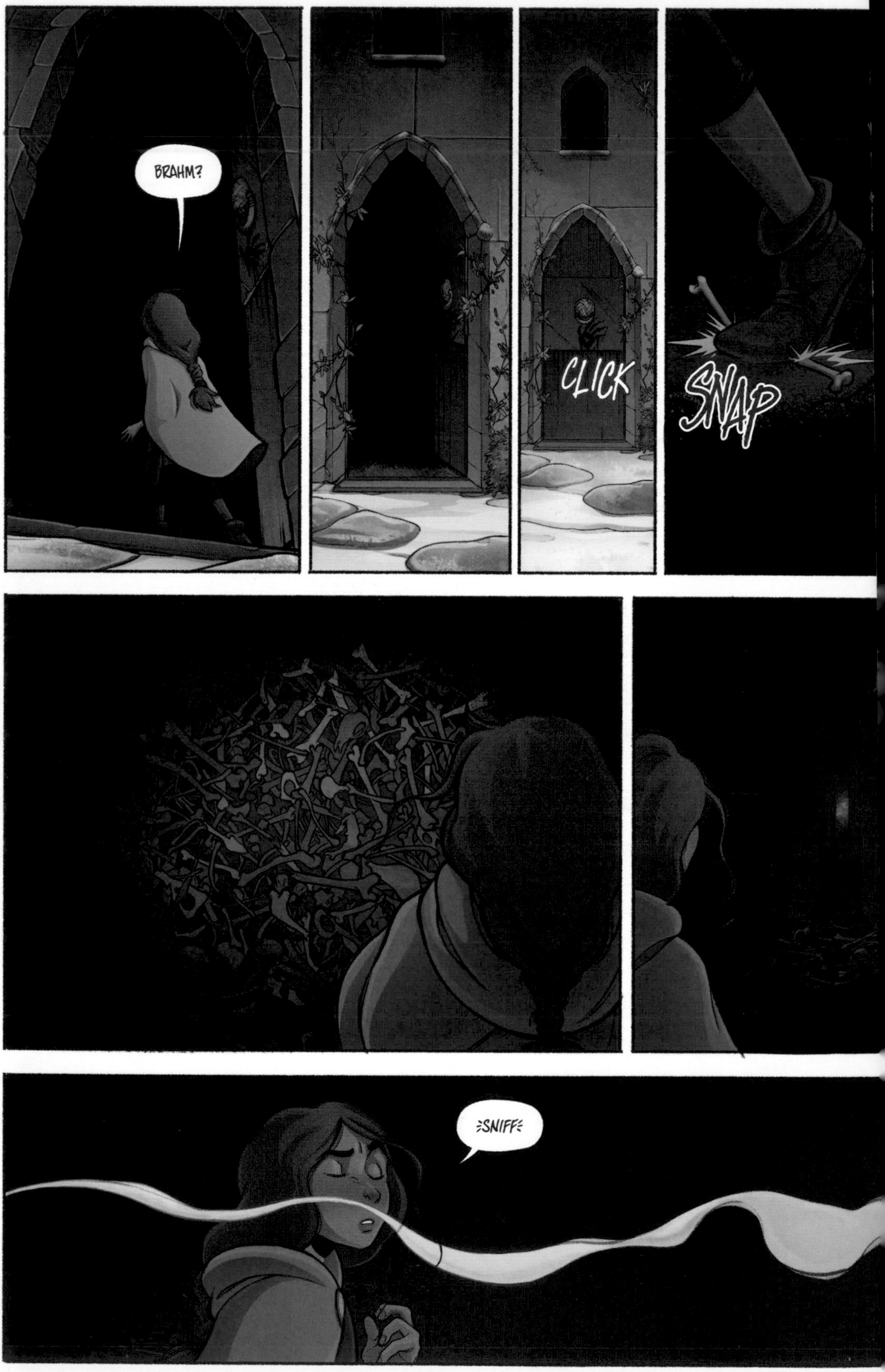
BRAHM?
CLICK
SNAP
SNIFF

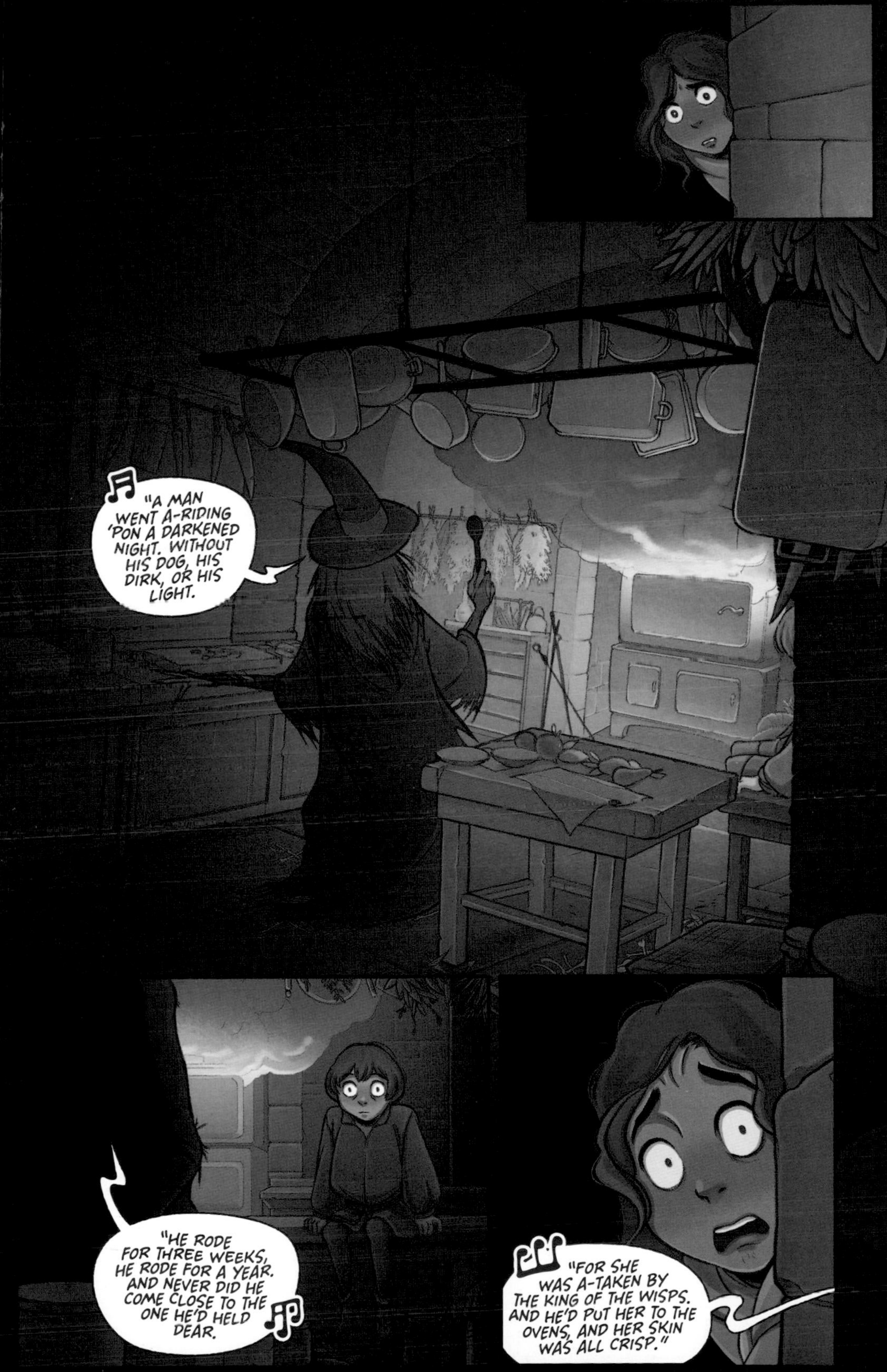
"A MAN WENT A-RIDING 'PON A DARKENED NIGHT. WITHOUT HIS DOG, HIS DIRK, OR HIS LIGHT.
"HE RODE FOR THREE WEEKS, HE RODE FOR A YEAR. AND NEVER DID HE COME CLOSE TO THE ONE HE'D HELD DEAR.
"FOR SHE WAS A-TAKEN BY THE KING OF THE WISPS. AND HE'D PUT HER TO THE OVENS, AND HER SKIN WAS ALL CRISP."

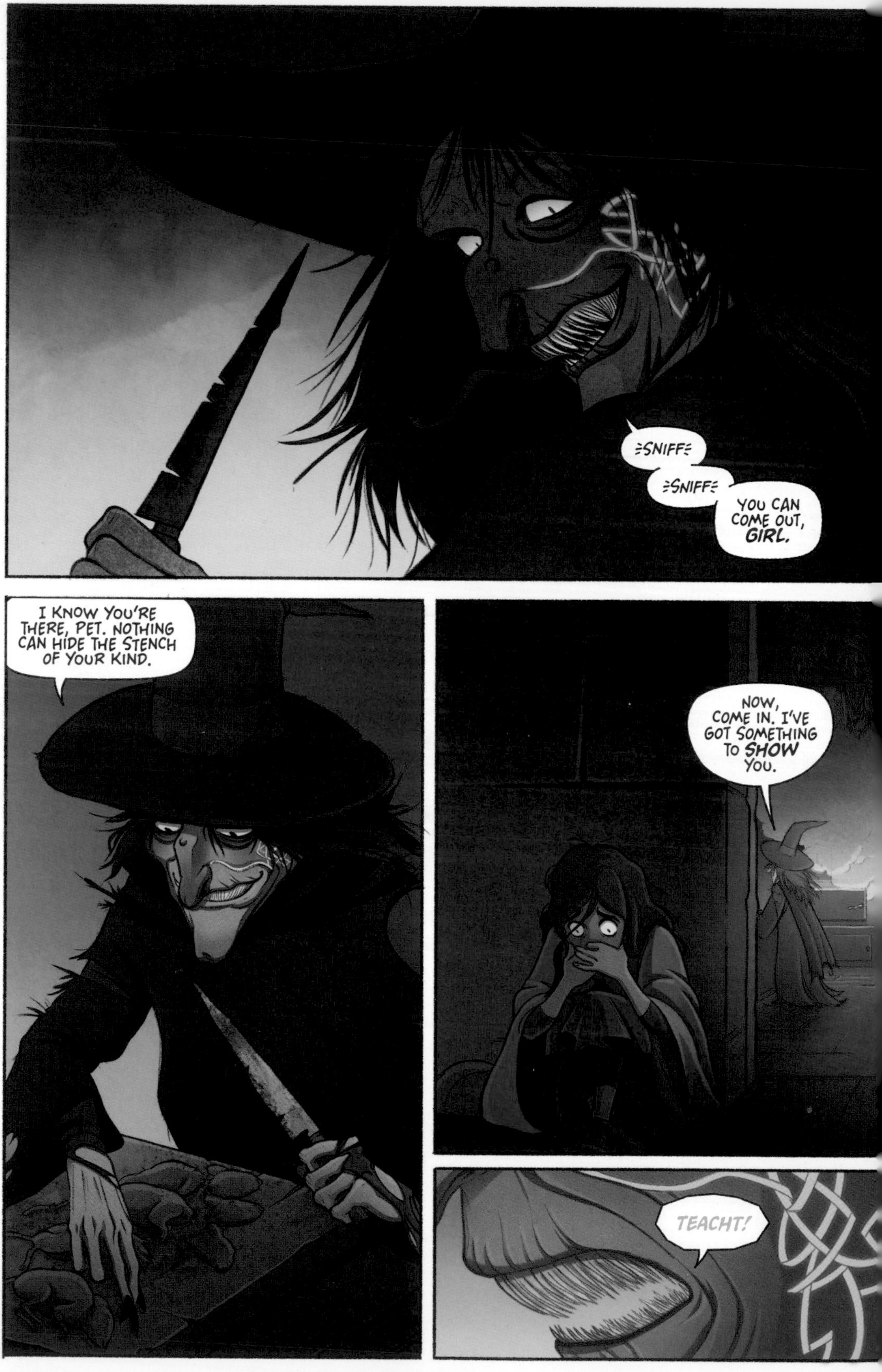

=SNIFF=
=SNIFF=
YOU CAN COME OUT, GIRL.
I KNOW YOU'RE THERE, PET. NOTHING CAN HIDE THE STENCH OF YOUR KIND.
NOW, COME IN. I'VE GOT SOMETHING TO SHOW YOU.
TEACHT!

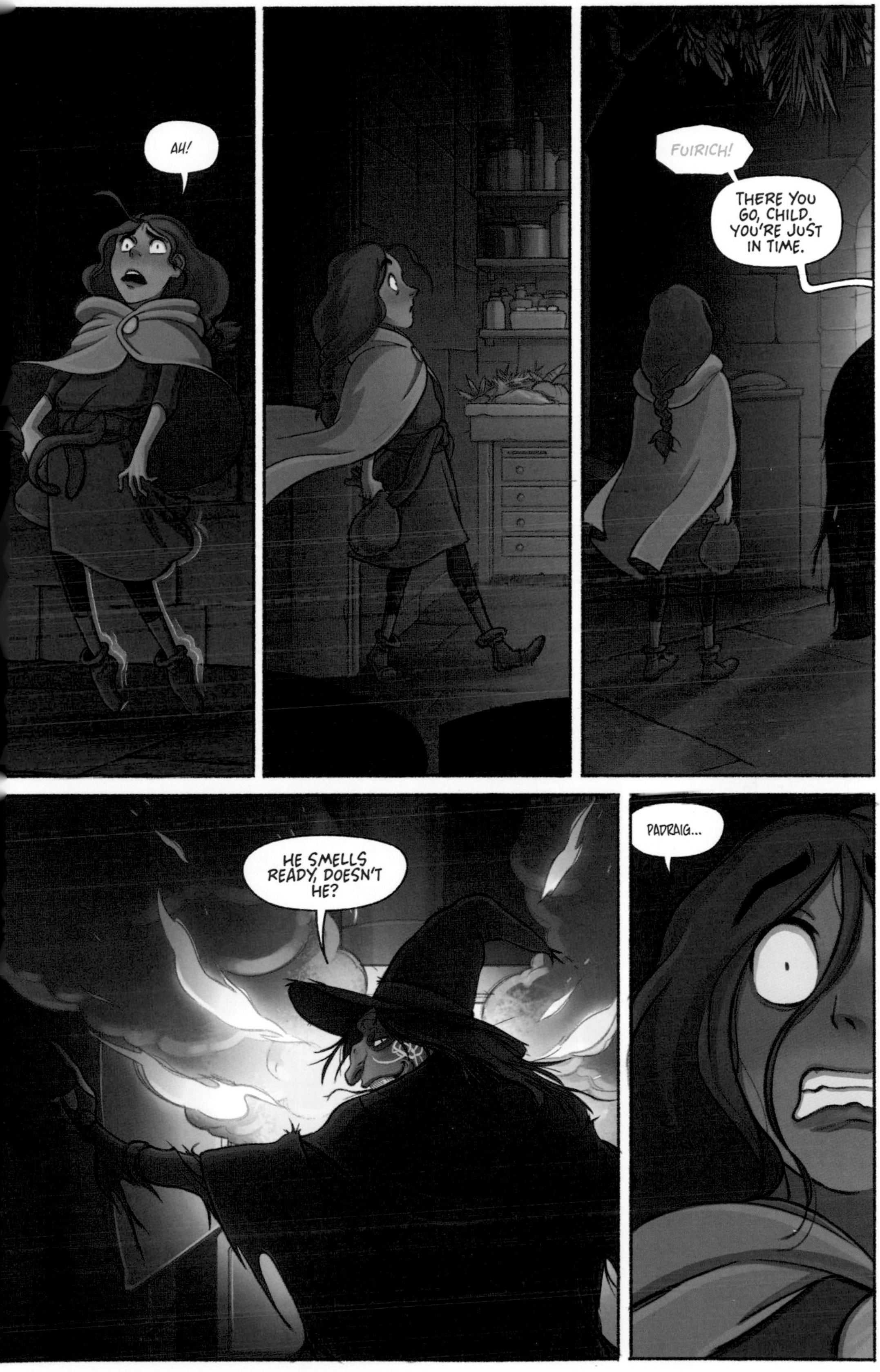
AH!
FUIRICH!
THERE YOU GO, CHILD. YOU'RE JUST IN TIME.
HE SMELLS READY, DOESN'T HE?
PADRAIG...

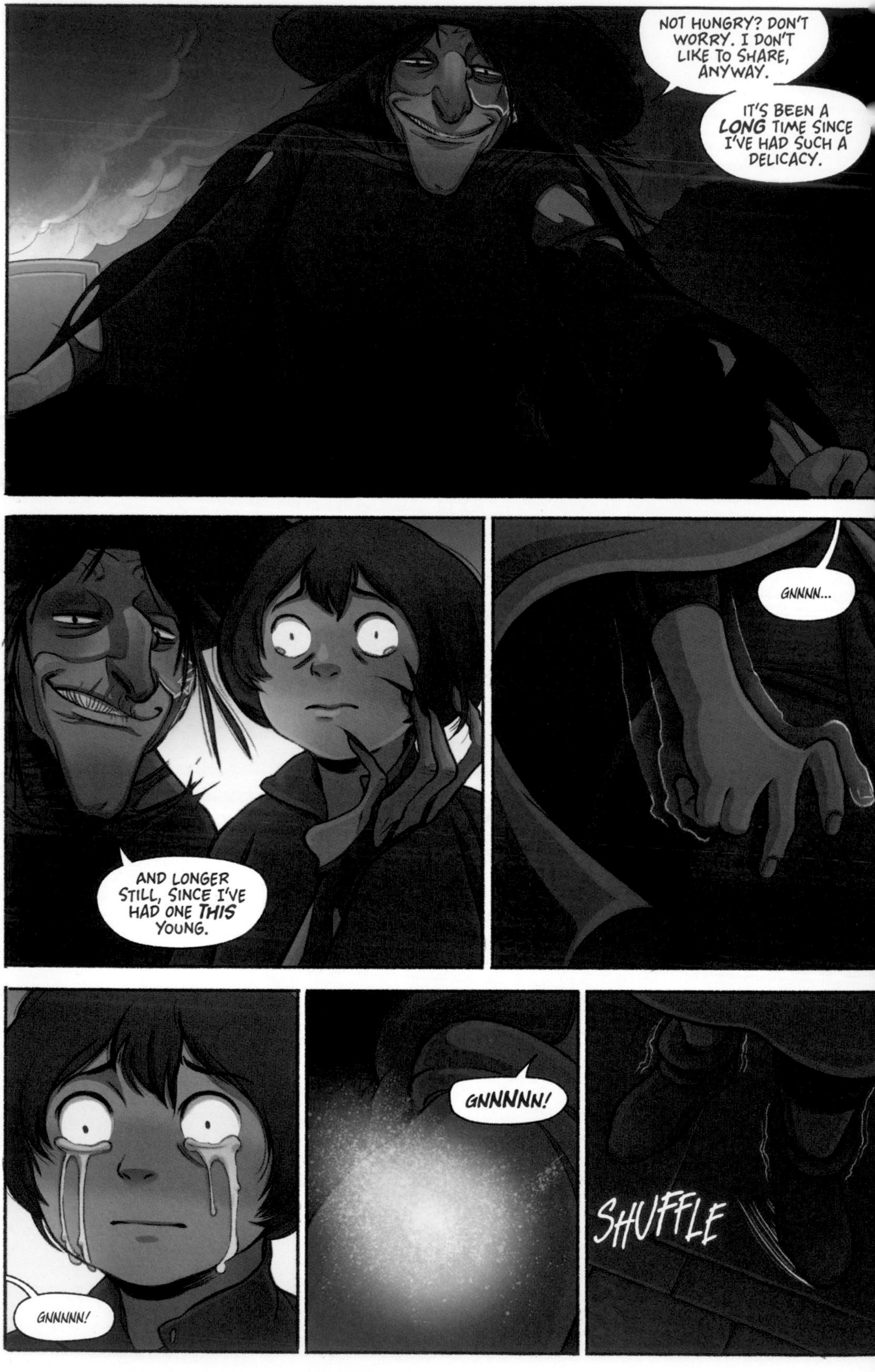
NOT HUNGRY? DON'T WORRY. I DON'T LIKE TO SHARE, ANYWAY.
IT'S BEEN A LONG TIME SINCE I'VE HAD SUCH A DELICACY.
AND LONGER STILL, SINCE I'VE HAD ONE THIS YOUNG.
GNNNN...
GNNNNN!
GNNNNN!
SHUFFLE

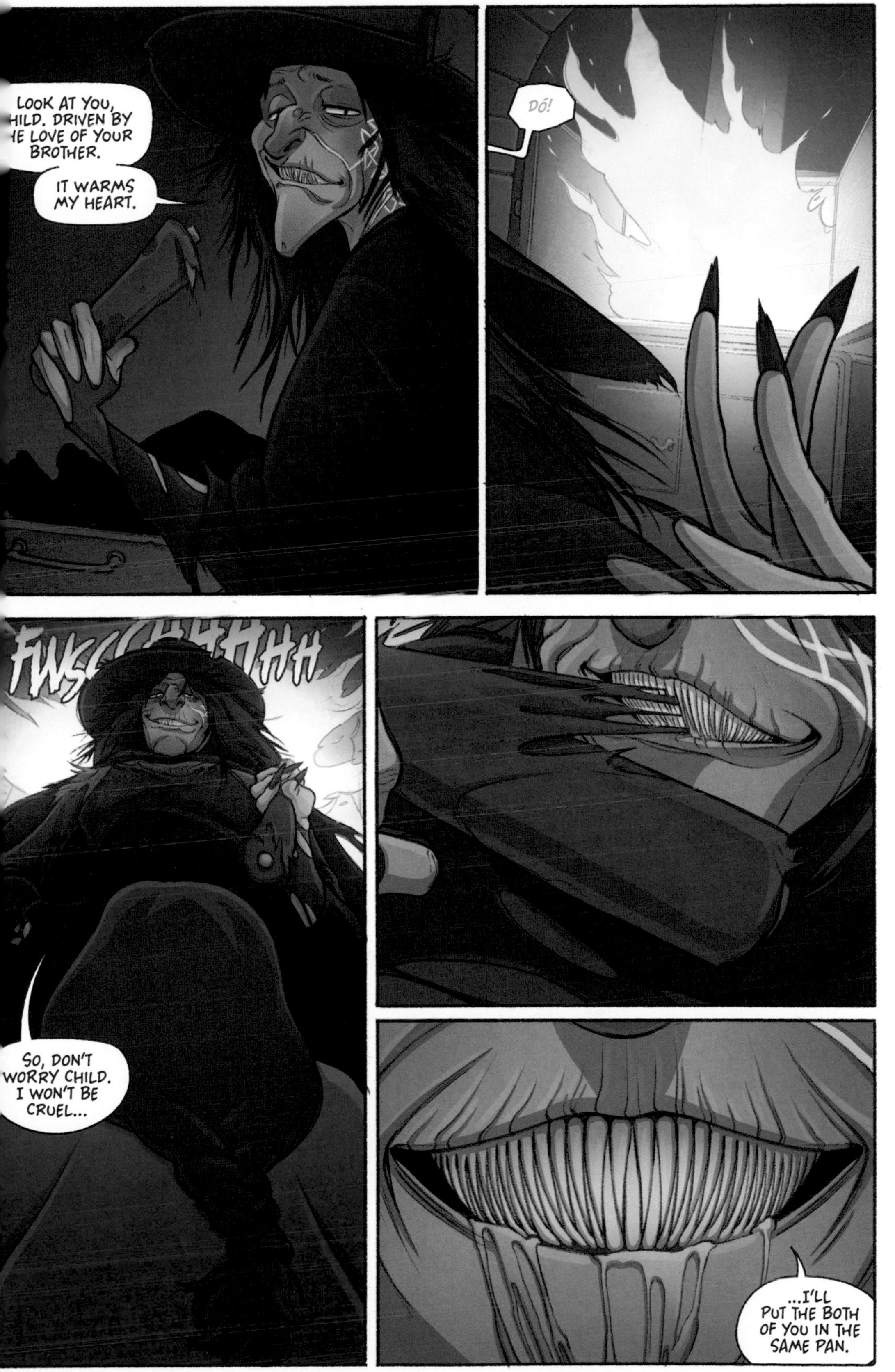
LOOK AT YOU, HILD. DRIVEN BY HE LOVE OF YOUR BROTHER.
IT WARMS MY HEART.
DÓ!
SO, DON'T WORRY CHILD. I WON'T BE CRUEL...
...I'LL PUT THE BOTH OF YOU IN THE SAME PAN.

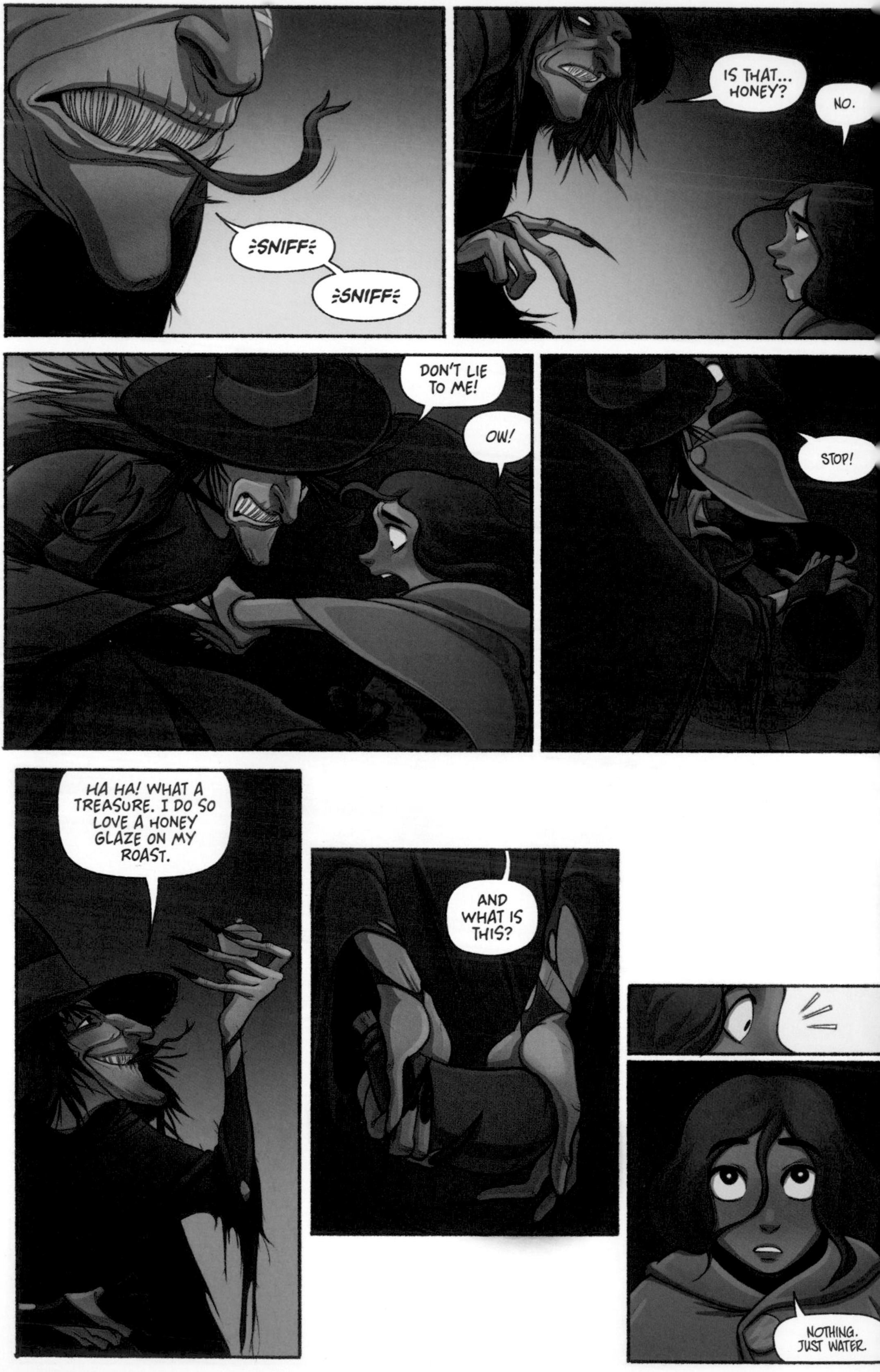
SNIFF
SNIFF
IS THAT... HONEY?
NO.
DON'T LIE TO ME!
OW!
STOP!
HA HA! WHAT A TREASURE. I DO SO LOVE A HONEY GLAZE ON MY ROAST.
AND WHAT IS THIS?
NOTHING. JUST WATER.

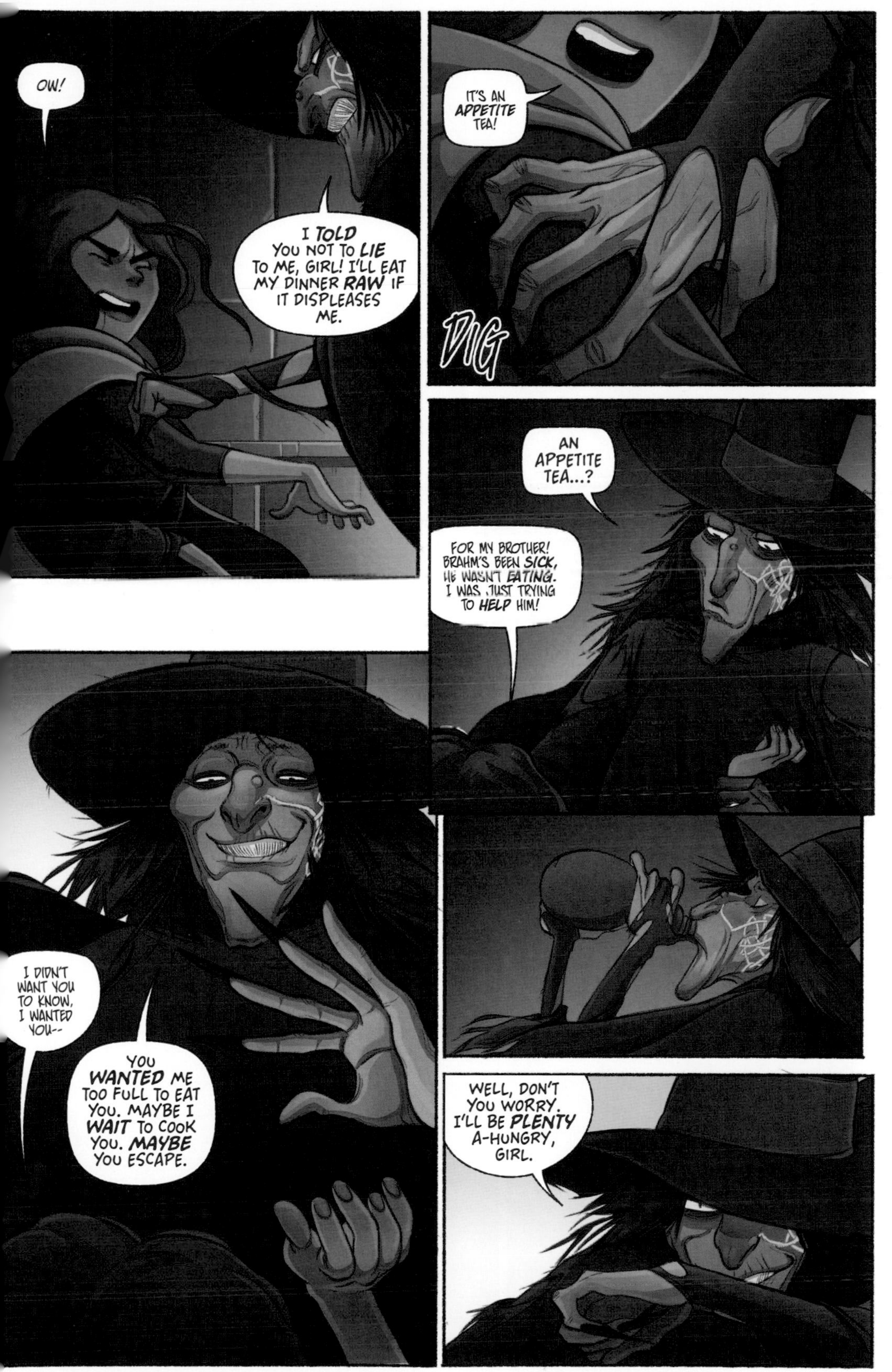
OW!
I TOLD YOU NOT TO LIE TO ME, GIRL! I'LL EAT MY DINNER RAW IF IT DISPLEASES ME.
IT'S AN APPETITE TEA!
DIG
AN APPETITE TEA...?
FOR MY BROTHER! BRAHM'S BEEN SICK, HE WASN'T EATING. I WAS JUST TRYING TO HELP HIM!
I DIDN'T WANT YOU TO KNOW, I WANTED YOU--
YOU WANTED ME TOO FULL TO EAT YOU. MAYBE I WAIT TO COOK YOU. MAYBE YOU ESCAPE.
WELL, DON'T YOU WORRY. I'LL BE PLENTY A-HUNGRY, GIRL.

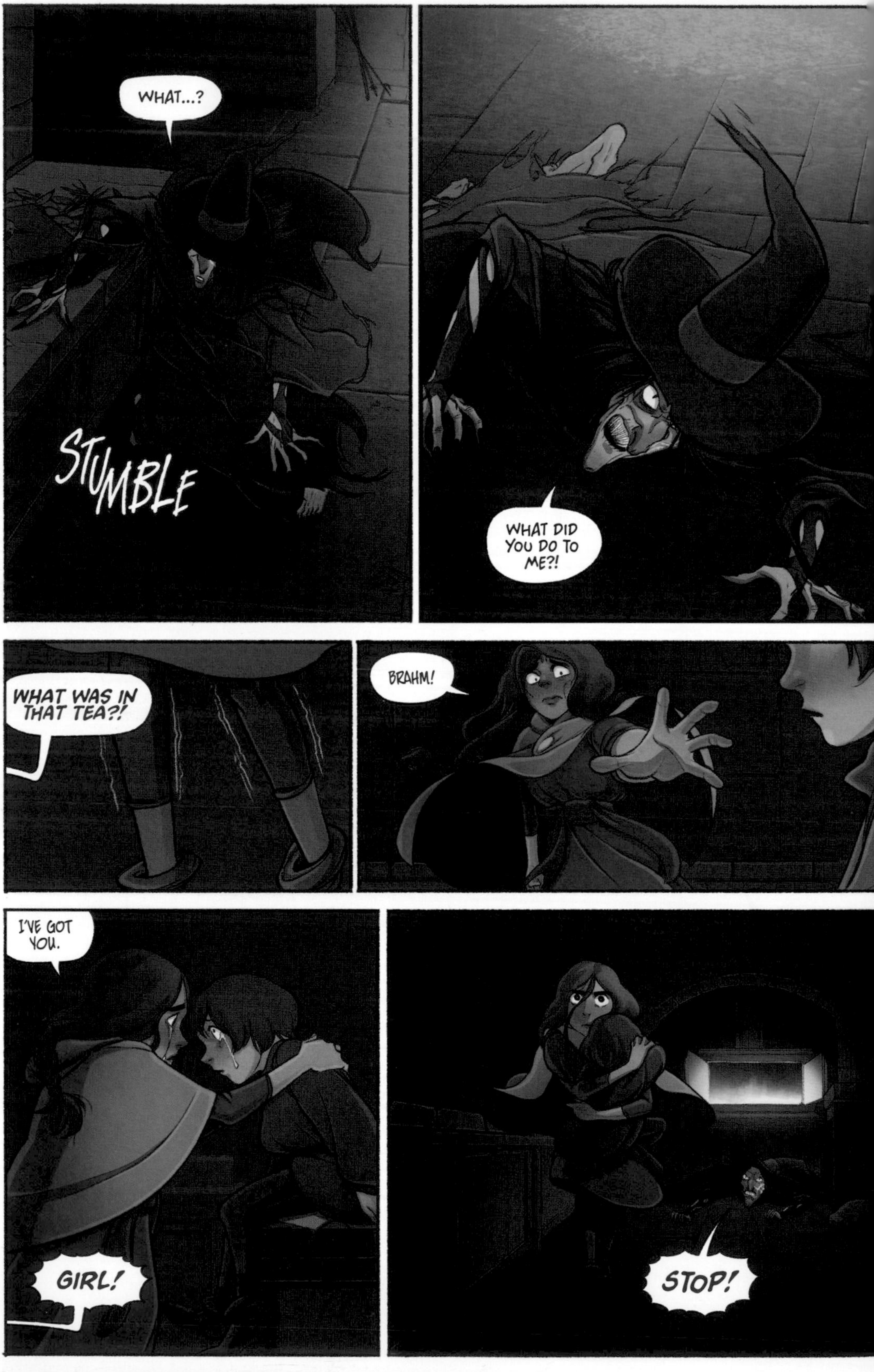
WHAT...?
STUMBLE
WHAT DID YOU DO TO ME?!
WHAT WAS IN THAT TEA?!
BRAHM!
I'VE GOT YOU.
GIRL!
STOP!

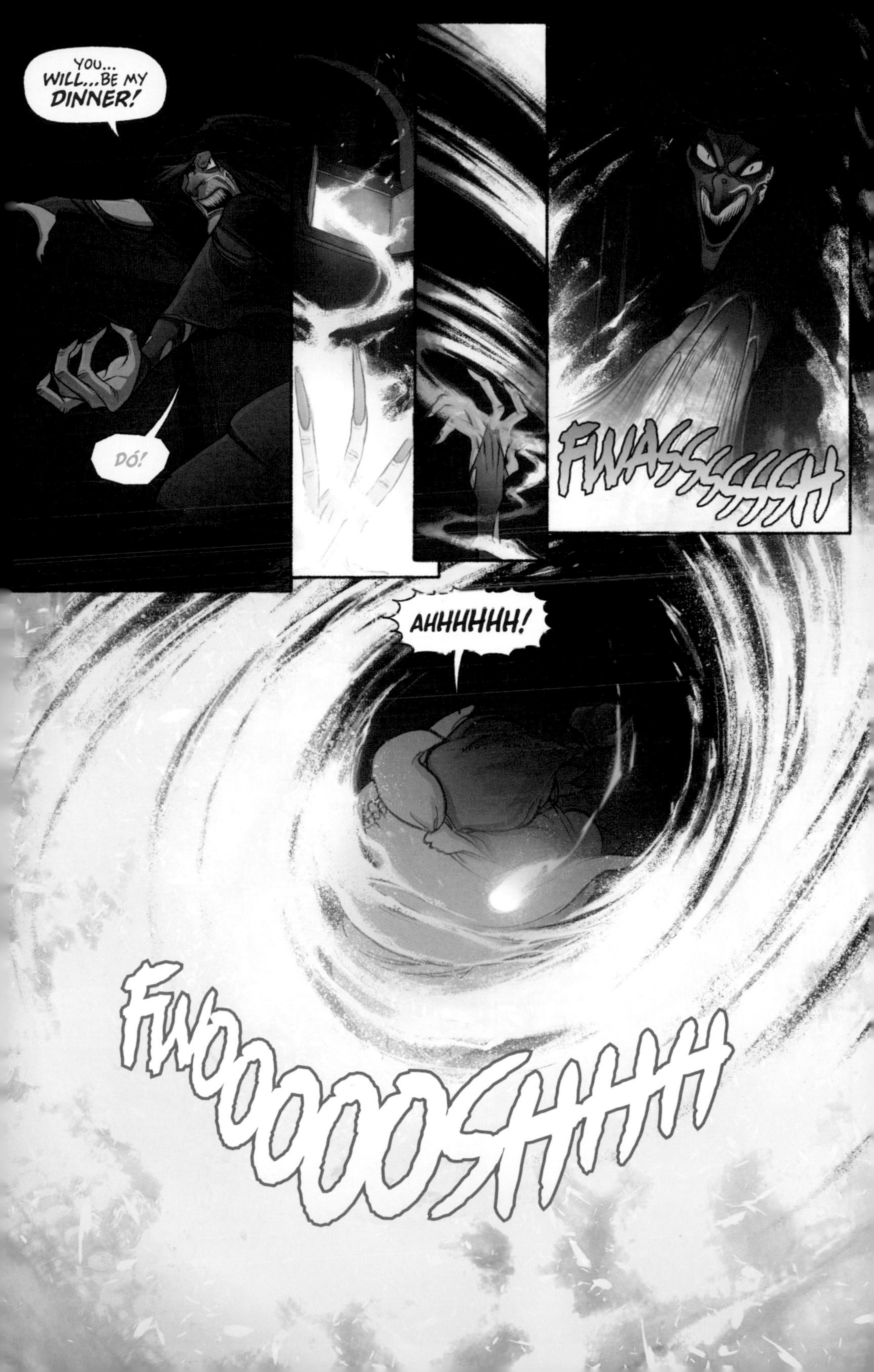
YOU... WILL...BE MY DINNER!
DÓ!
FWASSSSSSH
AHHHHHH!
FWOOOOOSHHHH

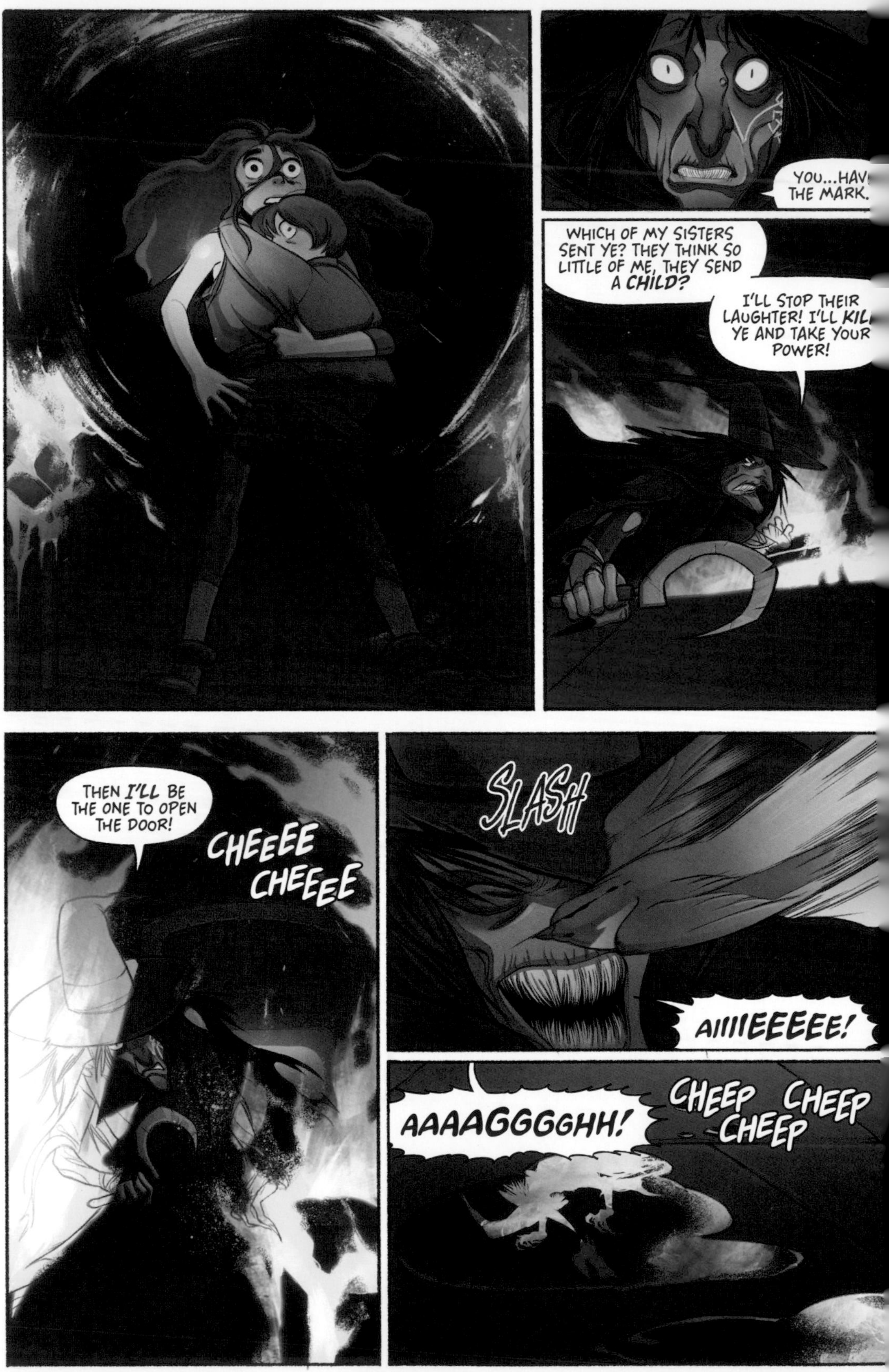
YOU...HAV
THE MARK.
WHICH OF MY SISTERS SENT YE? THEY THINK SO LITTLE OF ME, THEY SEND A CHILD?
I'LL STOP THEIR LAUGHTER! I'LL KIL
YE AND TAKE YOUR POWER!
THEN I'LL BE THE ONE TO OPEN THE DOOR!
CHEEEE CHEEEE
SLASH
AIIIEEEEE!
AAAAGGGGHH!
CHEEP CHEEP CHEEP

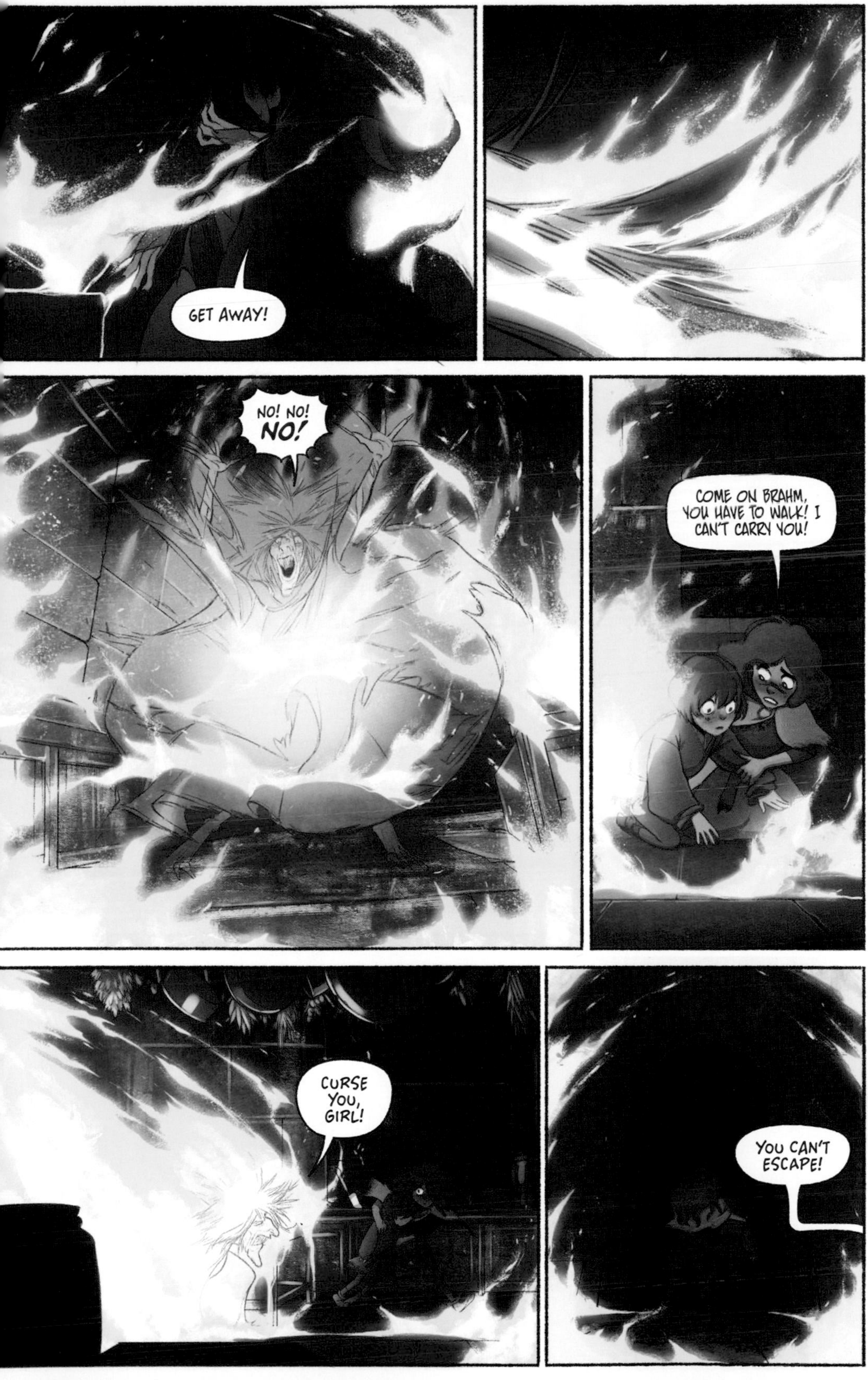
GET AWAY!
NO! NO! NO!
COME ON BRAHM, YOU HAVE TO WALK! I CAN'T CARRY YOU!
CURSE YOU, GIRL!
YOU CAN'T ESCAPE!

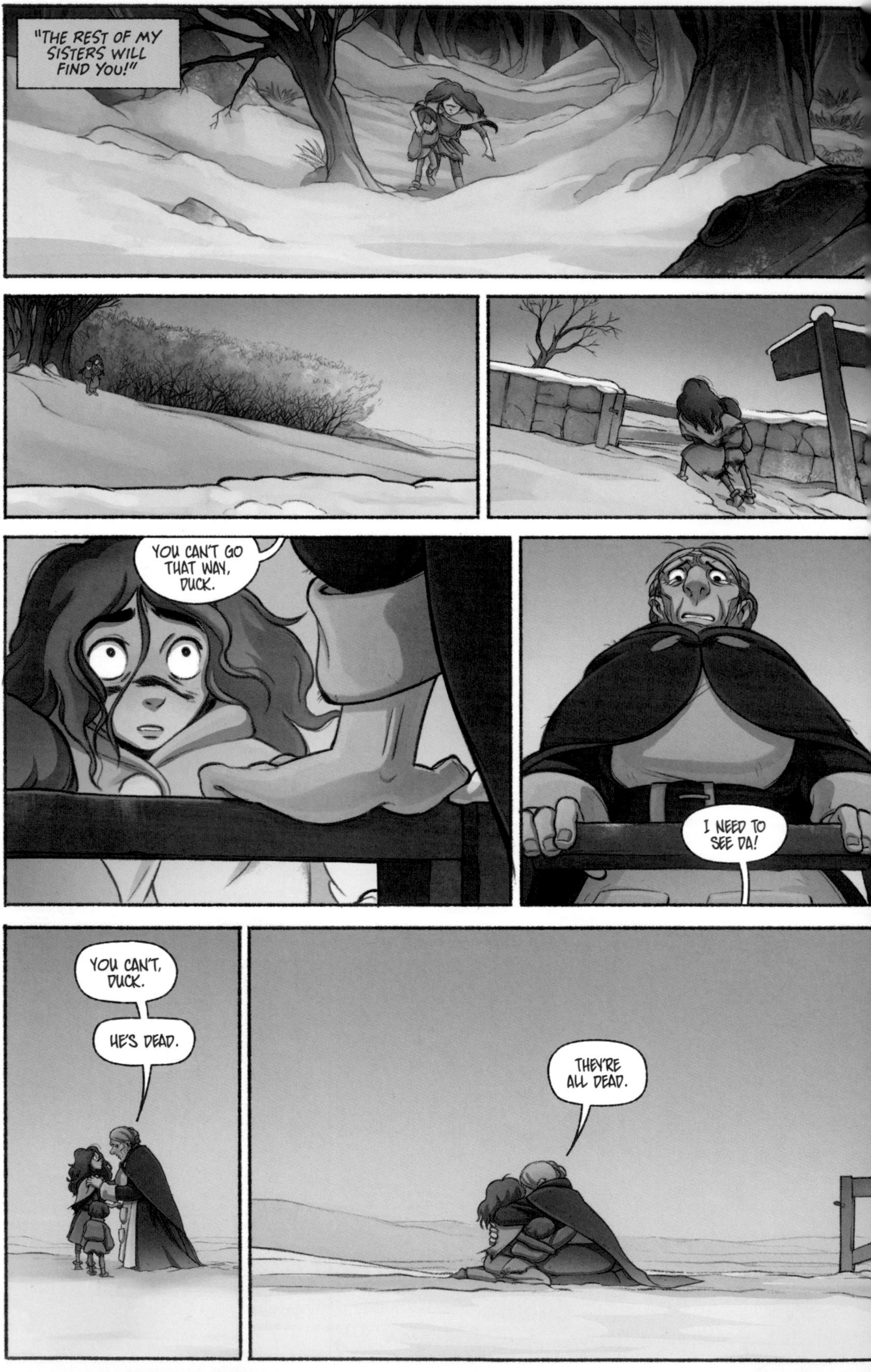
"THE REST OF MY SISTERS WILL FIND YOU!"
YOU CAN'T GO THAT WAY, DUCK.
I NEED TO SEE DA!
YOU CAN'T, DUCK.
HE'S DEAD.
THEY'RE ALL DEAD.

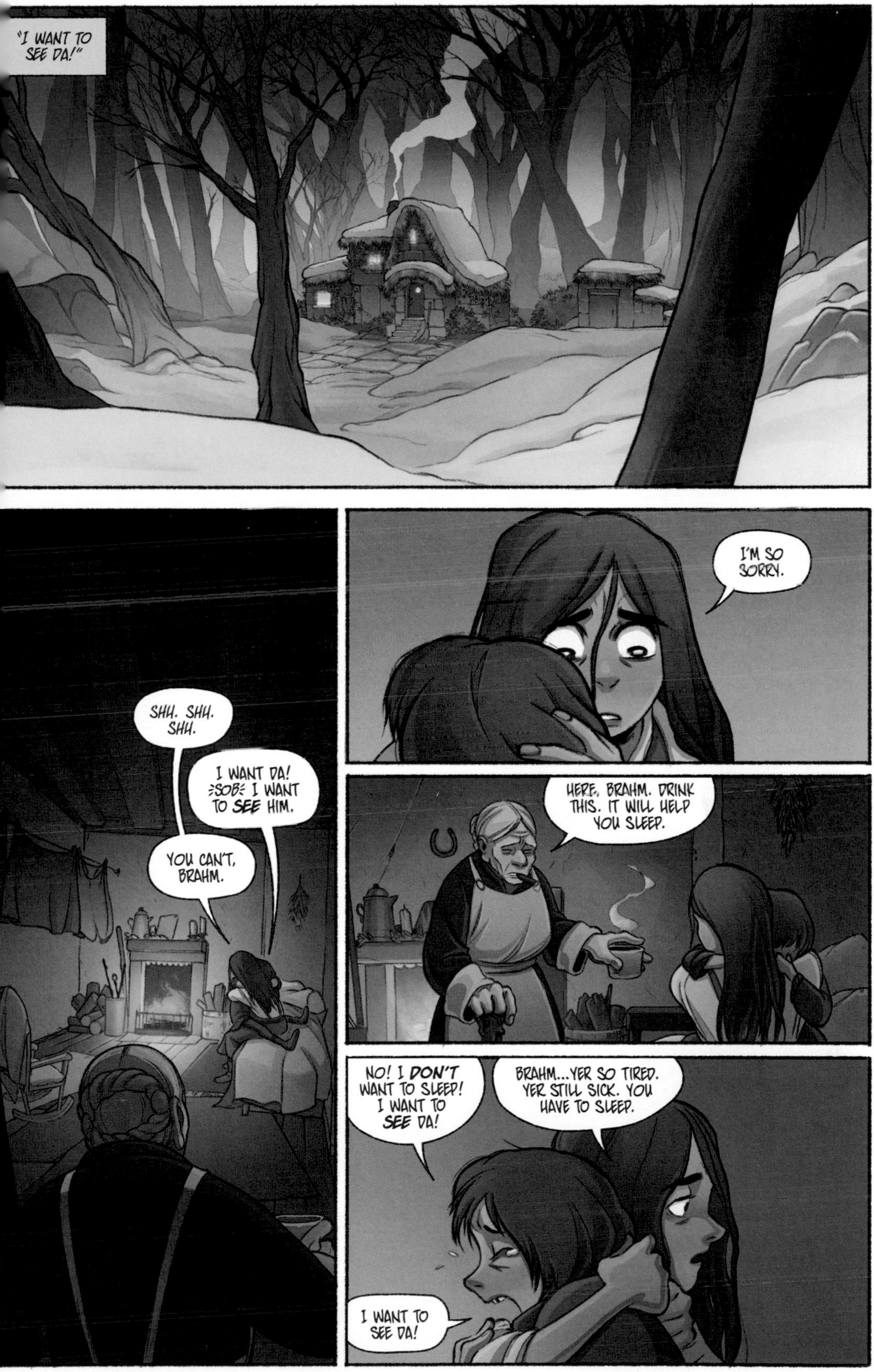
"I WANT TO SEE DA!"
SHH. SHH. SHH.
I WANT DA! *SOB* I WANT TO SEE HIM.
YOU CAN'T, BRAHM.
I'M SO SORRY.
HERE, BRAHM. DRINK THIS. IT WILL HELP YOU SLEEP.
NO! I DON'T WANT TO SLEEP! I WANT TO SEE DA!
BRAHM...YER SO TIRED. YER STILL SICK. YOU HAVE TO SLEEP.
I WANT TO SEE DA!

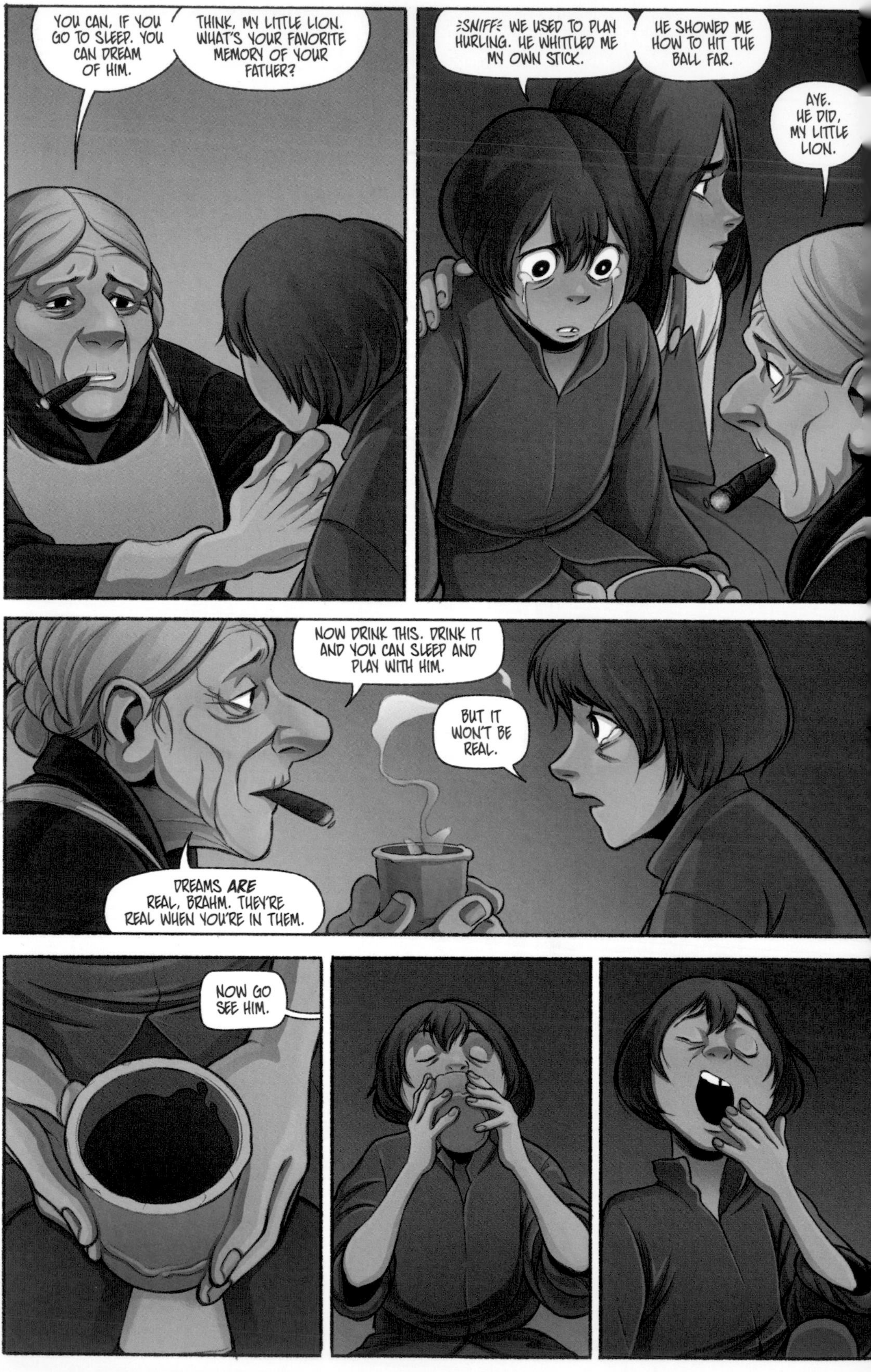
YOU CAN, IF YOU GO TO SLEEP. YOU CAN DREAM OF HIM.
THINK, MY LITTLE LION. WHAT'S YOUR FAVORITE MEMORY OF YOUR FATHER?
SNIFF WE USED TO PLAY HURLING. HE WHITTLED ME MY OWN STICK.
HE SHOWED ME HOW TO HIT THE BALL FAR.
AYE. HE DID, MY LITTLE LION.
NOW DRINK THIS. DRINK IT AND YOU CAN SLEEP AND PLAY WITH HIM.
BUT IT WON'T BE REAL.
DREAMS ARE REAL, BRAHM. THEY'RE REAL WHEN YOU'RE IN THEM.
NOW GO SEE HIM.

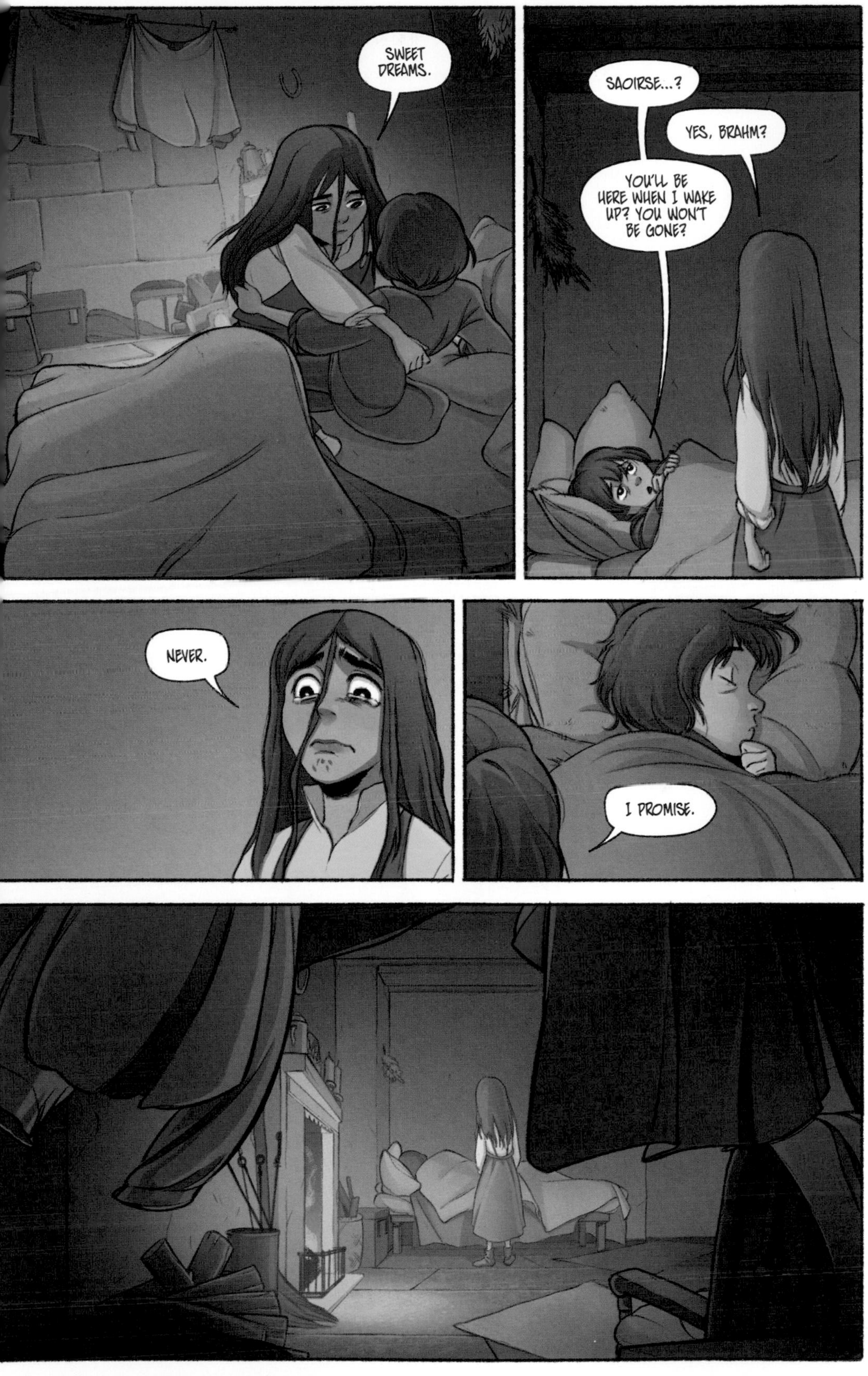
SWEET DREAMS.
SAOIRSE...?
YES, BRAHM?
YOU'LL BE HERE WHEN I WAKE UP? YOU WON'T BE GONE?
NEVER.
I PROMISE.

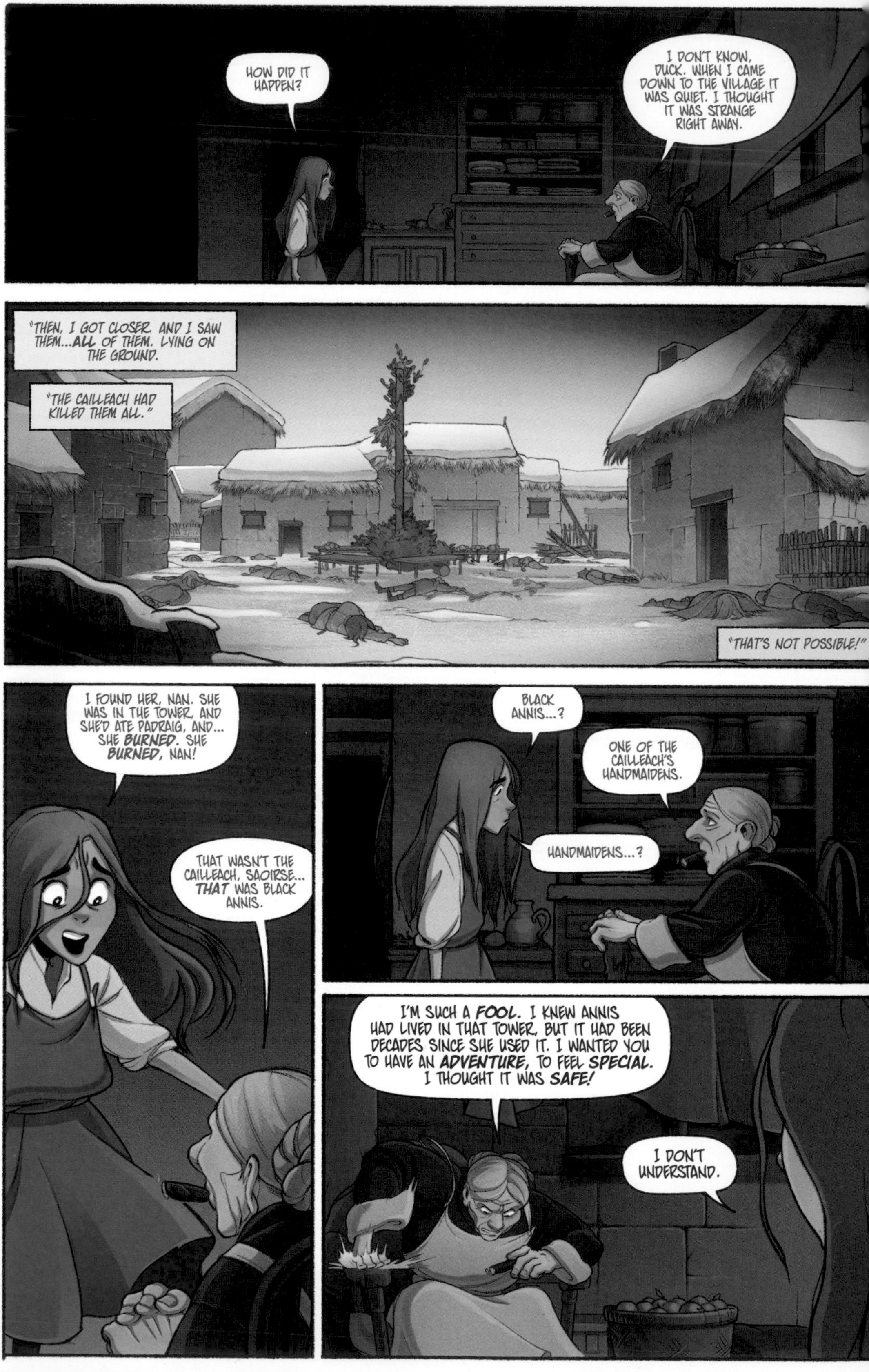
HOW DID IT HAPPEN?
I DON'T KNOW, DUCK. WHEN I CAME DOWN TO THE VILLAGE IT WAS QUIET. I THOUGHT IT WAS STRANGE RIGHT AWAY.
"THEN, I GOT CLOSER. AND I SAW THEM...ALL OF THEM. LYING ON THE GROUND.
"THE CAILLEACH HAD KILLED THEM ALL."
"THAT'S NOT POSSIBLE!"
I FOUND HER, NAN. SHE WAS IN THE TOWER, AND SHE'D ATE PADRAIG, AND... SHE BURNED. SHE BURNED, NAN!
THAT WASN'T THE CAILLEACH, SAOIRSE... THAT WAS BLACK ANNIS.
BLACK ANNIS...?
ONE OF THE CAILLEACH'S HANDMAIDENS.
HANDMAIDENS...?
I'M SUCH A FOOL. I KNEW ANNIS HAD LIVED IN THAT TOWER, BUT IT HAD BEEN DECADES SINCE SHE USED IT. I WANTED YOU TO HAVE AN ADVENTURE, TO FEEL SPECIAL. I THOUGHT IT WAS SAFE!
I DON'T UNDERSTAND.

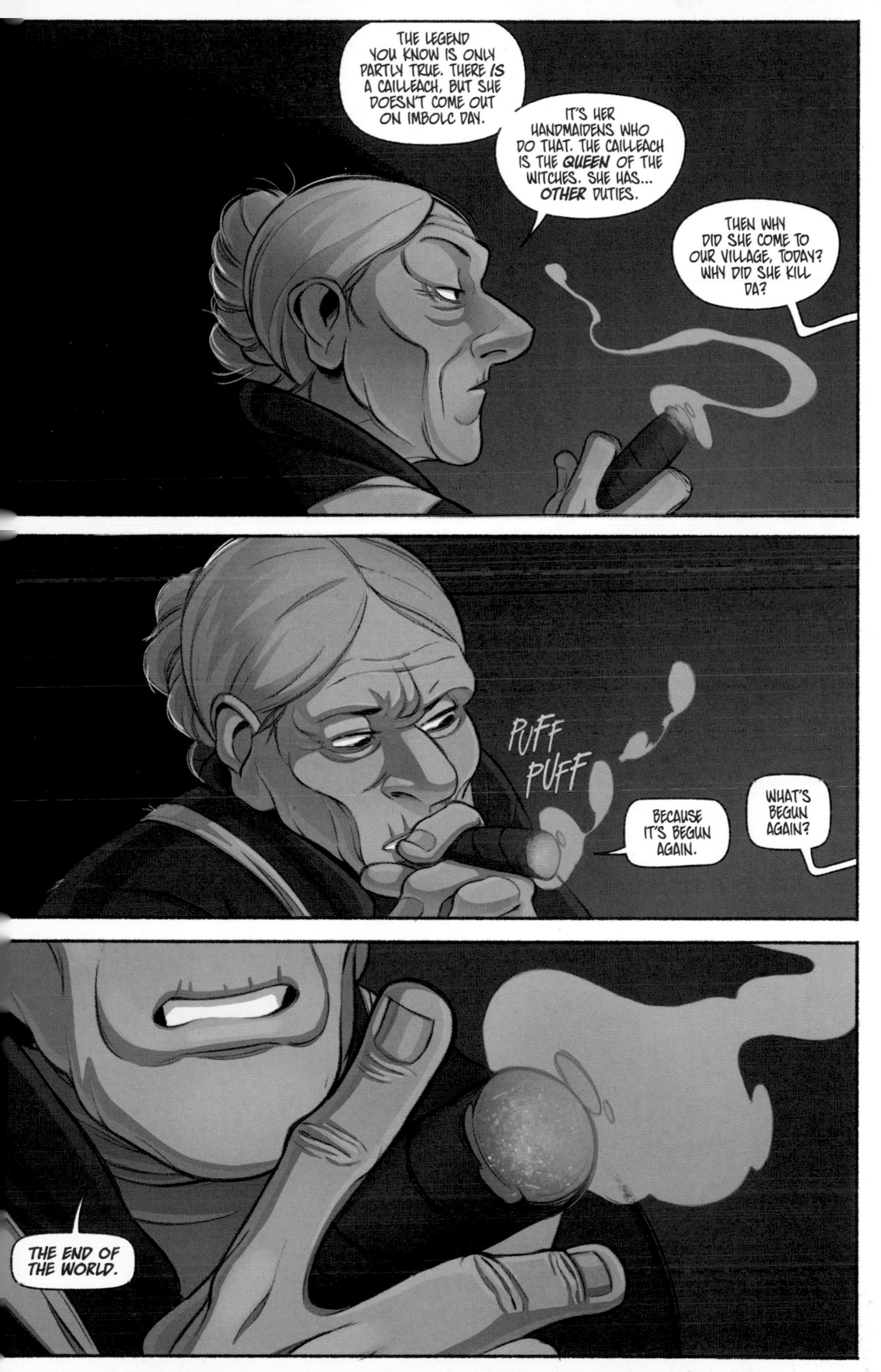
THE LEGEND YOU KNOW IS ONLY PARTLY TRUE. THERE *IS* A CAILLEACH, BUT SHE DOESN'T COME OUT ON IMBOLC DAY.
IT'S HER HANDMAIDENS WHO DO THAT. THE CAILLEACH IS THE ***QUEEN*** OF THE WITCHES. SHE HAS... ***OTHER*** DUTIES.
THEN WHY DID SHE COME TO OUR VILLAGE, TODAY? WHY DID SHE KILL DA?
PUFF
PUFF
BECAUSE IT'S BEGUN AGAIN.
WHAT'S BEGUN AGAIN?
THE END OF THE WORLD.

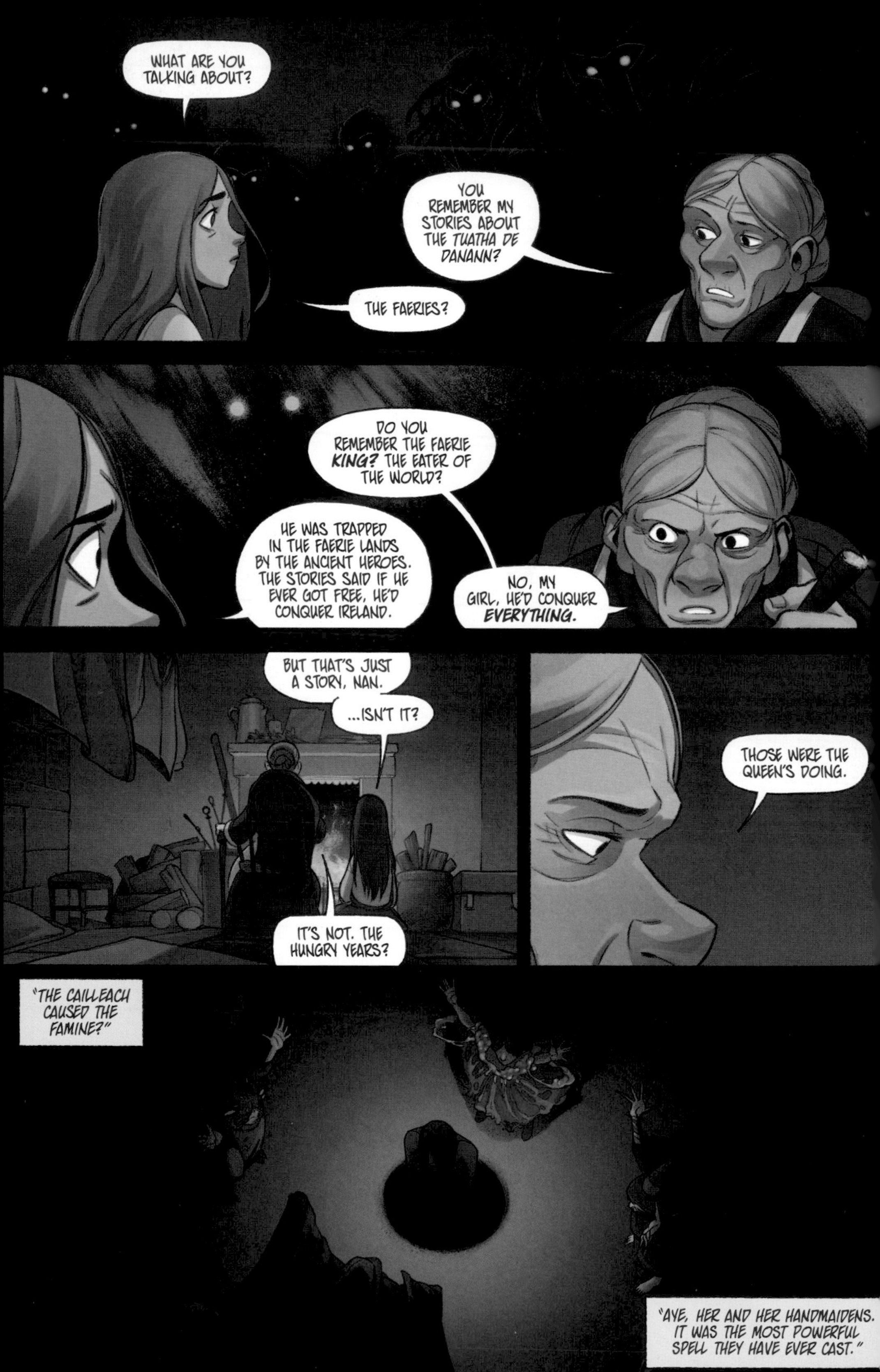
WHAT ARE YOU TALKING ABOUT?
YOU REMEMBER MY STORIES ABOUT THE *TUATHA DE DANANN*?
THE FAERIES?
DO YOU REMEMBER THE FAERIE **KING?** THE EATER OF THE WORLD?
HE WAS TRAPPED IN THE FAERIE LANDS BY THE ANCIENT HEROES. THE STORIES SAID IF HE EVER GOT FREE, HE'D CONQUER IRELAND.
NO, MY GIRL, HE'D CONQUER **EVERYTHING.**
BUT THAT'S JUST A STORY, NAN.
...ISN'T IT?
IT'S NOT. THE HUNGRY YEARS?
THOSE WERE THE QUEEN'S DOING.
"THE CAILLEACH CAUSED THE FAMINE?"
"AYE, HER AND HER HANDMAIDENS. IT WAS THE MOST POWERFUL SPELL THEY HAVE EVER CAST."

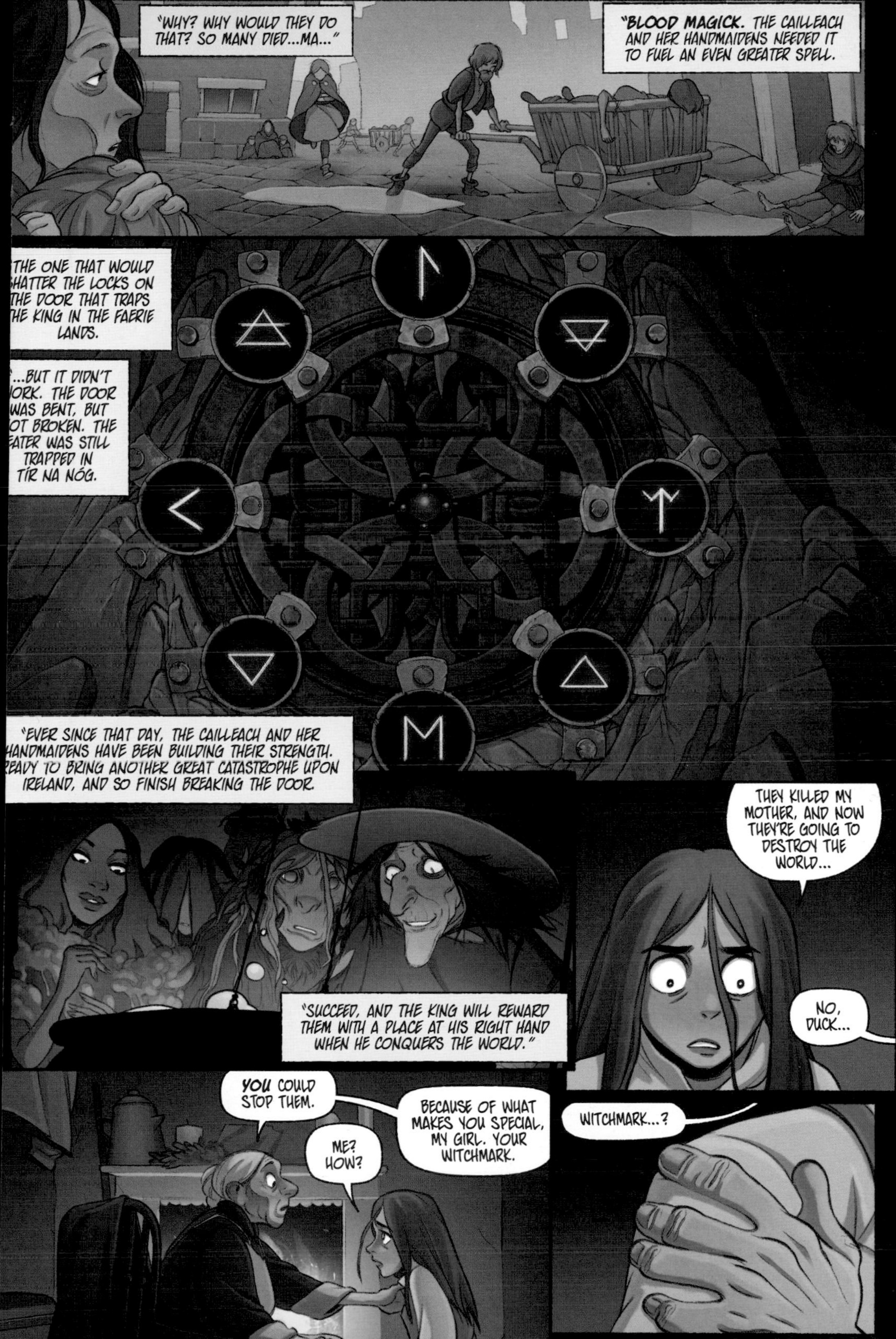
"WHY? WHY WOULD THEY DO THAT? SO MANY DIED...MA..."
"BLOOD MAGICK. THE CAILLEACH AND HER HANDMAIDENS NEEDED IT TO FUEL AN EVEN GREATER SPELL.
THE ONE THAT WOULD SHATTER THE LOCKS ON THE DOOR THAT TRAPS THE KING IN THE FAERIE LANDS.
...BUT IT DIDN'T WORK. THE DOOR WAS BENT, BUT OT BROKEN. THE EATER WAS STILL TRAPPED IN TÍR NA NÓG.
"EVER SINCE THAT DAY, THE CAILLEACH AND HER HANDMAIDENS HAVE BEEN BUILDING THEIR STRENGTH. READY TO BRING ANOTHER GREAT CATASTROPHE UPON IRELAND, AND SO FINISH BREAKING THE DOOR.
"SUCCEED, AND THE KING WILL REWARD THEM WITH A PLACE AT HIS RIGHT HAND WHEN HE CONQUERS THE WORLD."
THEY KILLED MY MOTHER, AND NOW THEY'RE GOING TO DESTROY THE WORLD...
NO, DUCK...
YOU COULD STOP THEM.
ME? HOW?
BECAUSE OF WHAT MAKES YOU SPECIAL, MY GIRL. YOUR WITCHMARK.
WITCHMARK...?

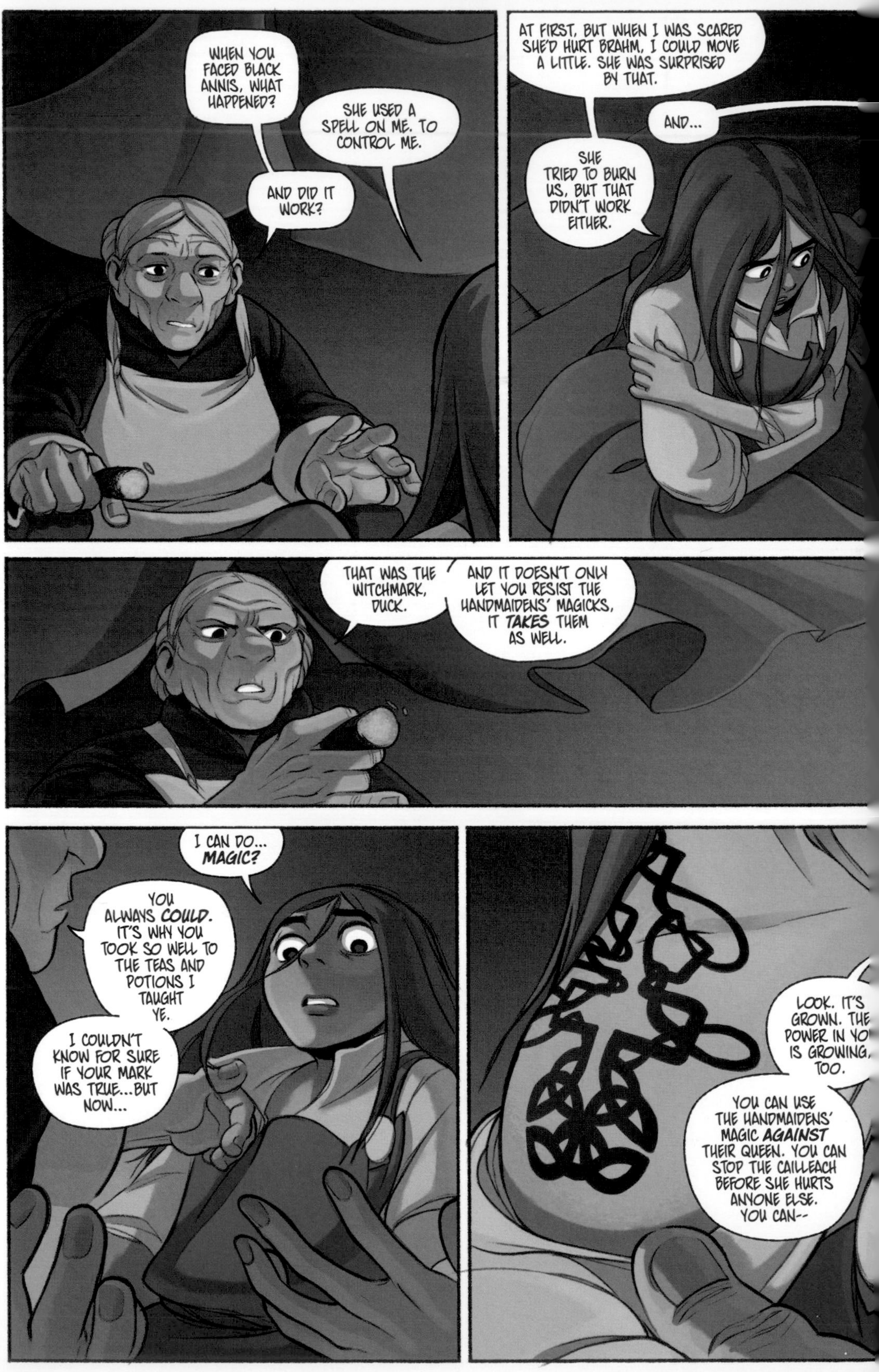
WHEN YOU FACED BLACK ANNIS, WHAT HAPPENED?
SHE USED A SPELL ON ME. TO CONTROL ME.
AND DID IT WORK?
AT FIRST, BUT WHEN I WAS SCARED SHE'D HURT BRAHM, I COULD MOVE A LITTLE. SHE WAS SURPRISED BY THAT.
AND...
SHE TRIED TO BURN US, BUT THAT DIDN'T WORK EITHER.
THAT WAS THE WITCHMARK, DUCK.
AND IT DOESN'T ONLY LET YOU RESIST THE HANDMAIDENS' MAGICKS, IT **TAKES** THEM AS WELL.
I CAN DO... **MAGIC?**
YOU ALWAYS **COULD**. IT'S WHY YOU TOOK SO WELL TO THE TEAS AND POTIONS I TAUGHT YE.
I COULDN'T KNOW FOR SURE IF YOUR MARK WAS TRUE...BUT NOW...
LOOK. IT'S GROWN. THE POWER IN YO IS GROWING, TOO.
YOU CAN USE THE HANDMAIDENS' MAGIC **AGAINST** THEIR QUEEN. YOU CAN STOP THE CAILLEACH BEFORE SHE HURTS ANYONE ELSE. YOU CAN--

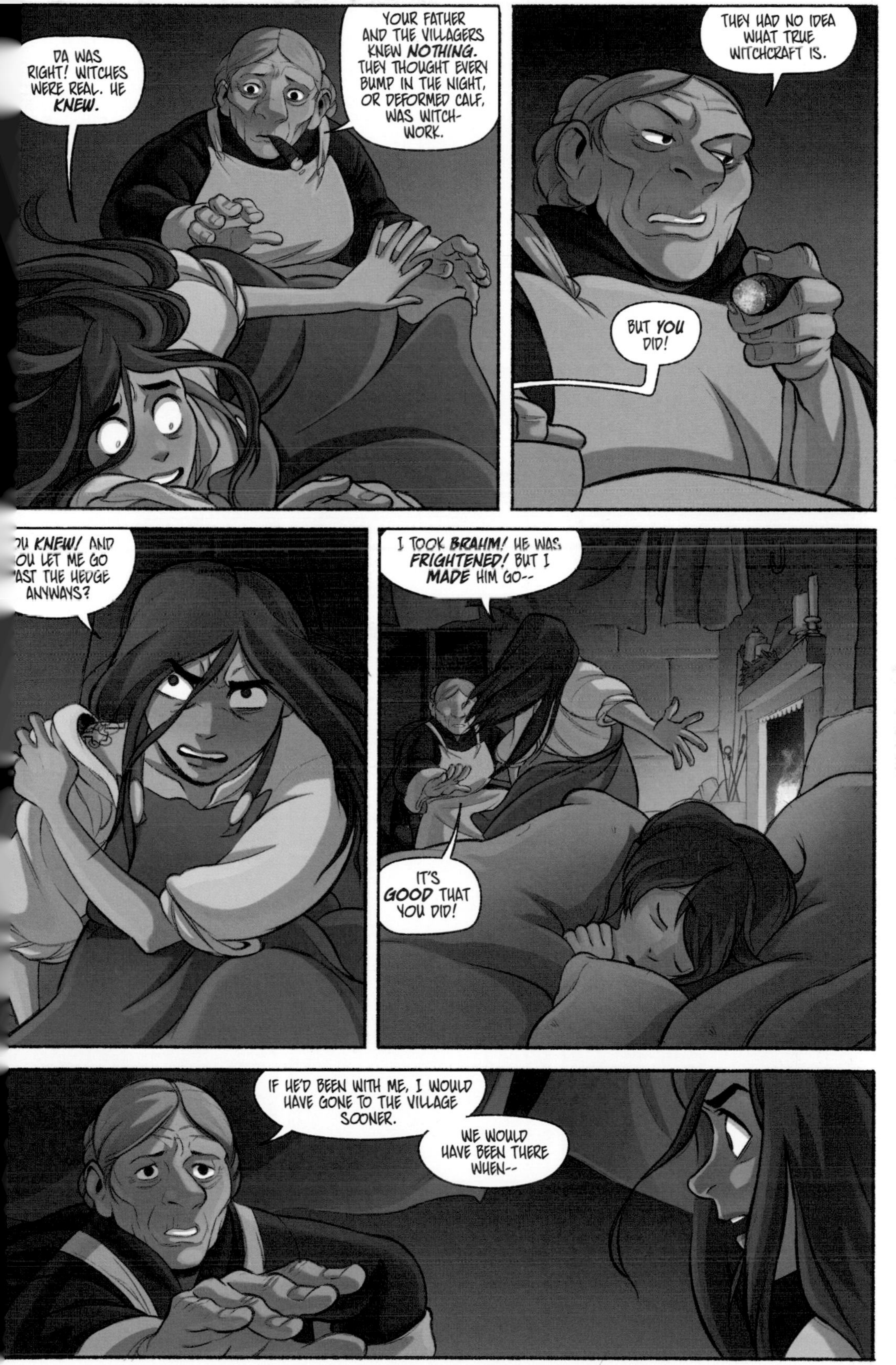
DA WAS RIGHT! WITCHES WERE REAL. HE KNEW.
YOUR FATHER AND THE VILLAGERS KNEW NOTHING. THEY THOUGHT EVERY BUMP IN THE NIGHT, OR DEFORMED CALF, WAS WITCH-WORK.
THEY HAD NO IDEA WHAT TRUE WITCHCRAFT IS.
BUT YOU DID!
OU KNEW! AND OU LET ME GO AST THE HEDGE ANYWAYS?
I TOOK BRAHM! HE WAS FRIGHTENED! BUT I MADE HIM GO--
IT'S GOOD THAT YOU DID!
IF HE'D BEEN WITH ME, I WOULD HAVE GONE TO THE VILLAGE SOONER.
WE WOULD HAVE BEEN THERE WHEN--

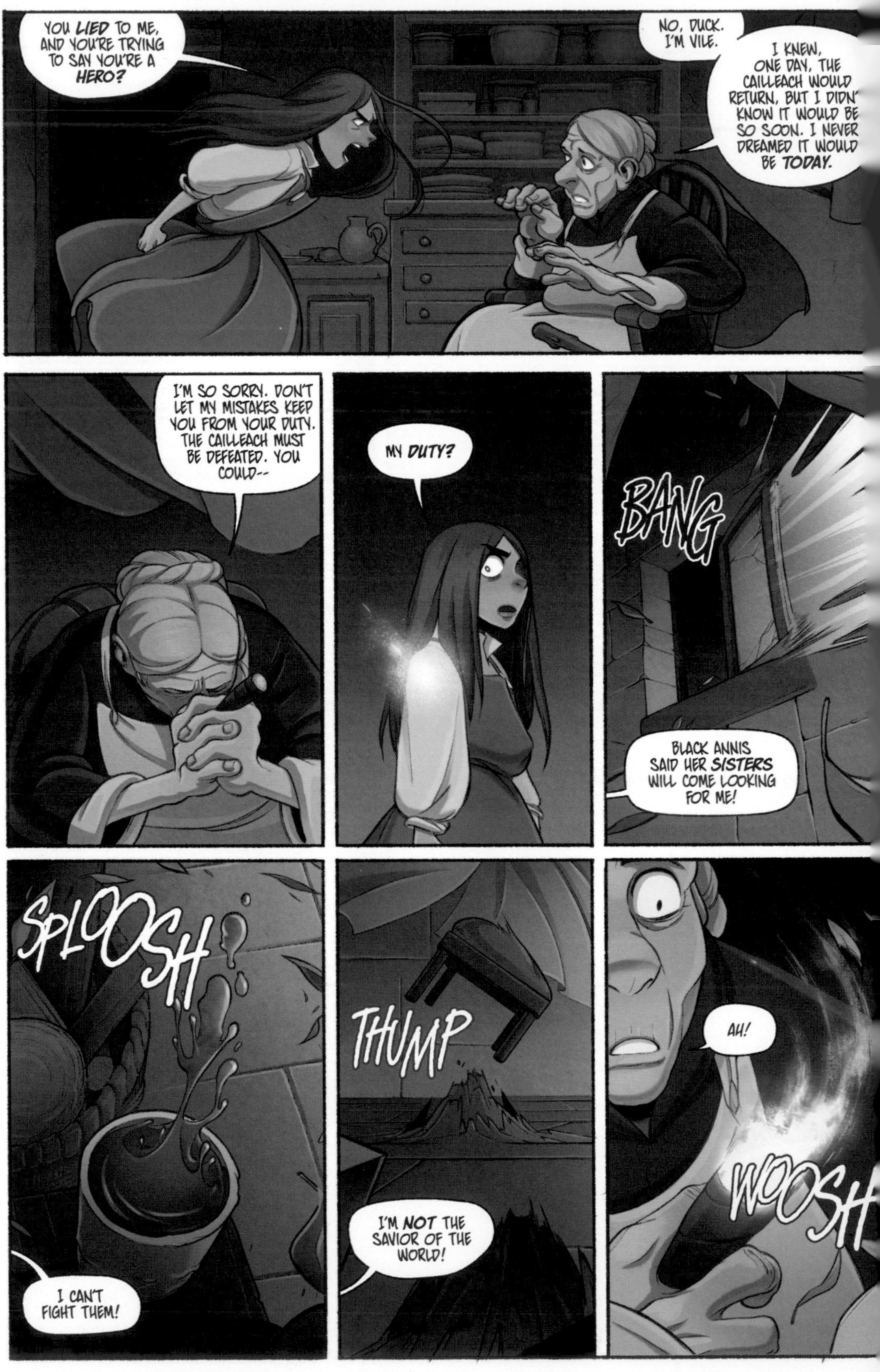
YOU LIED TO ME, AND YOU'RE TRYING TO SAY YOU'RE A HERO?
NO, DUCK. I'M VILE.
I KNEW, ONE DAY, THE CAILLEACH WOULD RETURN, BUT I DIDN' KNOW IT WOULD BE SO SOON. I NEVER DREAMED IT WOULD BE TODAY.
I'M SO SORRY. DON'T LET MY MISTAKES KEEP YOU FROM YOUR DUTY. THE CAILLEACH MUST BE DEFEATED. YOU COULD--
MY DUTY?
BANG
BLACK ANNIS SAID HER SISTERS WILL COME LOOKING FOR ME!
SPLOOSH
I CAN'T FIGHT THEM!
THUMP
I'M NOT THE SAVIOR OF THE WORLD!
AH!
WOOSH

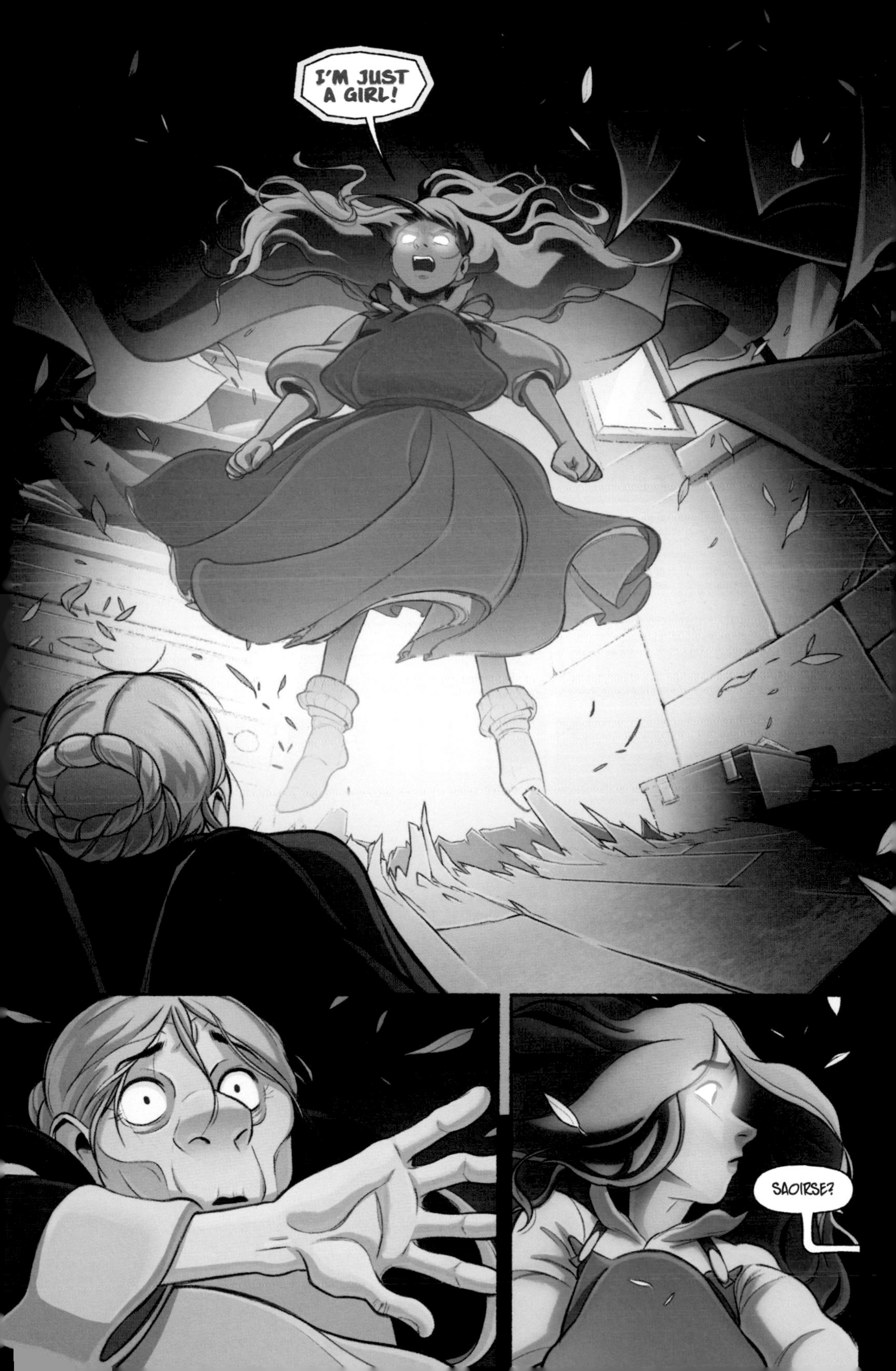
I'M JUST A GIRL!
SAOIRSE?

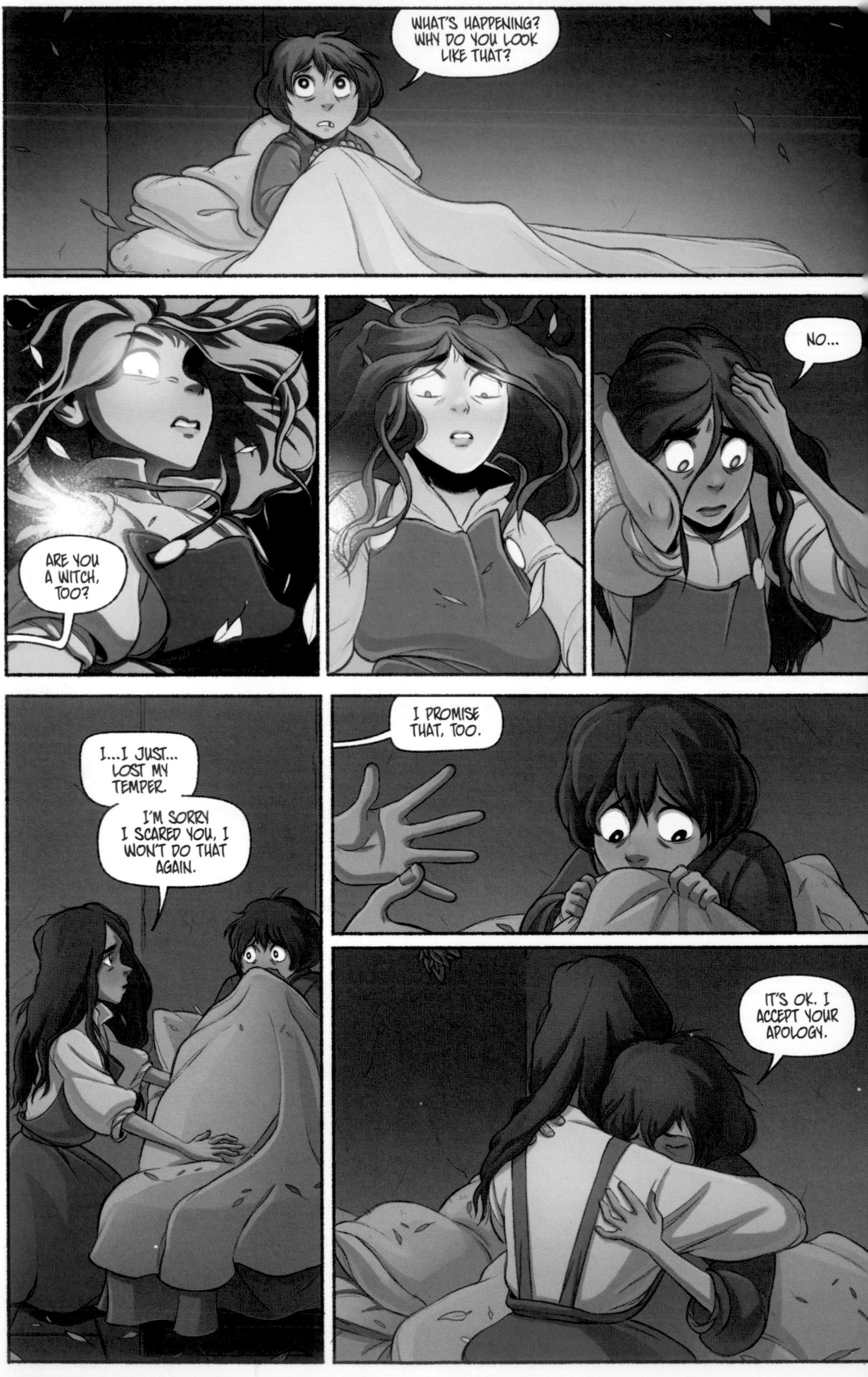
WHAT'S HAPPENING? WHY DO YOU LOOK LIKE THAT?
ARE YOU A WITCH, TOO?
NO...
I...I JUST... LOST MY TEMPER.
I'M SORRY I SCARED YOU, I WON'T DO THAT AGAIN.
I PROMISE THAT, TOO.
IT'S OK. I ACCEPT YOUR APOLOGY.

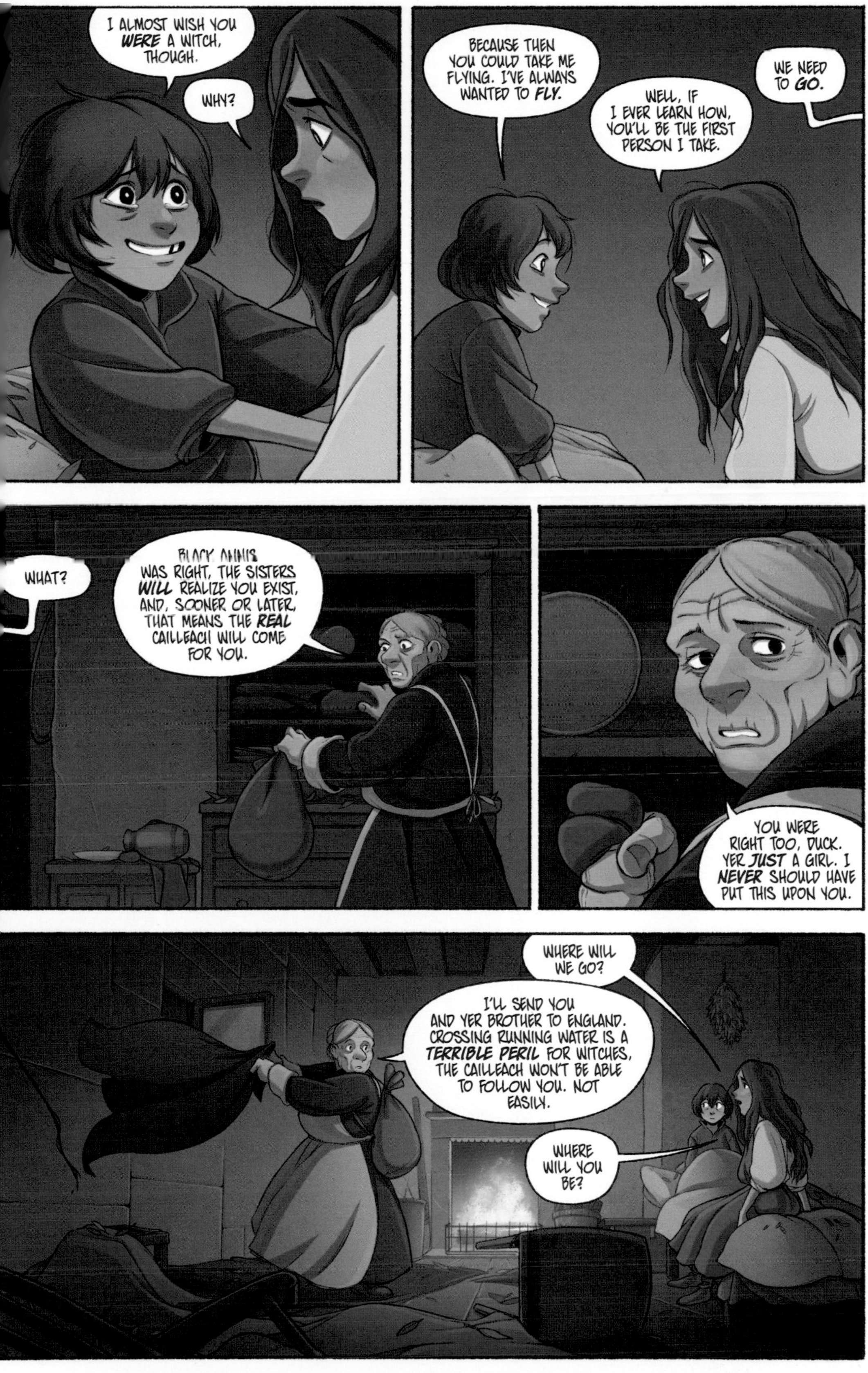

I ALMOST WISH YOU WERE A WITCH, THOUGH.
WHY?
BECAUSE THEN YOU COULD TAKE ME FLYING. I'VE ALWAYS WANTED TO FLY.
WELL, IF I EVER LEARN HOW, YOU'LL BE THE FIRST PERSON I TAKE.
WE NEED TO GO.
WHAT?
BLACK ANNIS WAS RIGHT, THE SISTERS WILL REALIZE YOU EXIST, AND, SOONER OR LATER, THAT MEANS THE REAL CAILLEACH WILL COME FOR YOU.
YOU WERE RIGHT TOO, DUCK. YER JUST A GIRL. I NEVER SHOULD HAVE PUT THIS UPON YOU.
WHERE WILL WE GO?
I'LL SEND YOU AND YER BROTHER TO ENGLAND. CROSSING RUNNING WATER IS A TERRIBLE PERIL FOR WITCHES, THE CAILLEACH WON'T BE ABLE TO FOLLOW YOU. NOT EASILY.
WHERE WILL YOU BE?

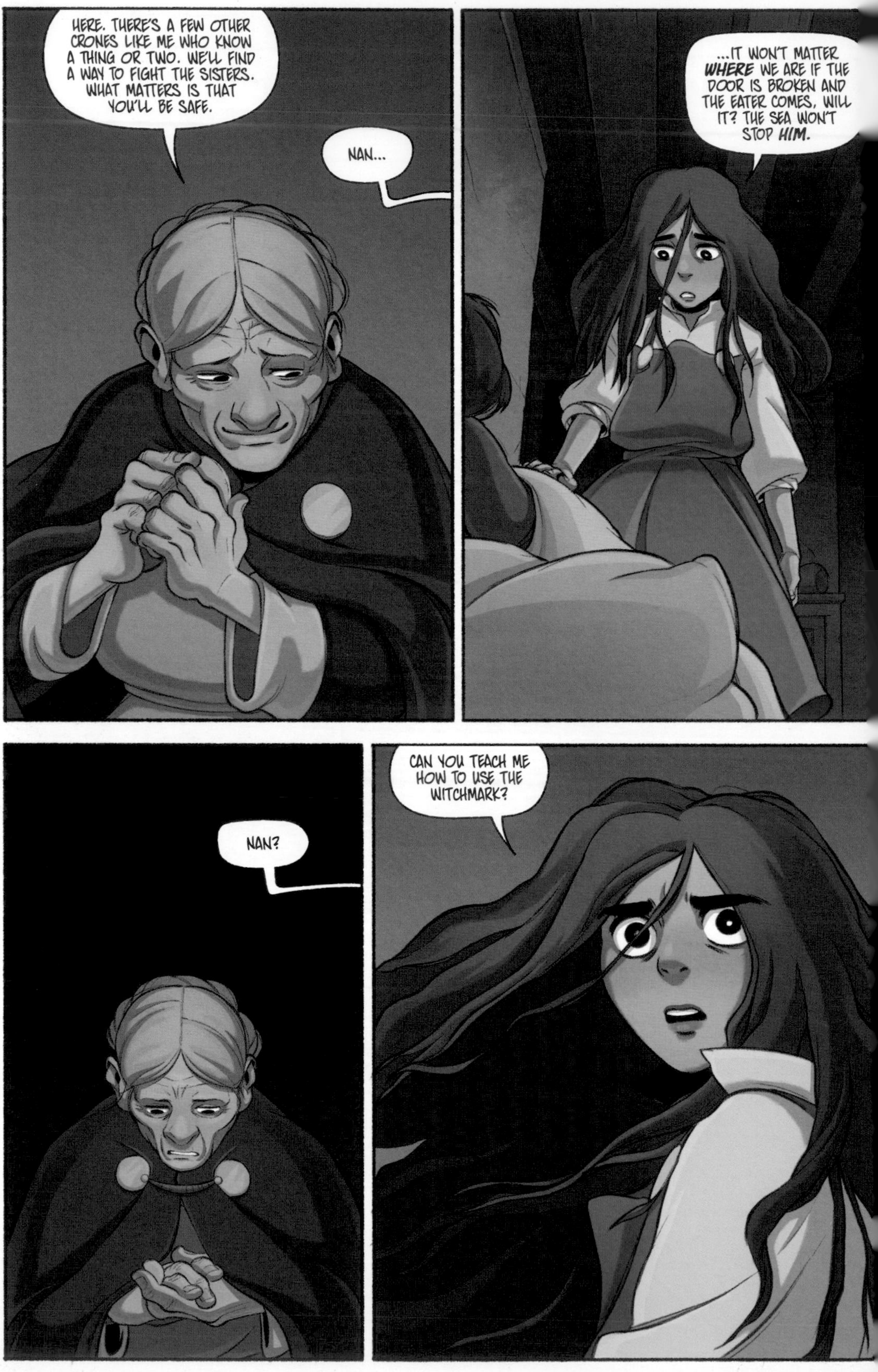
HERE. THERE'S A FEW OTHER CRONES LIKE ME WHO KNOW A THING OR TWO. WE'LL FIND A WAY TO FIGHT THE SISTERS. WHAT MATTERS IS THAT YOU'LL BE SAFE.
NAN...
...IT WON'T MATTER **WHERE** WE ARE IF THE DOOR IS BROKEN AND THE EATER COMES, WILL IT? THE SEA WON'T STOP **HIM**.
NAN?
CAN YOU TEACH ME HOW TO USE THE WITCHMARK?

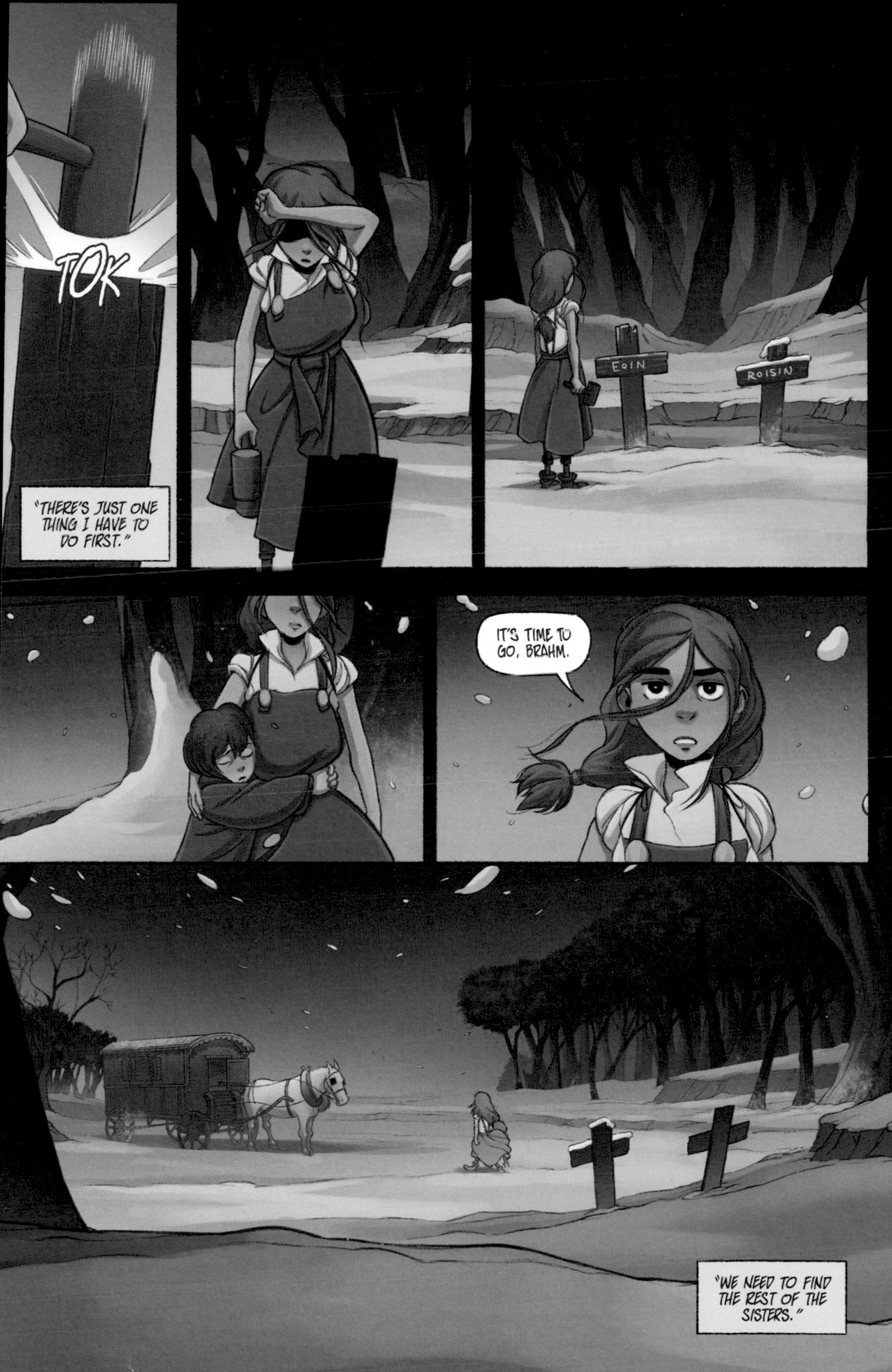
TOK
"THERE'S JUST ONE THING I HAVE TO DO FIRST."
EOIN
ROISIN
IT'S TIME TO GO, BRAHM.
"WE NEED TO FIND THE REST OF THE SISTERS."

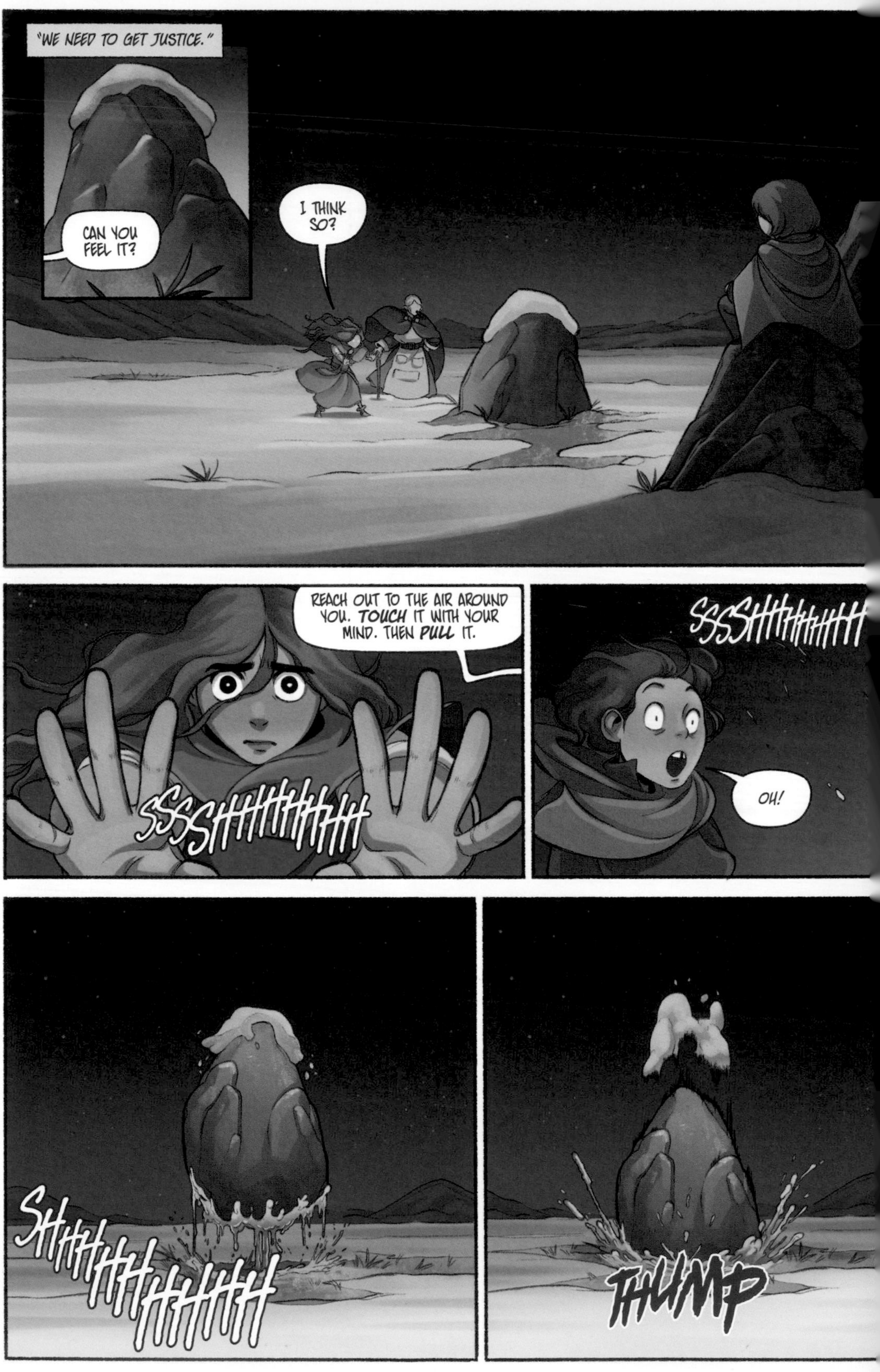
"WE NEED TO GET JUSTICE."
CAN YOU FEEL IT?
I THINK SO?
REACH OUT TO THE AIR AROUND YOU. TOUCH IT WITH YOUR MIND. THEN PULL IT.
SSSSHHHHHHHHHH
SSSSHHHHHHHHHHH
OH!
SHHHHHHHHHHHH
THUMP

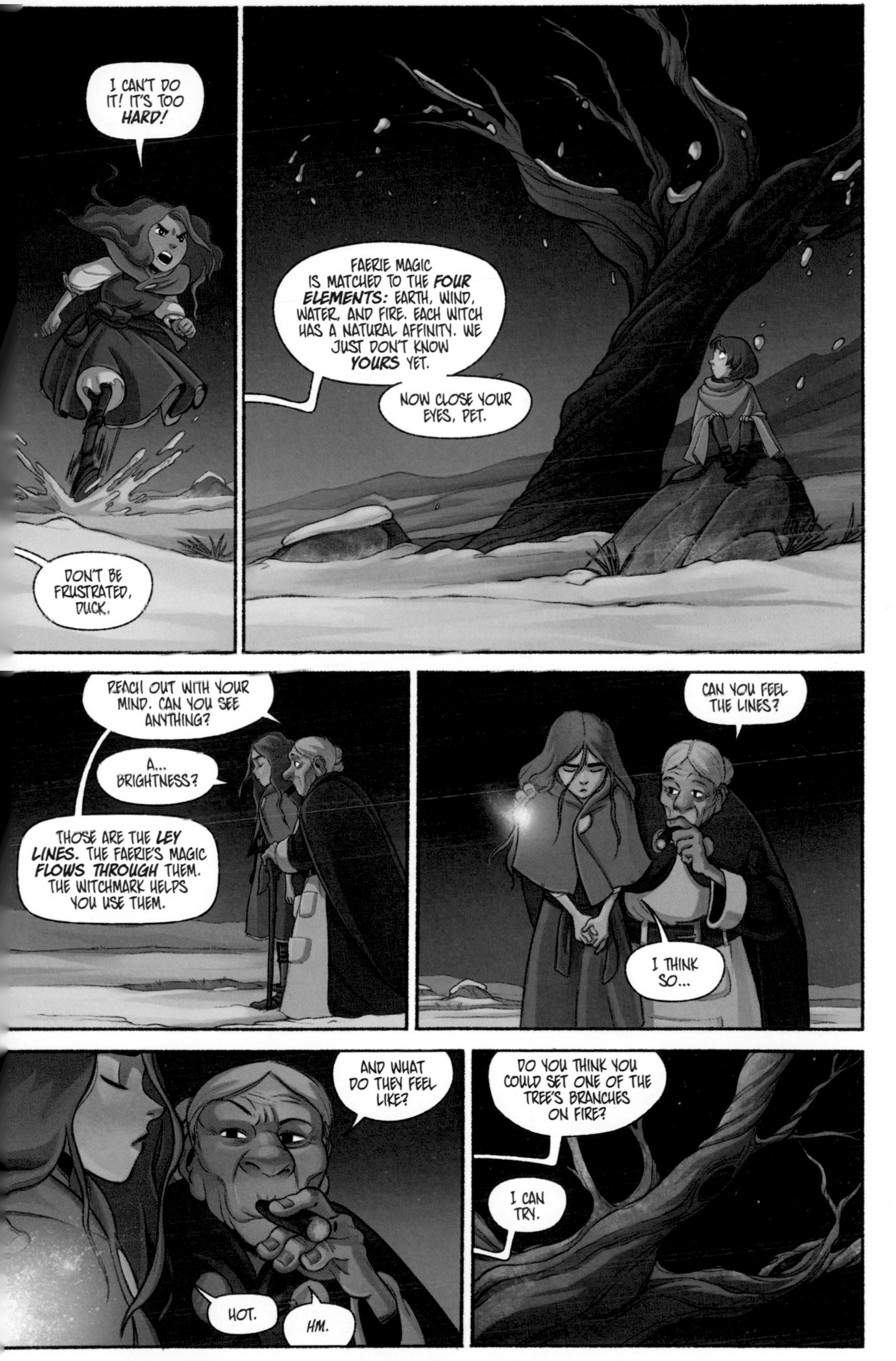

I CAN'T DO IT! IT'S TOO **HARD!**
DON'T BE FRUSTRATED, DUCK.
FAERIE MAGIC IS MATCHED TO THE **FOUR ELEMENTS:** EARTH, WIND, WATER, AND FIRE. EACH WITCH HAS A NATURAL AFFINITY. WE JUST DON'T KNOW **YOURS** YET.
NOW CLOSE YOUR EYES, PET.
REACH OUT WITH YOUR MIND. CAN YOU SEE ANYTHING?
A... BRIGHTNESS?
THOSE ARE THE **LEY LINES.** THE FAERIE'S MAGIC **FLOWS THROUGH** THEM. THE WITCHMARK HELPS YOU USE THEM.
CAN YOU FEEL THE LINES?
I THINK SO...
AND WHAT DO THEY FEEL LIKE?
HOT.
HM.
DO YOU THINK YOU COULD SET ONE OF THE TREE'S BRANCHES ON FIRE?
I CAN TRY.

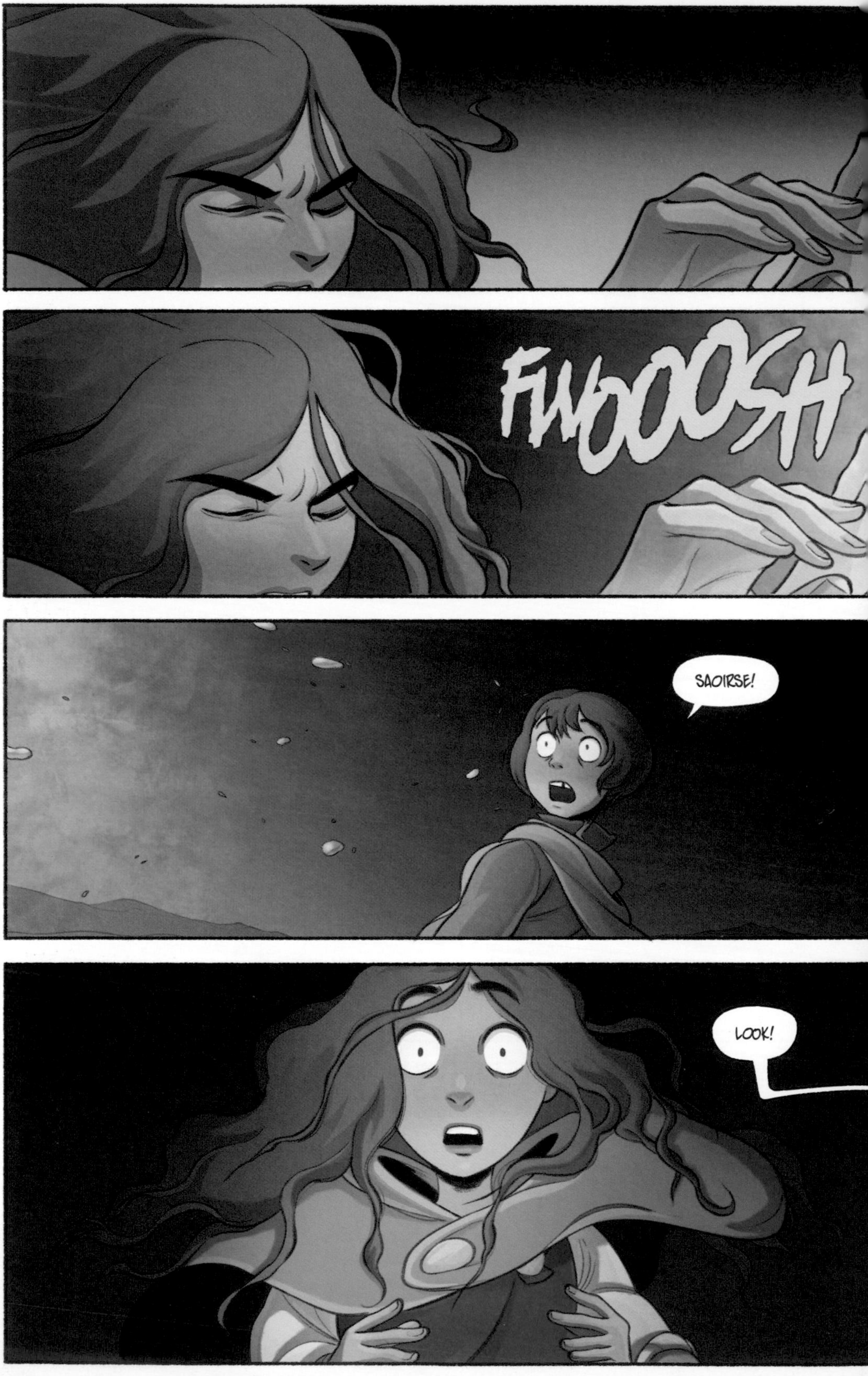
FWOOOSH
SAOIRSE!
LOOK!

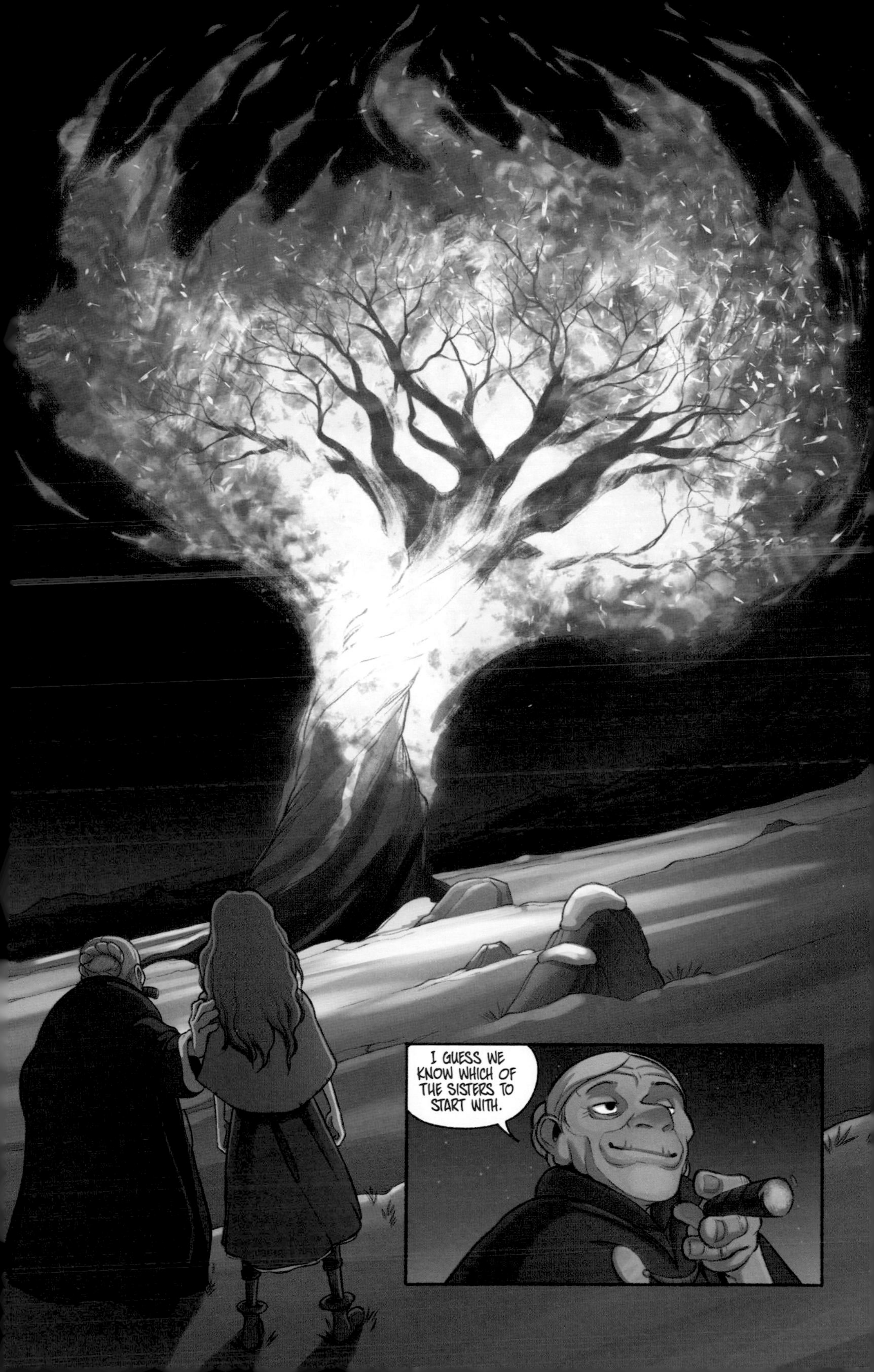
I GUESS WE KNOW WHICH OF THE SISTERS TO START WITH.

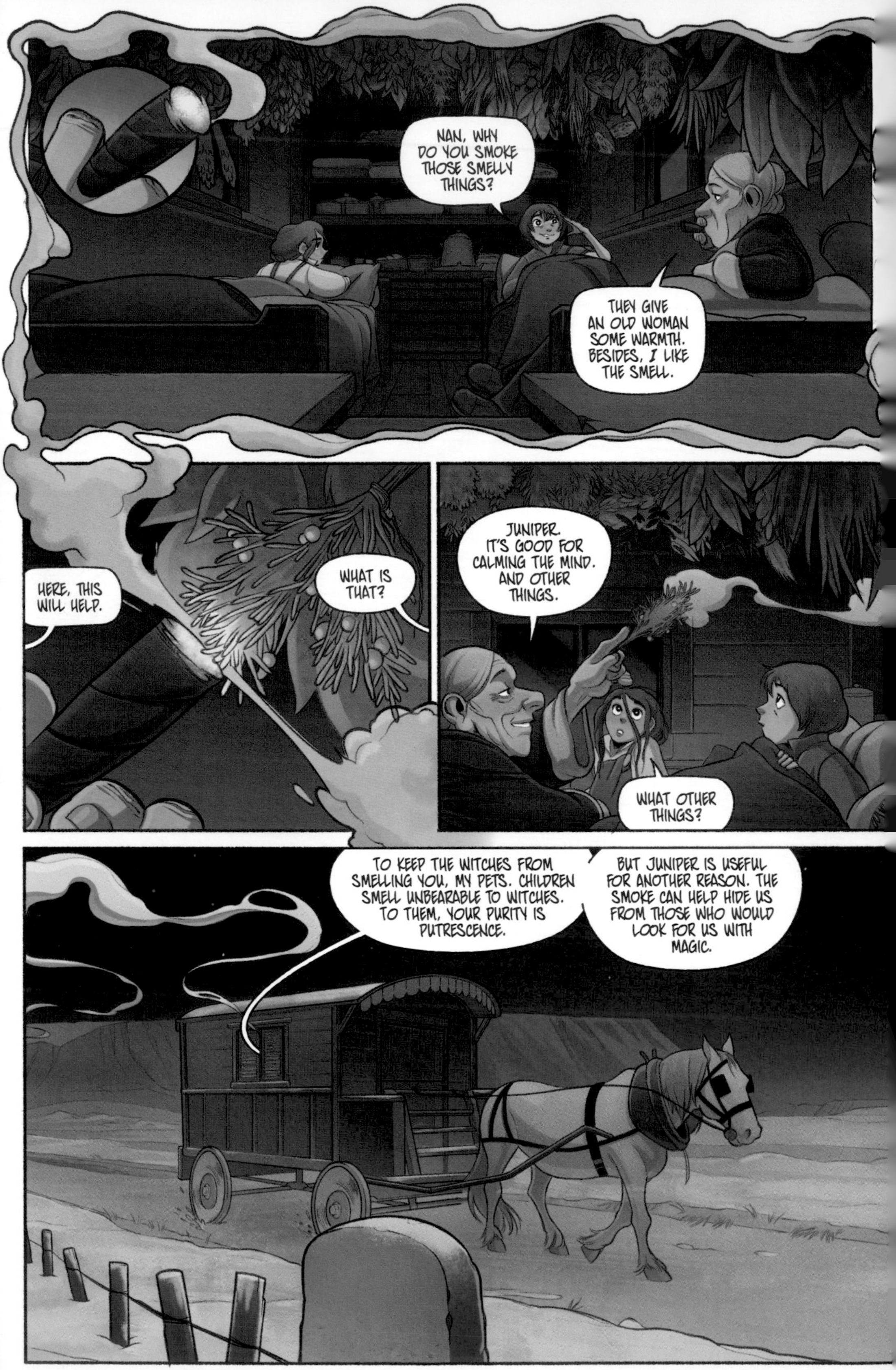
NAN, WHY DO YOU SMOKE THOSE SMELLY THINGS?
THEY GIVE AN OLD WOMAN SOME WARMTH. BESIDES, I LIKE THE SMELL.
HERE, THIS WILL HELP.
WHAT IS THAT?
JUNIPER. IT'S GOOD FOR CALMING THE MIND. AND OTHER THINGS.
WHAT OTHER THINGS?
TO KEEP THE WITCHES FROM SMELLING YOU, MY PETS. CHILDREN SMELL UNBEARABLE TO WITCHES. TO THEM, YOUR PURITY IS PUTRESCENCE.
BUT JUNIPER IS USEFUL FOR ANOTHER REASON. THE SMOKE CAN HELP HIDE US FROM THOSE WHO WOULD LOOK FOR US WITH MAGIC.

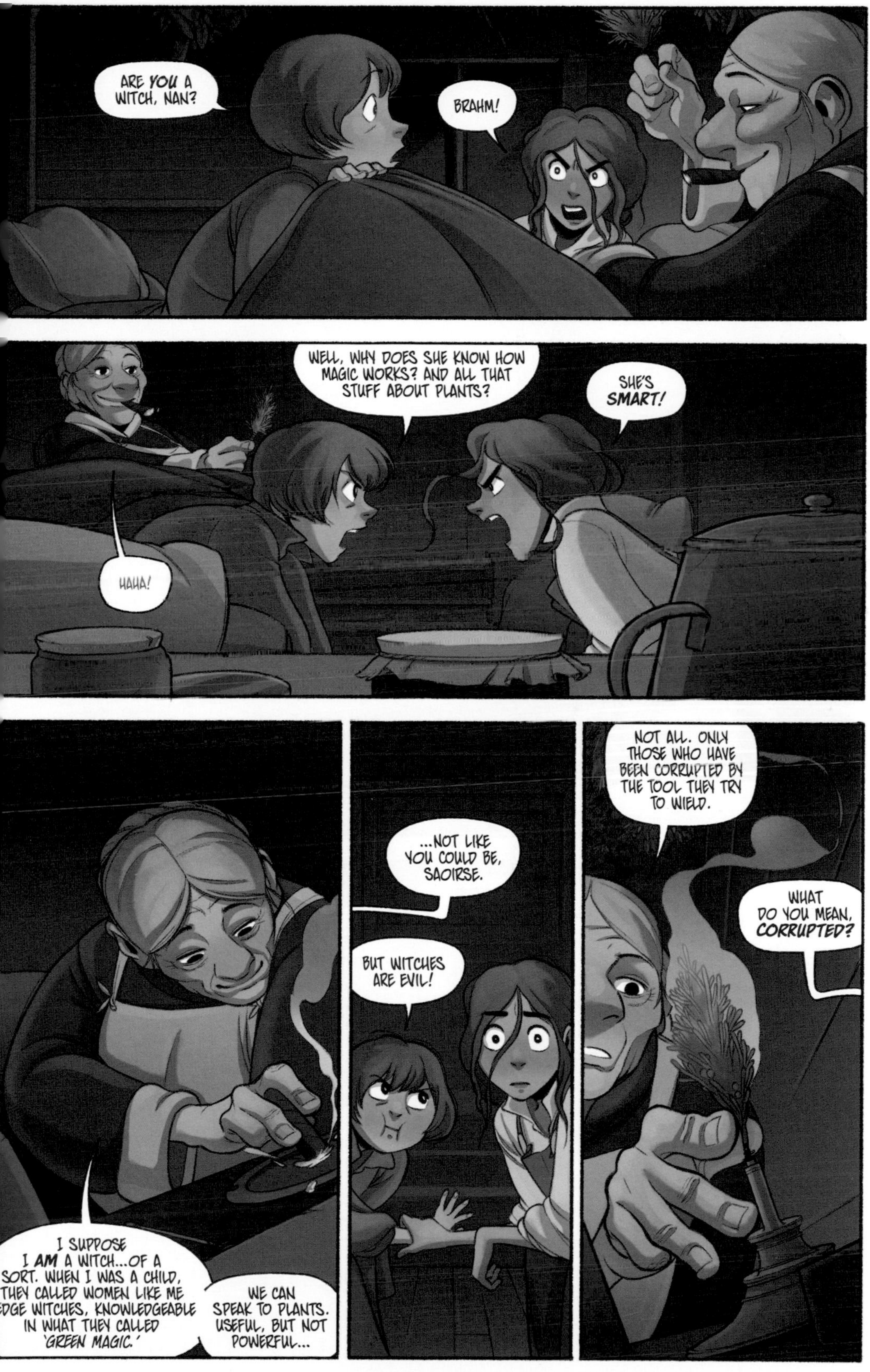
ARE YOU A WITCH, NAN?
BRAHM!
WELL, WHY DOES SHE KNOW HOW MAGIC WORKS? AND ALL THAT STUFF ABOUT PLANTS?
SHE'S SMART!
HAHA!
I SUPPOSE I AM A WITCH...OF A SORT. WHEN I WAS A CHILD, THEY CALLED WOMEN LIKE ME EDGE WITCHES, KNOWLEDGEABLE IN WHAT THEY CALLED 'GREEN MAGIC.'
WE CAN SPEAK TO PLANTS. USEFUL, BUT NOT POWERFUL...
...NOT LIKE YOU COULD BE, SAOIRSE.
BUT WITCHES ARE EVIL!
NOT ALL. ONLY THOSE WHO HAVE BEEN CORRUPTED BY THE TOOL THEY TRY TO WIELD.
WHAT DO YOU MEAN, CORRUPTED?

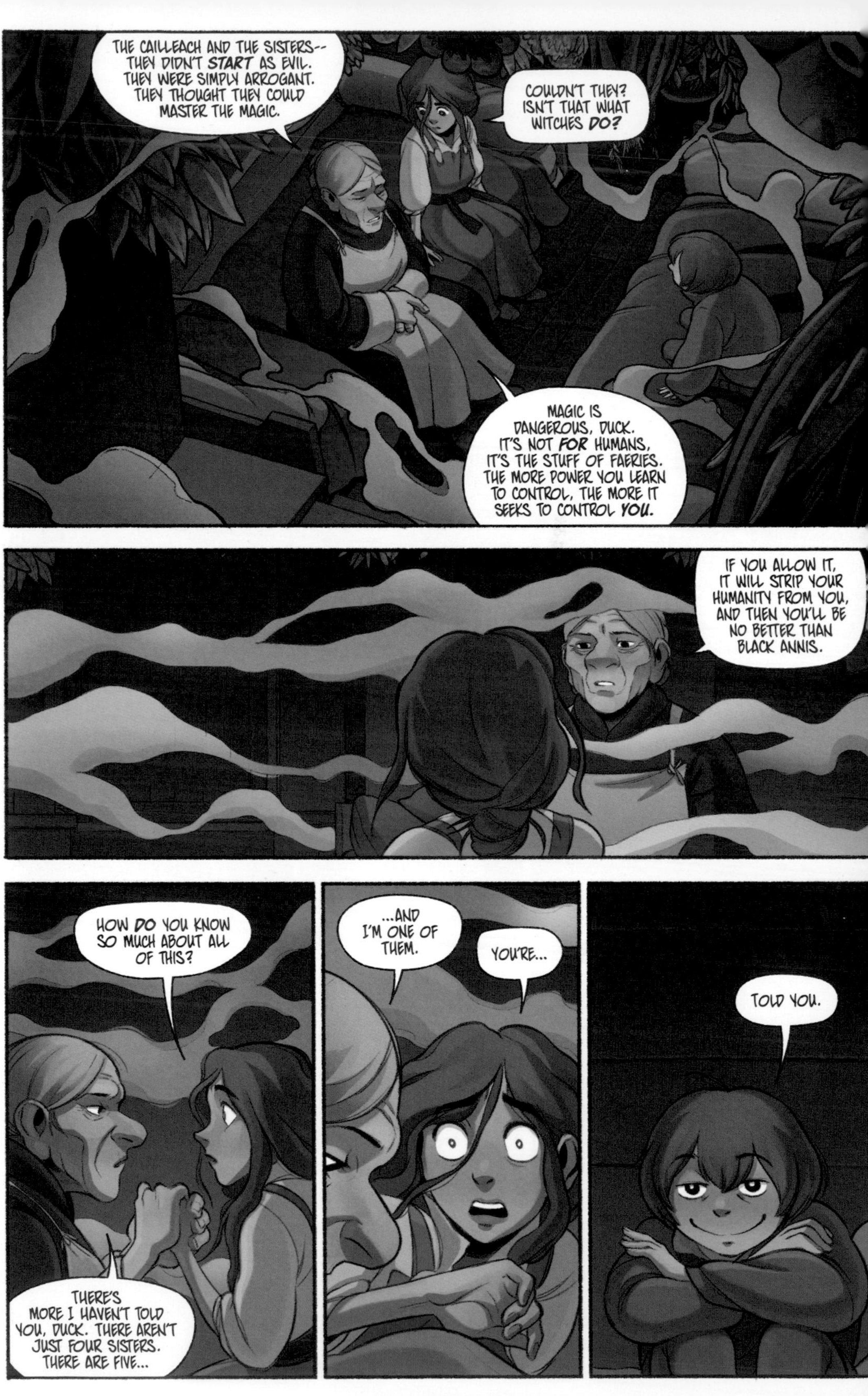
THE CAILLEACH AND THE SISTERS-- THEY DIDN'T START AS EVIL. THEY WERE SIMPLY ARROGANT. THEY THOUGHT THEY COULD MASTER THE MAGIC.
COULDN'T THEY? ISN'T THAT WHAT WITCHES DO?
MAGIC IS DANGEROUS, DUCK. IT'S NOT FOR HUMANS, IT'S THE STUFF OF FAERIES. THE MORE POWER YOU LEARN TO CONTROL, THE MORE IT SEEKS TO CONTROL YOU.
IF YOU ALLOW IT, IT WILL STRIP YOUR HUMANITY FROM YOU, AND THEN YOU'LL BE NO BETTER THAN BLACK ANNIS.
HOW DO YOU KNOW SO MUCH ABOUT ALL OF THIS?
THERE'S MORE I HAVEN'T TOLD YOU, DUCK. THERE AREN'T JUST FOUR SISTERS. THERE ARE FIVE...
...AND I'M ONE OF THEM.
YOU'RE...
TOLD YOU.

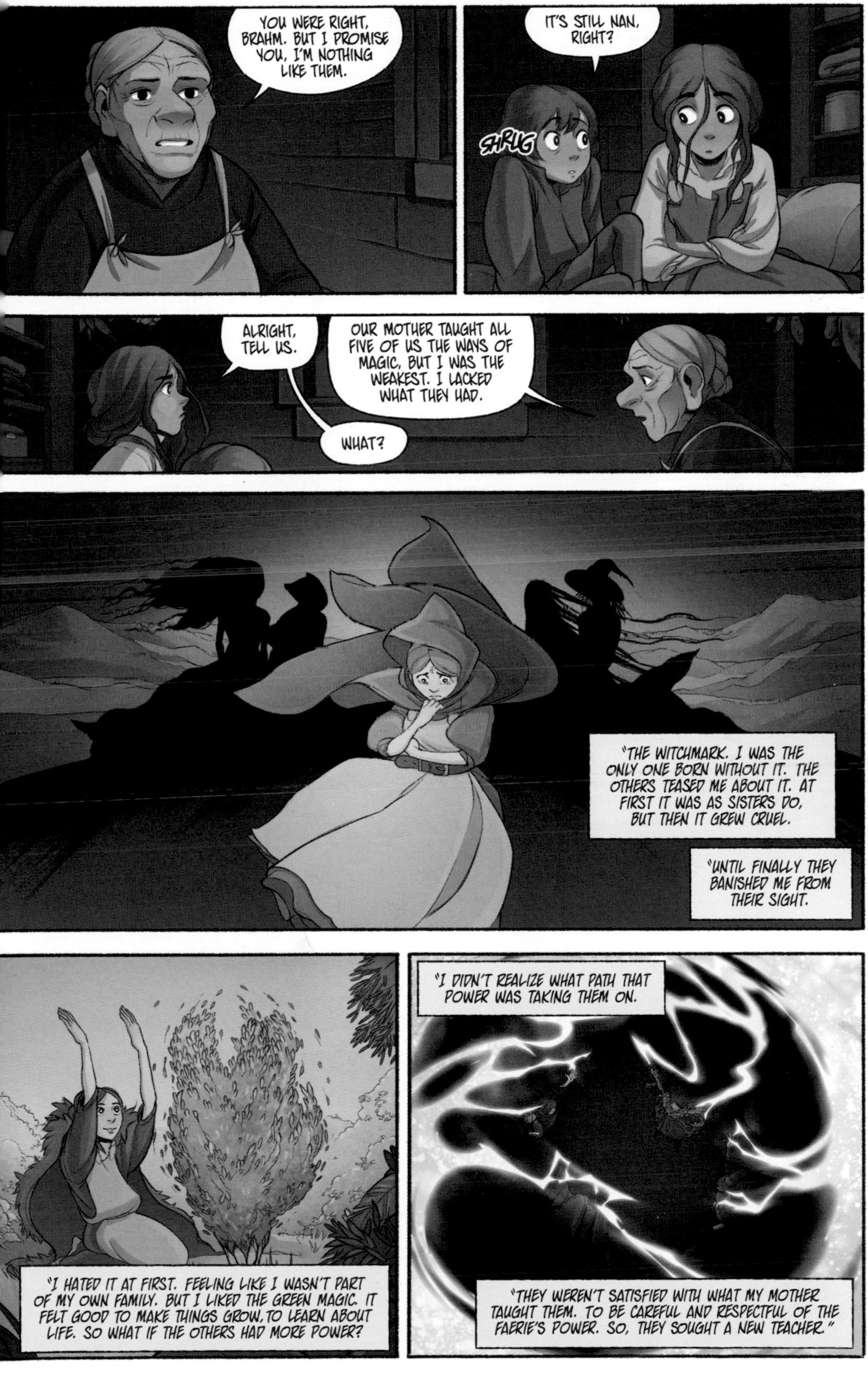
YOU WERE RIGHT, BRAHM. BUT I PROMISE YOU, I'M NOTHING LIKE THEM.
IT'S STILL NAN, RIGHT?
SHRUG
ALRIGHT, TELL US.
OUR MOTHER TAUGHT ALL FIVE OF US THE WAYS OF MAGIC, BUT I WAS THE WEAKEST. I LACKED WHAT THEY HAD.
WHAT?
"THE WITCHMARK. I WAS THE ONLY ONE BORN WITHOUT IT. THE OTHERS TEASED ME ABOUT IT. AT FIRST IT WAS AS SISTERS DO, BUT THEN IT GREW CRUEL.
"UNTIL FINALLY THEY BANISHED ME FROM THEIR SIGHT.
"I HATED IT AT FIRST. FEELING LIKE I WASN'T PART OF MY OWN FAMILY. BUT I LIKED THE GREEN MAGIC. IT FELT GOOD TO MAKE THINGS GROW, TO LEARN ABOUT LIFE. SO WHAT IF THE OTHERS HAD MORE POWER?
"I DIDN'T REALIZE WHAT PATH THAT POWER WAS TAKING THEM ON.
"THEY WEREN'T SATISFIED WITH WHAT MY MOTHER TAUGHT THEM. TO BE CAREFUL AND RESPECTFUL OF THE FAERIE'S POWER. SO, THEY SOUGHT A NEW TEACHER."

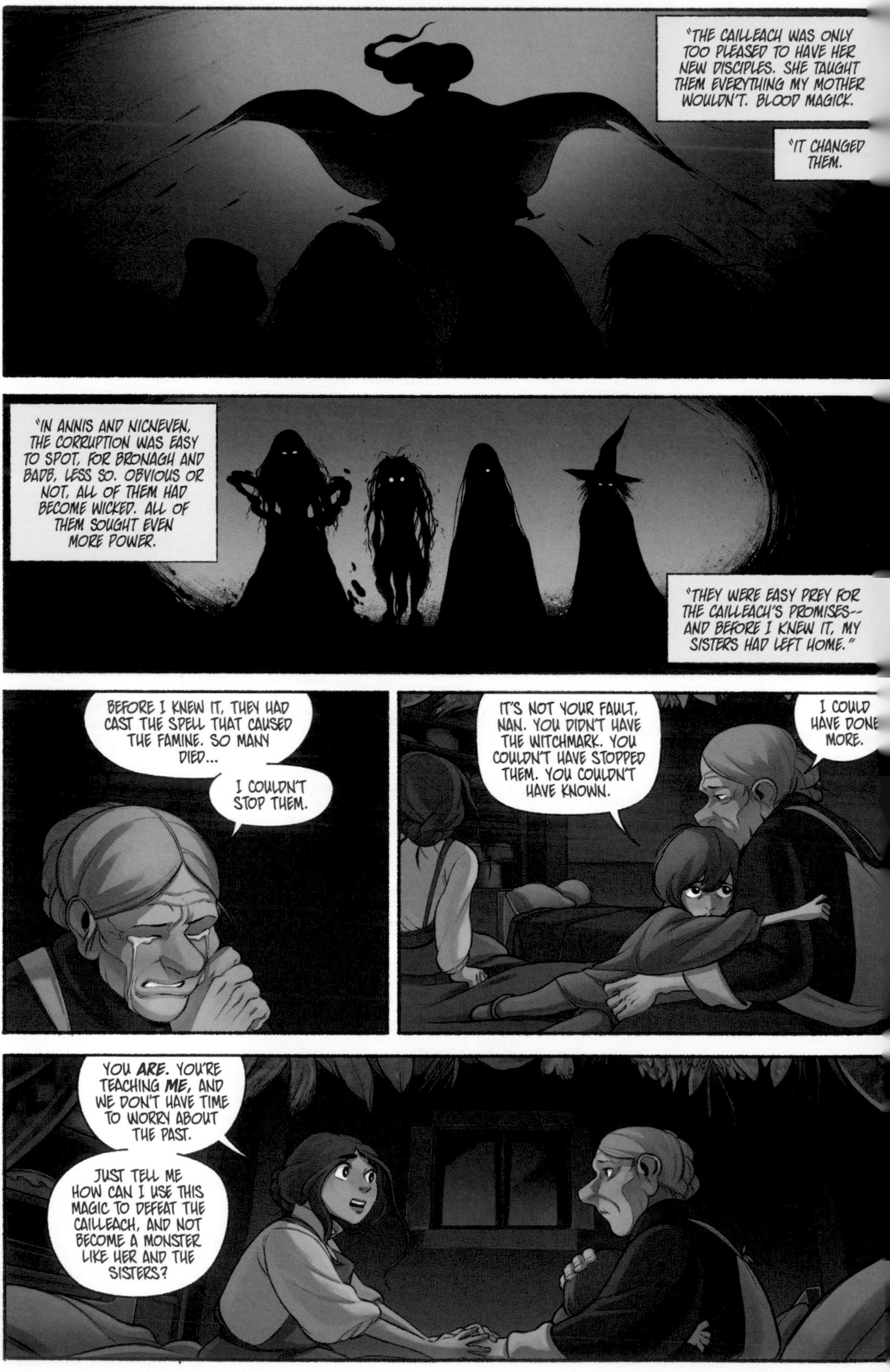
"THE CAILLEACH WAS ONLY TOO PLEASED TO HAVE HER NEW DISCIPLES. SHE TAUGHT THEM EVERYTHING MY MOTHER WOULDN'T. BLOOD MAGICK.
"IT CHANGED THEM.
"IN ANNIS AND NICNEVEN, THE CORRUPTION WAS EASY TO SPOT, FOR BRONAGH AND BADB, LESS SO. OBVIOUS OR NOT, ALL OF THEM HAD BECOME WICKED. ALL OF THEM SOUGHT EVEN MORE POWER.
"THEY WERE EASY PREY FOR THE CAILLEACH'S PROMISES--AND BEFORE I KNEW IT, MY SISTERS HAD LEFT HOME."
BEFORE I KNEW IT, THEY HAD CAST THE SPELL THAT CAUSED THE FAMINE. SO MANY DIED...
I COULDN'T STOP THEM.
IT'S NOT YOUR FAULT, NAN. YOU DIDN'T HAVE THE WITCHMARK. YOU COULDN'T HAVE STOPPED THEM. YOU COULDN'T HAVE KNOWN.
I COULD HAVE DONE MORE.
YOU ARE. YOU'RE TEACHING ME, AND WE DON'T HAVE TIME TO WORRY ABOUT THE PAST.
JUST TELL ME HOW CAN I USE THIS MAGIC TO DEFEAT THE CAILLEACH, AND NOT BECOME A MONSTER LIKE HER AND THE SISTERS?

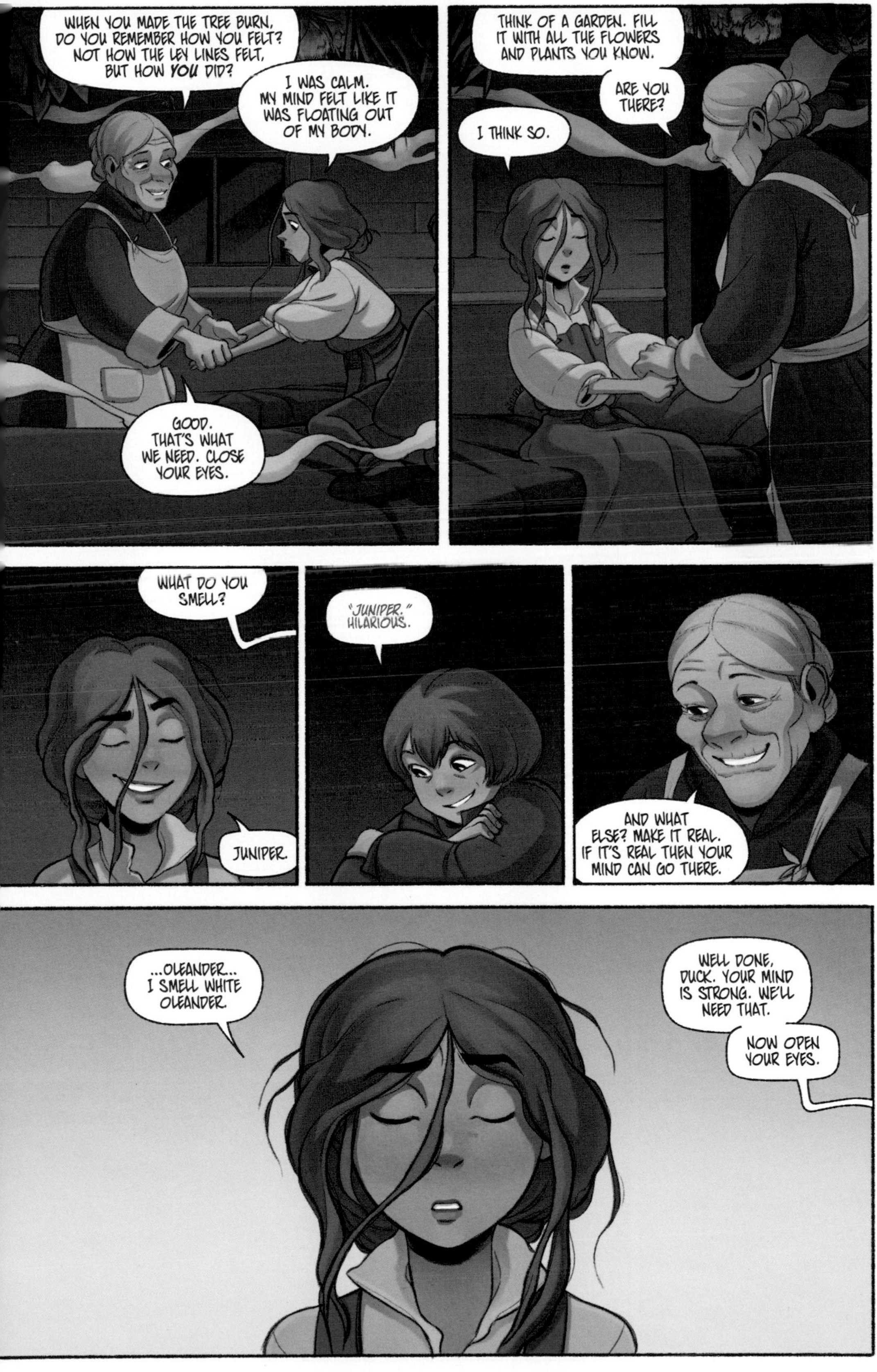
WHEN YOU MADE THE TREE BURN, DO YOU REMEMBER HOW YOU FELT? NOT HOW THE LEY LINES FELT, BUT HOW *YOU* DID?
I WAS CALM. MY MIND FELT LIKE IT WAS FLOATING OUT OF MY BODY.
GOOD. THAT'S WHAT WE NEED. CLOSE YOUR EYES.
THINK OF A GARDEN. FILL IT WITH ALL THE FLOWERS AND PLANTS YOU KNOW.
ARE YOU THERE?
I THINK SO.
WHAT DO YOU SMELL?
JUNIPER.
"JUNIPER." HILARIOUS.
AND WHAT ELSE? MAKE IT REAL. IF IT'S REAL THEN YOUR MIND CAN GO THERE.
...OLEANDER... I SMELL WHITE OLEANDER.
WELL DONE, DUCK. YOUR MIND IS STRONG. WE'LL NEED THAT.
NOW OPEN YOUR EYES.

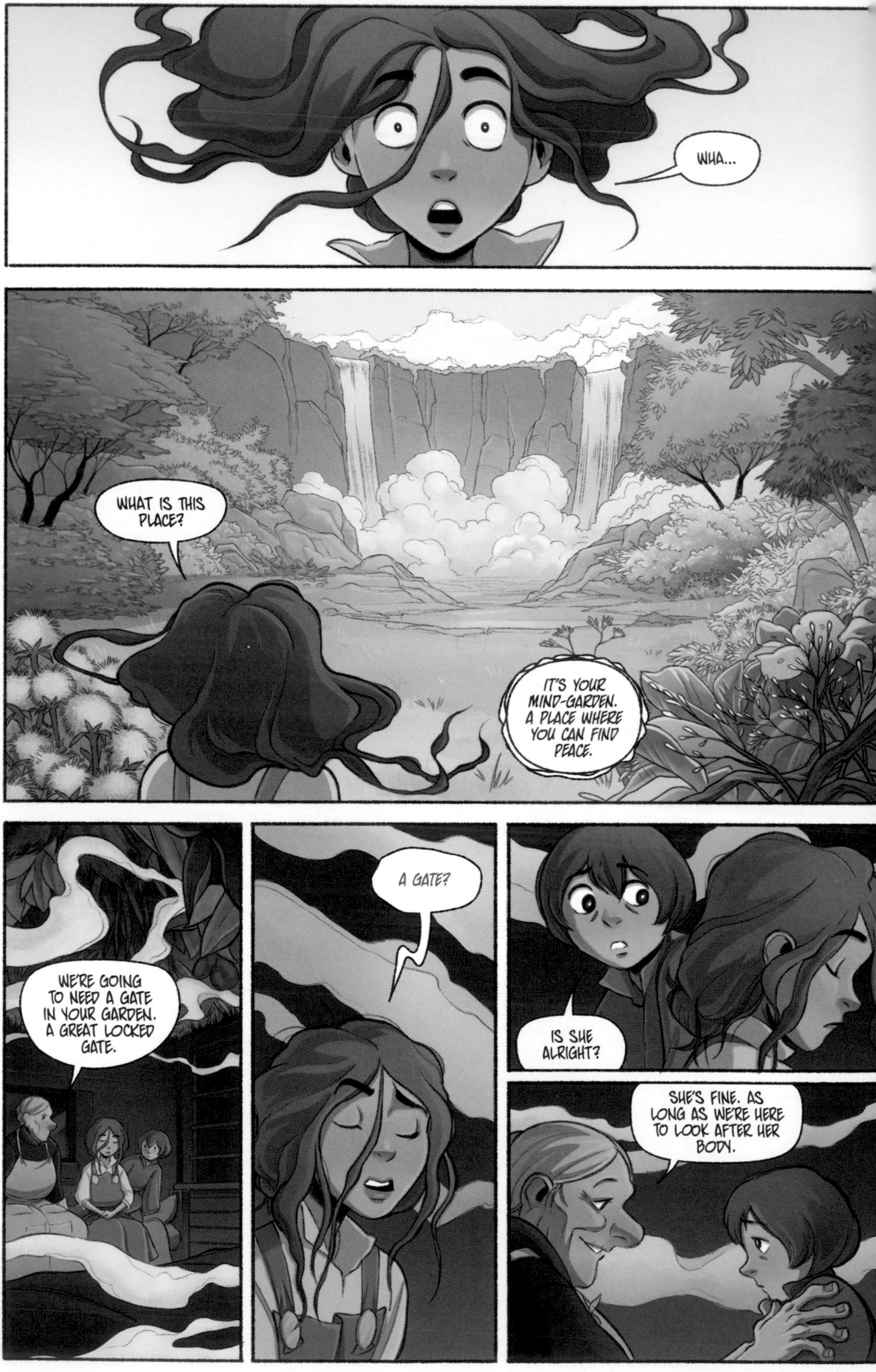
WHA...
WHAT IS THIS PLACE?
IT'S YOUR MIND-GARDEN. A PLACE WHERE YOU CAN FIND PEACE.
WE'RE GOING TO NEED A GATE IN YOUR GARDEN. A GREAT LOCKED GATE.
A GATE?
IS SHE ALRIGHT?
SHE'S FINE. AS LONG AS WE'RE HERE TO LOOK AFTER HER BODY.

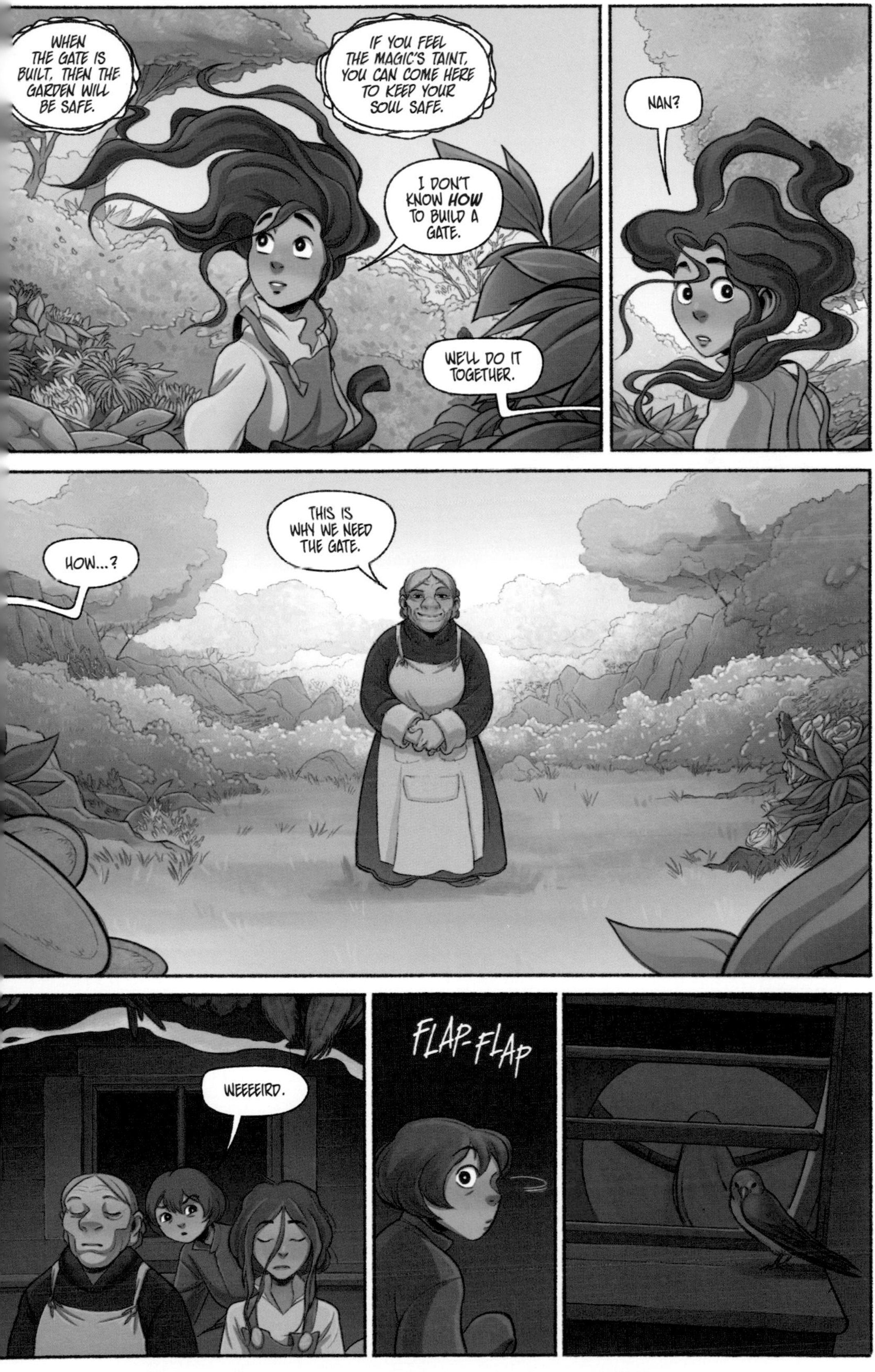
WHEN THE GATE IS BUILT, THEN THE GARDEN WILL BE SAFE.
IF YOU FEEL THE MAGIC'S TAINT, YOU CAN COME HERE TO KEEP YOUR SOUL SAFE.
I DON'T KNOW **HOW** TO BUILD A GATE.
WE'LL DO IT TOGETHER.
NAN?
HOW...?
THIS IS WHY WE NEED THE GATE.
WEEEEIRD.
FLAP-FLAP

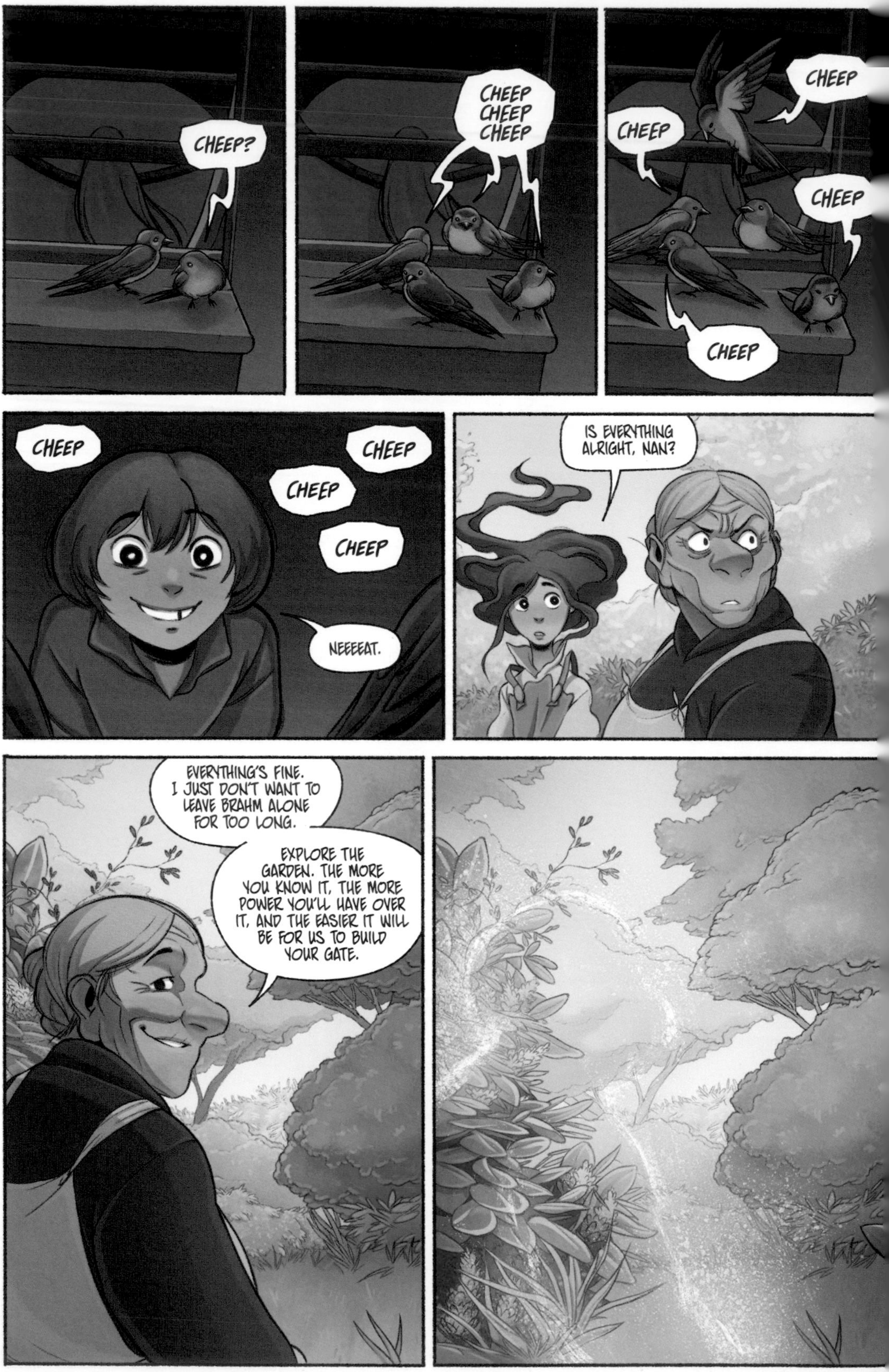
CHEEP?
CHEEP CHEEP CHEEP
CHEEP
CHEEP
CHEEP
CHEEP
CHEEP
CHEEP
CHEEP
CHEEP
NEEEEAT.
IS EVERYTHING ALRIGHT, NAN?
EVERYTHING'S FINE. I JUST DON'T WANT TO LEAVE BRAHM ALONE FOR TOO LONG.
EXPLORE THE GARDEN. THE MORE YOU KNOW IT, THE MORE POWER YOU'LL HAVE OVER IT, AND THE EASIER IT WILL BE FOR US TO BUILD YOUR GATE.

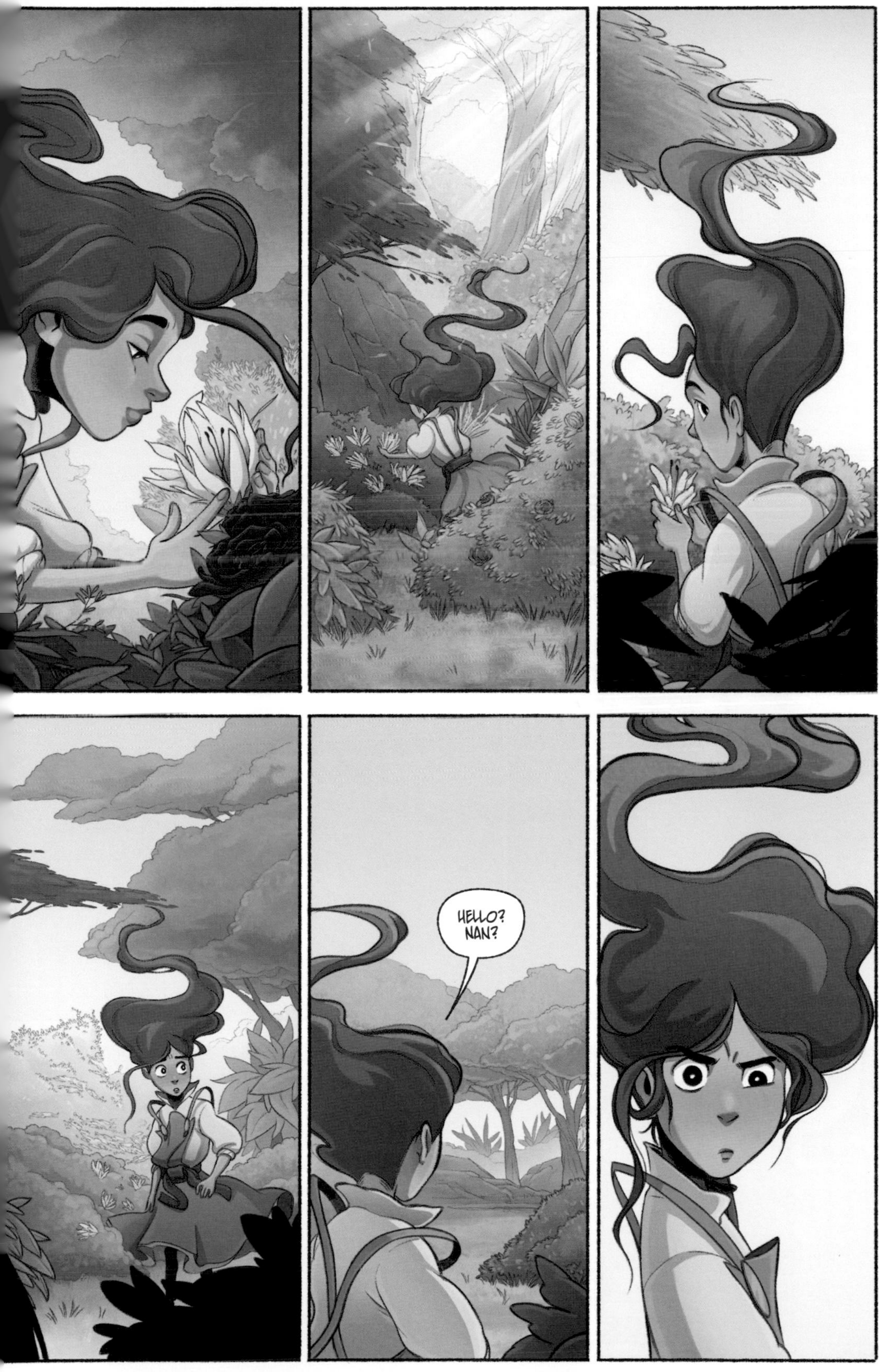
HELLO?
NAN?

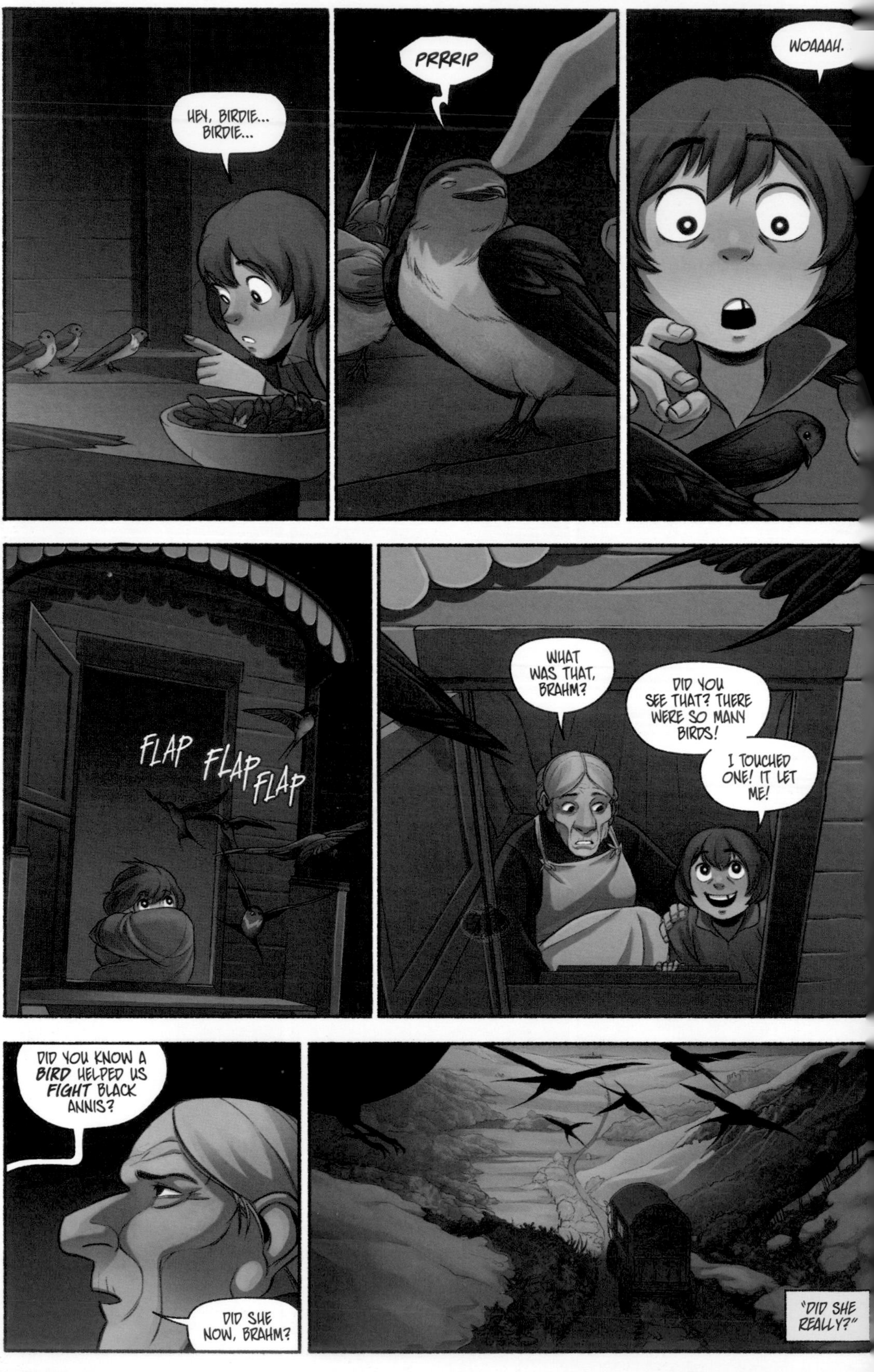
HEY, BIRDIE... BIRDIE...
PRRRIP
WOAAAH.
FLAP FLAP FLAP
WHAT WAS THAT, BRAHM?
DID YOU SEE THAT? THERE WERE SO MANY BIRDS!
I TOUCHED ONE! IT LET ME!
DID YOU KNOW A BIRD HELPED US FIGHT BLACK ANNIS?
DID SHE NOW, BRAHM?
"DID SHE REALLY?"

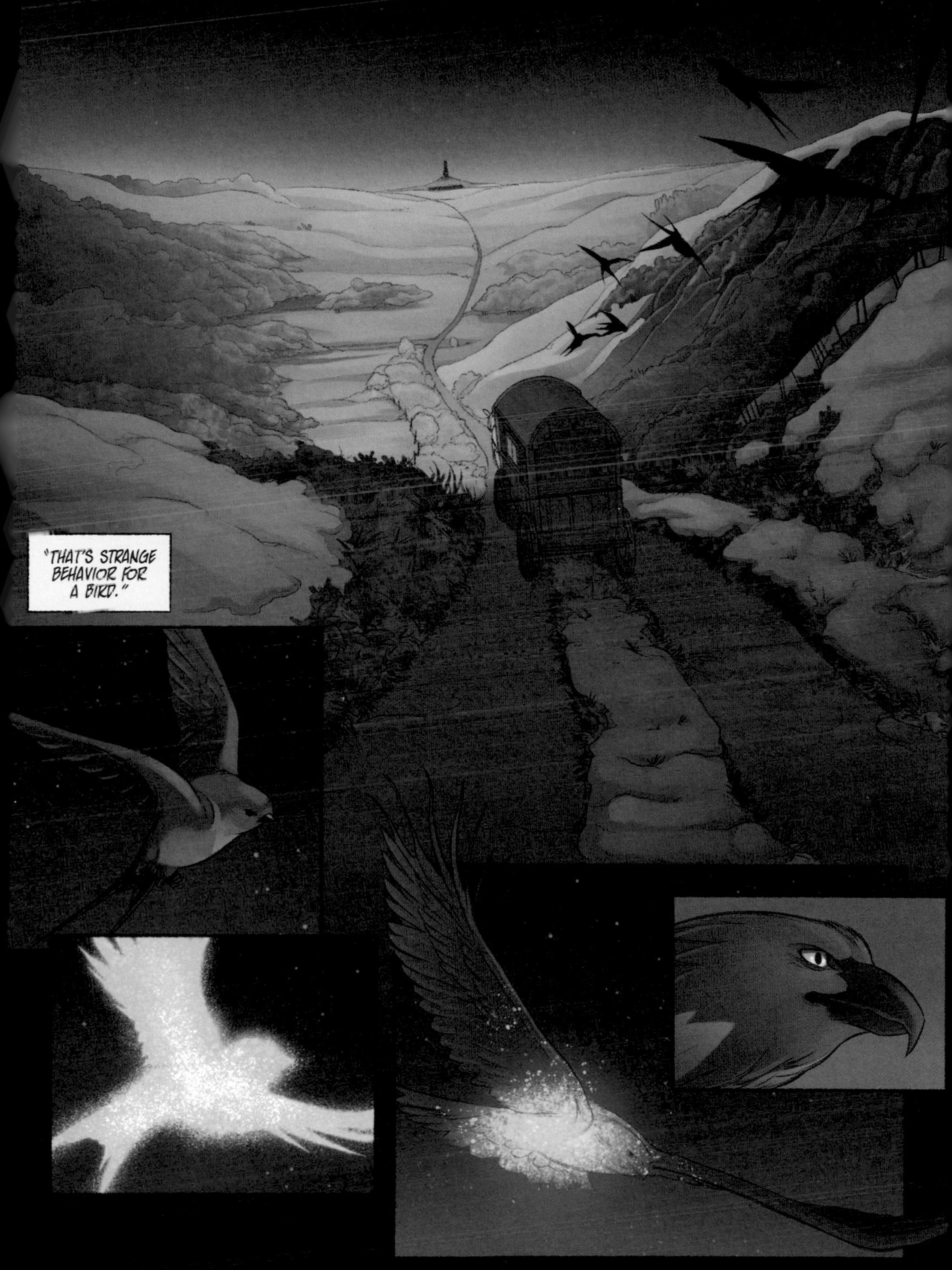
"THAT'S STRANGE BEHAVIOR FOR A BIRD."

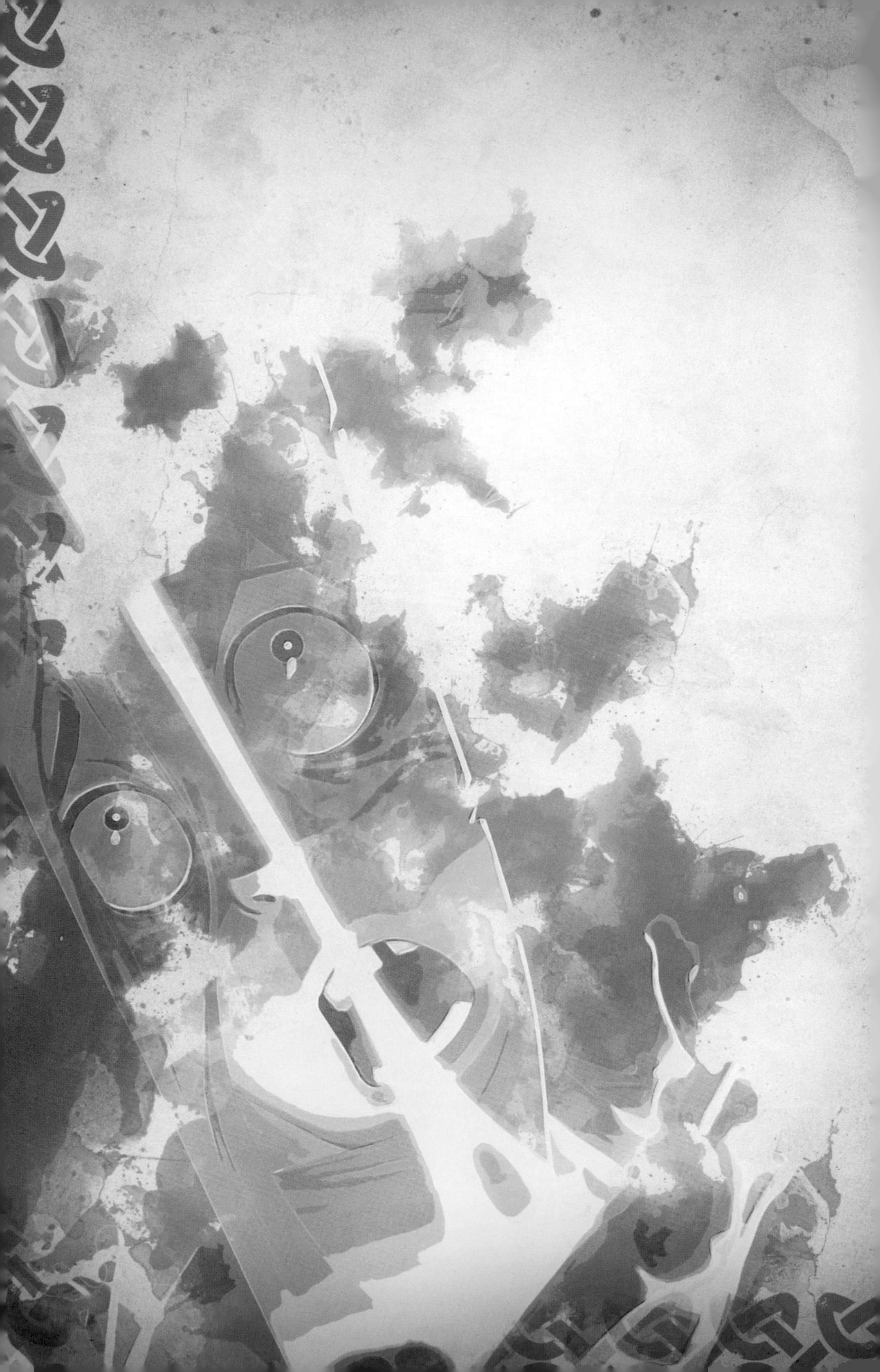

CHAPTER
THREE

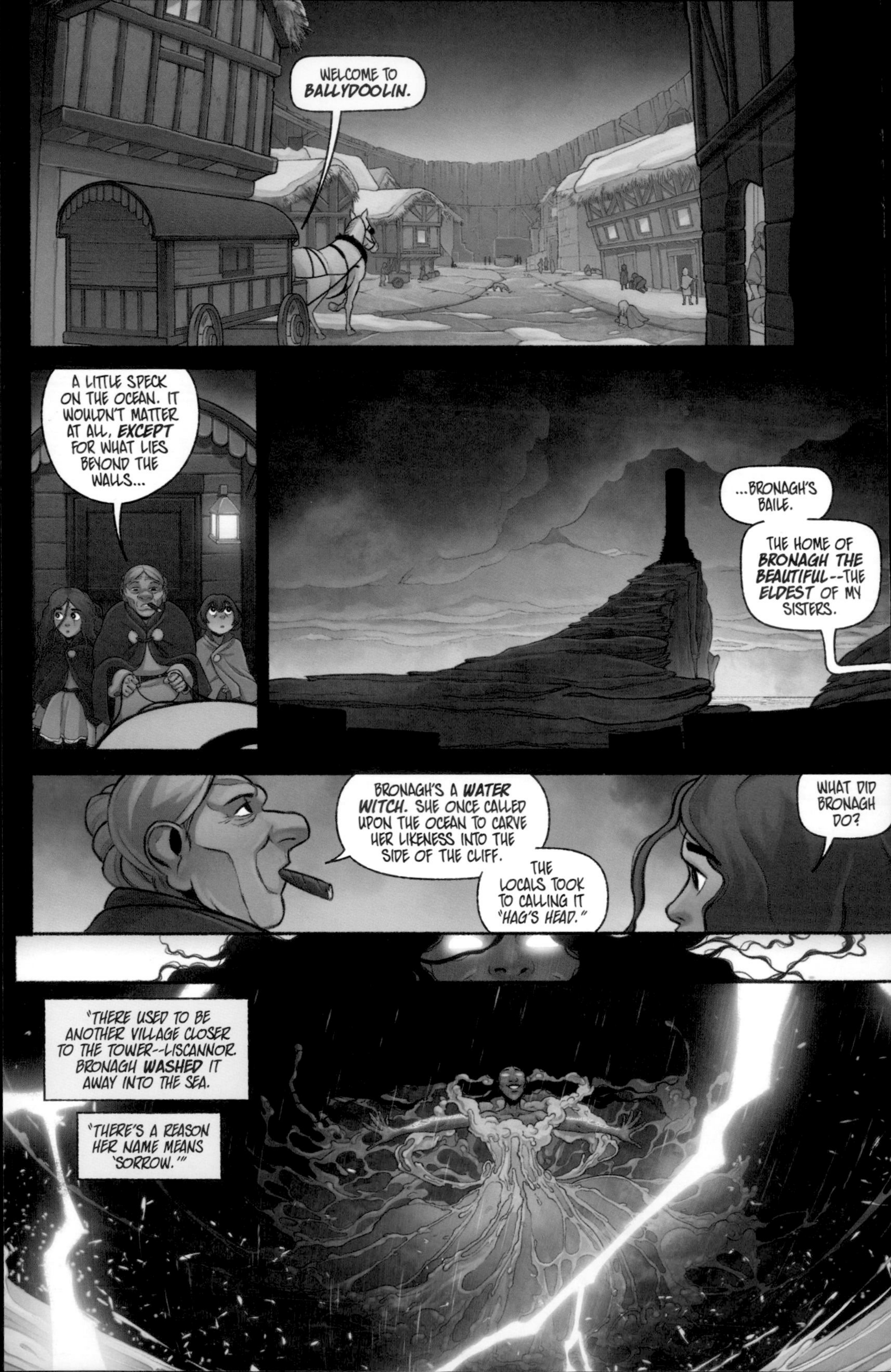
WELCOME TO BALLYDOOLIN.
A LITTLE SPECK ON THE OCEAN. IT WOULDN'T MATTER AT ALL, EXCEPT FOR WHAT LIES BEYOND THE WALLS...
...BRONAGH'S BAILE.
THE HOME OF BRONAGH THE BEAUTIFUL--THE ELDEST OF MY SISTERS.
BRONAGH'S A WATER WITCH. SHE ONCE CALLED UPON THE OCEAN TO CARVE HER LIKENESS INTO THE SIDE OF THE CLIFF.
THE LOCALS TOOK TO CALLING IT "HAG'S HEAD."
WHAT DID BRONAGH DO?
"THERE USED TO BE ANOTHER VILLAGE CLOSER TO THE TOWER--LISCANNOR. BRONAGH WASHED IT AWAY INTO THE SEA.
"THERE'S A REASON HER NAME MEANS 'SORROW.'"

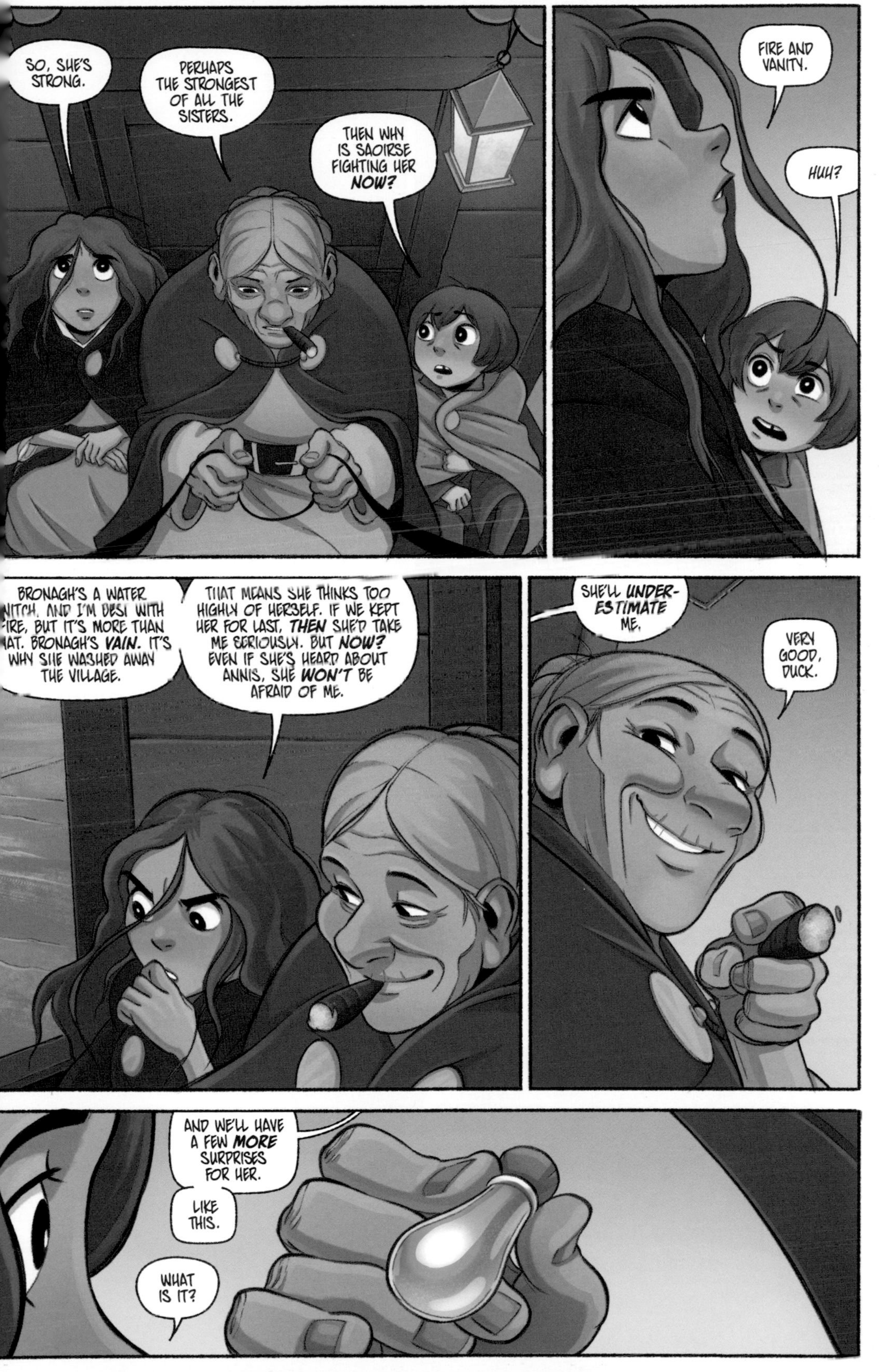
SO, SHE'S STRONG.
PERHAPS THE STRONGEST OF ALL THE SISTERS.
THEN WHY IS SAOIRSE FIGHTING HER NOW?
FIRE AND VANITY.
HUH?
BRONAGH'S A WATER WITCH, AND I'M BEST WITH FIRE, BUT IT'S MORE THAN THAT. BRONAGH'S VAIN. IT'S WHY SHE WASHED AWAY THE VILLAGE.
THAT MEANS SHE THINKS TOO HIGHLY OF HERSELF. IF WE KEPT HER FOR LAST, THEN SHE'D TAKE ME SERIOUSLY. BUT NOW? EVEN IF SHE'S HEARD ABOUT ANNIS, SHE WON'T BE AFRAID OF ME.
SHE'LL UNDER-ESTIMATE ME.
VERY GOOD, DUCK.
AND WE'LL HAVE A FEW MORE SURPRISES FOR HER.
LIKE THIS.
WHAT IS IT?

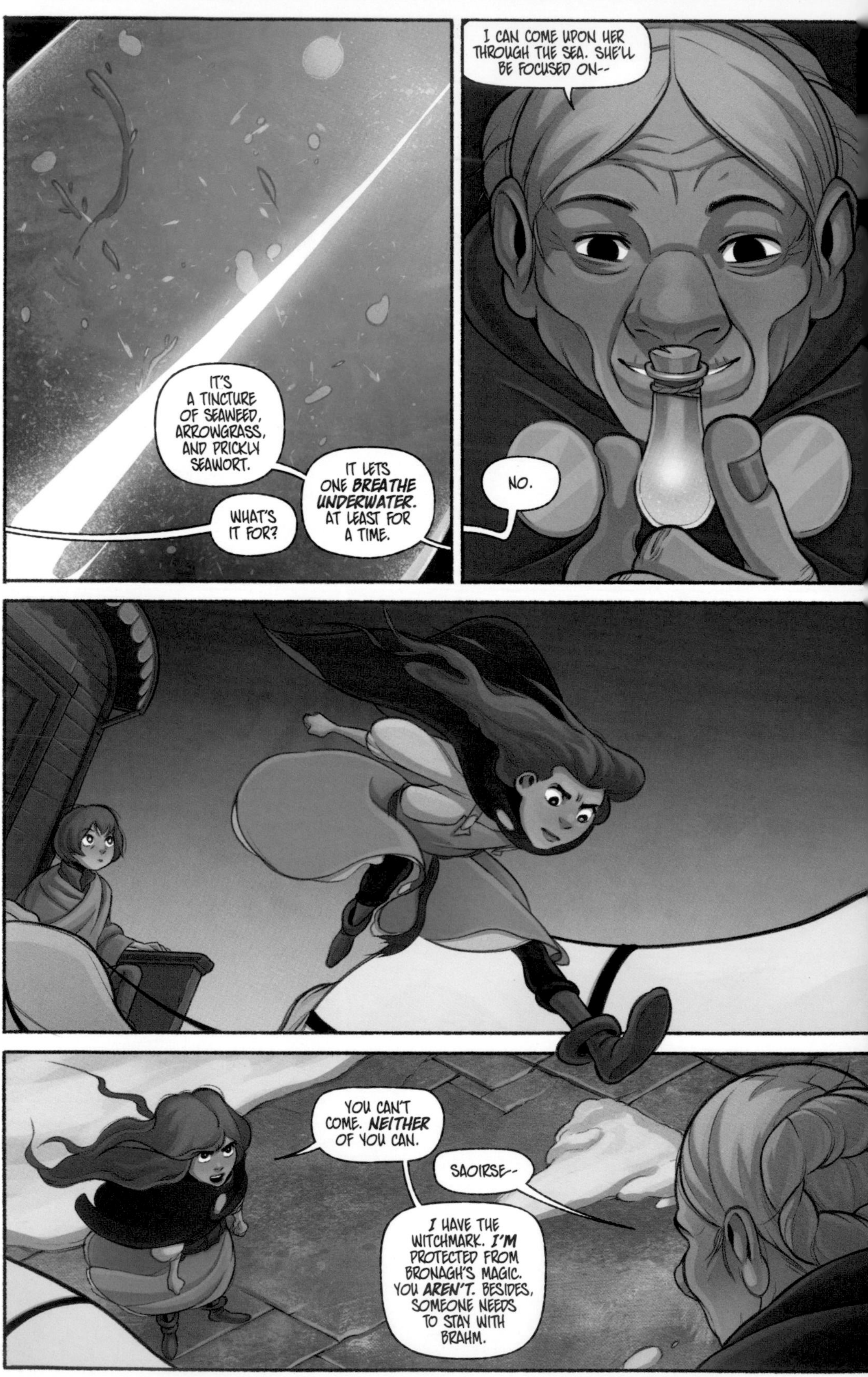
I CAN COME UPON HER THROUGH THE SEA. SHE'LL BE FOCUSED ON--
IT'S A TINCTURE OF SEAWEED, ARROWGRASS, AND PRICKLY SEAWORT.
WHAT'S IT FOR?
IT LETS ONE **BREATHE UNDERWATER.** AT LEAST FOR A TIME.
NO.
YOU CAN'T COME. **NEITHER** OF YOU CAN.
SAOIRSE--
I HAVE THE WITCHMARK. ***I'M*** PROTECTED FROM BRONAGH'S MAGIC. YOU ***AREN'T.*** BESIDES, SOMEONE NEEDS TO STAY WITH BRAHM.

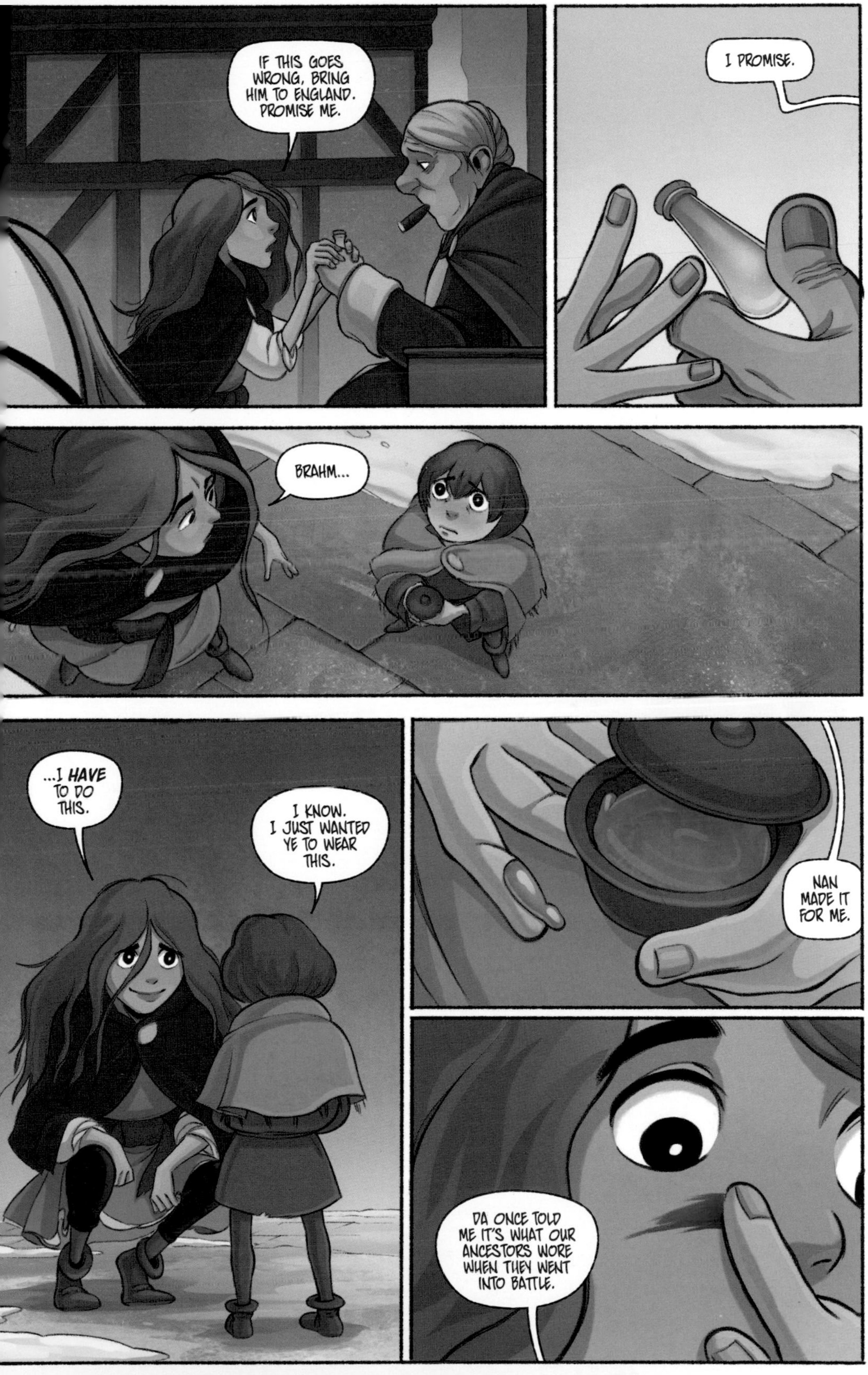
IF THIS GOES WRONG, BRING HIM TO ENGLAND. PROMISE ME.
I PROMISE.
BRAHM...
...I HAVE TO DO THIS.
I KNOW. I JUST WANTED YE TO WEAR THIS.
NAN MADE IT FOR ME.
DA ONCE TOLD ME IT'S WHAT OUR ANCESTORS WORE WHEN THEY WENT INTO BATTLE.

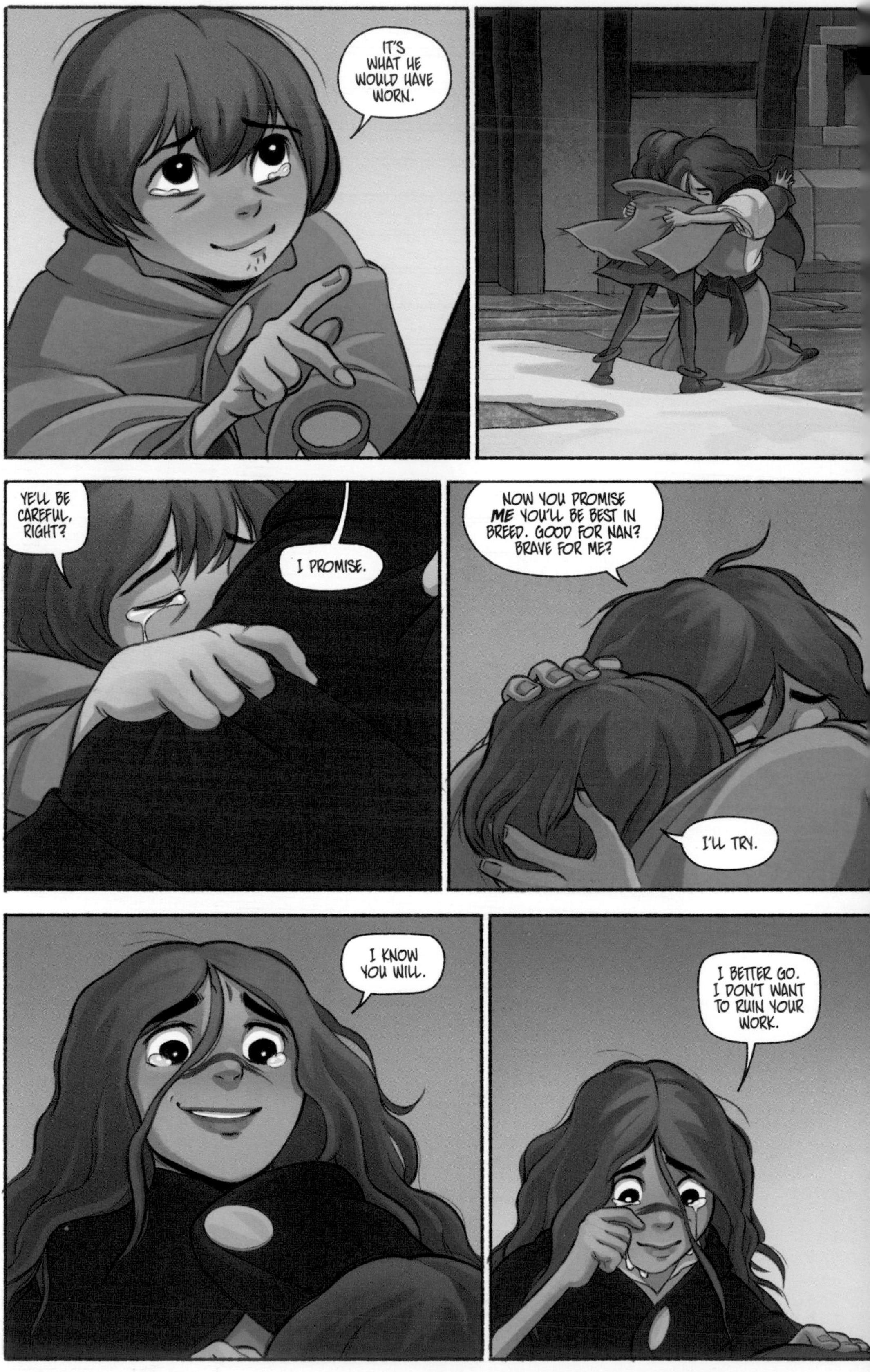
IT'S WHAT HE WOULD HAVE WORN.
YE'LL BE CAREFUL, RIGHT?
I PROMISE.
NOW YOU PROMISE **ME** YOU'LL BE BEST IN BREED. GOOD FOR NAN? BRAVE FOR ME?
I'LL TRY.
I KNOW YOU WILL.
I BETTER GO. I DON'T WANT TO RUIN YOUR WORK.

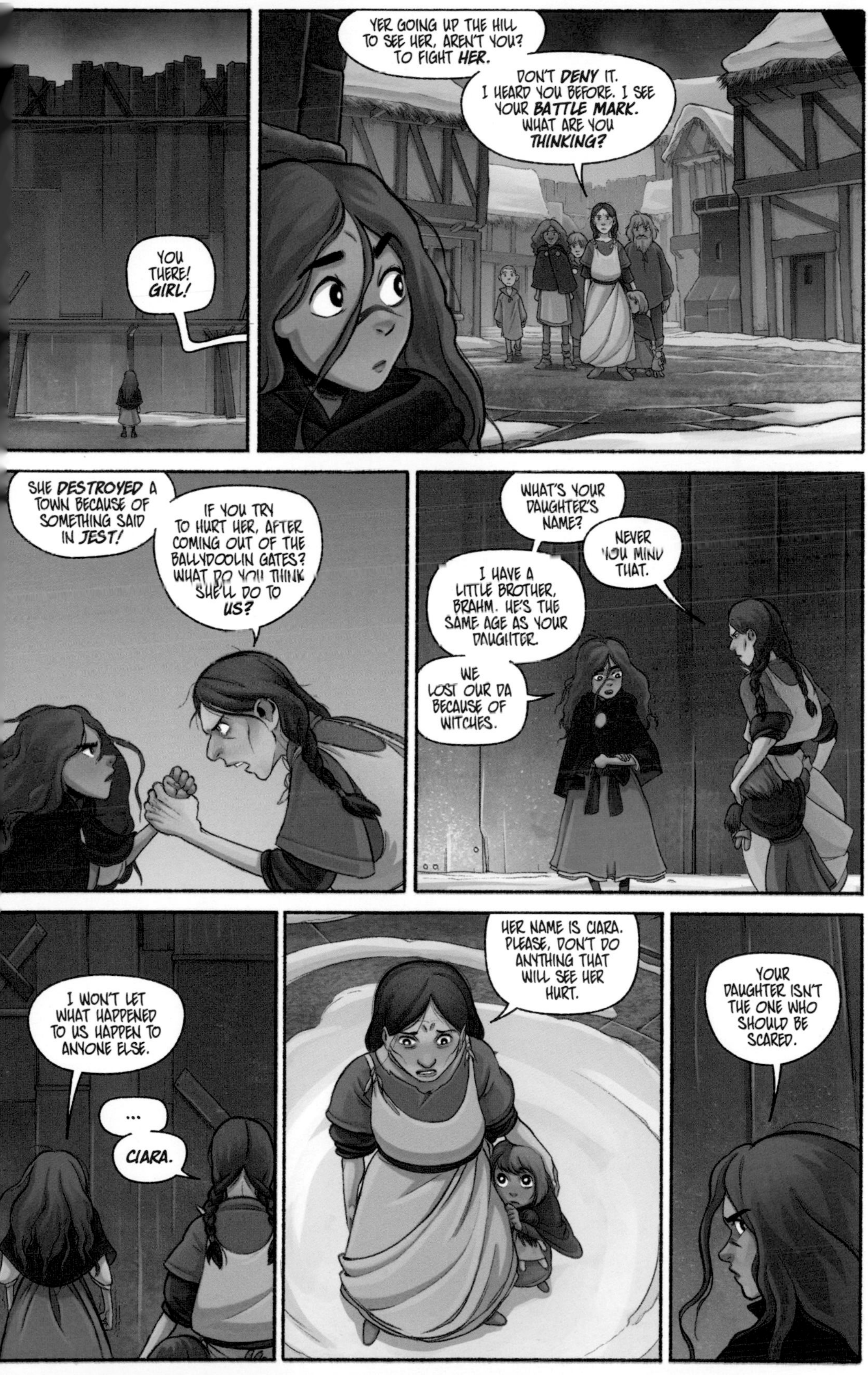
YOU THERE! GIRL!
YER GOING UP THE HILL TO SEE HER, AREN'T YOU? TO FIGHT HER.
DON'T DENY IT. I HEARD YOU BEFORE. I SEE YOUR BATTLE MARK. WHAT ARE YOU THINKING?
SHE DESTROYED A TOWN BECAUSE OF SOMETHING SAID IN JEST!
IF YOU TRY TO HURT HER, AFTER COMING OUT OF THE BALLYDOOLIN GATES? WHAT DO YOU THINK SHE'LL DO TO US?
WHAT'S YOUR DAUGHTER'S NAME?
NEVER YOU MIND THAT.
I HAVE A LITTLE BROTHER, BRAHM. HE'S THE SAME AGE AS YOUR DAUGHTER.
WE LOST OUR DA BECAUSE OF WITCHES.
I WON'T LET WHAT HAPPENED TO US HAPPEN TO ANYONE ELSE.
...
CIARA.
HER NAME IS CIARA. PLEASE, DON'T DO ANYTHING THAT WILL SEE HER HURT.
YOUR DAUGHTER ISN'T THE ONE WHO SHOULD BE SCARED.

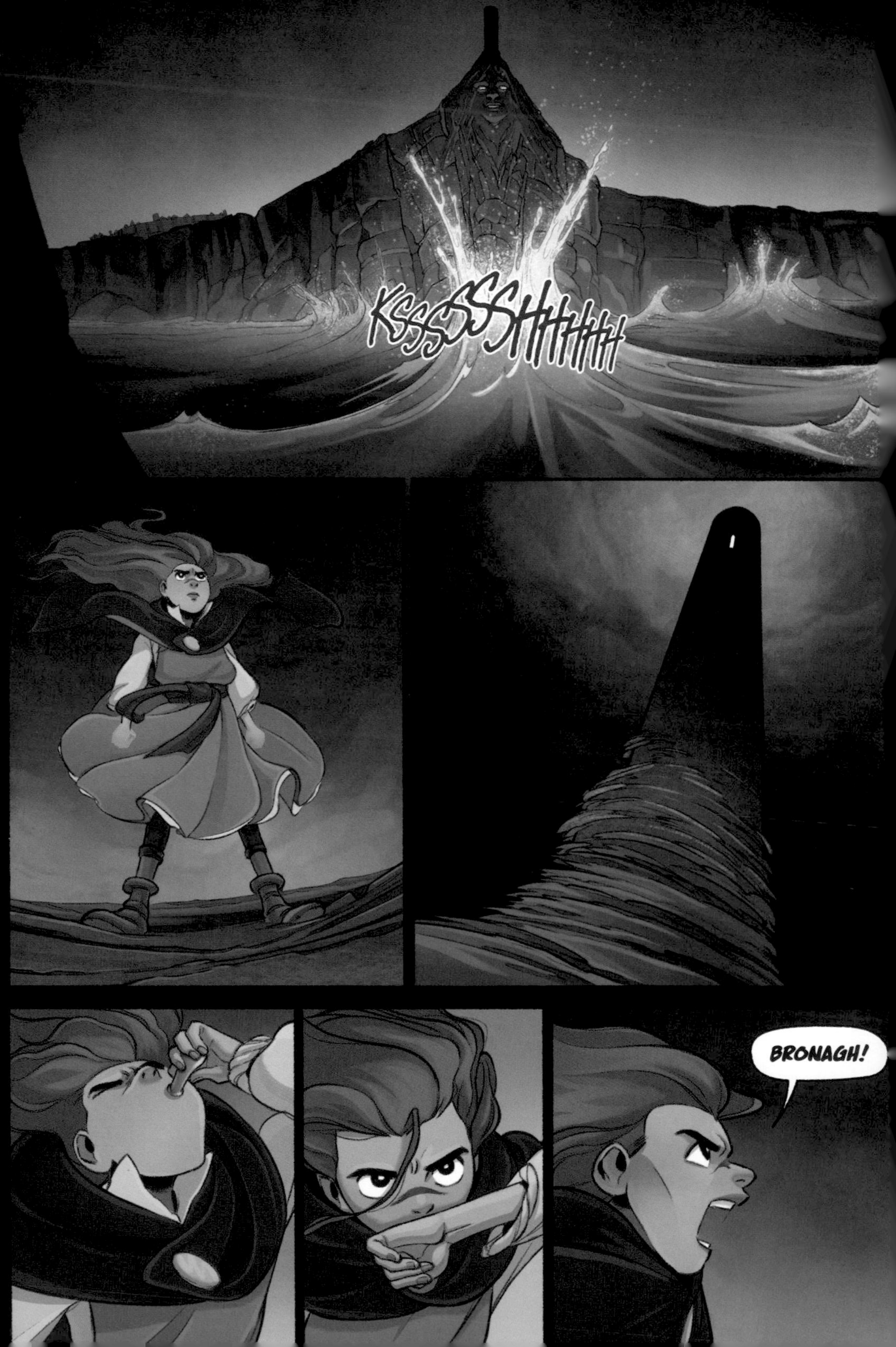
KSSSSSSHHHHHH
BRONAGH!

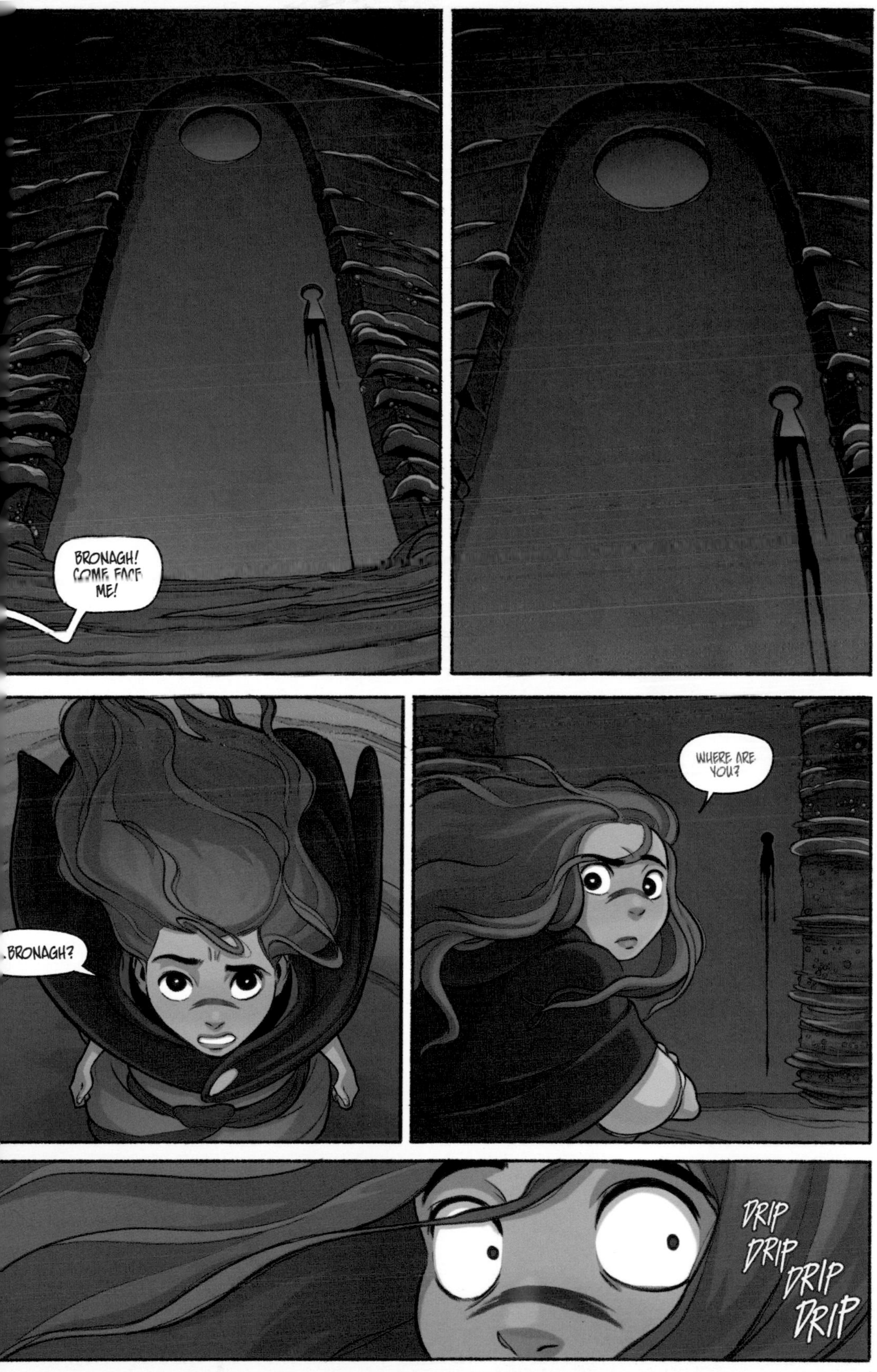
BRONAGH! COME FACE ME!
.BRONAGH?
WHERE ARE YOU?
DRIP
DRIP
DRIP
DRIP

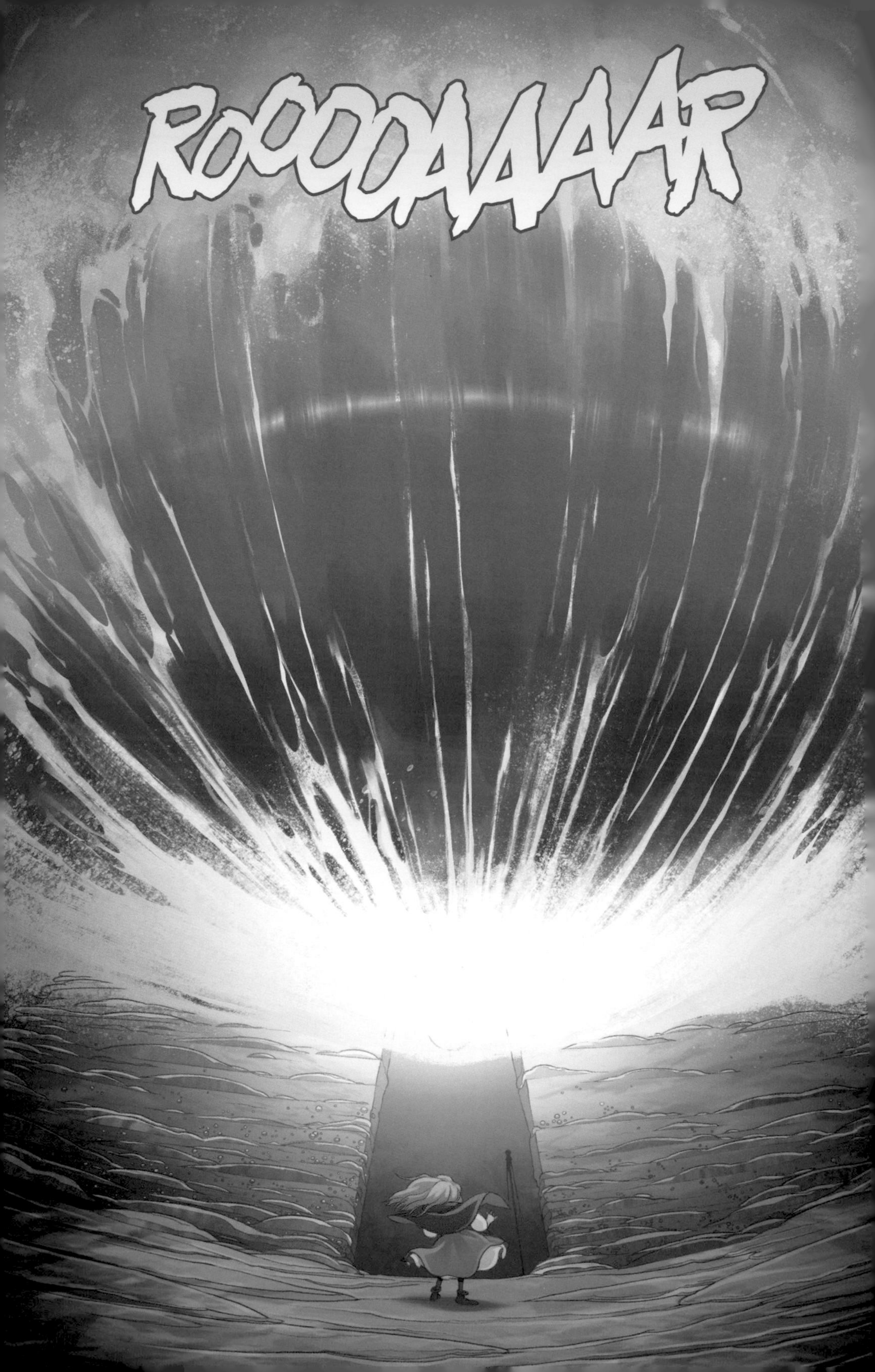
ROOOOAAAAR

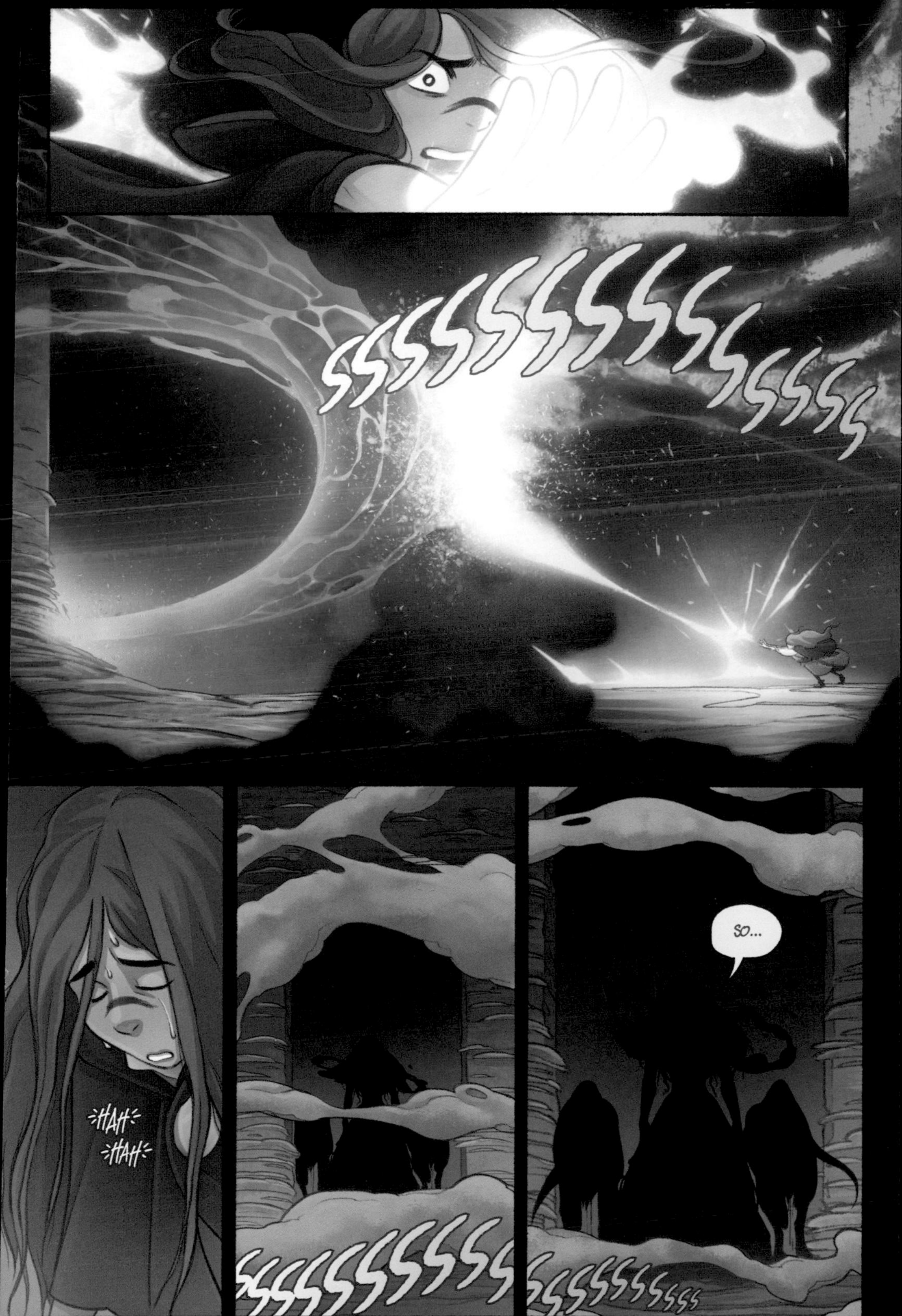
SSSSSSSSSSSSSSSSS
HAH
HAH
SO...
SSSSSSSSSSSS
SSSSSSSSSSSS

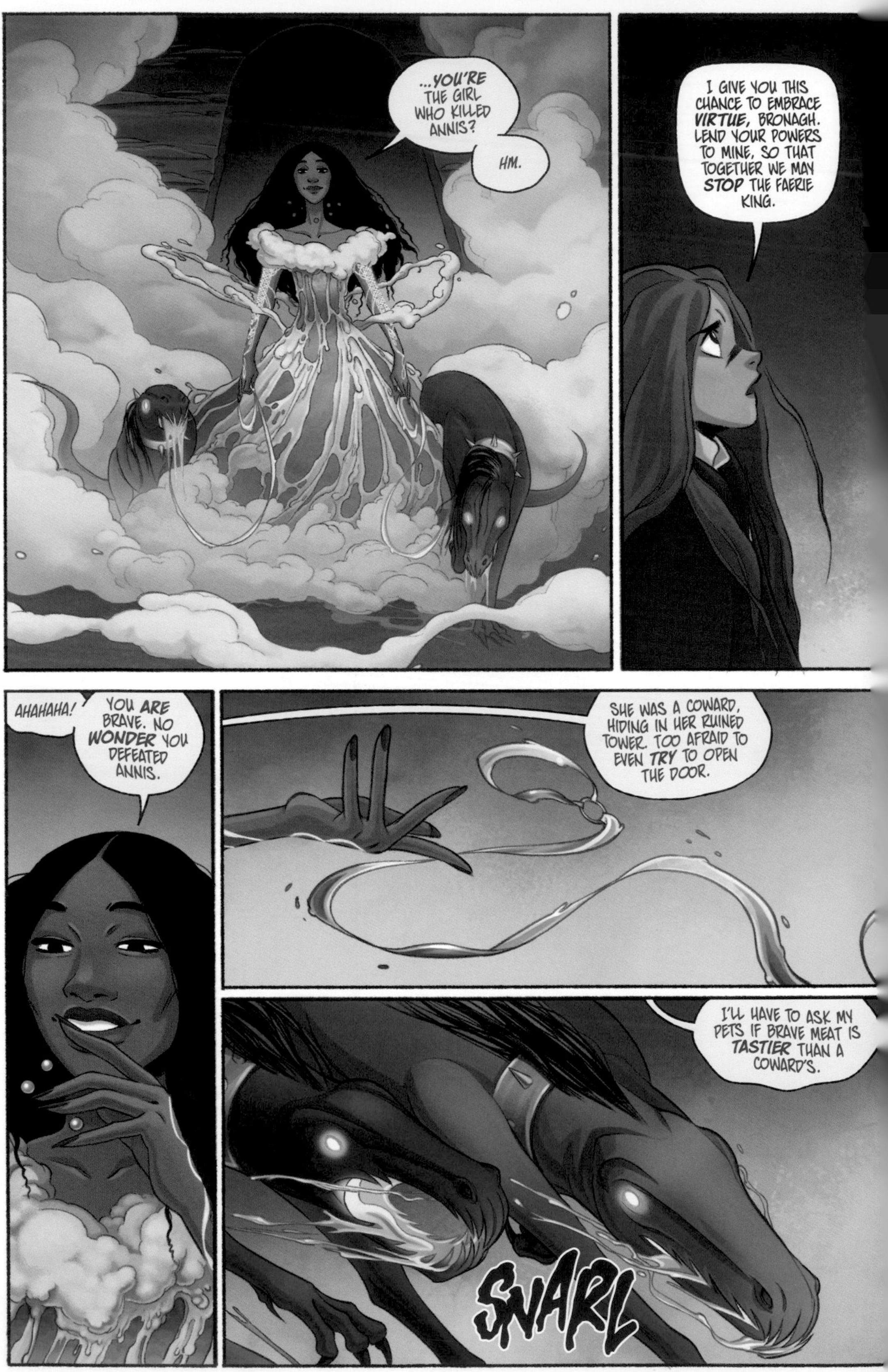
...YOU'RE THE GIRL WHO KILLED ANNIS?
HM.
I GIVE YOU THIS CHANCE TO EMBRACE VIRTUE, BRONAGH. LEND YOUR POWERS TO MINE, SO THAT TOGETHER WE MAY STOP THE FAERIE KING.
AHAHAHA!
YOU ARE BRAVE. NO WONDER YOU DEFEATED ANNIS.
SHE WAS A COWARD, HIDING IN HER RUINED TOWER. TOO AFRAID TO EVEN TRY TO OPEN THE DOOR.
I'LL HAVE TO ASK MY PETS IF BRAVE MEAT IS TASTIER THAN A COWARD'S.
SNARL

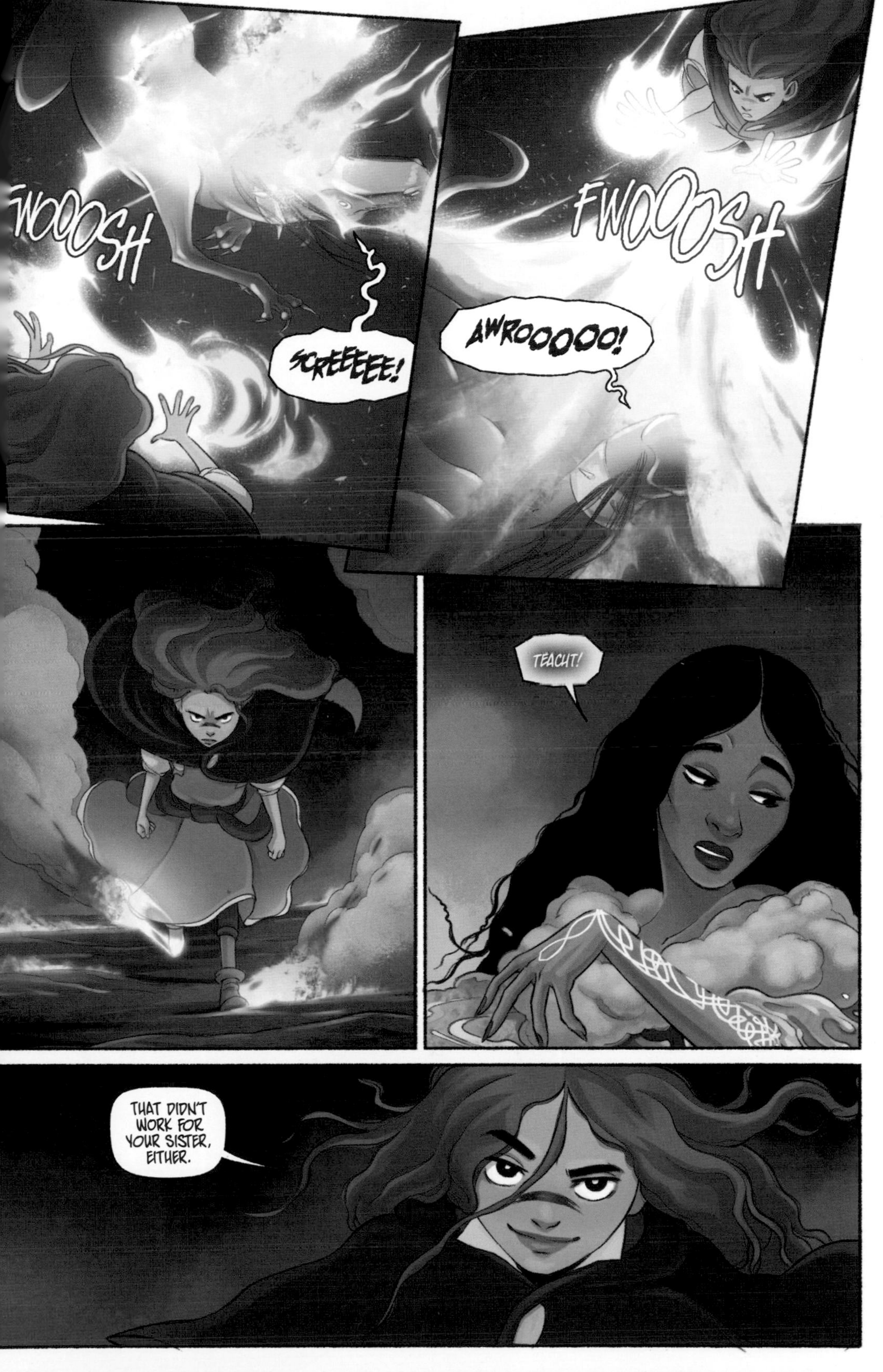
FWOOOSH
SCREEEEEE!
FWOOOOSH
AWROOOOO!
TEACHT!
THAT DIDN'T WORK FOR YOUR SISTER, EITHER.

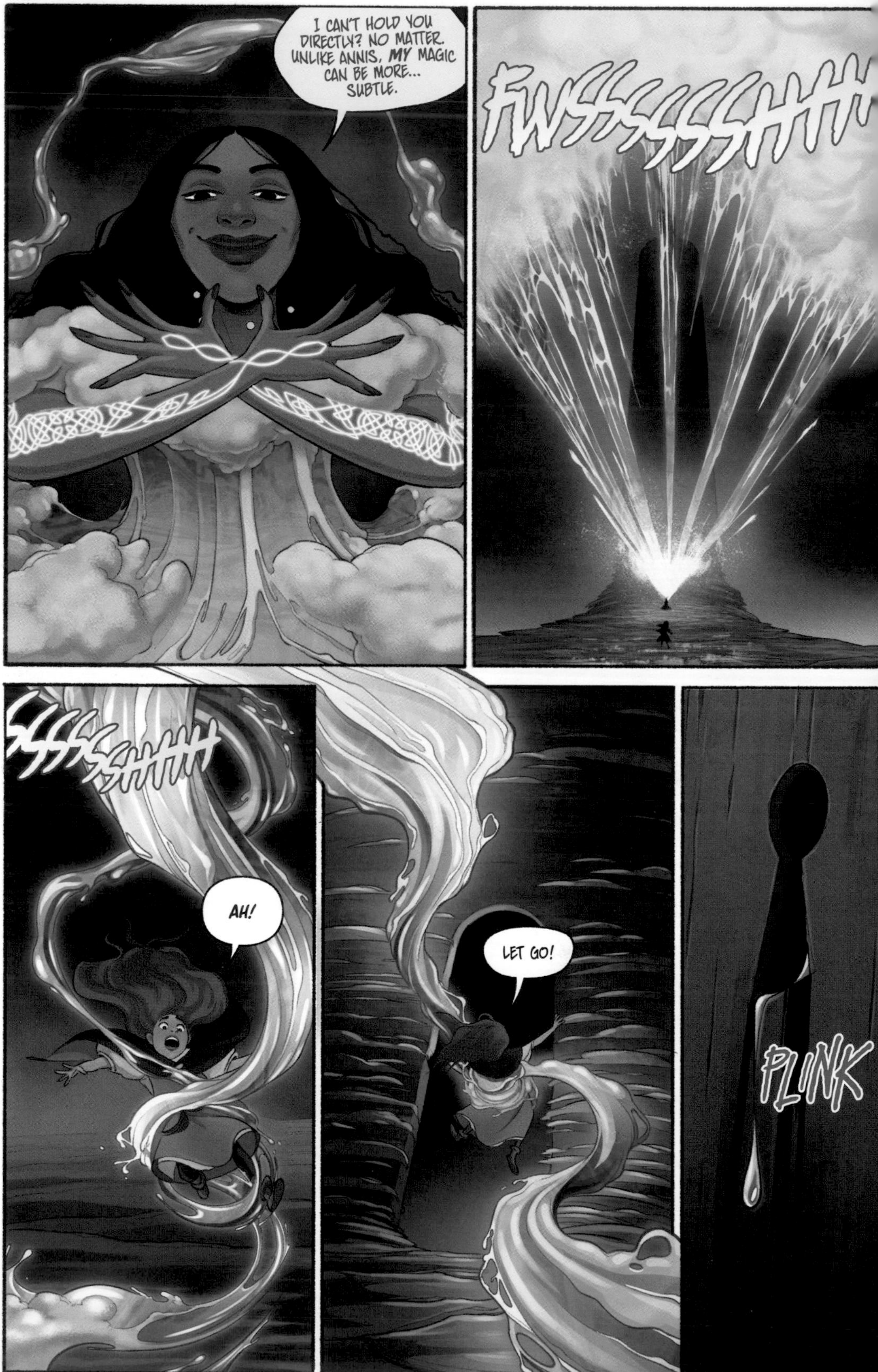
I CAN'T HOLD YOU DIRECTLY? NO MATTER. UNLIKE ANNIS, **MY** MAGIC CAN BE MORE... SUBTLE.
FWSSSSSSHHH
SSSSSHHHH
AH!
LET GO!
PLINK

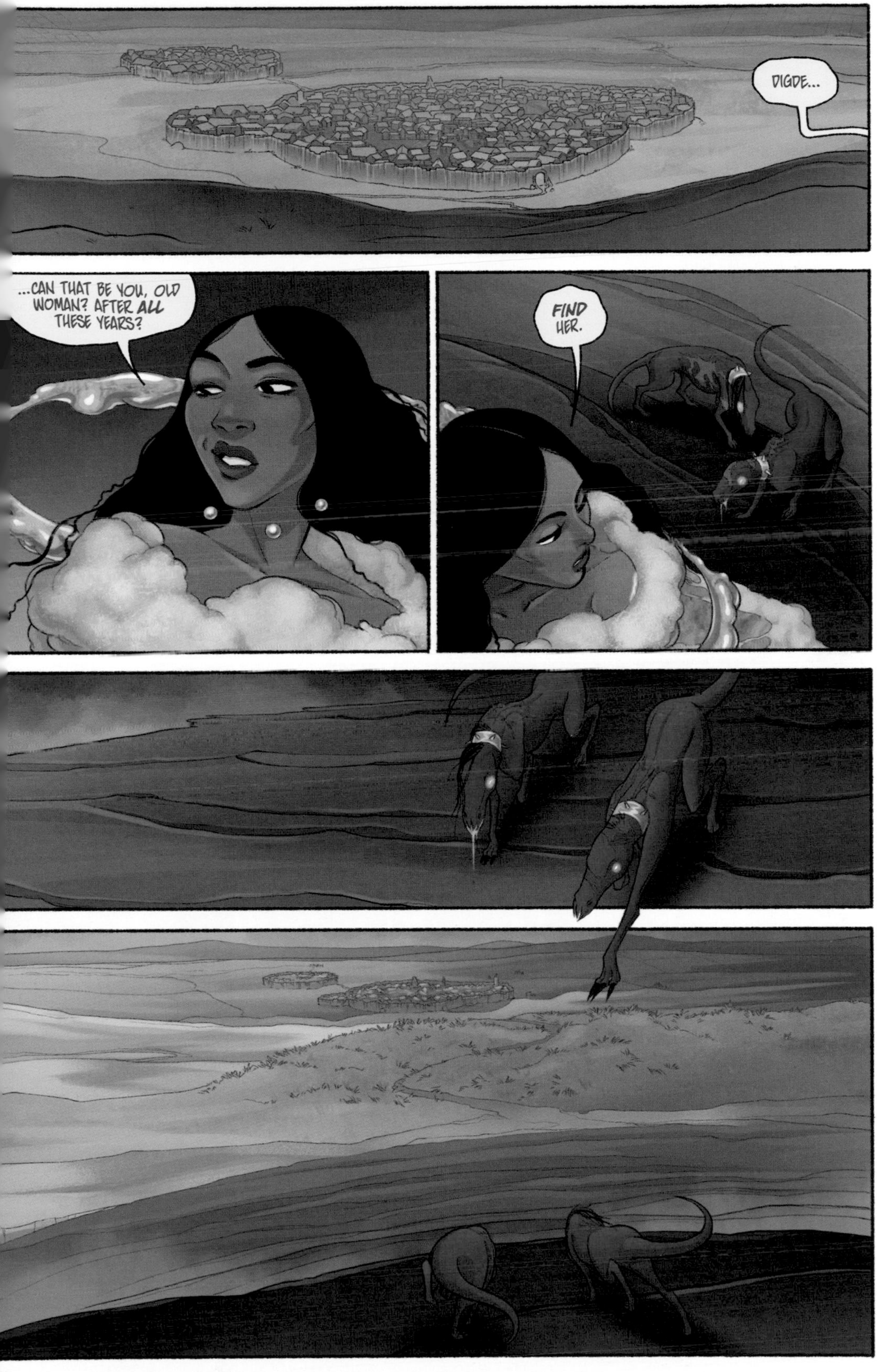
DIGDE...
...CAN THAT BE YOU, OLD WOMAN? AFTER ALL THESE YEARS?
FIND HER.

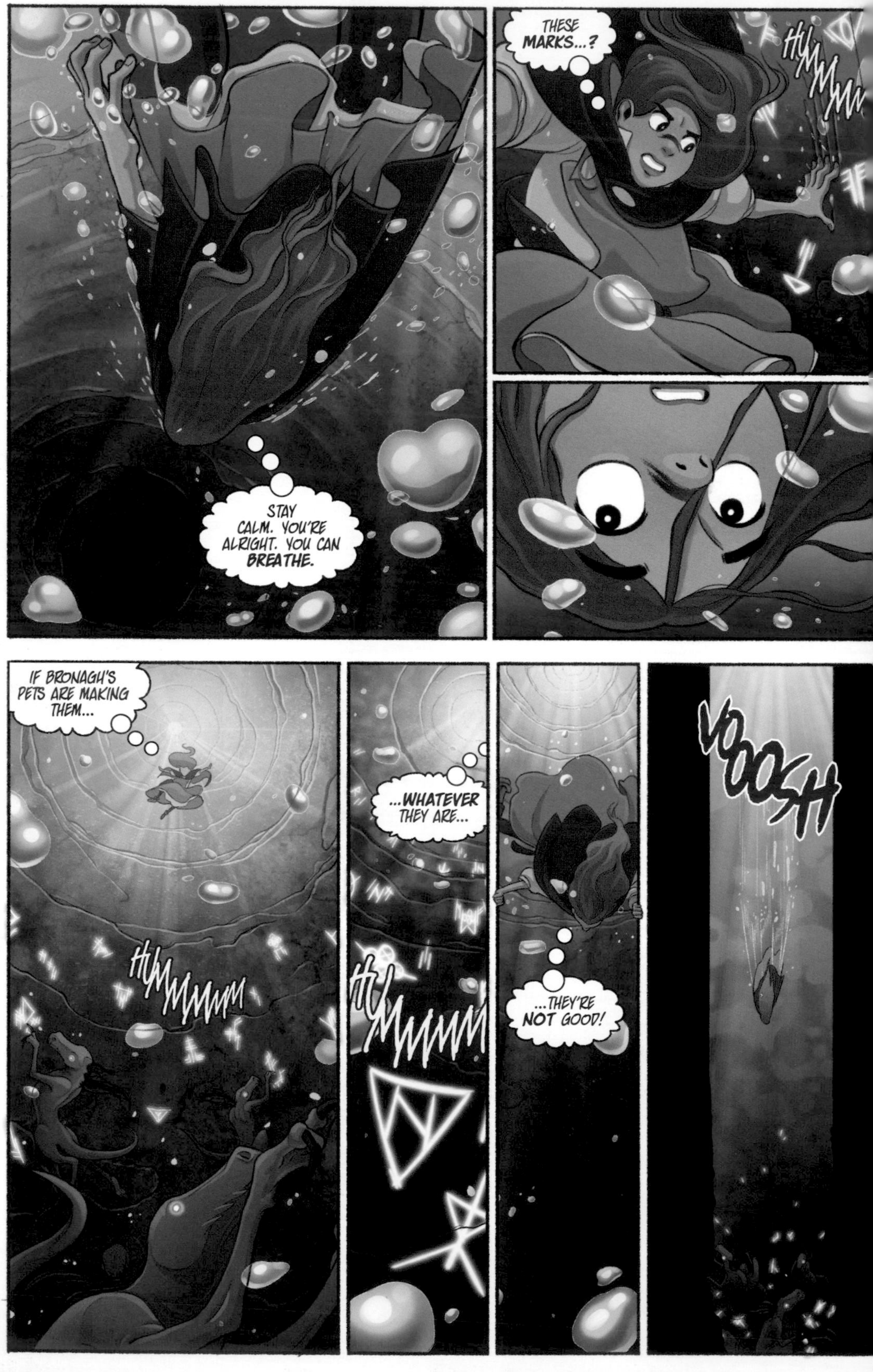
STAY CALM. YOU'RE ALRIGHT. YOU CAN BREATHE.
THESE MARKS...?
HUMMMM
IF BRONAGH'S PETS ARE MAKING THEM...
HUMMMM
...WHATEVER THEY ARE...
HUMMMM
...THEY'RE NOT GOOD!
VOOOSH

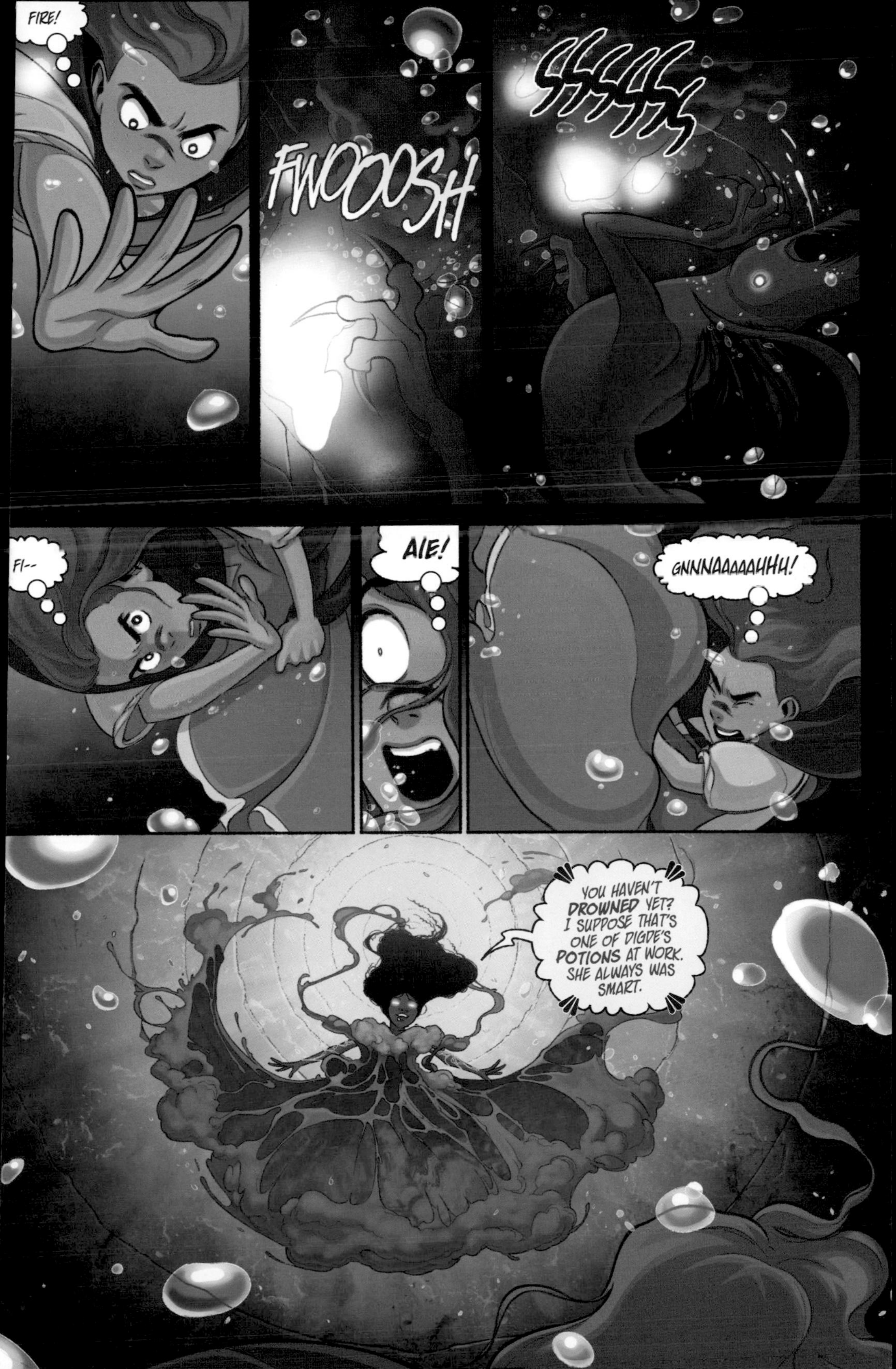
FIRE!
FWOOOSH
SSSSSS
FI--
AIE!
GNNNAAAAAHHH!
YOU HAVEN'T DROWNED YET? I SUPPOSE THAT'S ONE OF DIGDE'S POTIONS AT WORK. SHE ALWAYS WAS SMART.

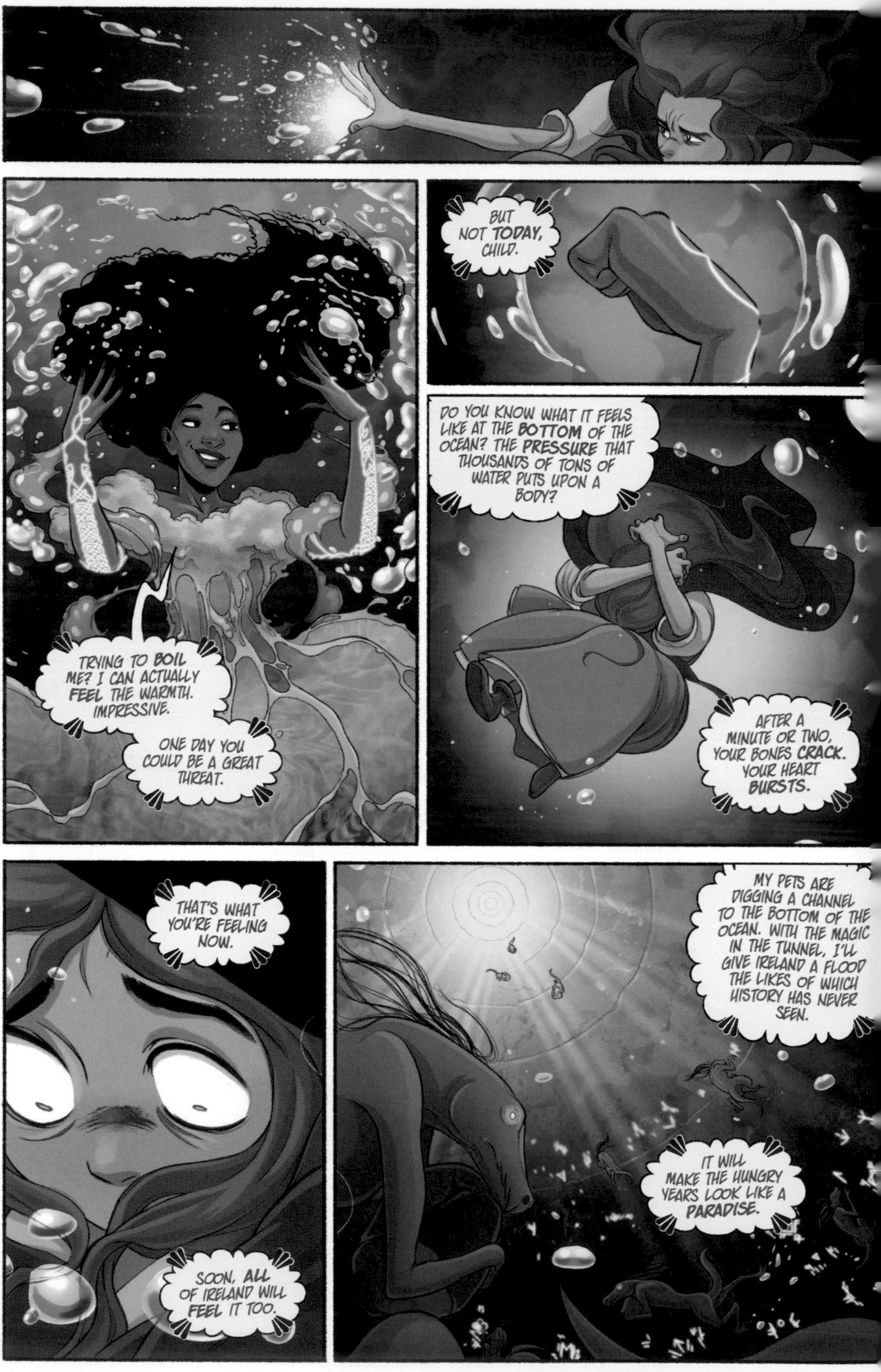

TRYING TO BOIL ME? I CAN ACTUALLY FEEL THE WARMTH. IMPRESSIVE.
ONE DAY YOU COULD BE A GREAT THREAT.
BUT NOT TODAY, CHILD.
DO YOU KNOW WHAT IT FEELS LIKE AT THE BOTTOM OF THE OCEAN? THE PRESSURE THAT THOUSANDS OF TONS OF WATER PUTS UPON A BODY?
AFTER A MINUTE OR TWO, YOUR BONES CRACK. YOUR HEART BURSTS.
THAT'S WHAT YOU'RE FEELING NOW.
SOON, ALL OF IRELAND WILL FEEL IT TOO.
MY PETS ARE DIGGING A CHANNEL TO THE BOTTOM OF THE OCEAN. WITH THE MAGIC IN THE TUNNEL, I'LL GIVE IRELAND A FLOOD THE LIKES OF WHICH HISTORY HAS NEVER SEEN.
IT WILL MAKE THE HUNGRY YEARS LOOK LIKE A PARADISE.

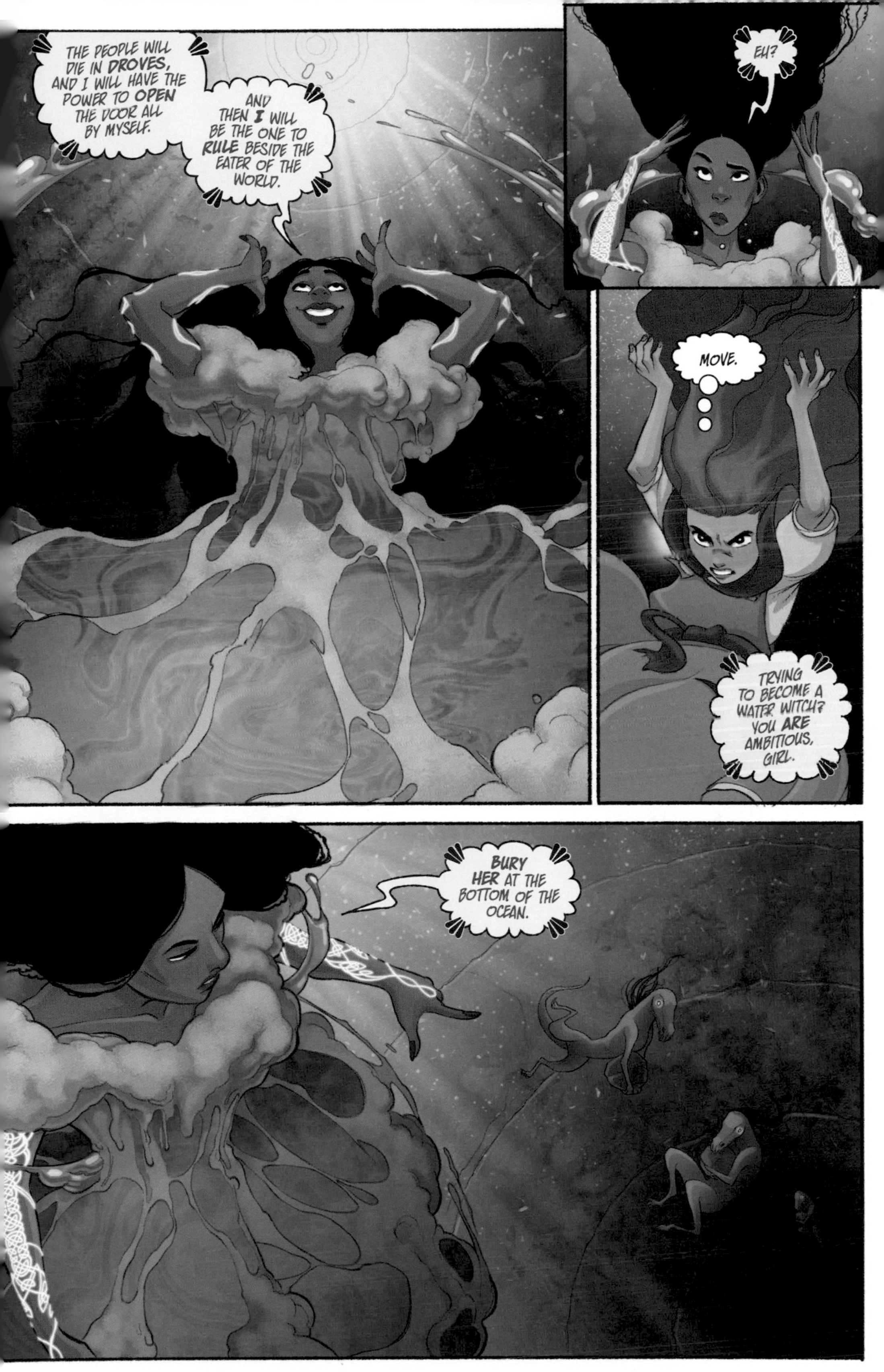
THE PEOPLE WILL DIE IN DROVES, AND I WILL HAVE THE POWER TO OPEN THE DOOR ALL BY MYSELF.
AND THEN I WILL BE THE ONE TO RULE BESIDE THE EATER OF THE WORLD.
EH?
MOVE.
TRYING TO BECOME A WATER WITCH? YOU ARE AMBITIOUS, GIRL.
BURY HER AT THE BOTTOM OF THE OCEAN.

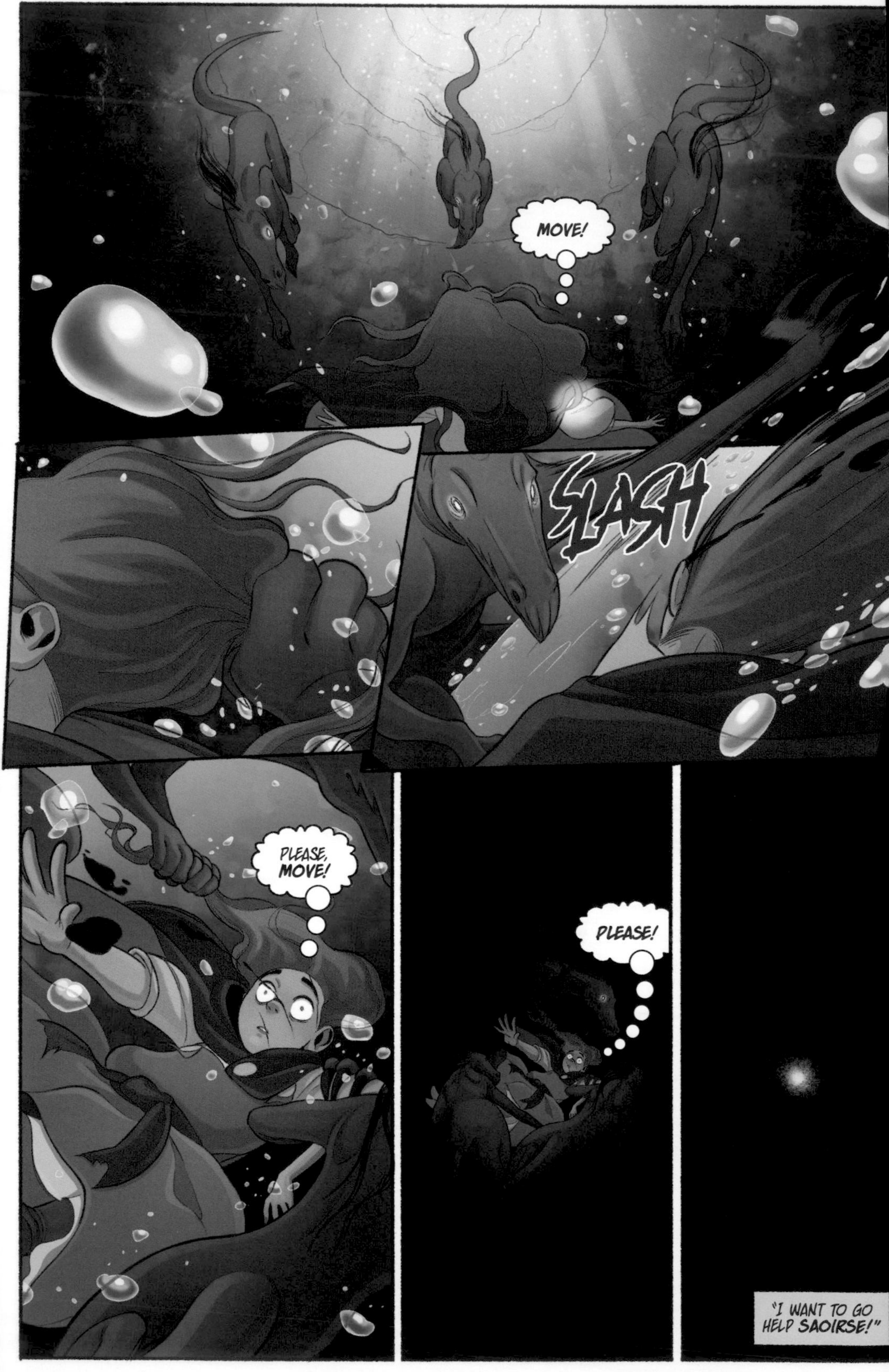
MOVE!
SLASH
PLEASE, MOVE!
PLEASE!
"I WANT TO GO HELP SAOIRSE!"

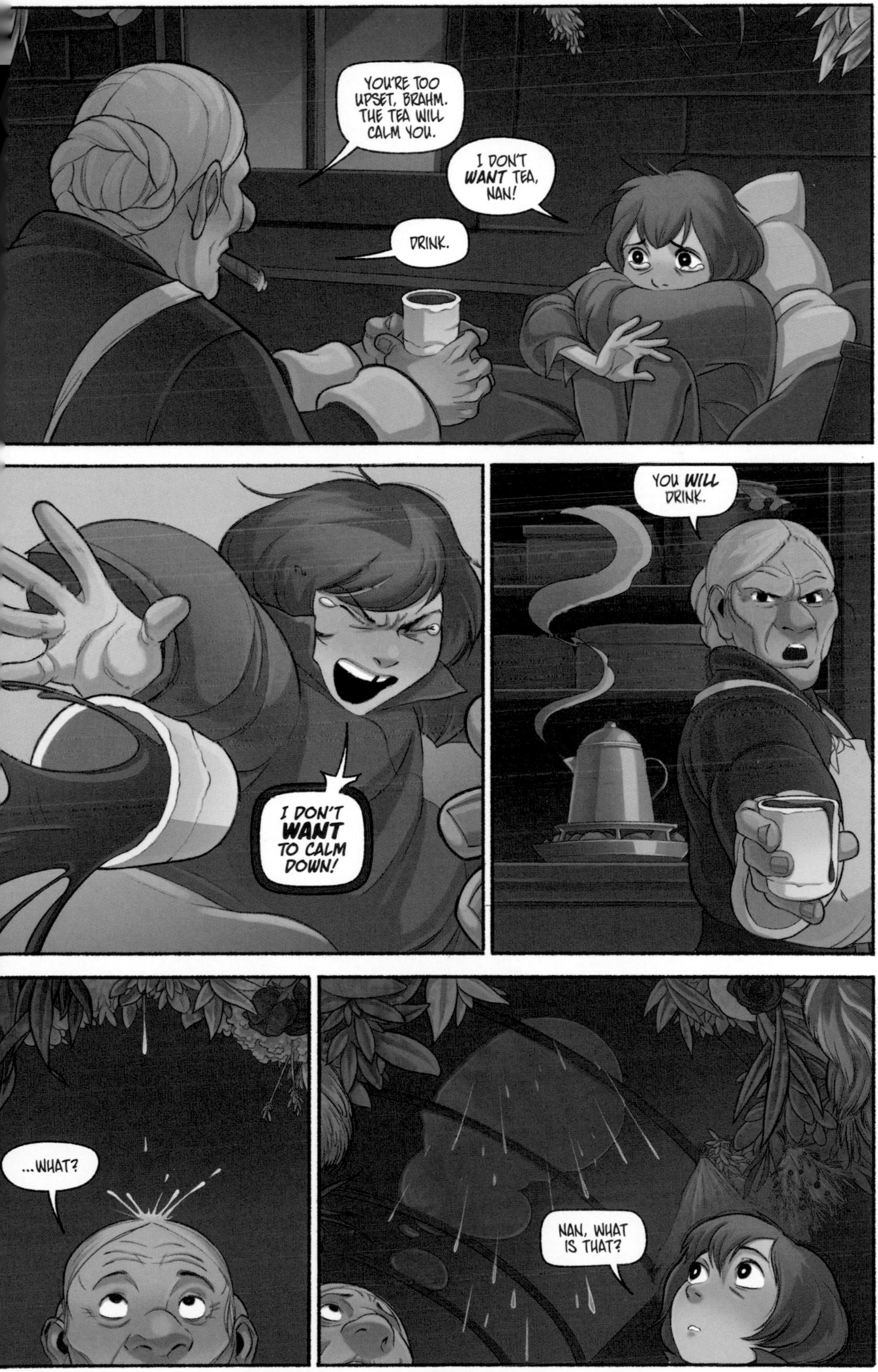
YOU'RE TOO UPSET, BRAHM. THE TEA WILL CALM YOU.
I DON'T WANT TEA, NAN!
DRINK.
I DON'T WANT TO CALM DOWN!
YOU WILL DRINK.
...WHAT?
NAN, WHAT IS THAT?

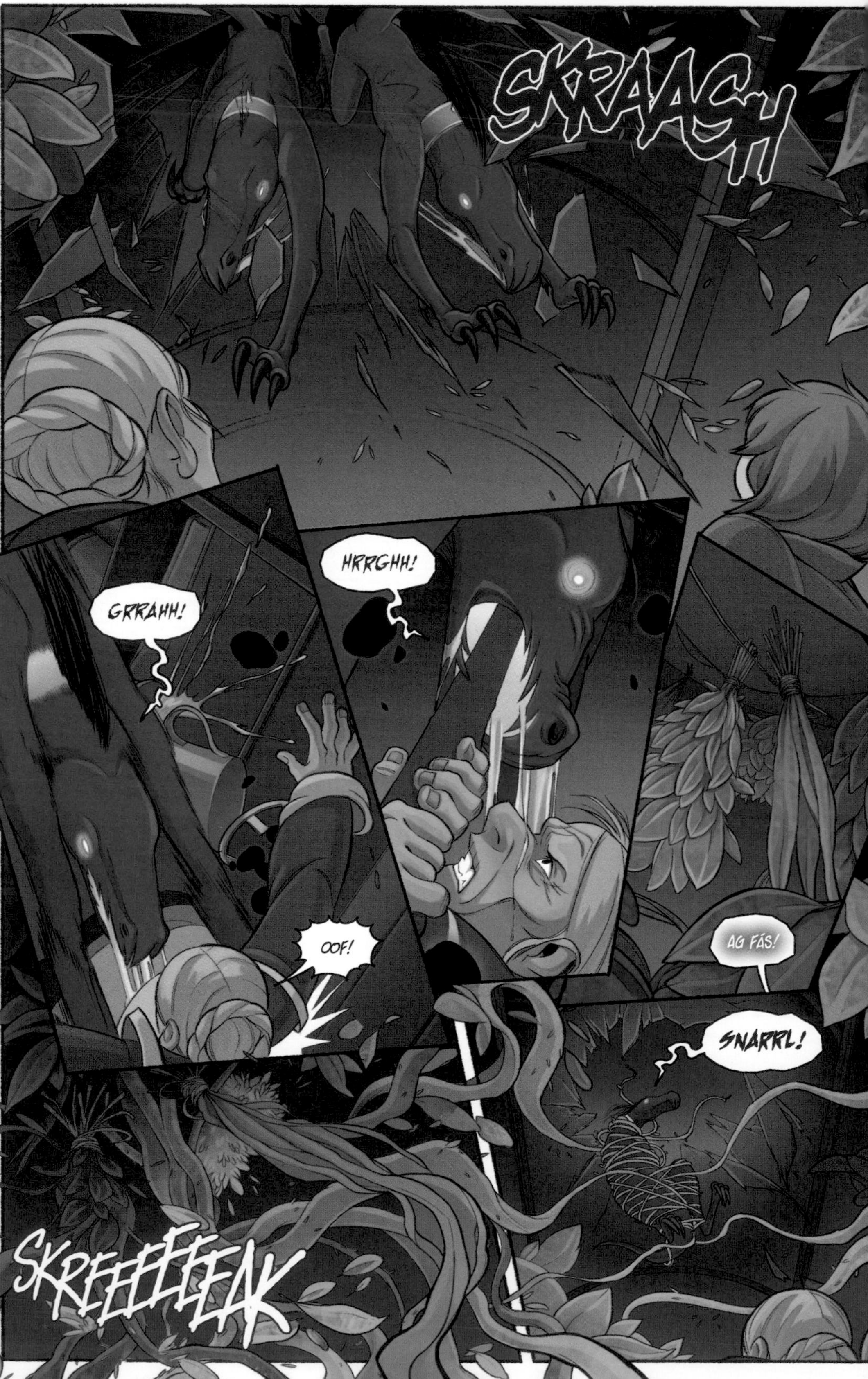
SKRAACH
GRRAHH!
HRRGHH!
OOF!
AG FÁS!
SNARRL!
SKREEEEEAK

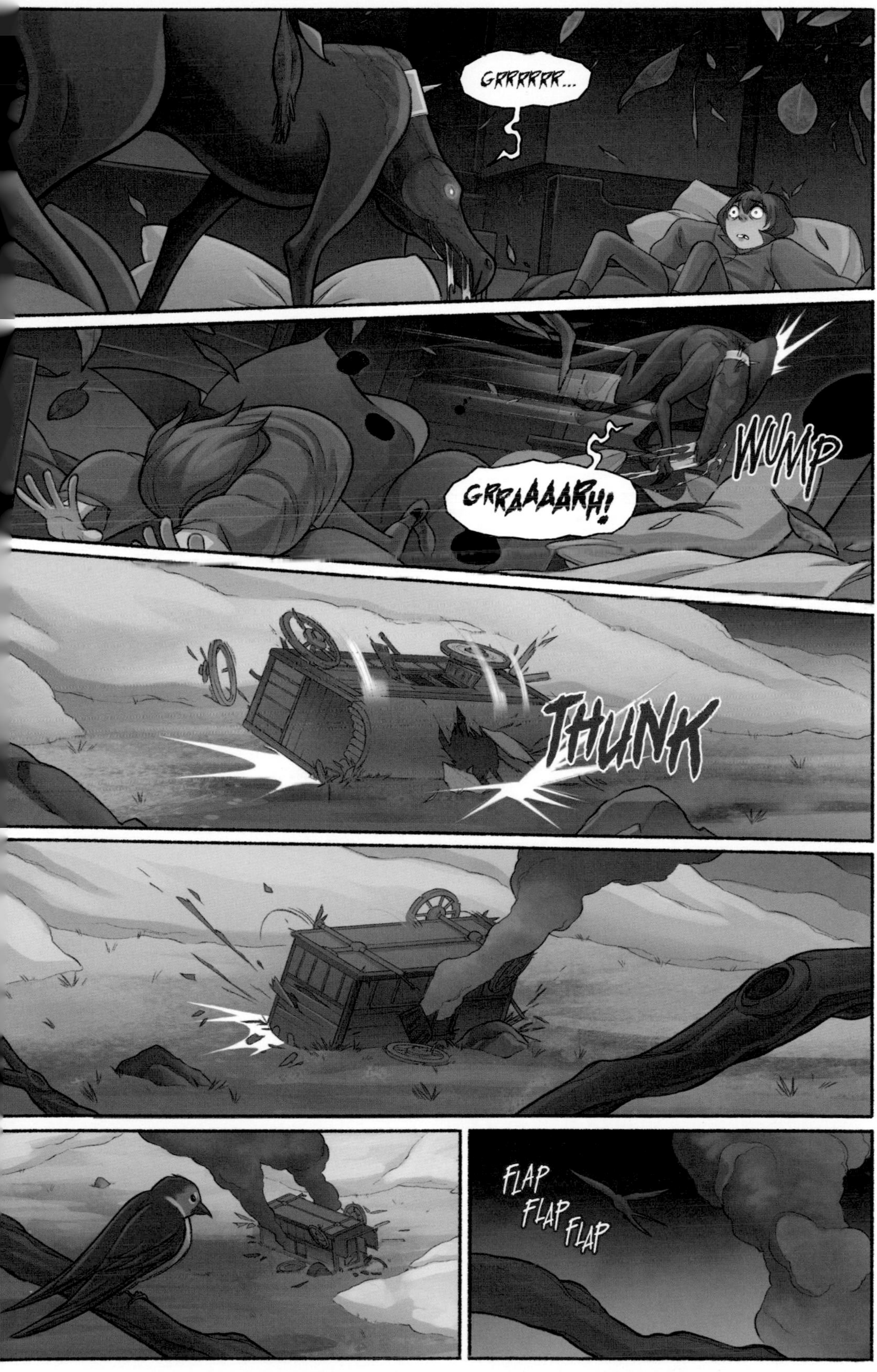
GRRRRRR...
GRRAAAARH!
WUMP
THUNK
FLAP
FLAP
FLAP

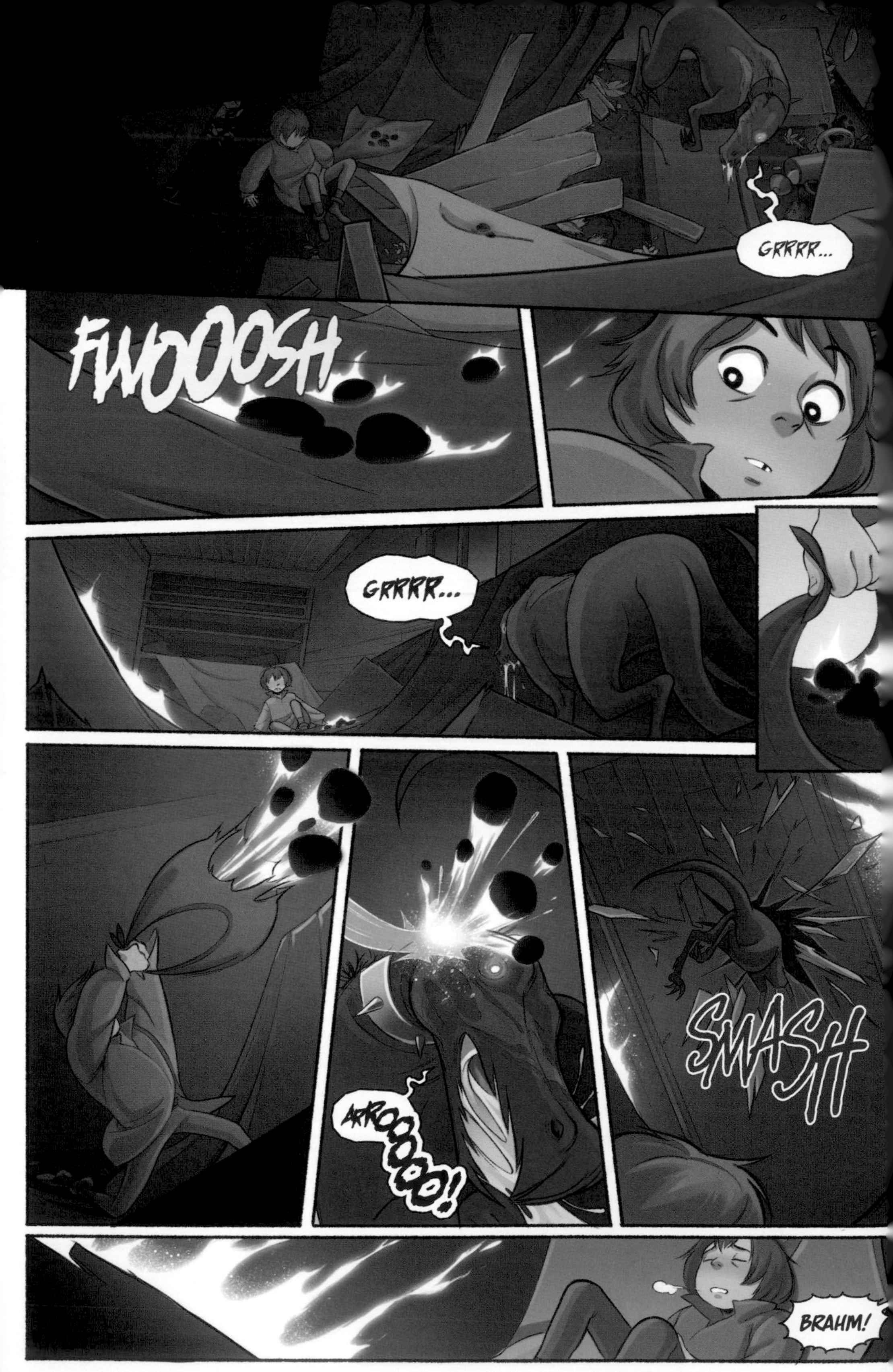
GRRRR...
FWOOOSH
GRRRR...
ARROOOOOO!
SMASH
BRAHM!

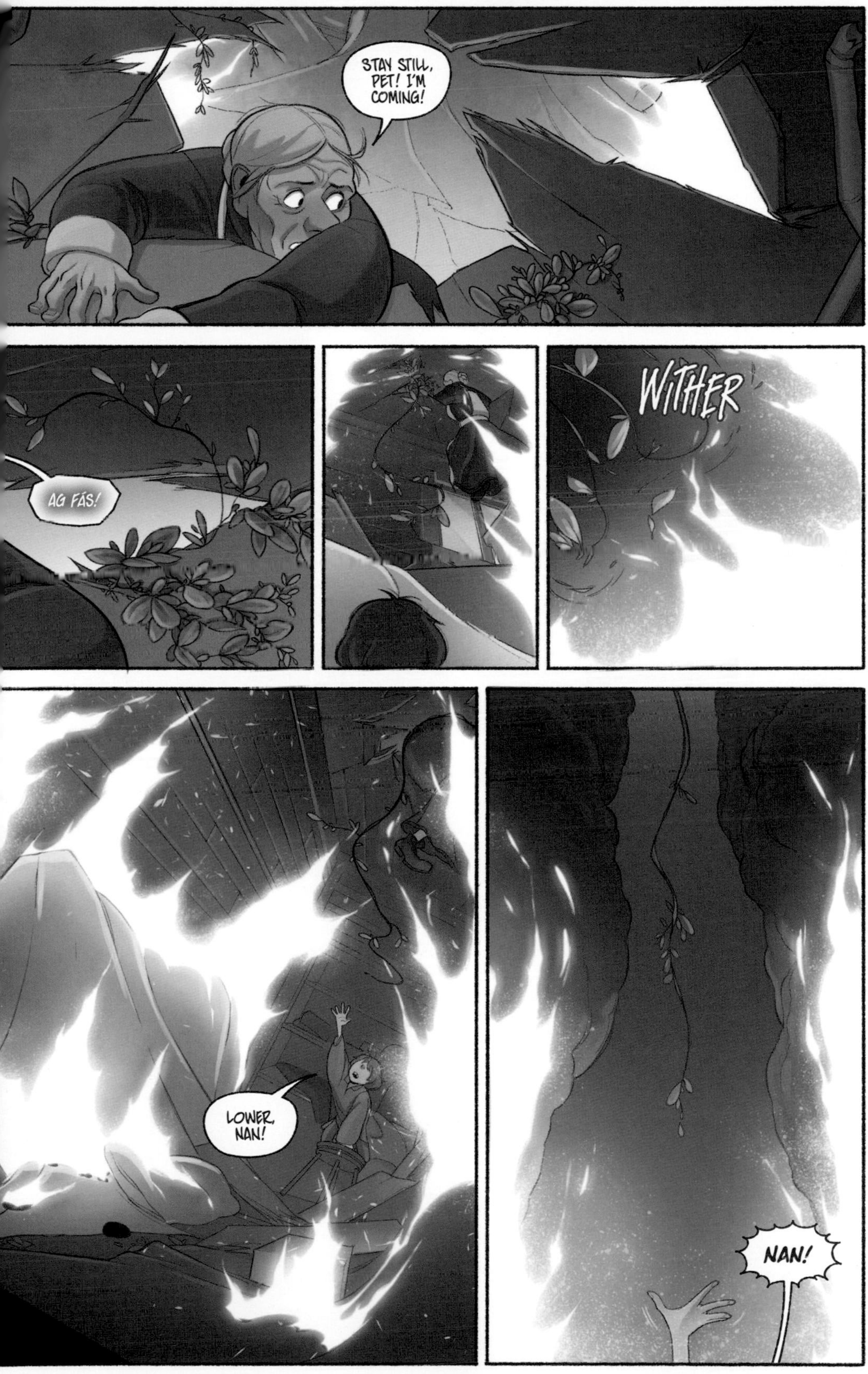
STAY STILL, PET! I'M COMING!
AG FÁS!
WITHER
LOWER, NAN!
NAN!

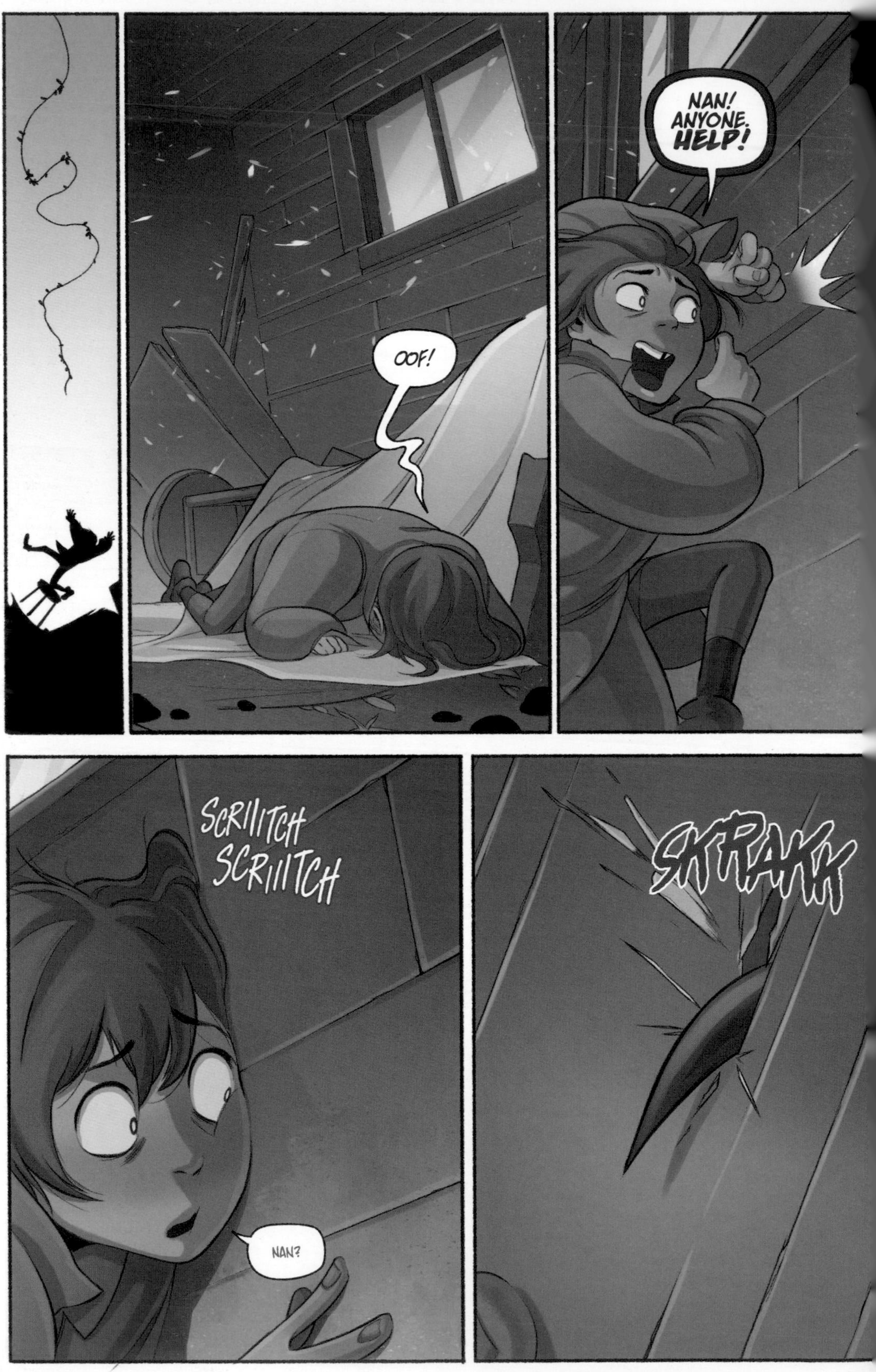
OOF!
NAN! ANYONE. HELP!
SCRIIITCH SCRIIITCH
NAN?
SKRAKK

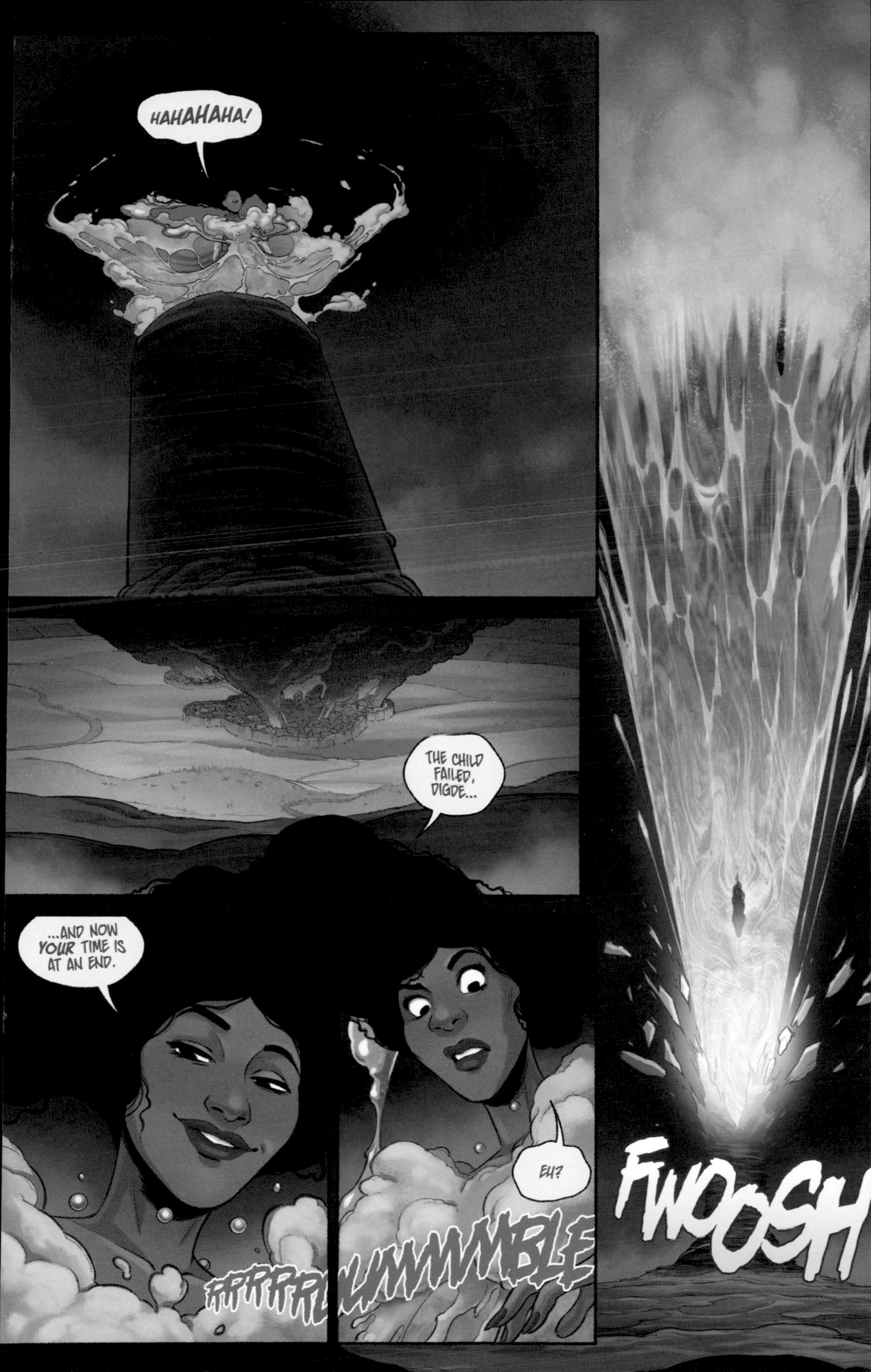
HAHAHAHA!
THE CHILD FAILED, DIGDE...
...AND NOW YOUR TIME IS AT AN END.
EH?
RRRRRUMMMMBLE
FWOOSH

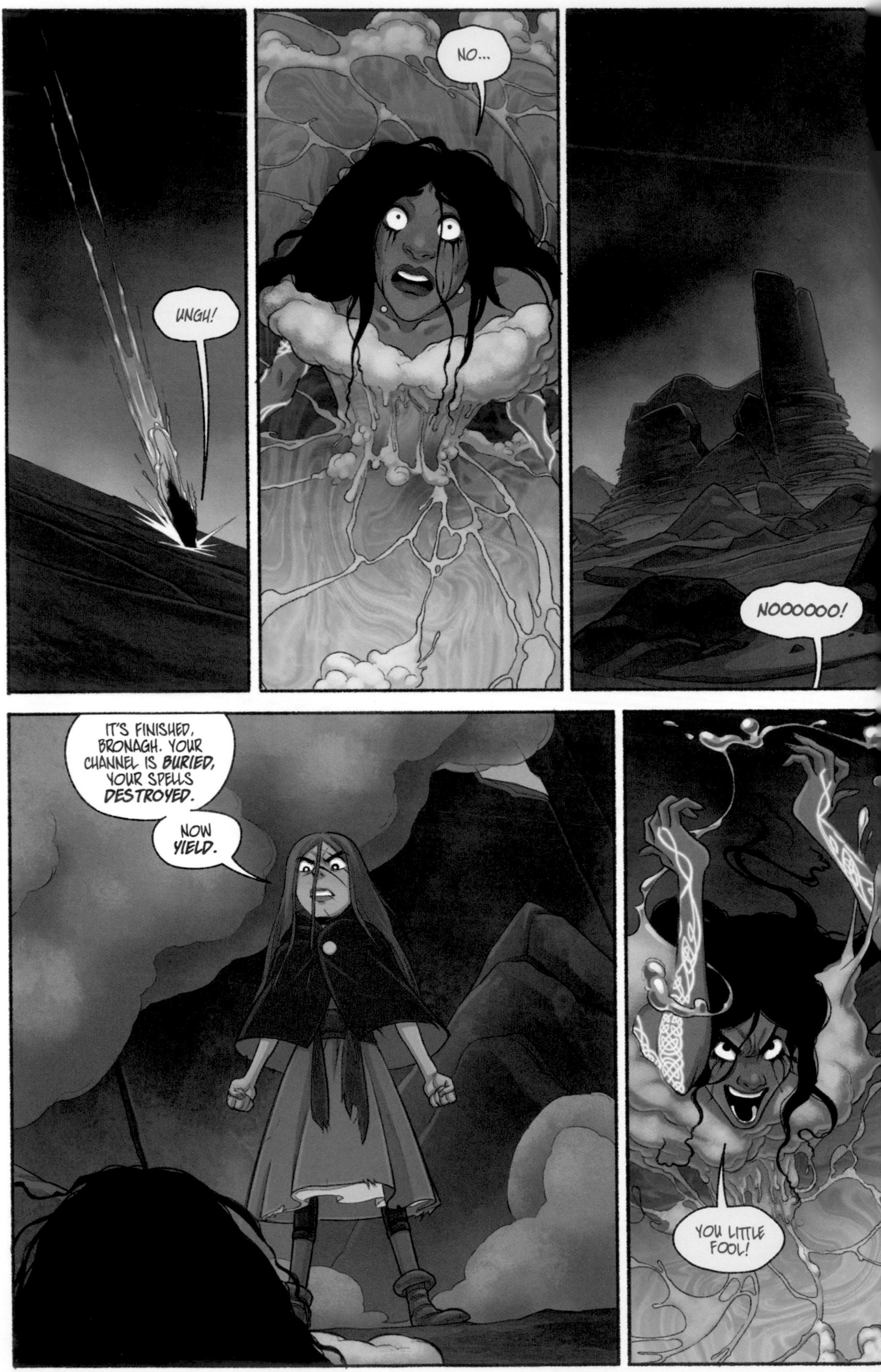
UNGH!
NO...
NOOOOOO!
IT'S FINISHED, BRONAGH. YOUR CHANNEL IS BURIED, YOUR SPELLS DESTROYED.
NOW YIELD.
YOU LITTLE FOOL!

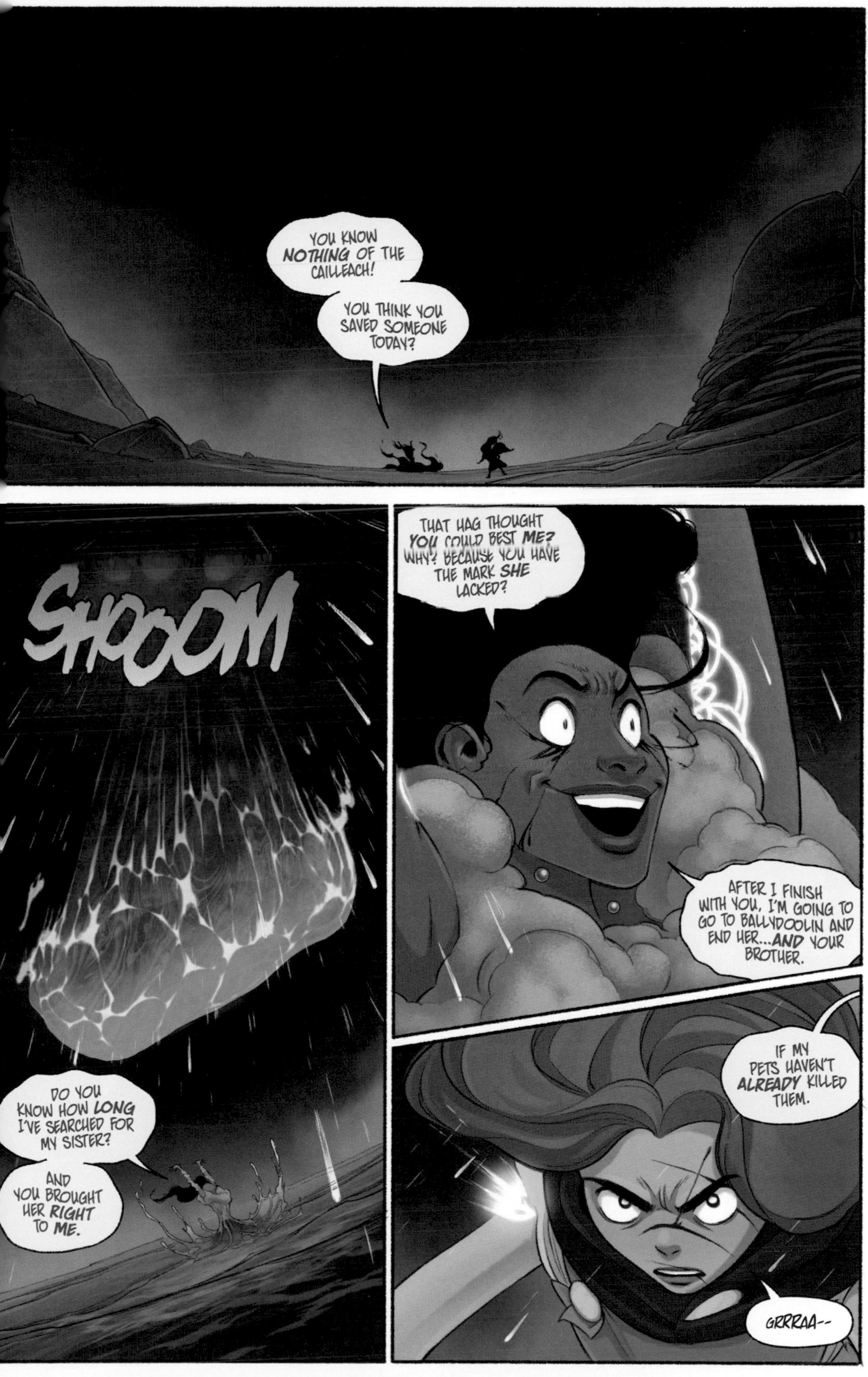
YOU KNOW NOTHING OF THE CAILLEACH!
YOU THINK YOU SAVED SOMEONE TODAY?
SHOOOM
DO YOU KNOW HOW LONG I'VE SEARCHED FOR MY SISTER?
AND YOU BROUGHT HER RIGHT TO ME.
THAT HAG THOUGHT YOU COULD BEST ME? WHY? BECAUSE YOU HAVE THE MARK SHE LACKED?
AFTER I FINISH WITH YOU, I'M GOING TO GO TO BALLYDOOLIN AND END HER...AND YOUR BROTHER.
IF MY PETS HAVEN'T ALREADY KILLED THEM.
GRRRAA--

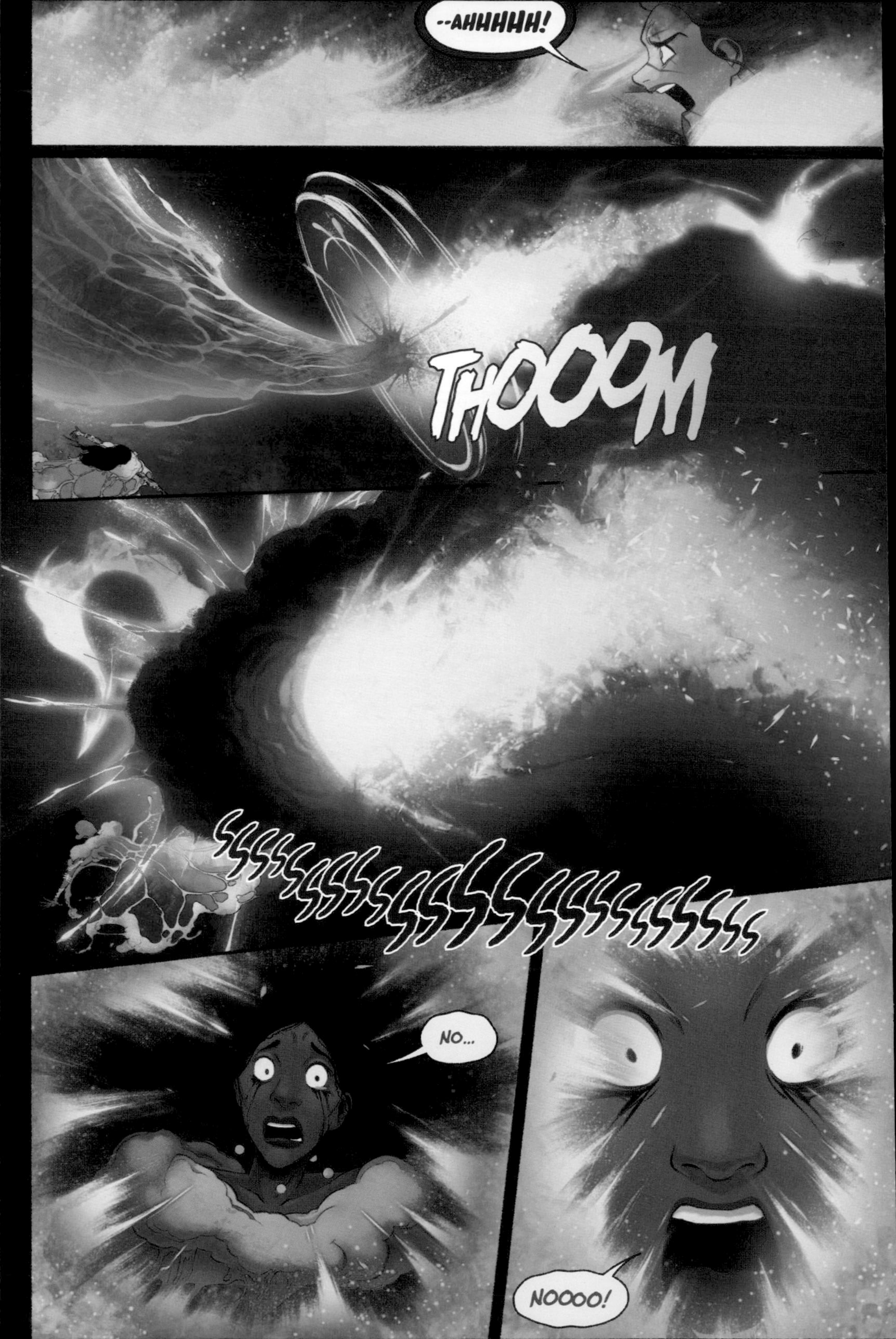
--AHHHHH!
THOOOM
SSSSSSSSSSSSSSSSSSSSSSSSSSSSS
NO...
NOOOO!

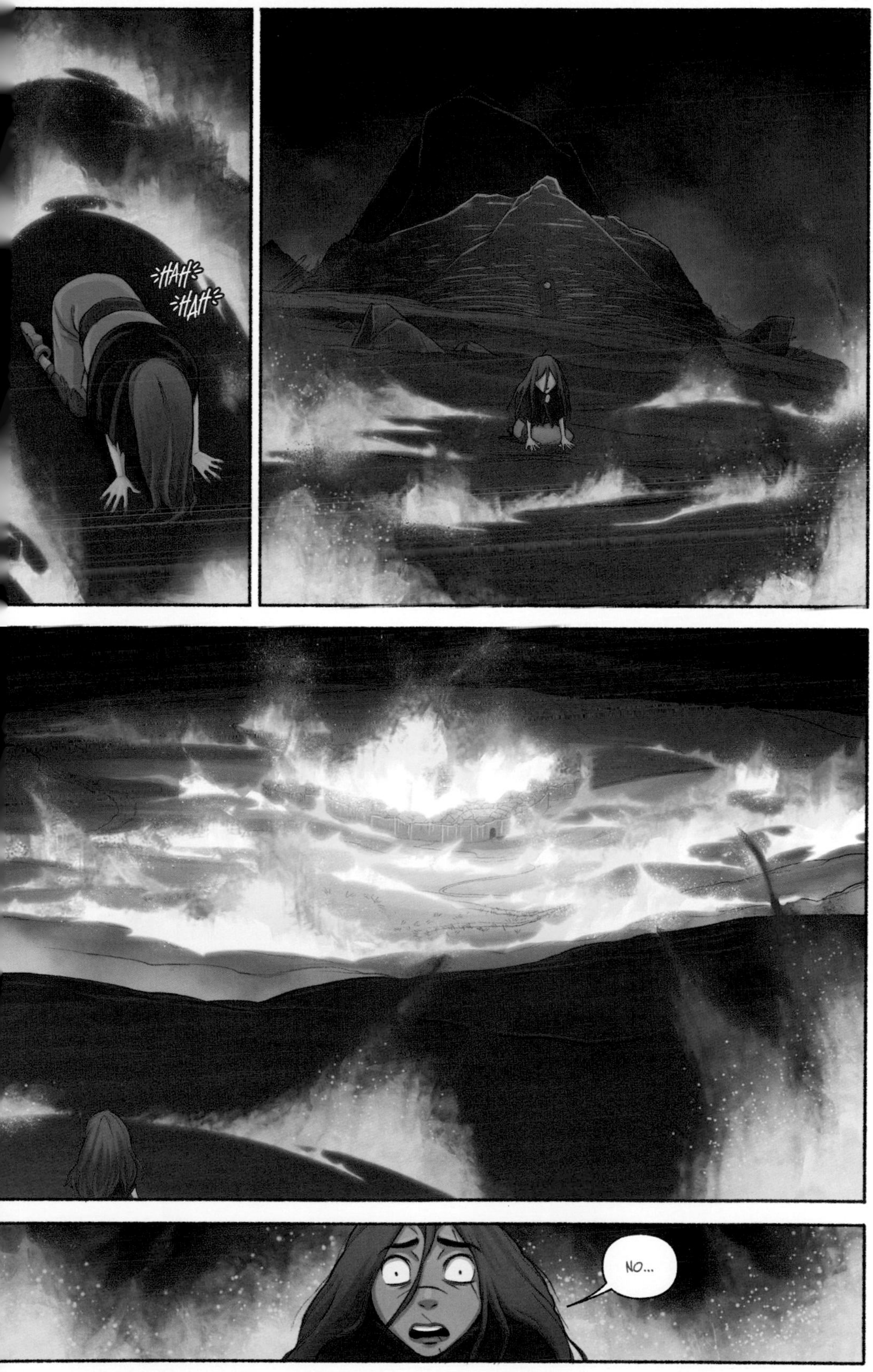
HAH
HAH
NO...

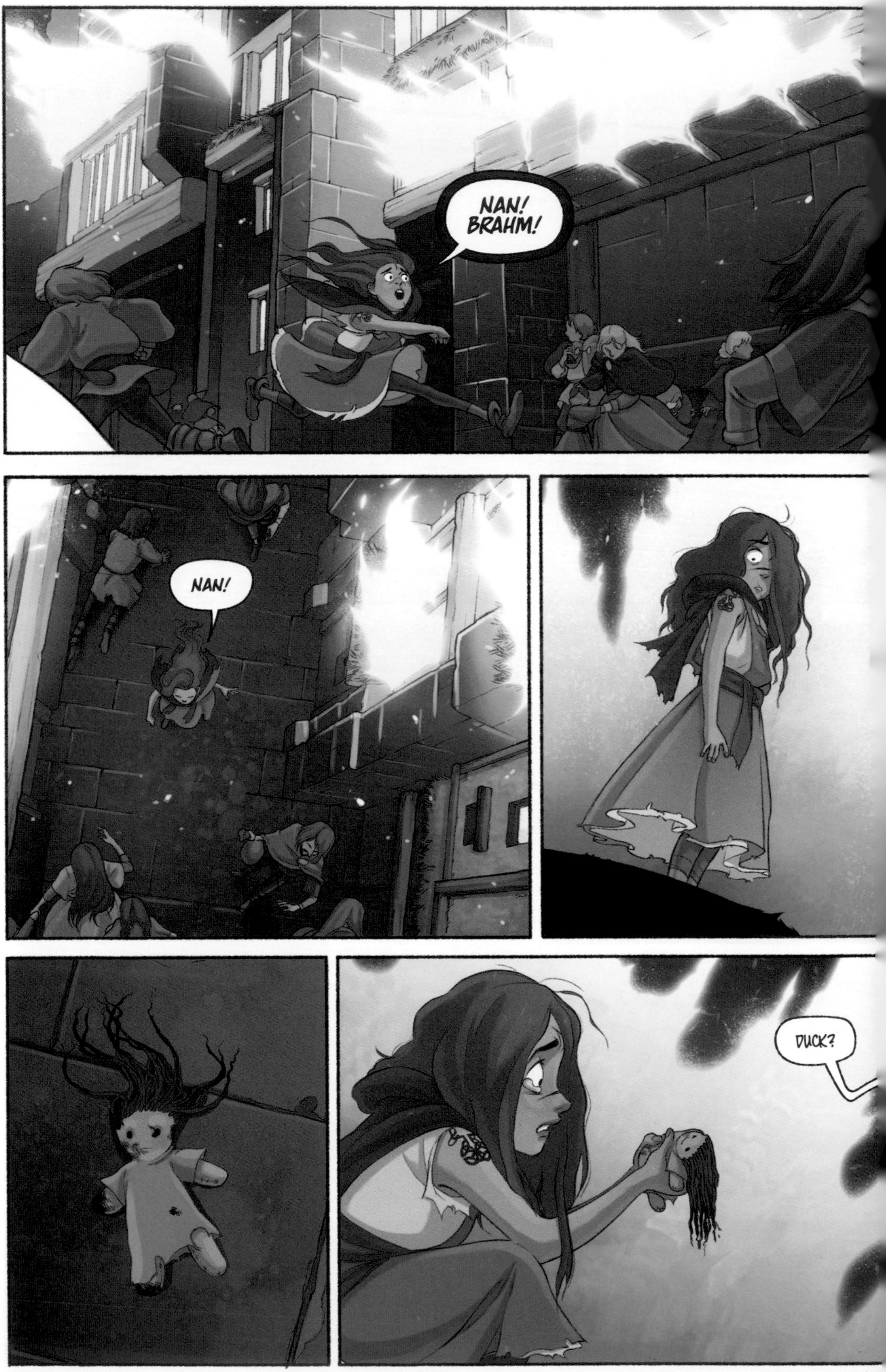
NAN! BRAHM!
NAN!
DUCK?

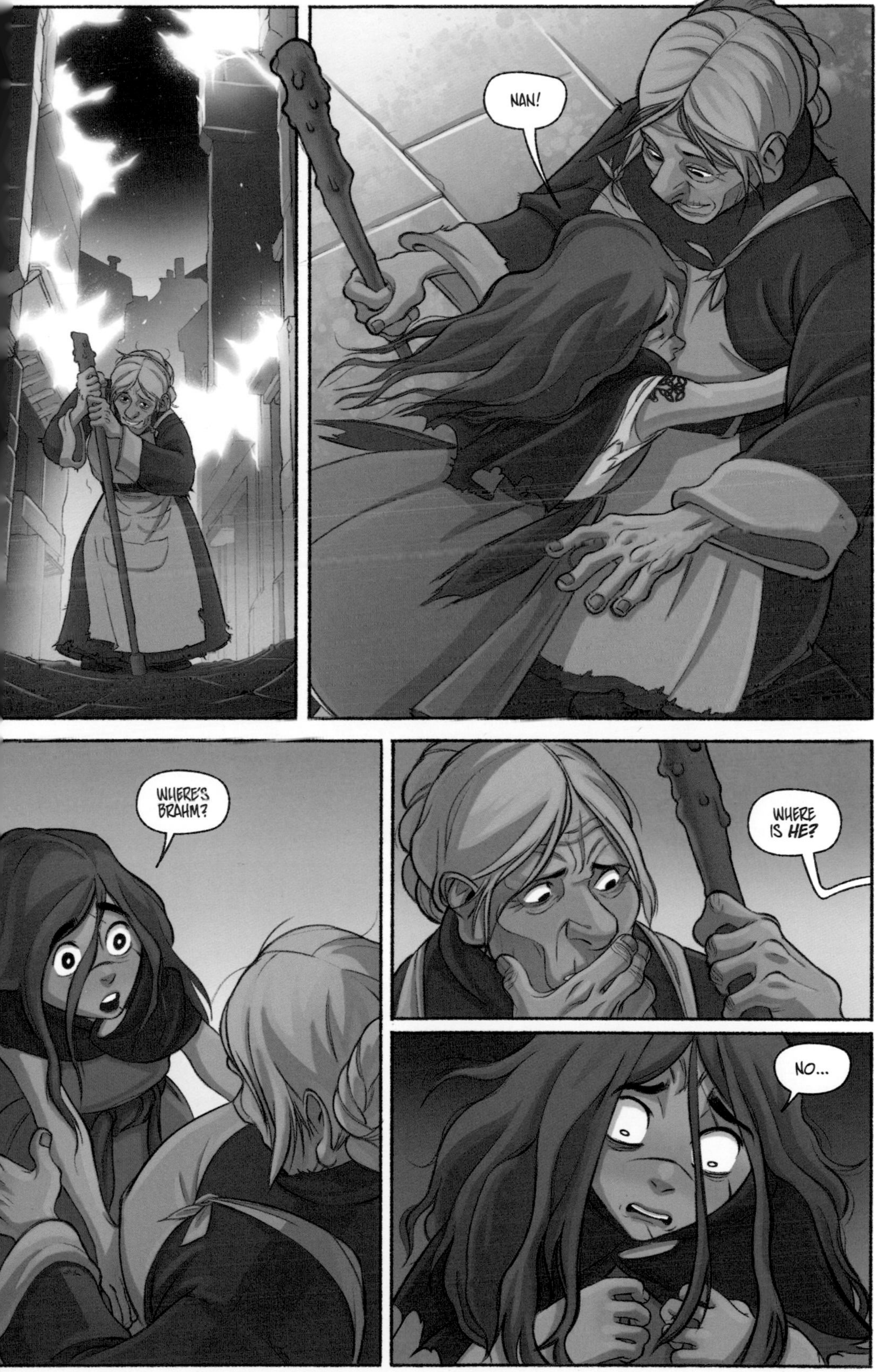
NAN!
WHERE'S BRAHM?
WHERE IS HE?
NO...

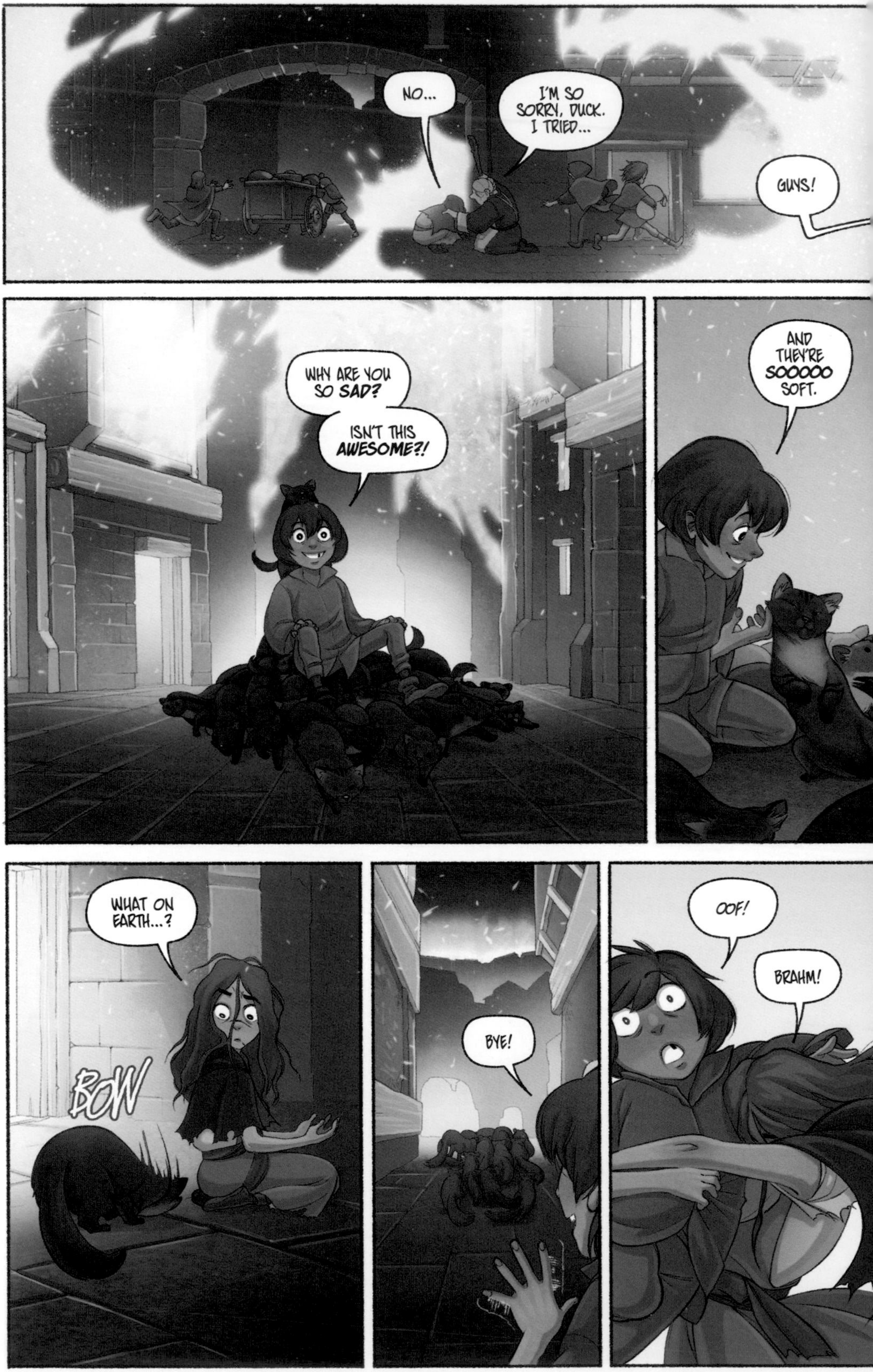
NO...
I'M SO SORRY, DUCK. I TRIED...
GUYS!
WHY ARE YOU SO SAD?
ISN'T THIS AWESOME?!
AND THEY'RE SOOOOO SOFT.
WHAT ON EARTH...?
BOW
BYE!
OOF!
BRAHM!

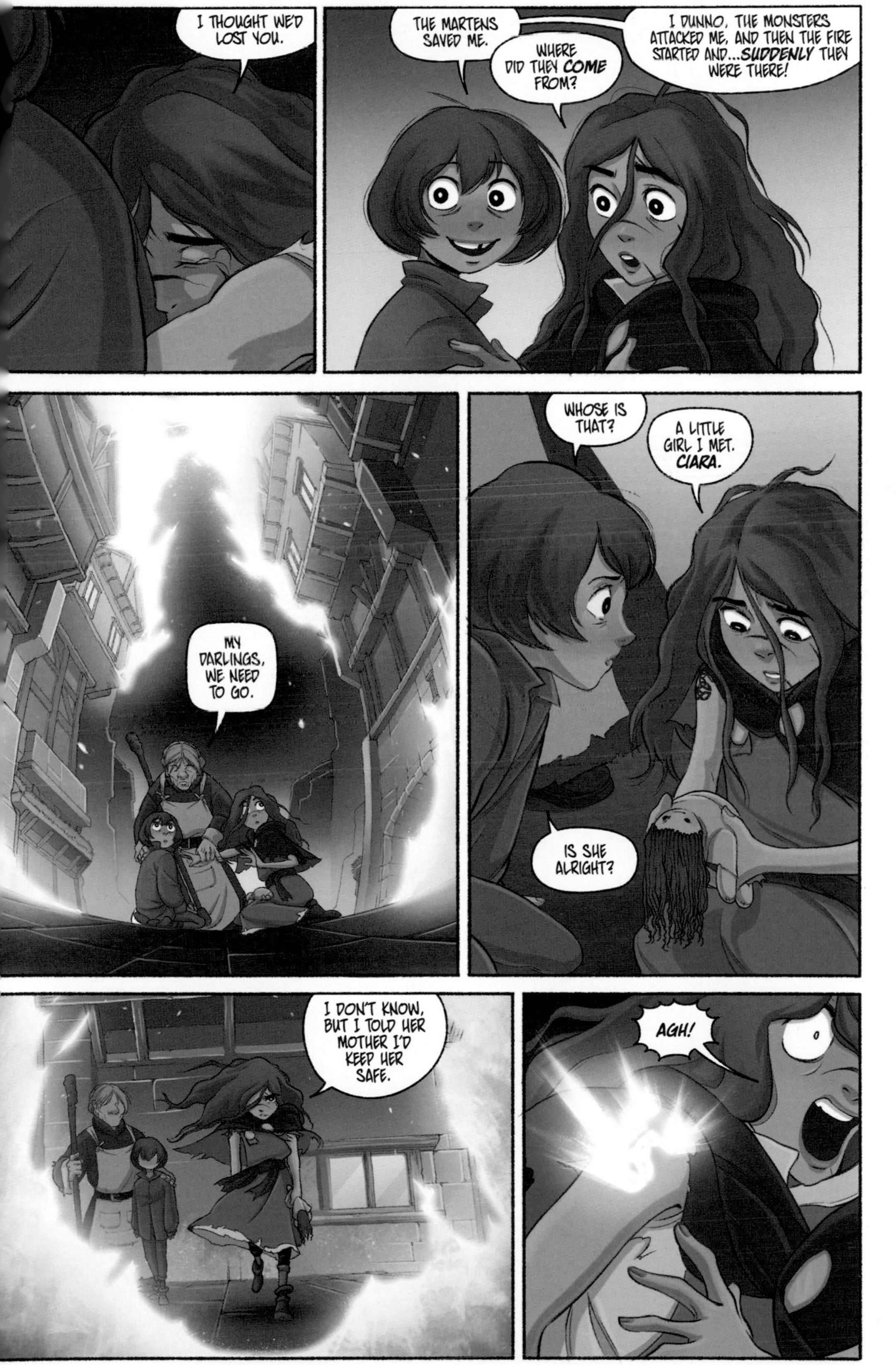
I THOUGHT WE'D LOST YOU.
THE MARTENS SAVED ME.
WHERE DID THEY COME FROM?
I DUNNO, THE MONSTERS ATTACKED ME, AND THEN THE FIRE STARTED AND...SUDDENLY THEY WERE THERE!
MY DARLINGS, WE NEED TO GO.
WHOSE IS THAT?
A LITTLE GIRL I MET. CIARA.
IS SHE ALRIGHT?
I DON'T KNOW, BUT I TOLD HER MOTHER I'D KEEP HER SAFE.
AGH!

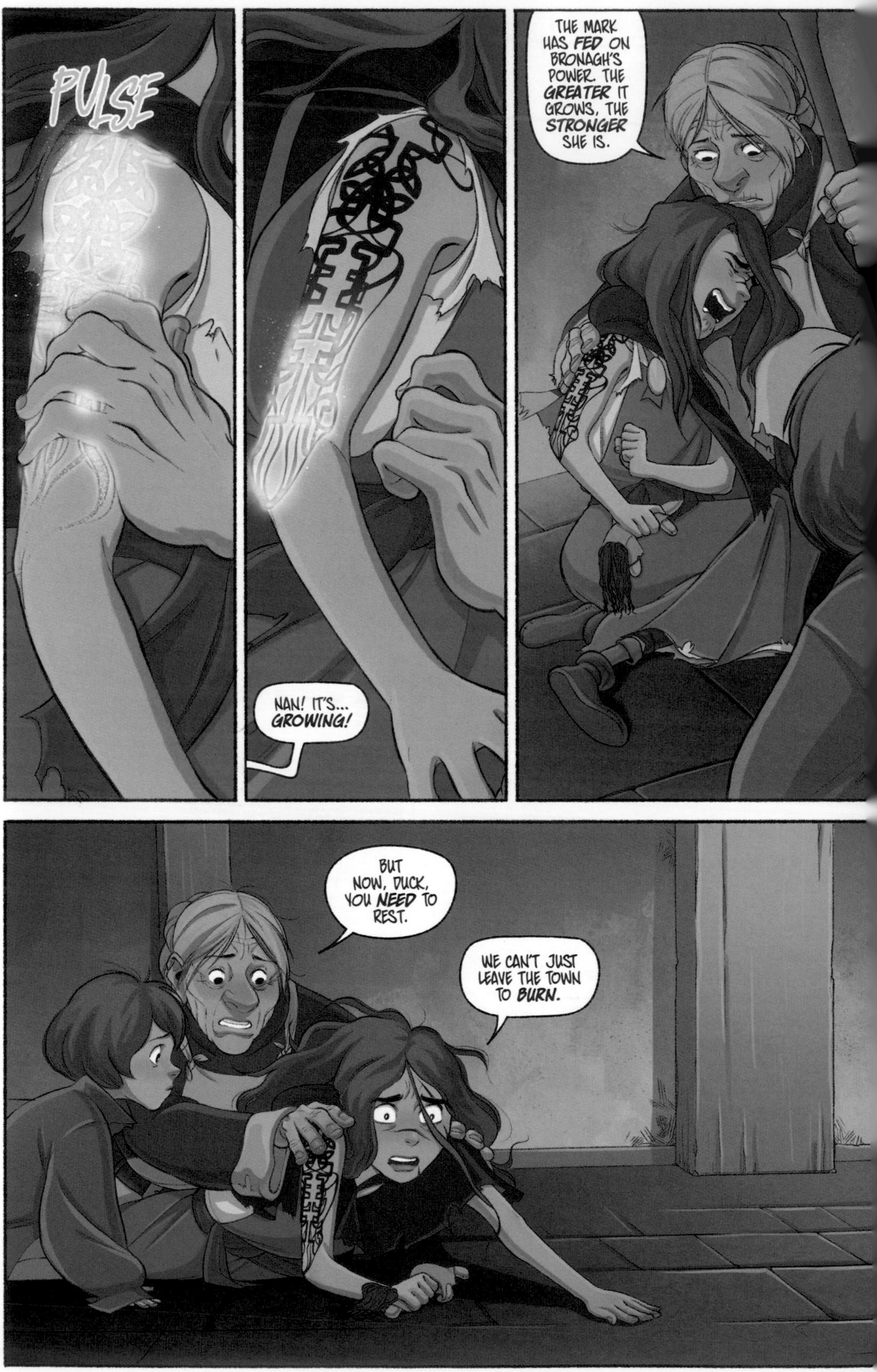
PULSE
NAN! IT'S... GROWING!
THE MARK HAS FED ON BRONAGH'S POWER. THE GREATER IT GROWS, THE STRONGER SHE IS.
BUT NOW, DUCK, YOU NEED TO REST.
WE CAN'T JUST LEAVE THE TOWN TO BURN.

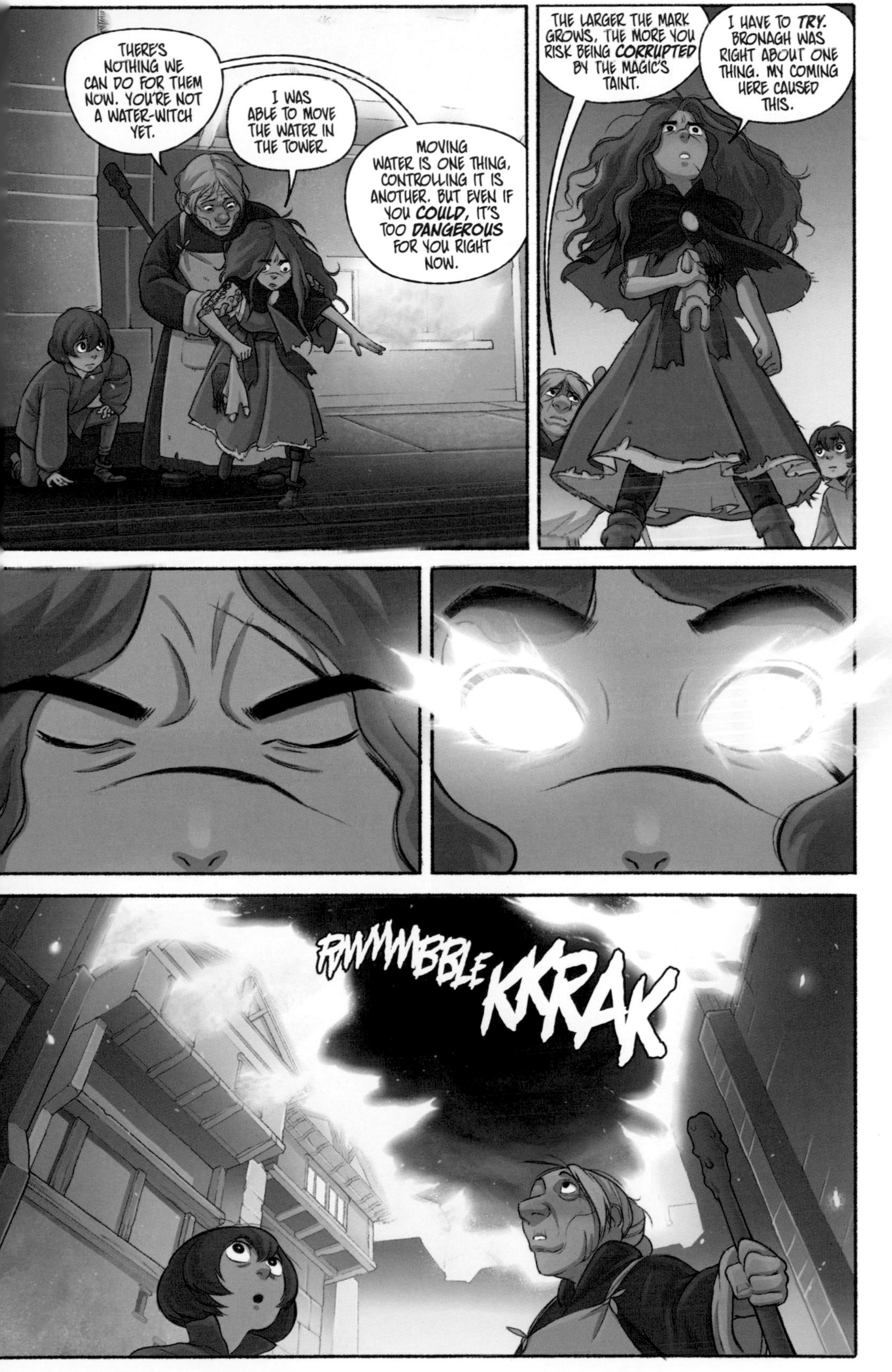
THERE'S NOTHING WE CAN DO FOR THEM NOW. YOU'RE NOT A WATER-WITCH YET.
I WAS ABLE TO MOVE THE WATER IN THE TOWER.
MOVING WATER IS ONE THING, CONTROLLING IT IS ANOTHER. BUT EVEN IF YOU COULD, IT'S TOO DANGEROUS FOR YOU RIGHT NOW.
THE LARGER THE MARK GROWS, THE MORE YOU RISK BEING CORRUPTED BY THE MAGIC'S TAINT.
I HAVE TO TRY. BRONAGH WAS RIGHT ABOUT ONE THING. MY COMING HERE CAUSED THIS.
RMMMBBLE
KKRAK

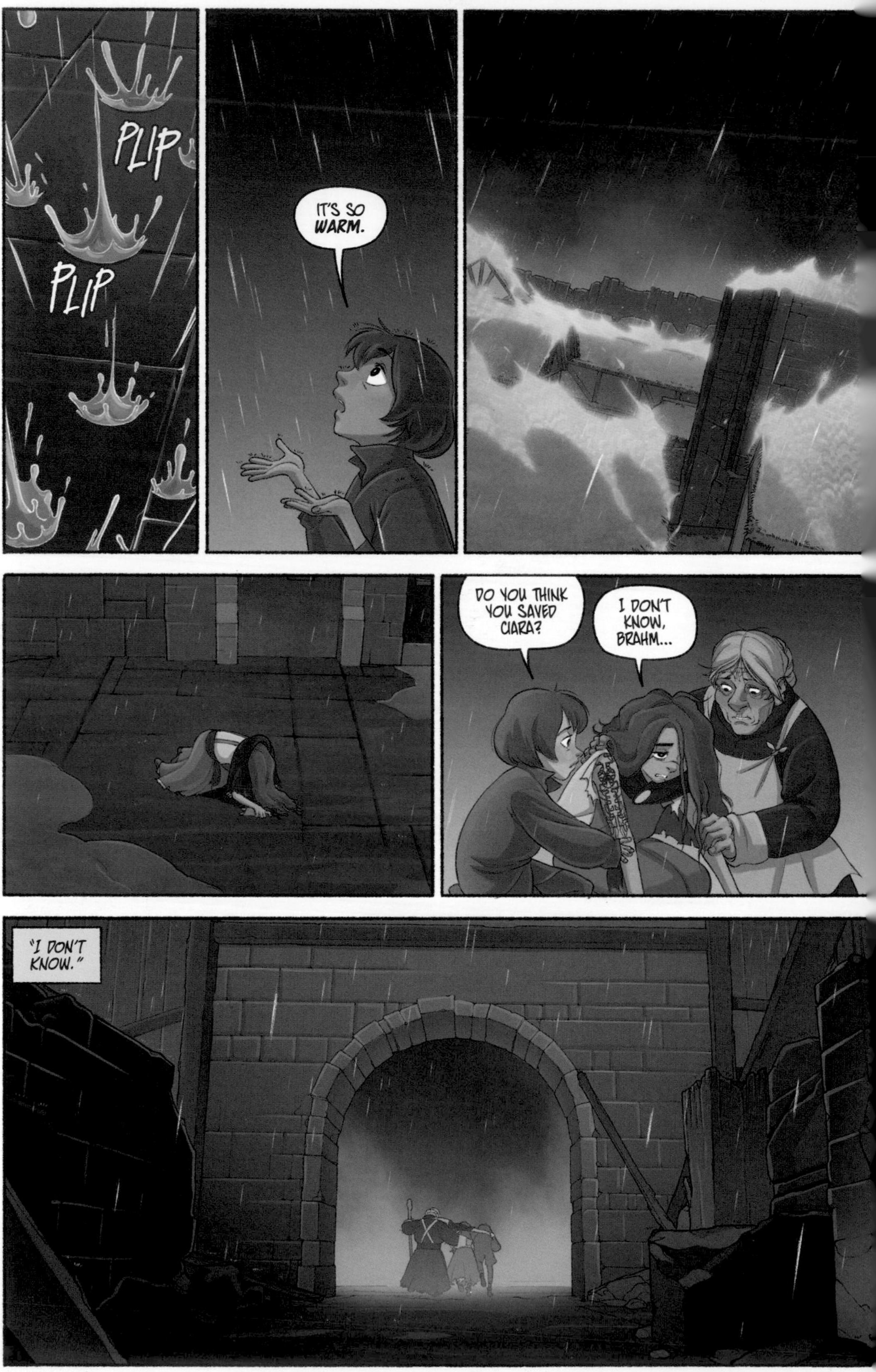
PLIP
PLIP
IT'S SO WARM.
DO YOU THINK YOU SAVED CIARA?
I DON'T KNOW, BRAHM...
"I DON'T KNOW."

CHAPTER
FOUR

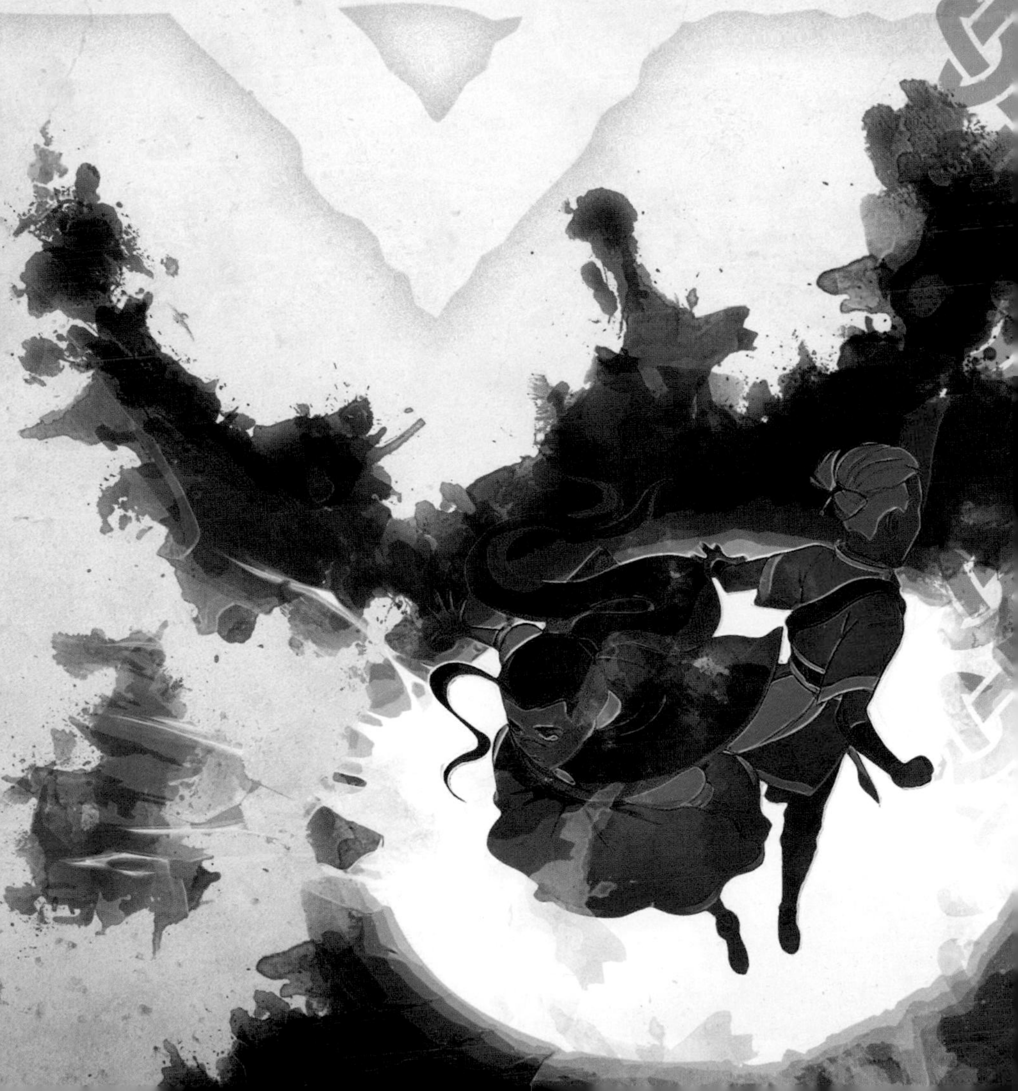

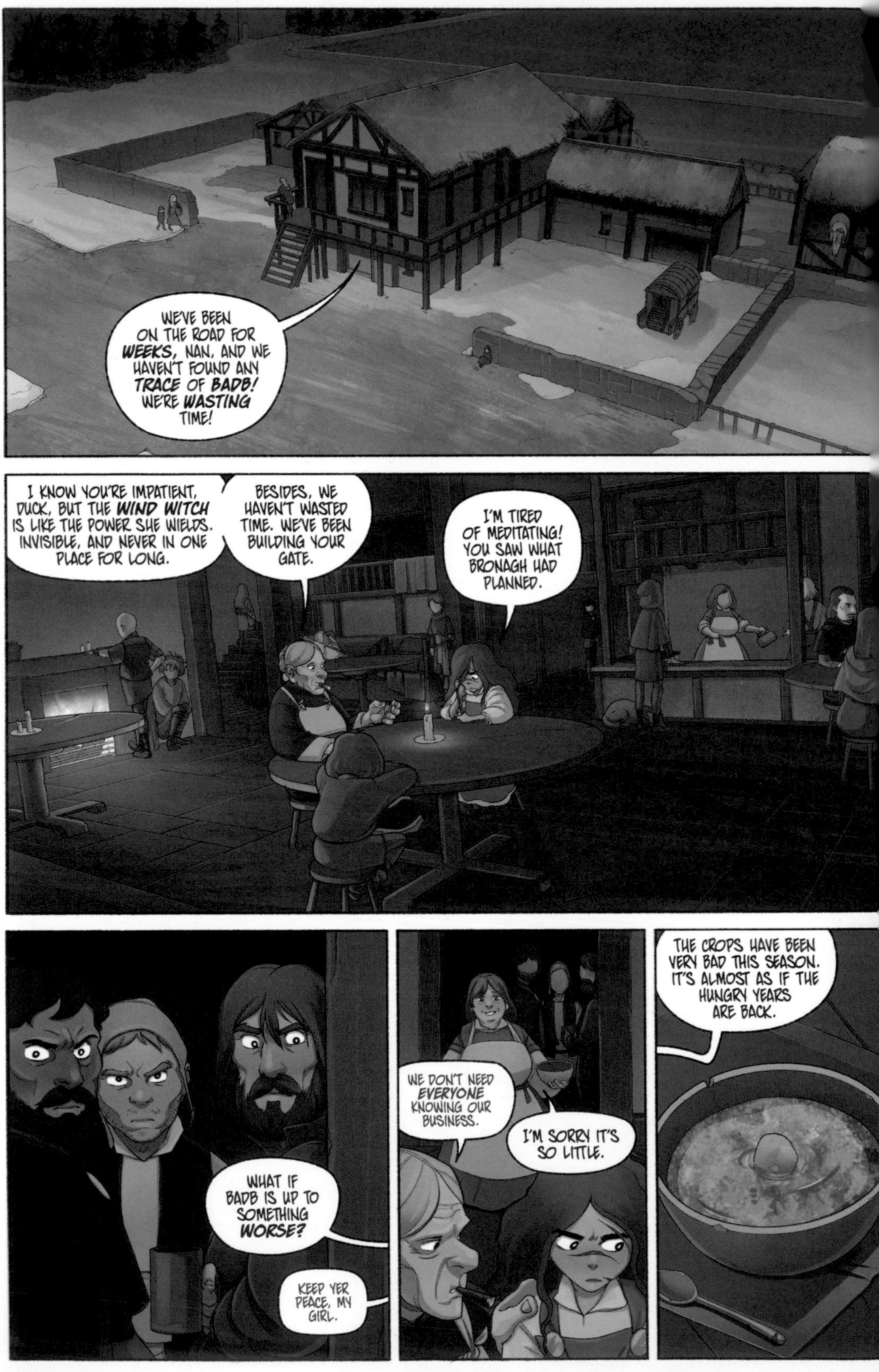

WE'VE BEEN ON THE ROAD FOR WEEKS, NAN, AND WE HAVEN'T FOUND ANY TRACE OF BADB! WE'RE WASTING TIME!
I KNOW YOU'RE IMPATIENT, DUCK, BUT THE WIND WITCH IS LIKE THE POWER SHE WIELDS. INVISIBLE, AND NEVER IN ONE PLACE FOR LONG.
BESIDES, WE HAVEN'T WASTED TIME. WE'VE BEEN BUILDING YOUR GATE.
I'M TIRED OF MEDITATING! YOU SAW WHAT BRONAGH HAD PLANNED.
WHAT IF BADB IS UP TO SOMETHING WORSE?
KEEP YER PEACE, MY GIRL.
WE DON'T NEED EVERYONE KNOWING OUR BUSINESS.
I'M SORRY IT'S SO LITTLE.
THE CROPS HAVE BEEN VERY BAD THIS SEASON. IT'S ALMOST AS IF THE HUNGRY YEARS ARE BACK.

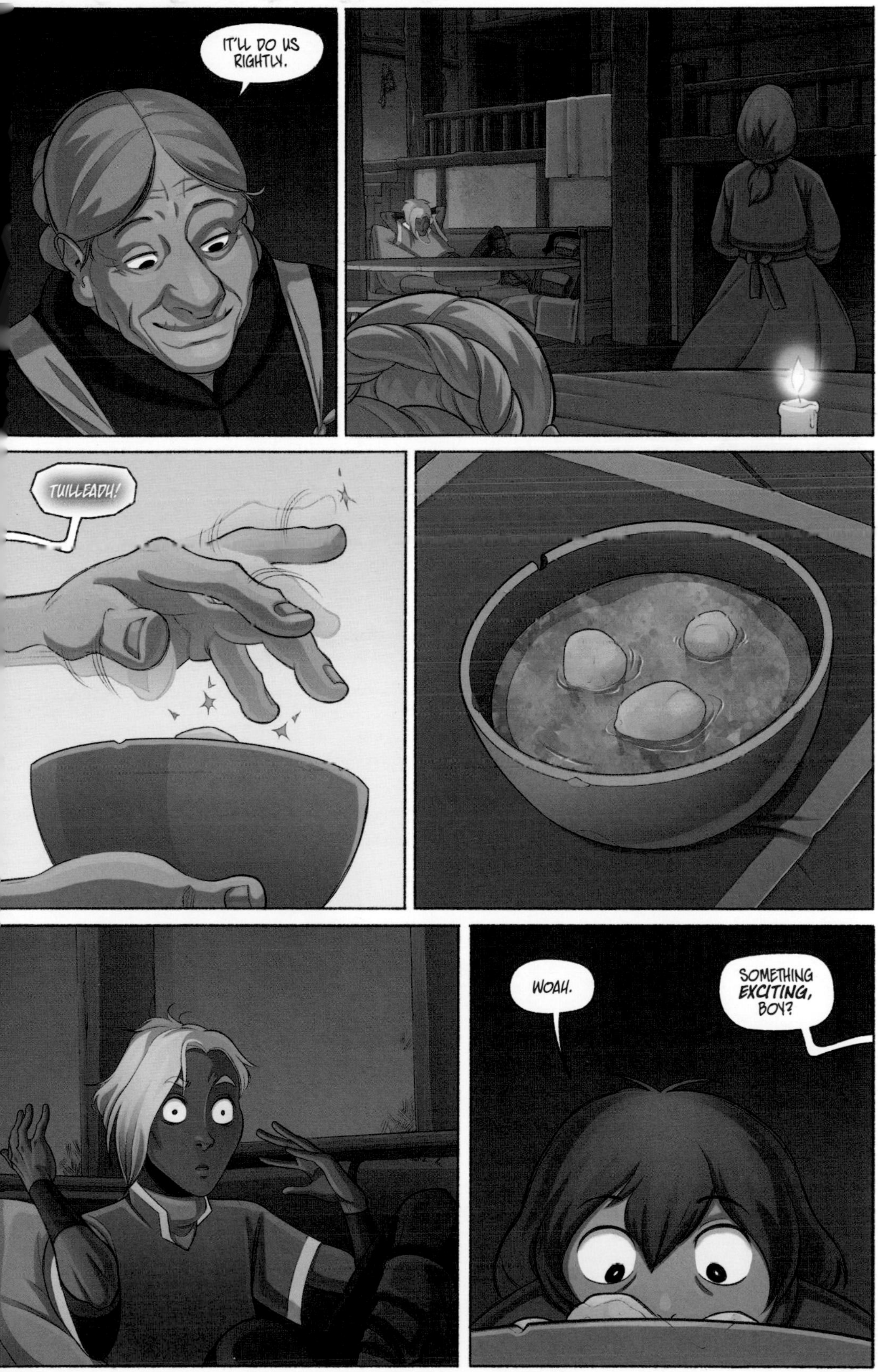
IT'LL DO US RIGHTLY.
TUILLEADH!
WOAH.
SOMETHING EXCITING, BOY?

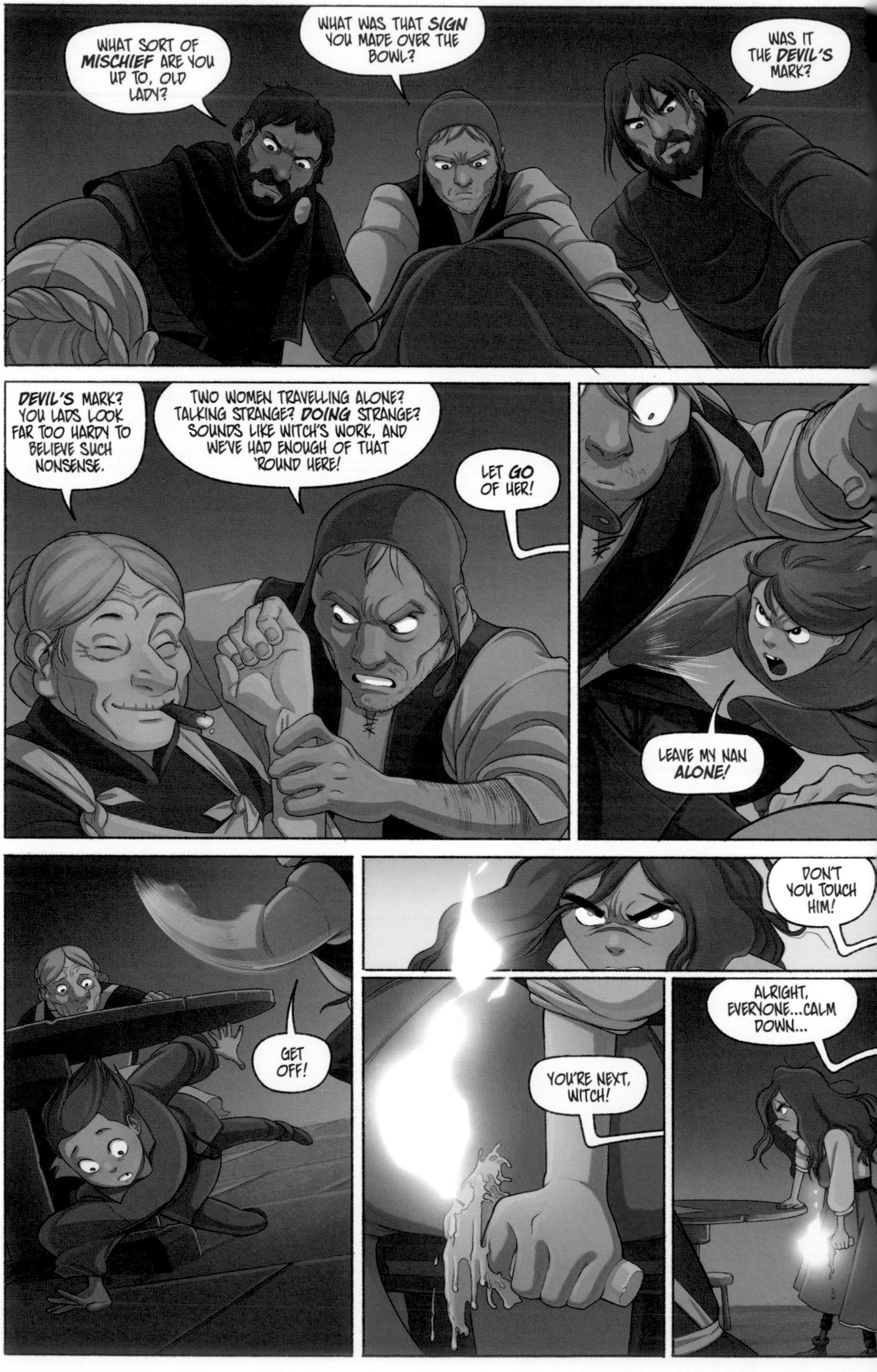
WHAT SORT OF MISCHIEF ARE YOU UP TO, OLD LADY?
WHAT WAS THAT SIGN YOU MADE OVER THE BOWL?
WAS IT THE DEVIL'S MARK?
DEVIL'S MARK? YOU LADS LOOK FAR TOO HARDY TO BELIEVE SUCH NONSENSE.
TWO WOMEN TRAVELLING ALONE? TALKING STRANGE? DOING STRANGE? SOUNDS LIKE WITCH'S WORK, AND WE'VE HAD ENOUGH OF THAT 'ROUND HERE!
LET GO OF HER!
LEAVE MY NAN ALONE!
GET OFF!
DON'T YOU TOUCH HIM!
YOU'RE NEXT, WITCH!
ALRIGHT, EVERYONE...CALM DOWN...

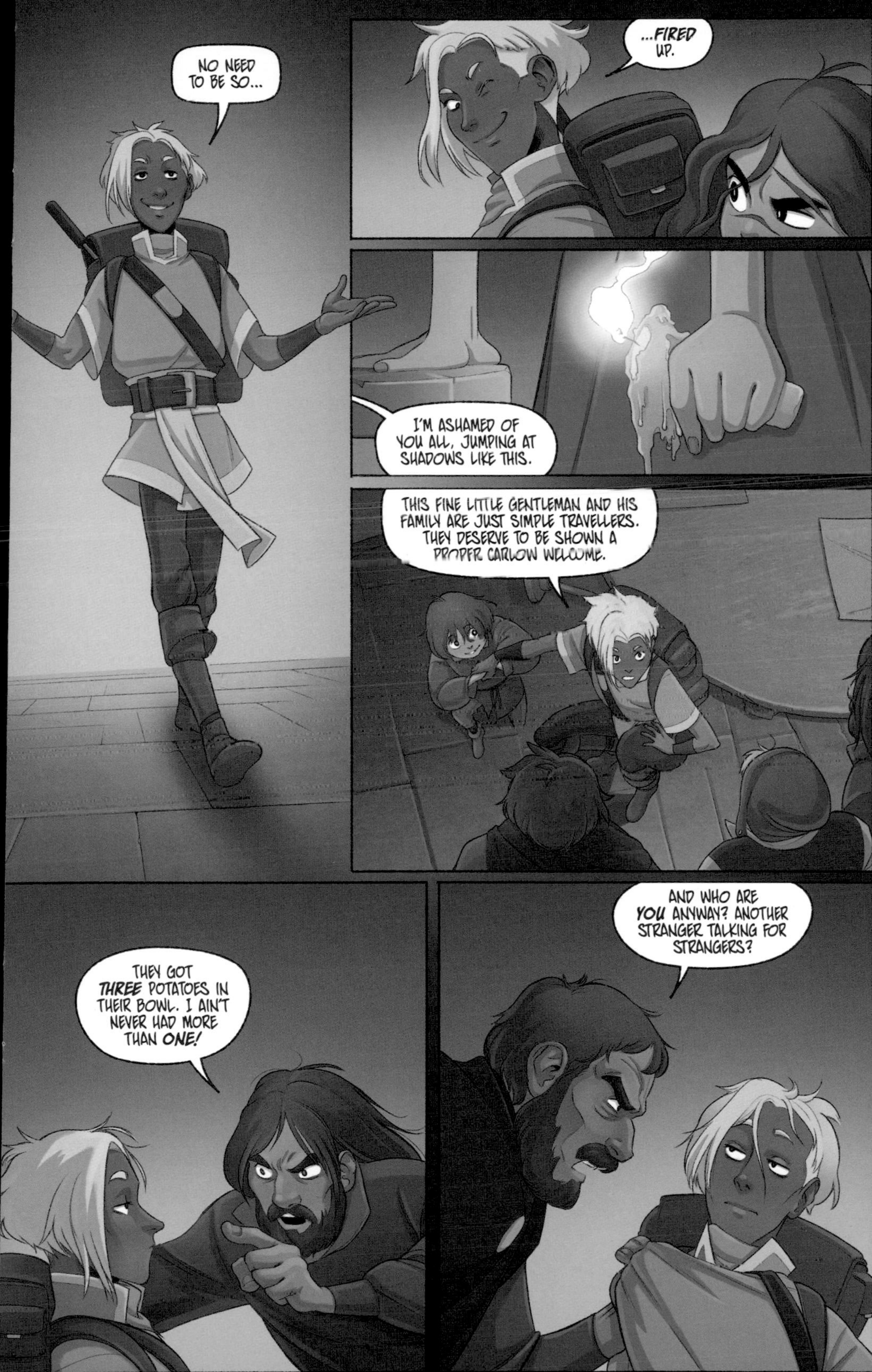
NO NEED TO BE SO...
...FIRED UP.
I'M ASHAMED OF YOU ALL, JUMPING AT SHADOWS LIKE THIS.
THIS FINE LITTLE GENTLEMAN AND HIS FAMILY ARE JUST SIMPLE TRAVELLERS. THEY DESERVE TO BE SHOWN A PROPER CARLOW WELCOME.
THEY GOT THREE POTATOES IN THEIR BOWL. I AIN'T NEVER HAD MORE THAN ONE!
AND WHO ARE YOU ANYWAY? ANOTHER STRANGER TALKING FOR STRANGERS?

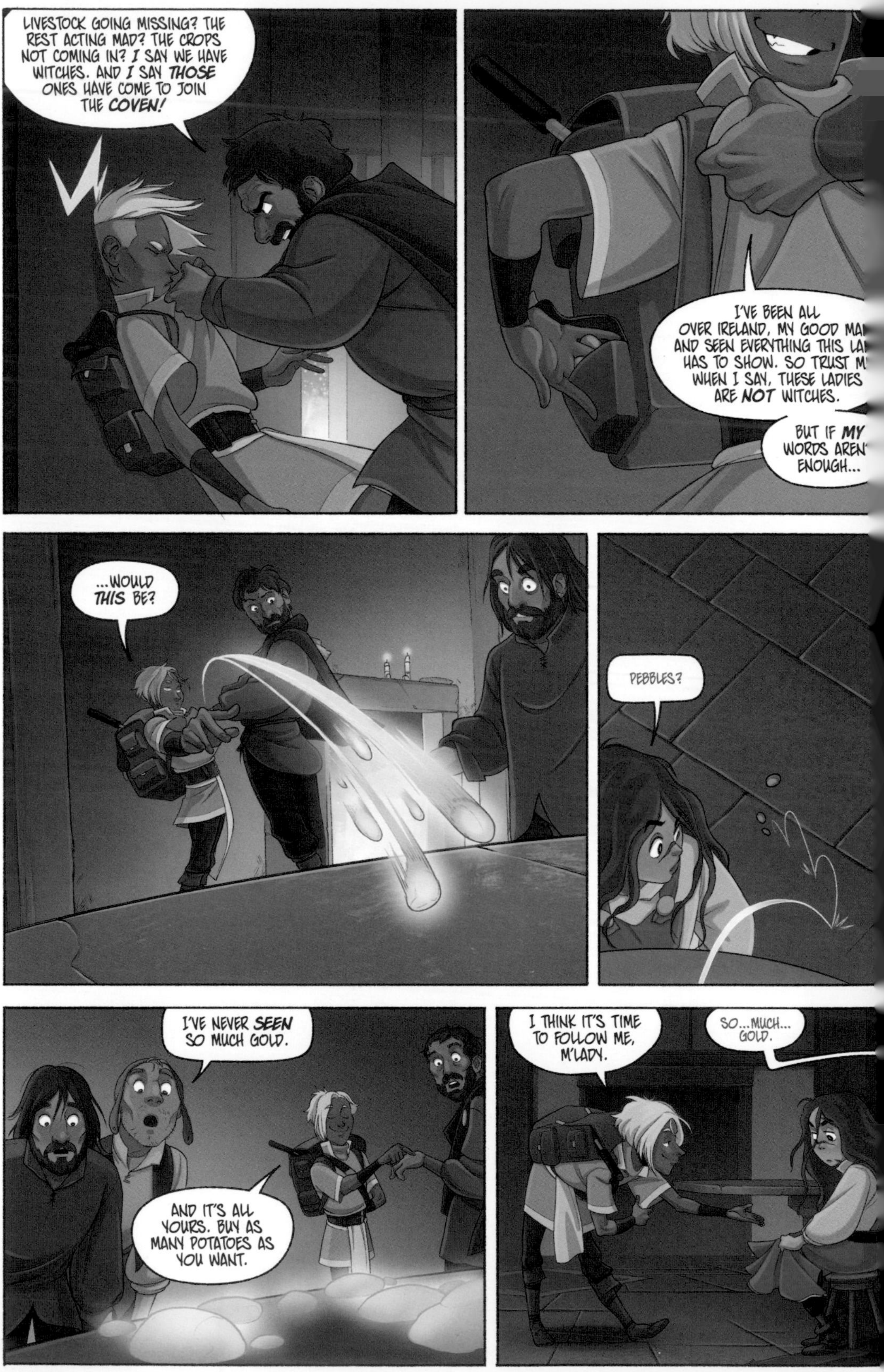
LIVESTOCK GOING MISSING? THE REST ACTING MAD? THE CROPS NOT COMING IN? I SAY WE HAVE WITCHES. AND I SAY THOSE ONES HAVE COME TO JOIN THE COVEN!
I'VE BEEN ALL OVER IRELAND, MY GOOD MA AND SEEN EVERYTHING THIS LA HAS TO SHOW. SO TRUST M WHEN I SAY, THESE LADIES ARE NOT WITCHES.
BUT IF MY WORDS AREN ENOUGH...
...WOULD THIS BE?
PEBBLES?
I'VE NEVER SEEN SO MUCH GOLD.
AND IT'S ALL YOURS. BUY AS MANY POTATOES AS YOU WANT.
I THINK IT'S TIME TO FOLLOW ME, M'LADY.
SO...MUCH... GOLD.

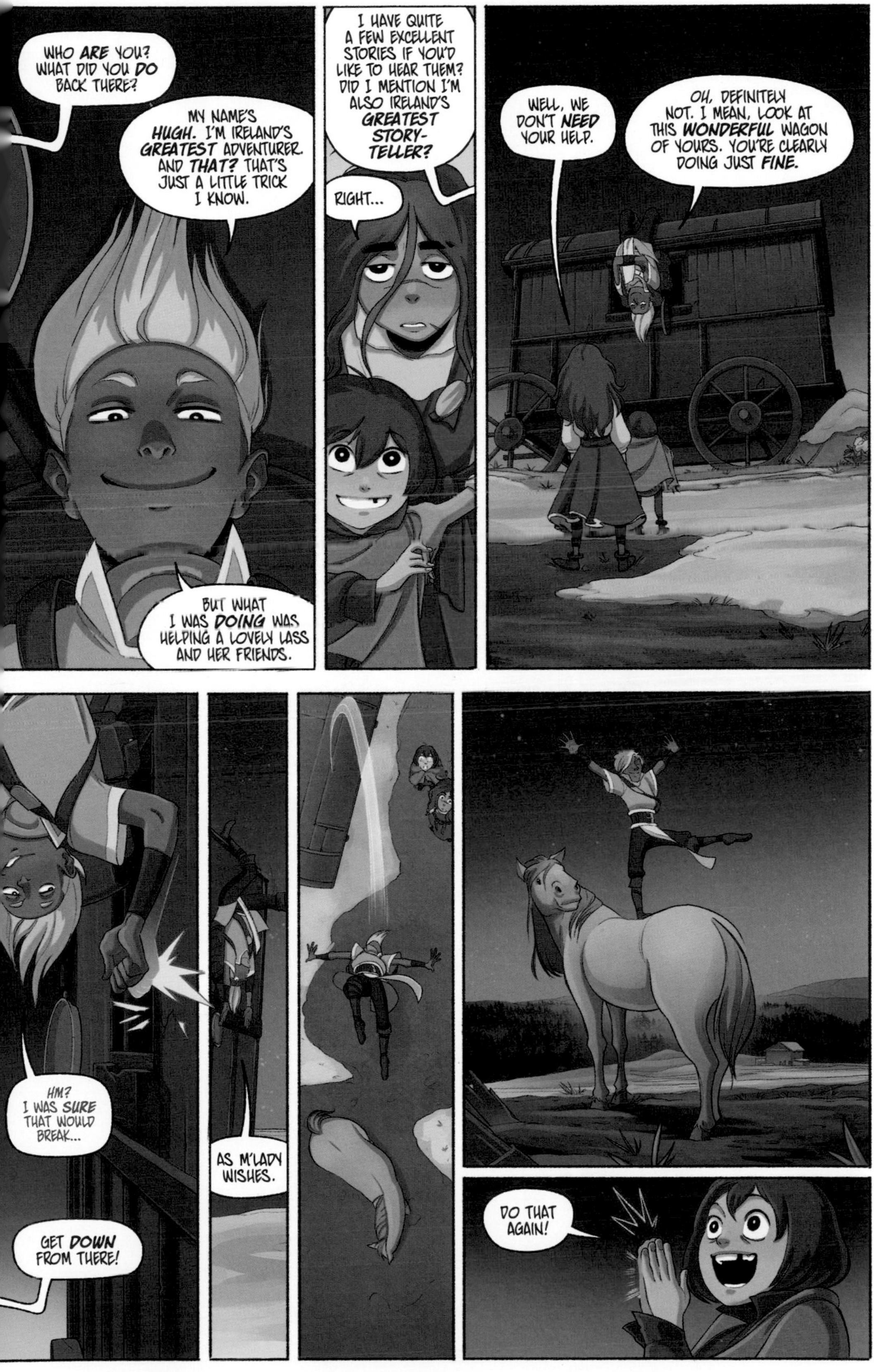
WHO ARE YOU? WHAT DID YOU DO BACK THERE?
MY NAME'S HUGH. I'M IRELAND'S GREATEST ADVENTURER. AND THAT? THAT'S JUST A LITTLE TRICK I KNOW.
BUT WHAT I WAS DOING WAS HELPING A LOVELY LASS AND HER FRIENDS.
I HAVE QUITE A FEW EXCELLENT STORIES IF YOU'D LIKE TO HEAR THEM? DID I MENTION I'M ALSO IRELAND'S GREATEST STORY-TELLER?
RIGHT...
WELL, WE DON'T NEED YOUR HELP.
OH, DEFINITELY NOT. I MEAN, LOOK AT THIS WONDERFUL WAGON OF YOURS. YOU'RE CLEARLY DOING JUST FINE.
HM? I WAS SURE THAT WOULD BREAK...
GET DOWN FROM THERE!
AS M'LADY WISHES.
DO THAT AGAIN!

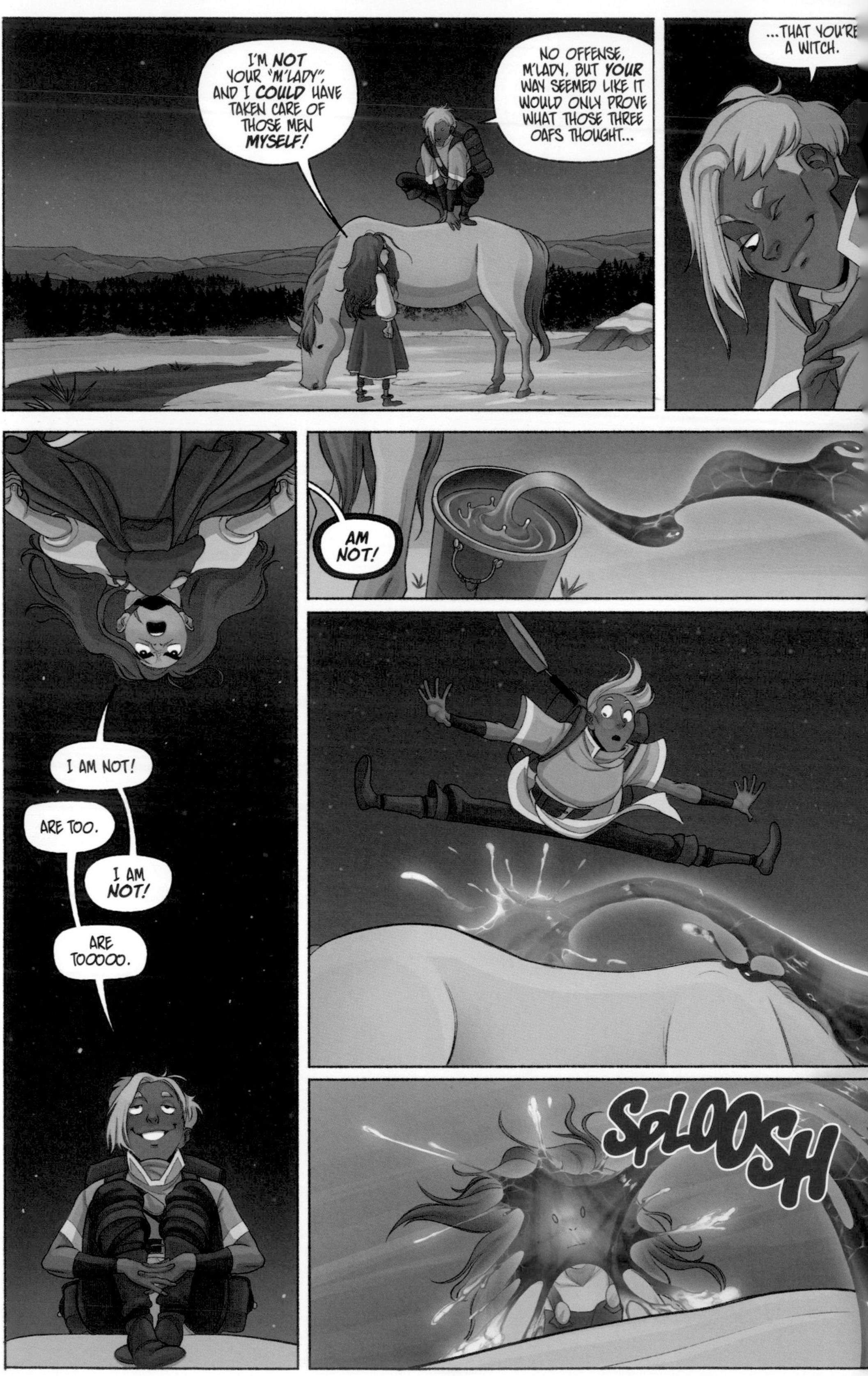
I'M NOT YOUR "M'LADY", AND I COULD HAVE TAKEN CARE OF THOSE MEN MYSELF!
NO OFFENSE, M'LADY, BUT YOUR WAY SEEMED LIKE IT WOULD ONLY PROVE WHAT THOSE THREE OAFS THOUGHT...
...THAT YOU'RE A WITCH.
AM NOT!
I AM NOT!
ARE TOO.
I AM NOT!
ARE TOOOOO.
SPLOOSH

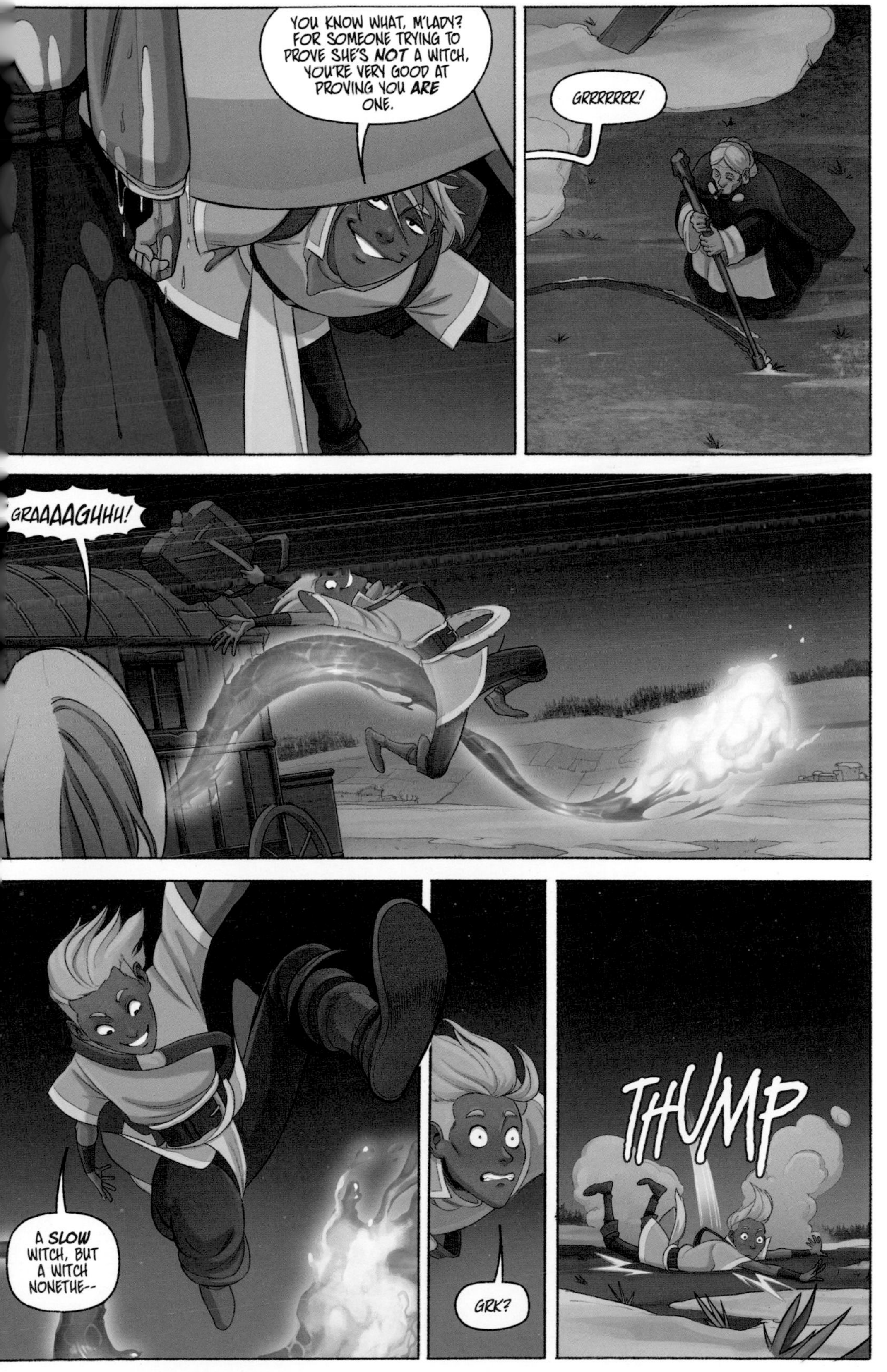
YOU KNOW WHAT, M'LADY? FOR SOMEONE TRYING TO PROVE SHE'S NOT A WITCH, YOU'RE VERY GOOD AT PROVING YOU ARE ONE.
GRRRRRRR!
GRAAAAGHHH!
A SLOW WITCH, BUT A WITCH NONETHE--
GRK?
THUMP

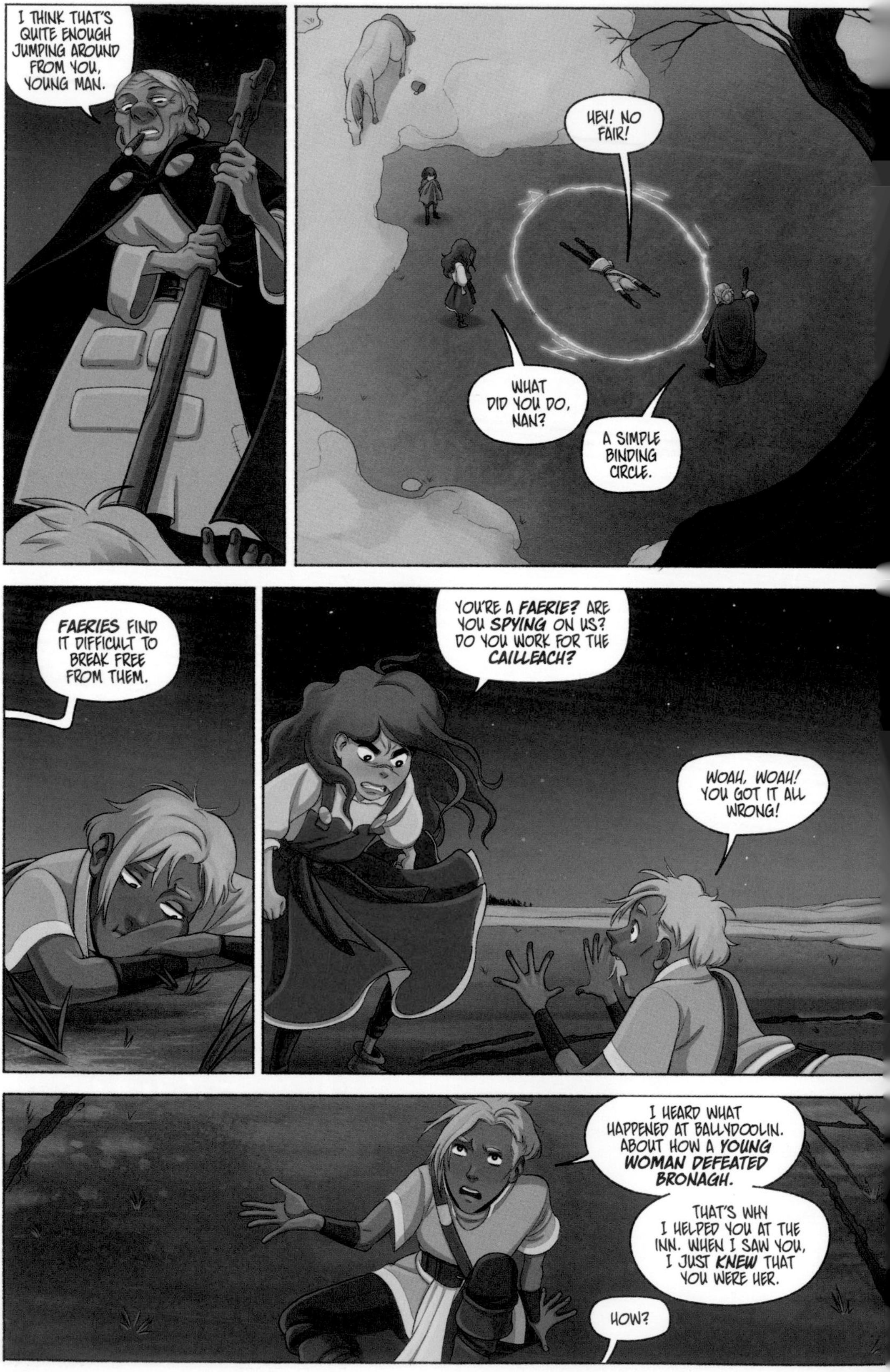
I THINK THAT'S QUITE ENOUGH JUMPING AROUND FROM YOU, YOUNG MAN.
HEY! NO FAIR!
WHAT DID YOU DO, NAN?
A SIMPLE BINDING CIRCLE.
FAERIES FIND IT DIFFICULT TO BREAK FREE FROM THEM.
YOU'RE A FAERIE? ARE YOU SPYING ON US? DO YOU WORK FOR THE CAILLEACH?
WOAH, WOAH! YOU GOT IT ALL WRONG!
I HEARD WHAT HAPPENED AT BALLYDOOLIN. ABOUT HOW A YOUNG WOMAN DEFEATED BRONAGH.
THAT'S WHY I HELPED YOU AT THE INN. WHEN I SAW YOU, I JUST KNEW THAT YOU WERE HER.
HOW?

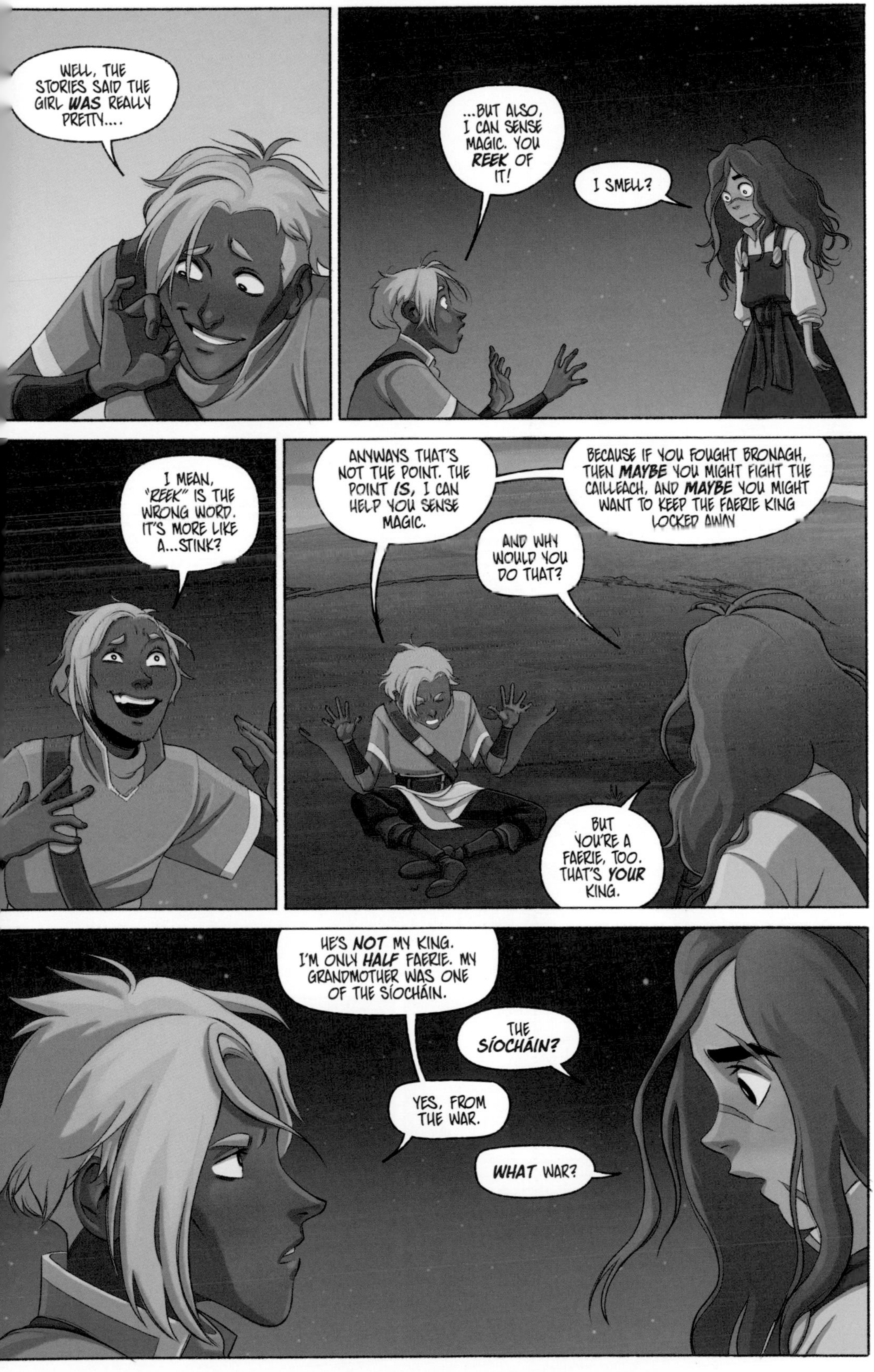
WELL, THE STORIES SAID THE GIRL WAS REALLY PRETTY....
...BUT ALSO, I CAN SENSE MAGIC. YOU REEK OF IT!
I SMELL?
I MEAN, "REEK" IS THE WRONG WORD. IT'S MORE LIKE A...STINK?
ANYWAYS THAT'S NOT THE POINT. THE POINT IS, I CAN HELP YOU SENSE MAGIC.
BECAUSE IF YOU FOUGHT BRONAGH, THEN MAYBE YOU MIGHT FIGHT THE CAILLEACH, AND MAYBE YOU MIGHT WANT TO KEEP THE FAERIE KING LOCKED AWAY
AND WHY WOULD YOU DO THAT?
BUT YOU'RE A FAERIE, TOO. THAT'S YOUR KING.
HE'S NOT MY KING. I'M ONLY HALF FAERIE. MY GRANDMOTHER WAS ONE OF THE SÍOCHÁIN.
THE SÍOCHÁIN?
YES, FROM THE WAR.
WHAT WAR?

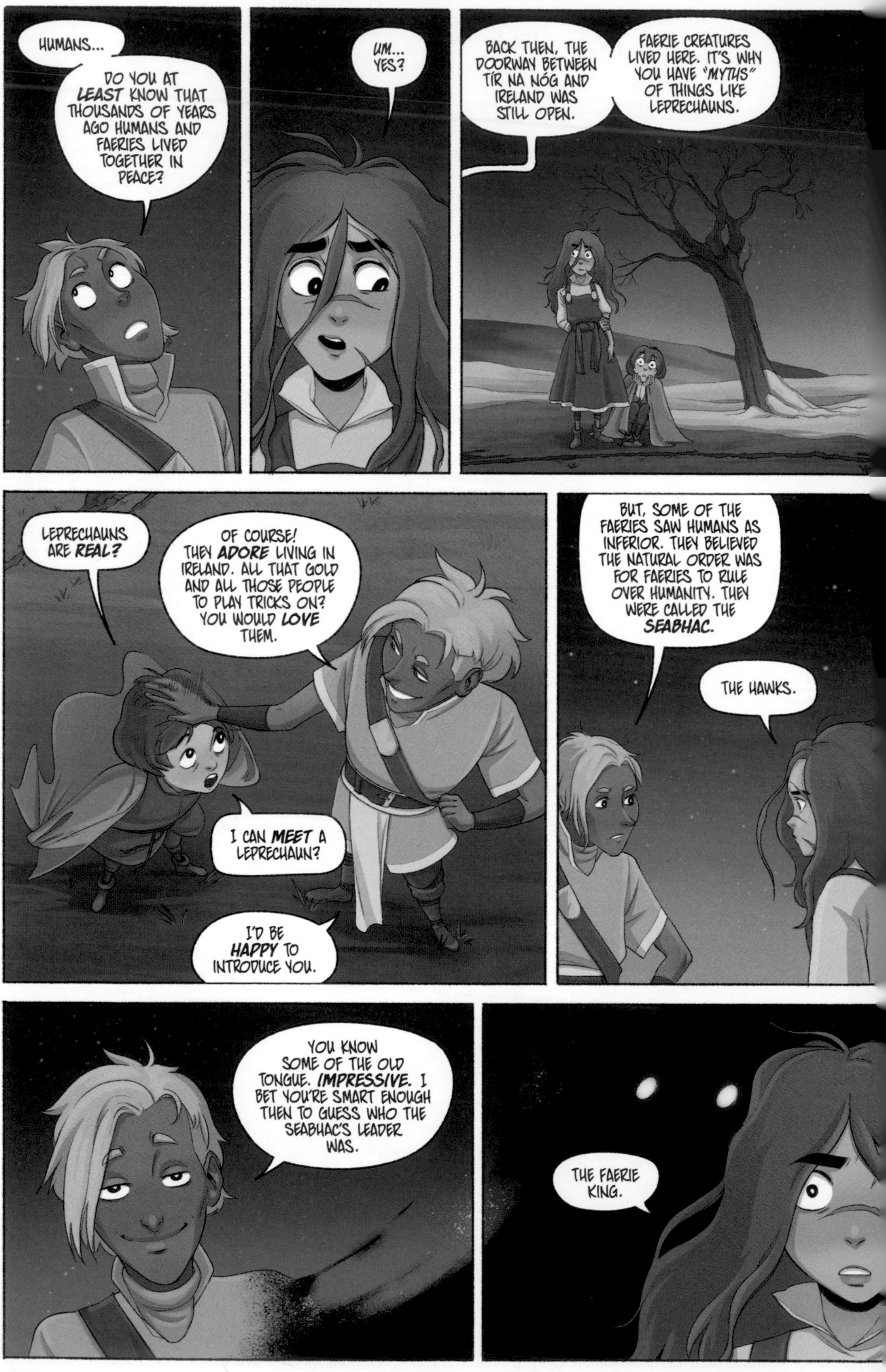

HUMANS...
DO YOU AT LEAST KNOW THAT THOUSANDS OF YEARS AGO HUMANS AND FAERIES LIVED TOGETHER IN PEACE?
UM... YES?
BACK THEN, THE DOORWAY BETWEEN TÍR NA NÓG AND IRELAND WAS STILL OPEN.
FAERIE CREATURES LIVED HERE. IT'S WHY YOU HAVE "MYTHS" OF THINGS LIKE LEPRECHAUNS.
LEPRECHAUNS ARE REAL?
OF COURSE! THEY ADORE LIVING IN IRELAND. ALL THAT GOLD AND ALL THOSE PEOPLE TO PLAY TRICKS ON? YOU WOULD LOVE THEM.
I CAN MEET A LEPRECHAUN?
I'D BE HAPPY TO INTRODUCE YOU.
BUT, SOME OF THE FAERIES SAW HUMANS AS INFERIOR. THEY BELIEVED THE NATURAL ORDER WAS FOR FAERIES TO RULE OVER HUMANITY. THEY WERE CALLED THE SEABHAC.
THE HAWKS.
YOU KNOW SOME OF THE OLD TONGUE. IMPRESSIVE. I BET YOU'RE SMART ENOUGH THEN TO GUESS WHO THE SEABHAC'S LEADER WAS.
THE FAERIE KING.

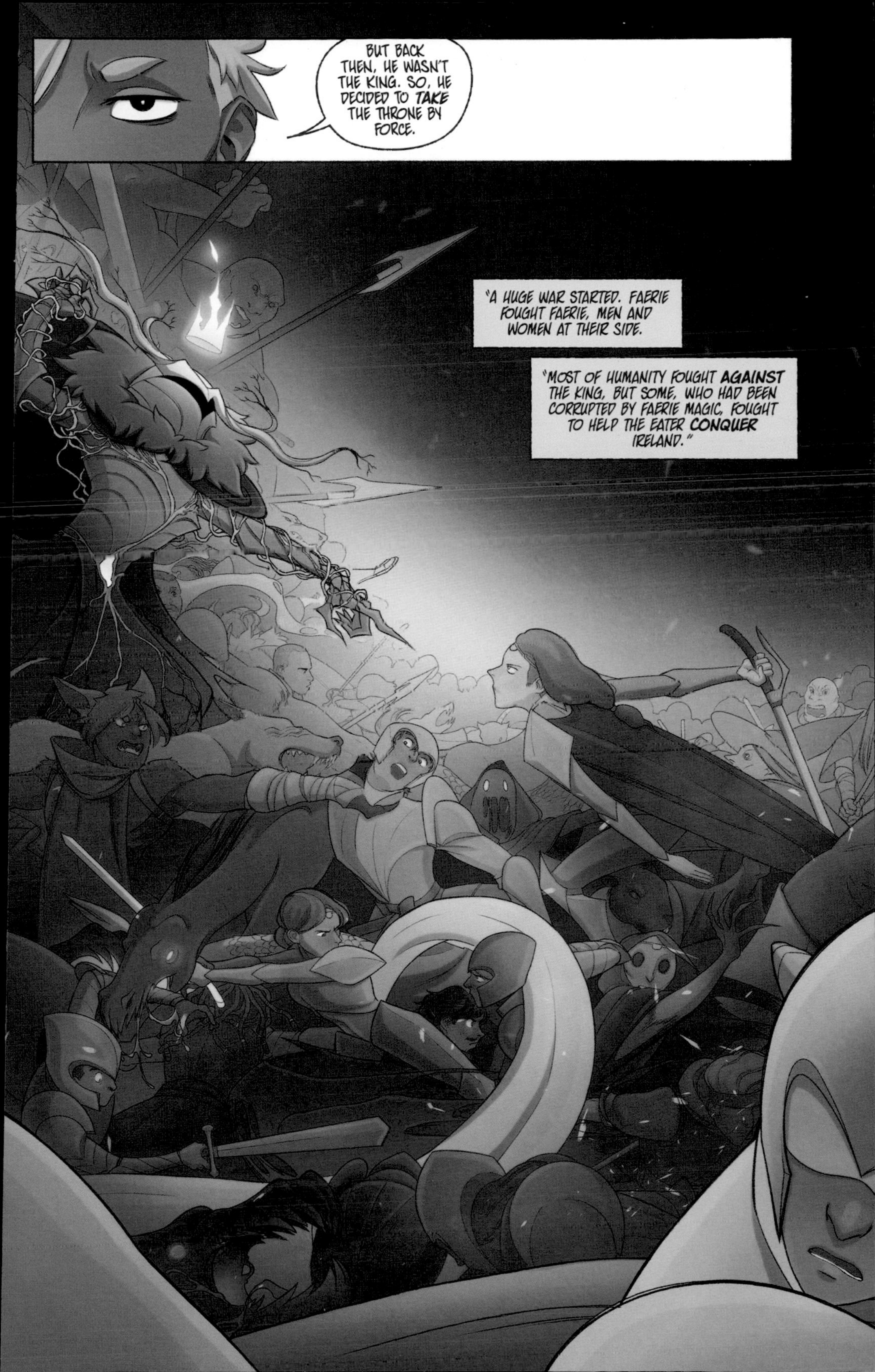
BUT BACK THEN, HE WASN'T THE KING. SO, HE DECIDED TO TAKE THE THRONE BY FORCE.
"A HUGE WAR STARTED. FAERIE FOUGHT FAERIE, MEN AND WOMEN AT THEIR SIDE.
"MOST OF HUMANITY FOUGHT AGAINST THE KING, BUT SOME, WHO HAD BEEN CORRUPTED BY FAERIE MAGIC, FOUGHT TO HELP THE EATER CONQUER IRELAND."

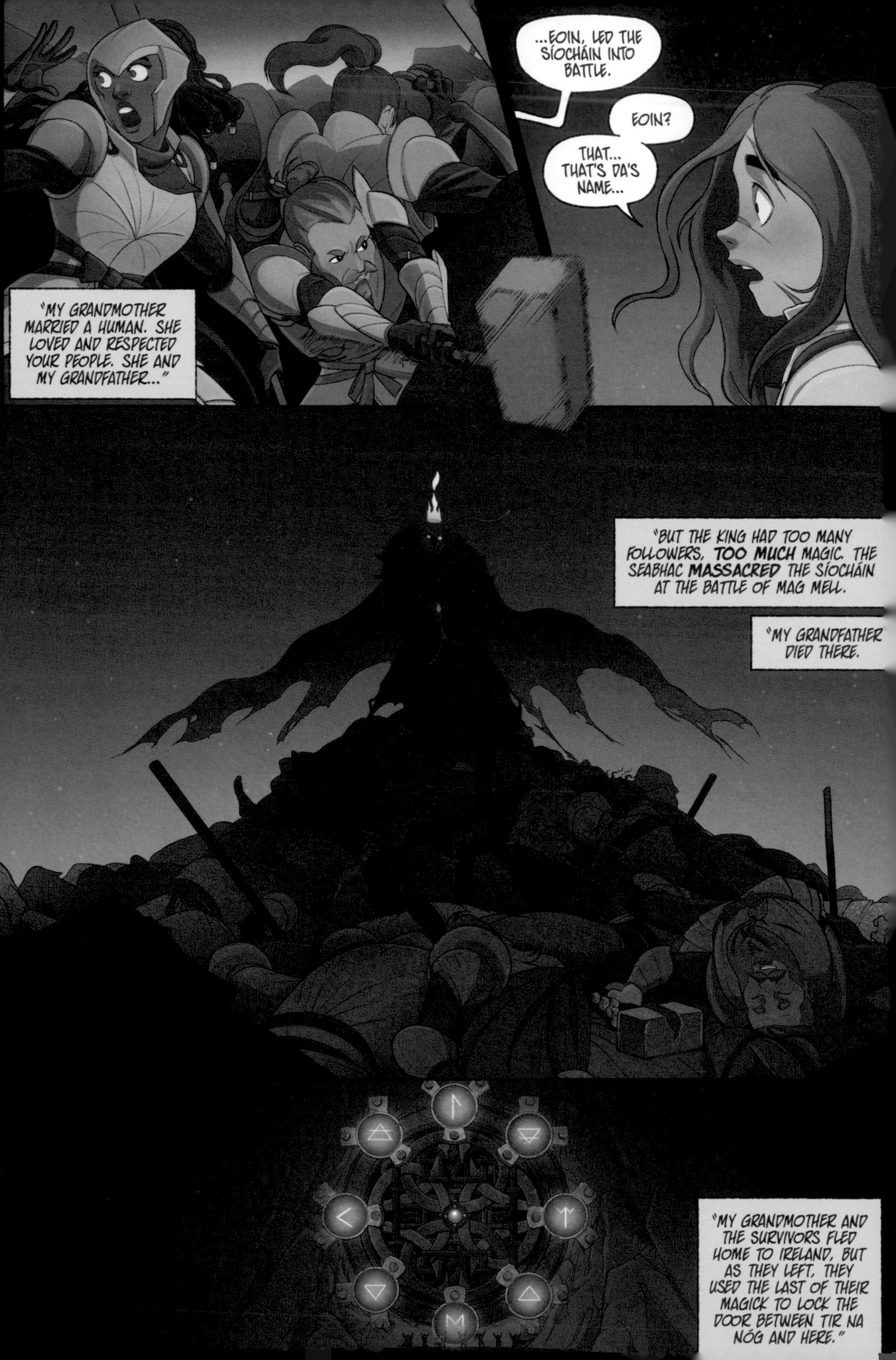

"MY GRANDMOTHER MARRIED A HUMAN. SHE LOVED AND RESPECTED YOUR PEOPLE. SHE AND MY GRANDFATHER..."
...EOIN, LED THE SÍOCHÁIN INTO BATTLE.
EOIN?
THAT... THAT'S DA'S NAME...
"BUT THE KING HAD TOO MANY FOLLOWERS, TOO MUCH MAGIC. THE SEABHAC MASSACRED THE SÍOCHÁIN AT THE BATTLE OF MAG MELL.
"MY GRANDFATHER DIED THERE.
"MY GRANDMOTHER AND THE SURVIVORS FLED HOME TO IRELAND, BUT AS THEY LEFT, THEY USED THE LAST OF THEIR MAGICK TO LOCK THE DOOR BETWEEN TIR NA NÓG AND HERE."

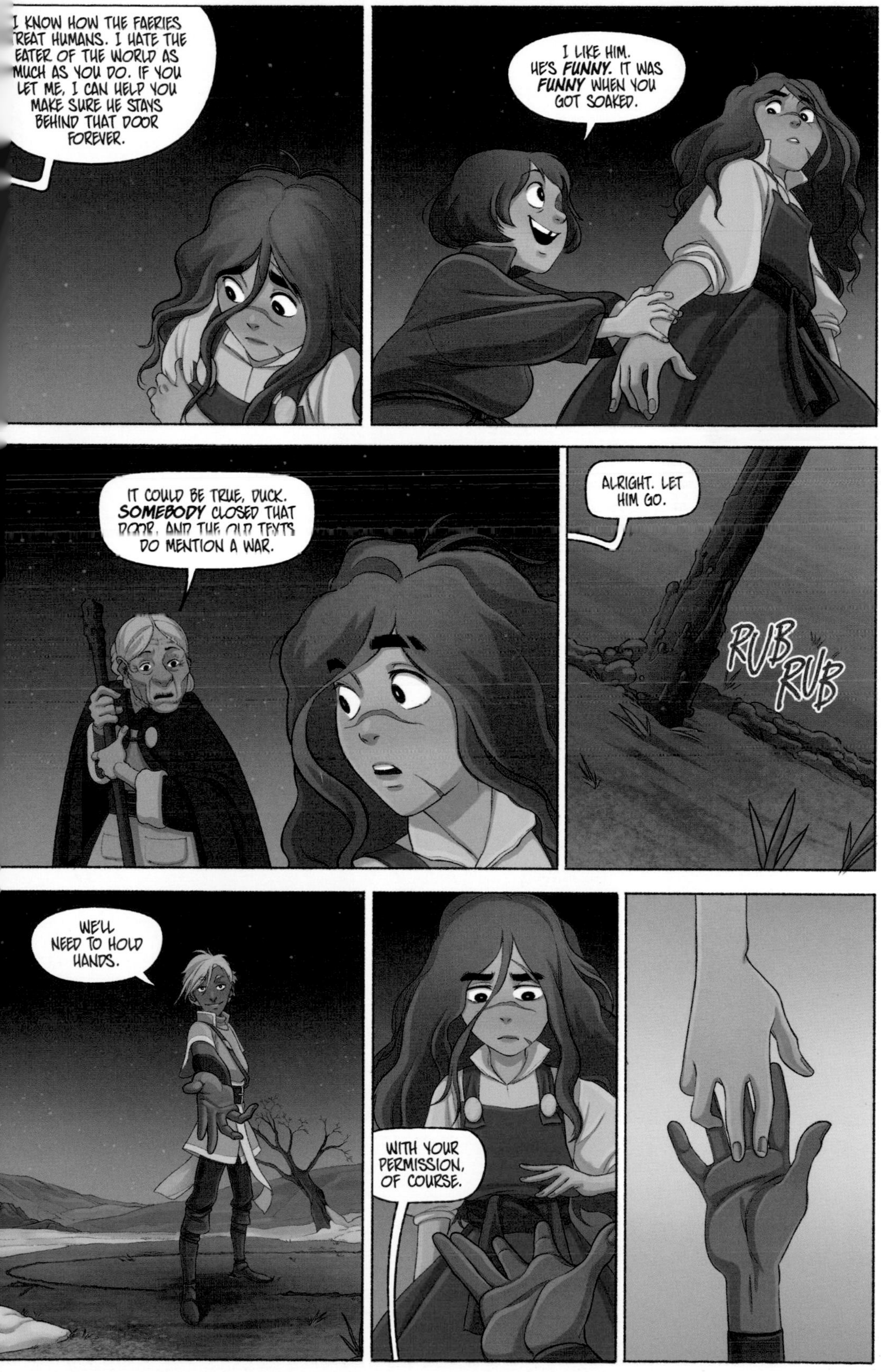
I KNOW HOW THE FAERIES TREAT HUMANS. I HATE THE EATER OF THE WORLD AS MUCH AS YOU DO. IF YOU LET ME, I CAN HELP YOU MAKE SURE HE STAYS BEHIND THAT DOOR FOREVER.
I LIKE HIM. HE'S FUNNY. IT WAS FUNNY WHEN YOU GOT SOAKED.
IT COULD BE TRUE, DUCK. SOMEBODY CLOSED THAT DOOR. AND THE OLD TEXTS DO MENTION A WAR.
ALRIGHT. LET HIM GO.
RUB RUB
WE'LL NEED TO HOLD HANDS.
WITH YOUR PERMISSION, OF COURSE.

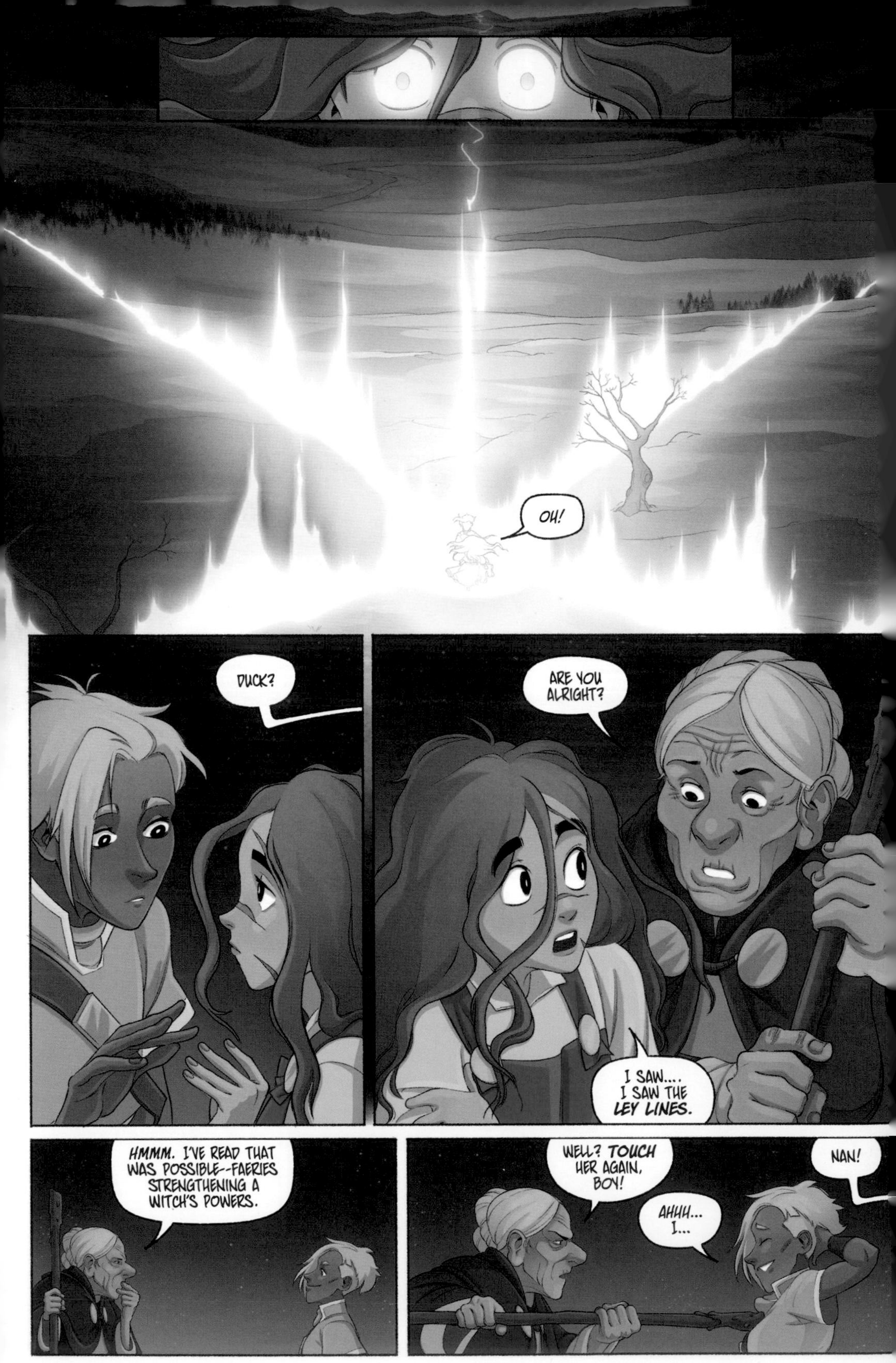
OH!
DUCK?
ARE YOU ALRIGHT?
I SAW.... I SAW THE LEY LINES.
HMMM. I'VE READ THAT WAS POSSIBLE--FAERIES STRENGTHENING A WITCH'S POWERS.
WELL? TOUCH HER AGAIN, BOY!
NAN!
AHHH... I...

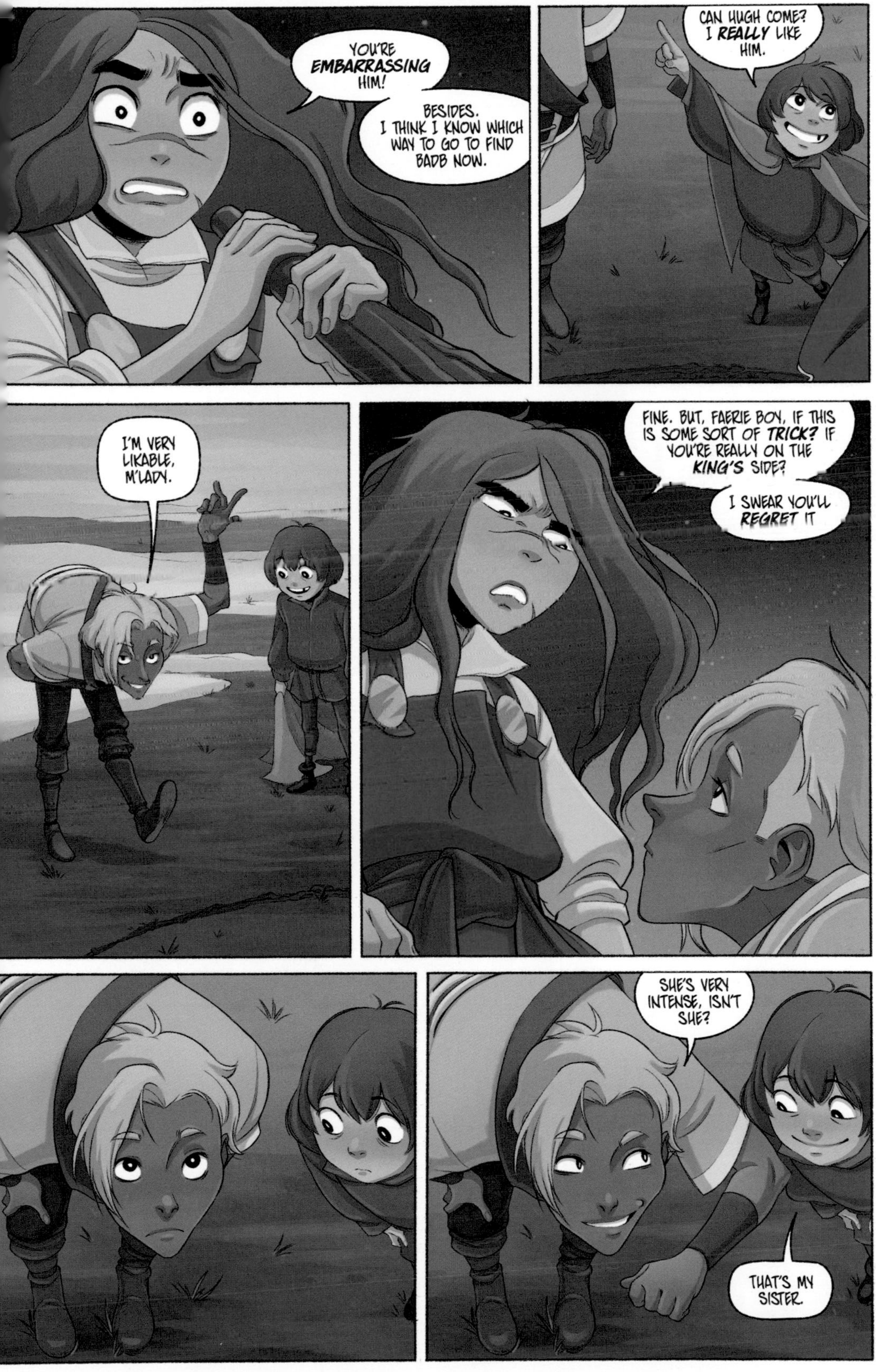
YOU'RE EMBARRASSING HIM!
BESIDES. I THINK I KNOW WHICH WAY TO GO TO FIND BADB NOW.
CAN HUGH COME? I REALLY LIKE HIM.
I'M VERY LIKABLE, M'LADY.
FINE. BUT, FAERIE BOY, IF THIS IS SOME SORT OF TRICK? IF YOU'RE REALLY ON THE KING'S SIDE?
I SWEAR YOU'LL REGRET IT
SHE'S VERY INTENSE, ISN'T SHE?
THAT'S MY SISTER.

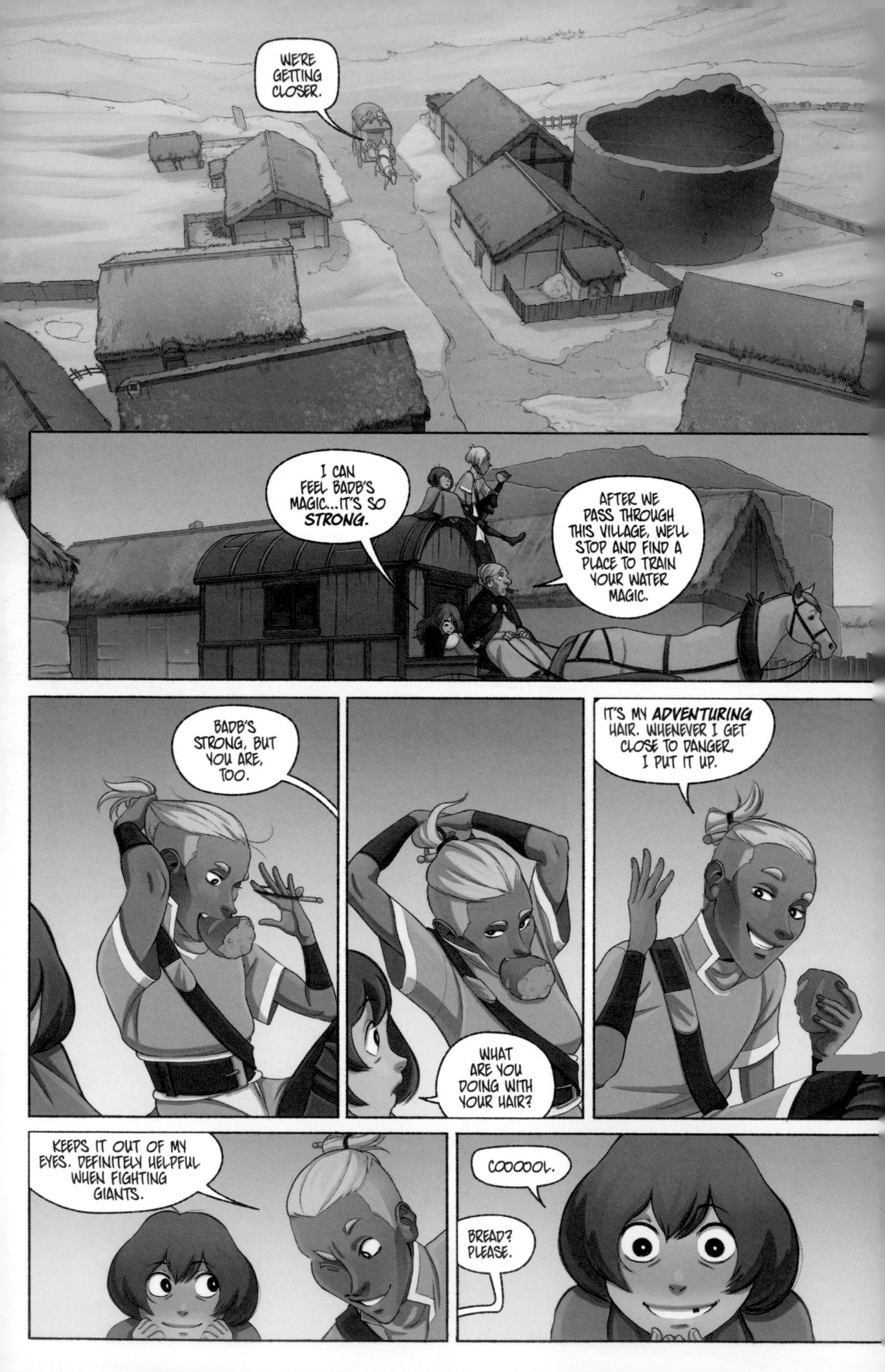
WE'RE GETTING CLOSER.
I CAN FEEL BADB'S MAGIC...IT'S SO **STRONG.**
AFTER WE PASS THROUGH THIS VILLAGE, WE'LL STOP AND FIND A PLACE TO TRAIN YOUR WATER MAGIC.
BADB'S STRONG, BUT YOU ARE, TOO.
WHAT ARE YOU DOING WITH YOUR HAIR?
IT'S MY **ADVENTURING** HAIR. WHENEVER I GET CLOSE TO DANGER, I PUT IT UP.
KEEPS IT OUT OF MY EYES. DEFINITELY HELPFUL WHEN FIGHTING GIANTS.
COOOOOL.
BREAD? PLEASE.

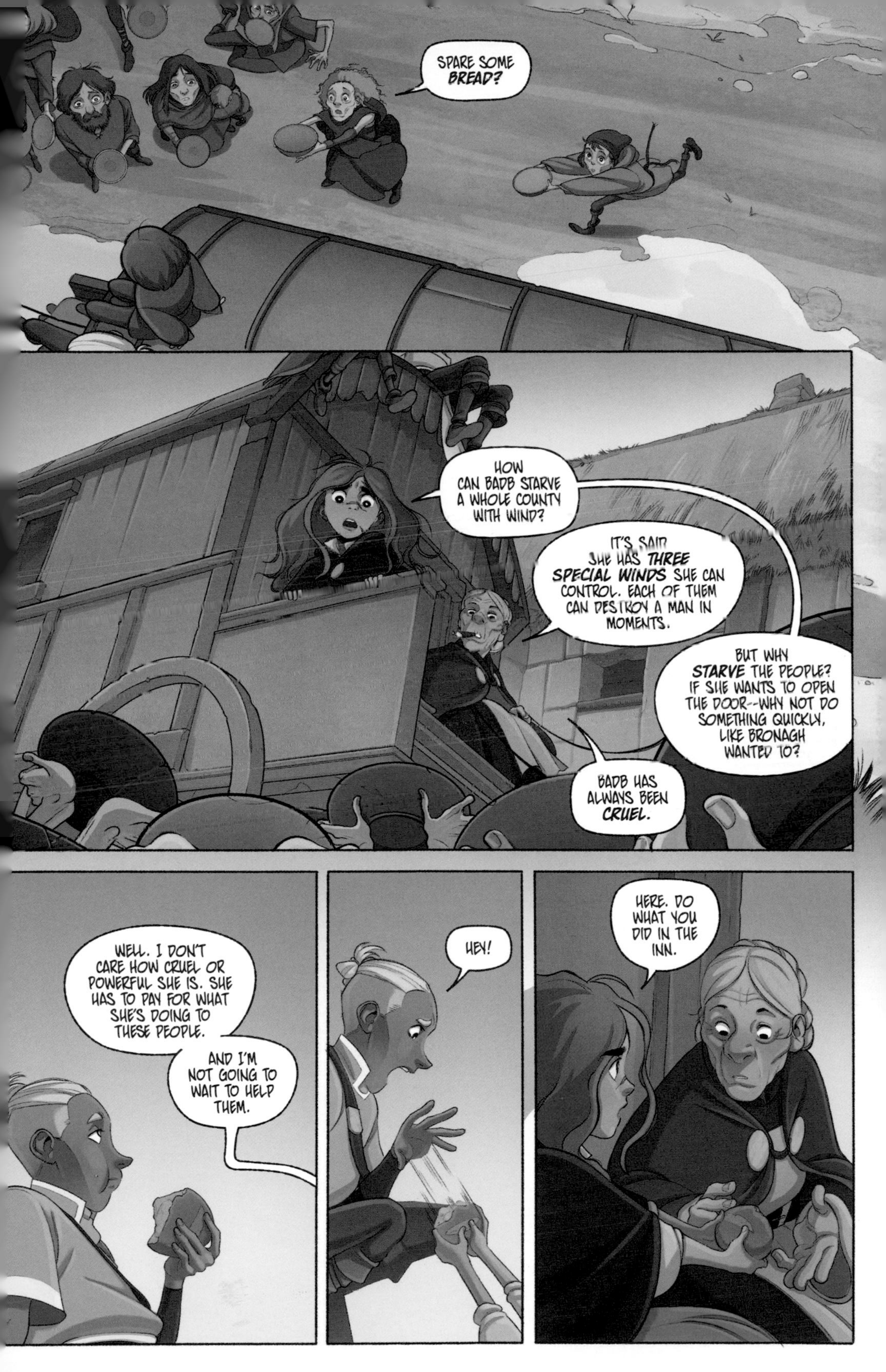
SPARE SOME BREAD?
HOW CAN BADB STARVE A WHOLE COUNTY WITH WIND?
IT'S SAID SHE HAS THREE SPECIAL WINDS SHE CAN CONTROL. EACH OF THEM CAN DESTROY A MAN IN MOMENTS.
BUT WHY STARVE THE PEOPLE? IF SHE WANTS TO OPEN THE DOOR--WHY NOT DO SOMETHING QUICKLY, LIKE BRONAGH WANTED TO?
BADB HAS ALWAYS BEEN CRUEL.
WELL. I DON'T CARE HOW CRUEL OR POWERFUL SHE IS. SHE HAS TO PAY FOR WHAT SHE'S DOING TO THESE PEOPLE.
AND I'M NOT GOING TO WAIT TO HELP THEM.
HEY!
HERE. DO WHAT YOU DID IN THE INN.

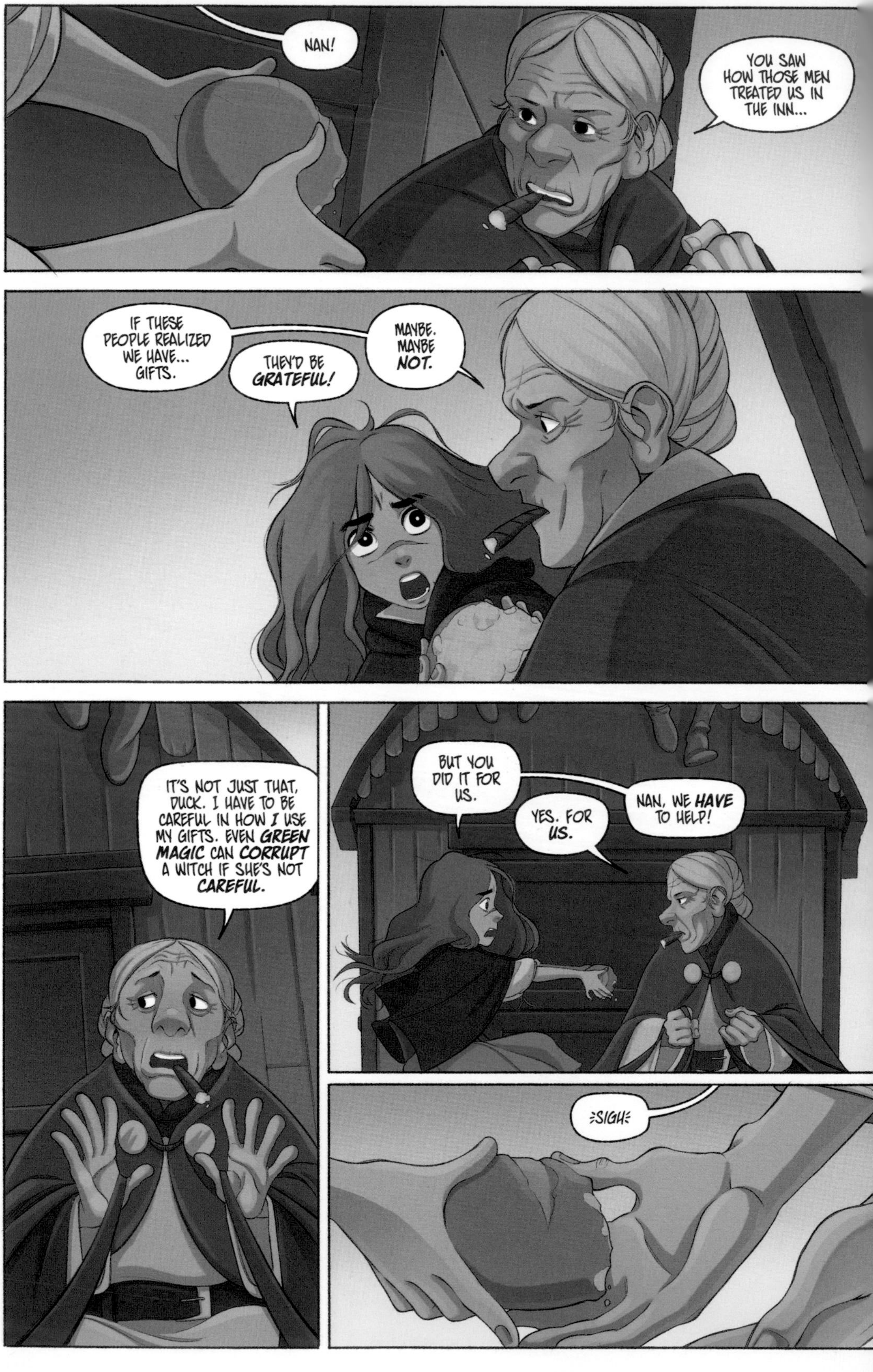
NAN!
YOU SAW HOW THOSE MEN TREATED US IN THE INN...
IF THESE PEOPLE REALIZED WE HAVE... GIFTS.
THEY'D BE **GRATEFUL!**
MAYBE. MAYBE **NOT.**
IT'S NOT JUST THAT, DUCK. I HAVE TO BE CAREFUL IN HOW *I* USE MY GIFTS. EVEN **GREEN MAGIC** CAN **CORRUPT** A WITCH IF SHE'S NOT **CAREFUL.**
BUT YOU DID IT FOR US.
YES. FOR **US.**
NAN, WE **HAVE** TO HELP!
SIGH

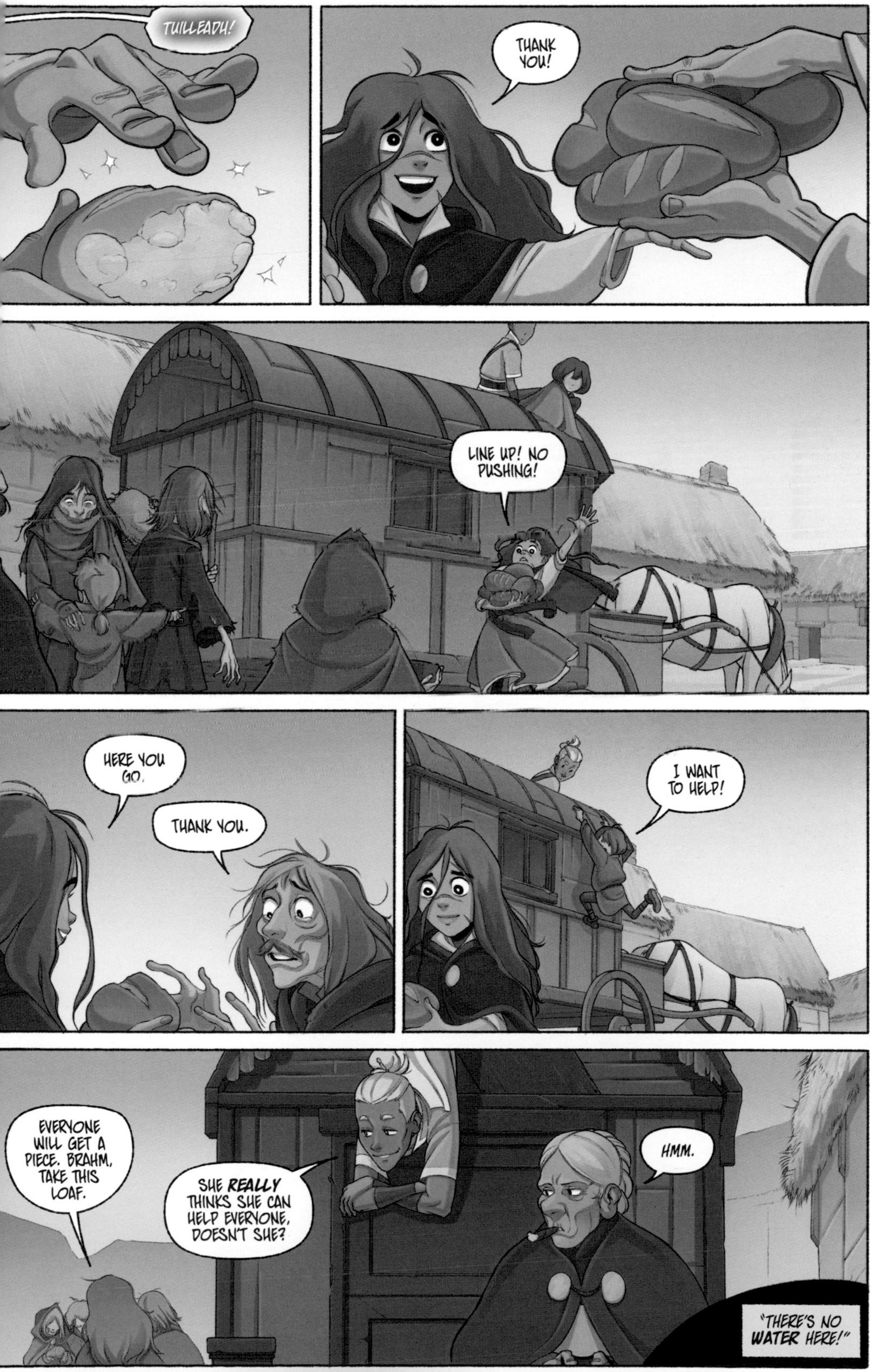
TUILLEADH!
THANK YOU!
LINE UP! NO PUSHING!
HERE YOU GO.
THANK YOU.
I WANT TO HELP!
EVERYONE WILL GET A PIECE. BRAHM, TAKE THIS LOAF.
SHE **REALLY** THINKS SHE CAN HELP EVERYONE, DOESN'T SHE?
HMM.
"THERE'S NO **WATER** HERE!"

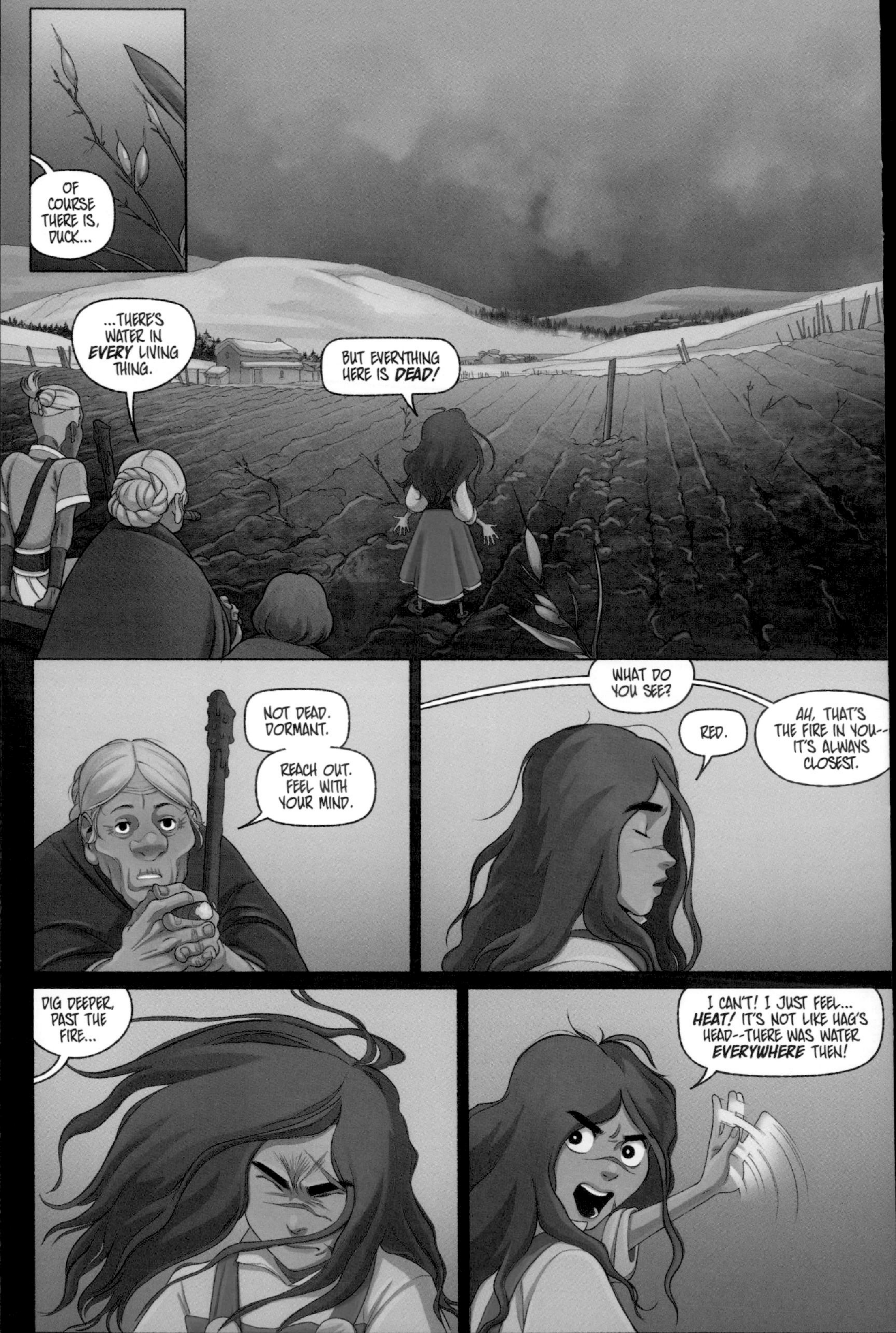
OF COURSE THERE IS, DUCK...
...THERE'S WATER IN EVERY LIVING THING.
BUT EVERYTHING HERE IS DEAD!
NOT DEAD. DORMANT.
REACH OUT. FEEL WITH YOUR MIND.
WHAT DO YOU SEE?
RED.
AH, THAT'S THE FIRE IN YOU--IT'S ALWAYS CLOSEST.
DIG DEEPER, PAST THE FIRE...
I CAN'T! I JUST FEEL... HEAT! IT'S NOT LIKE HAG'S HEAD--THERE WAS WATER EVERYWHERE THEN!

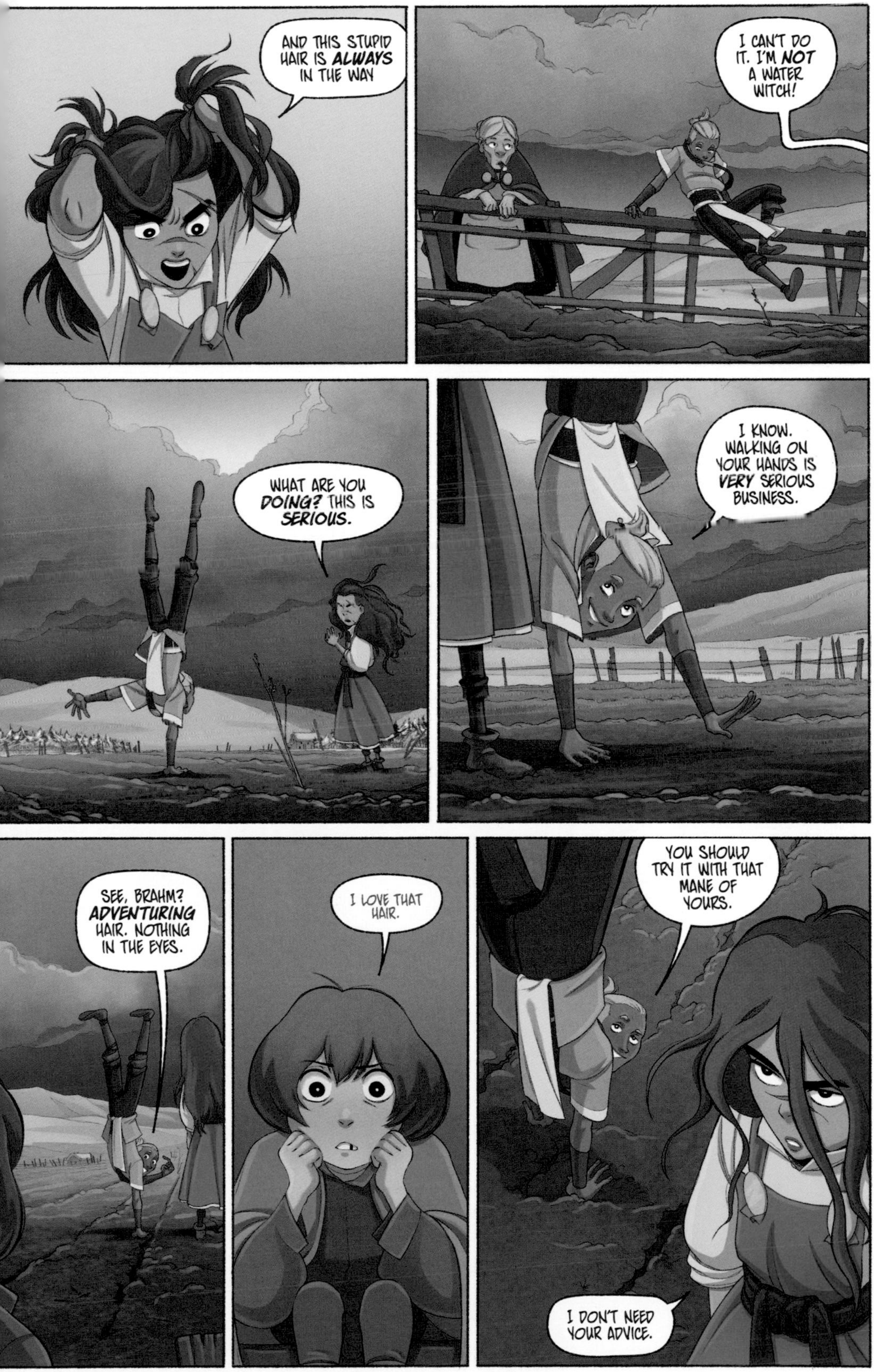
AND THIS STUPID HAIR IS **ALWAYS** IN THE WAY
I CAN'T DO IT. I'M **NOT** A WATER WITCH!
WHAT ARE YOU **DOING?** THIS IS **SERIOUS.**
I KNOW. WALKING ON YOUR HANDS IS **VERY** SERIOUS BUSINESS.
SEE, BRAHM? **ADVENTURING** HAIR. NOTHING IN THE EYES.
I LOVE THAT HAIR.
YOU SHOULD TRY IT WITH THAT MANE OF YOURS.
I DON'T NEED YOUR ADVICE.

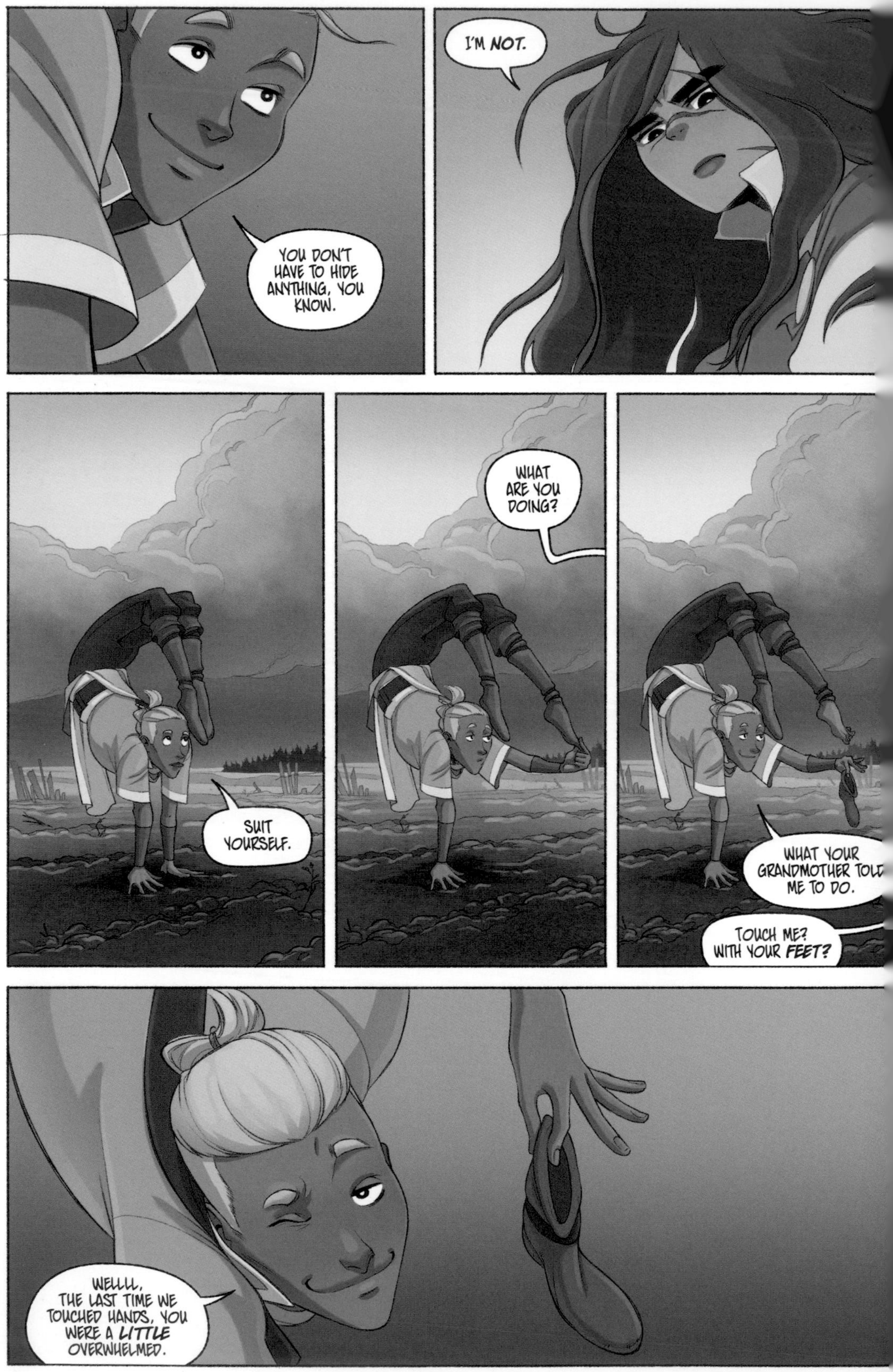
YOU DON'T HAVE TO HIDE ANYTHING, YOU KNOW.
I'M NOT.
SUIT YOURSELF.
WHAT ARE YOU DOING?
WHAT YOUR GRANDMOTHER TOLD ME TO DO.
TOUCH ME? WITH YOUR FEET?
WELLLL, THE LAST TIME WE TOUCHED HANDS, YOU WERE A LITTLE OVERWHELMED.

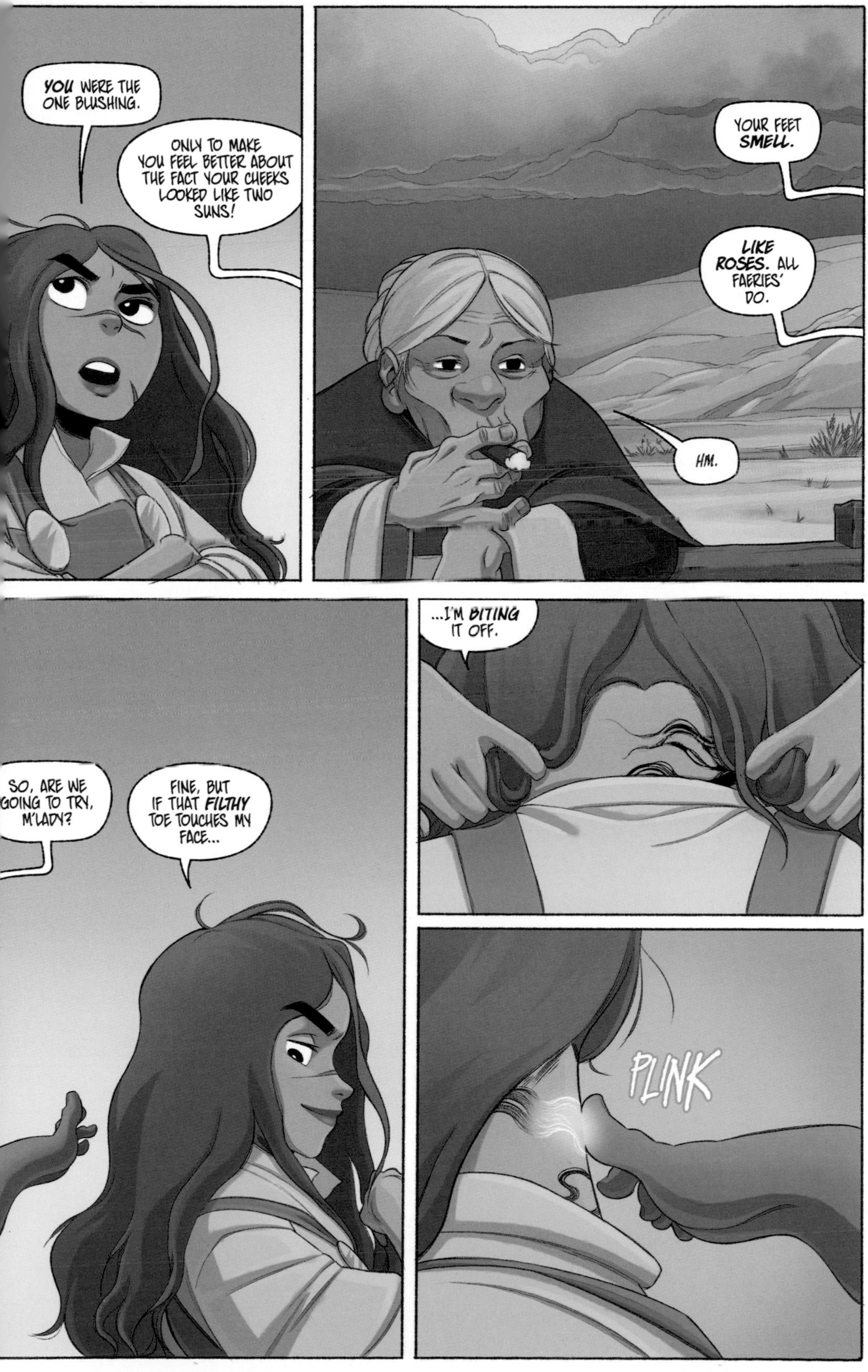
YOU WERE THE ONE BLUSHING.
ONLY TO MAKE YOU FEEL BETTER ABOUT THE FACT YOUR CHEEKS LOOKED LIKE TWO SUNS!
YOUR FEET SMELL.
LIKE ROSES. ALL FAERIES' DO.
HM.
SO, ARE WE GOING TO TRY, M'LADY?
FINE, BUT IF THAT FILTHY TOE TOUCHES MY FACE...
...I'M BITING IT OFF.
PLINK

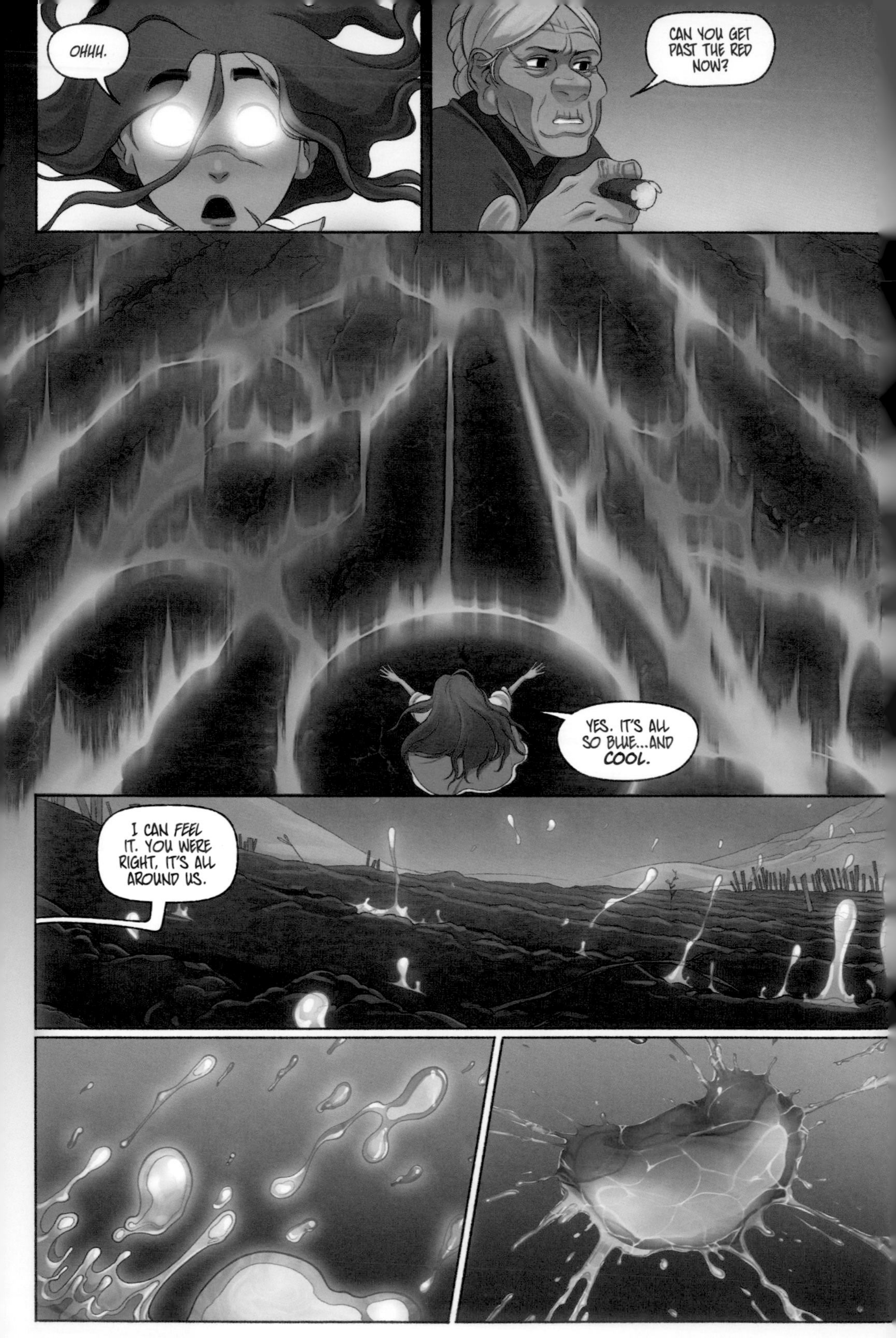
OHHH.
CAN YOU GET PAST THE RED NOW?
YES. IT'S ALL SO BLUE...AND COOL.
I CAN FEEL IT. YOU WERE RIGHT, IT'S ALL AROUND US.

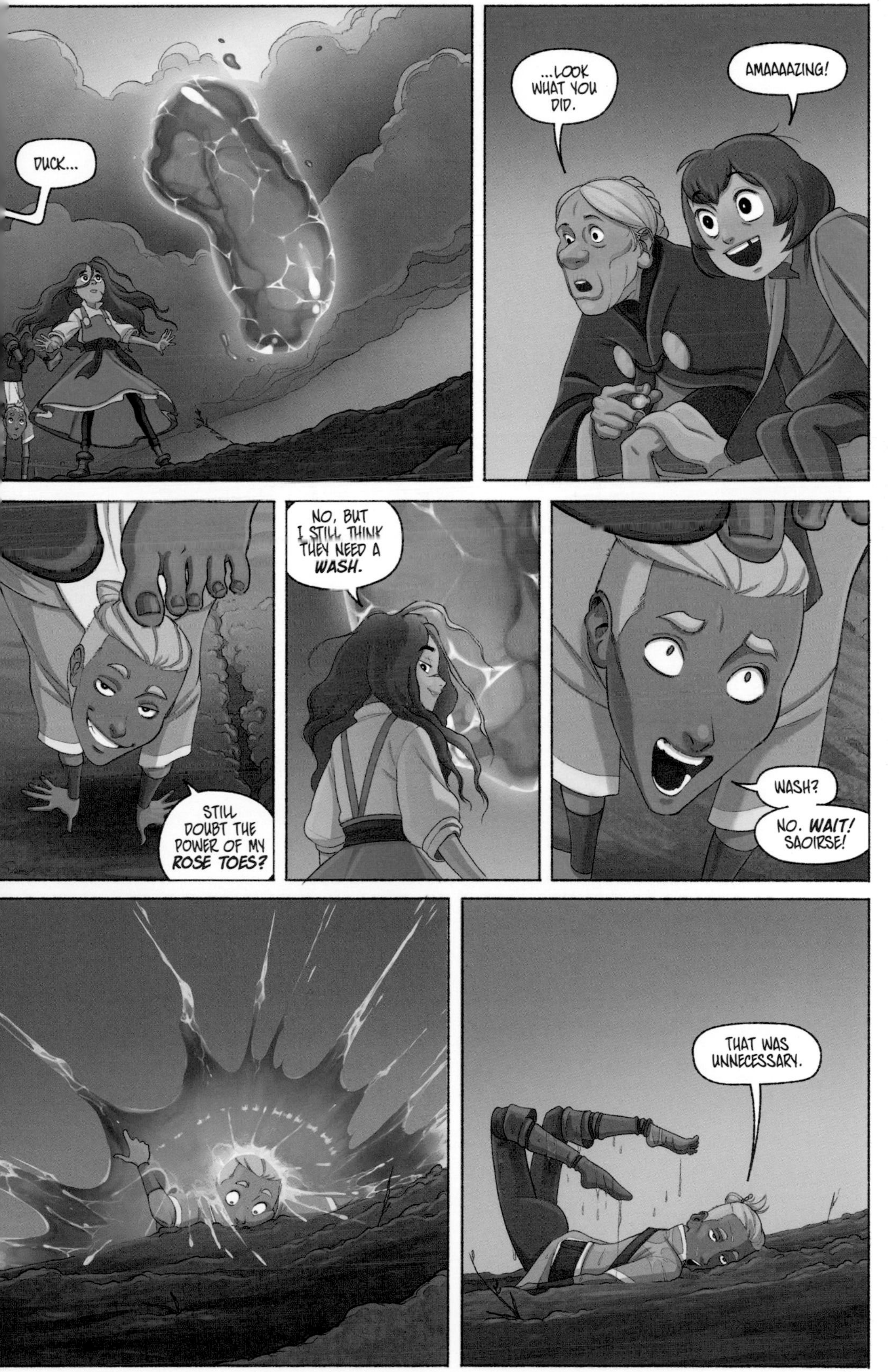
DUCK...
...LOOK WHAT YOU DID.
AMAAAAZING!
STILL DOUBT THE POWER OF MY ROSE TOES?
NO, BUT I STILL THINK THEY NEED A WASH.
WASH?
NO. WAIT! SAOIRSE!
THAT WAS UNNECESSARY.

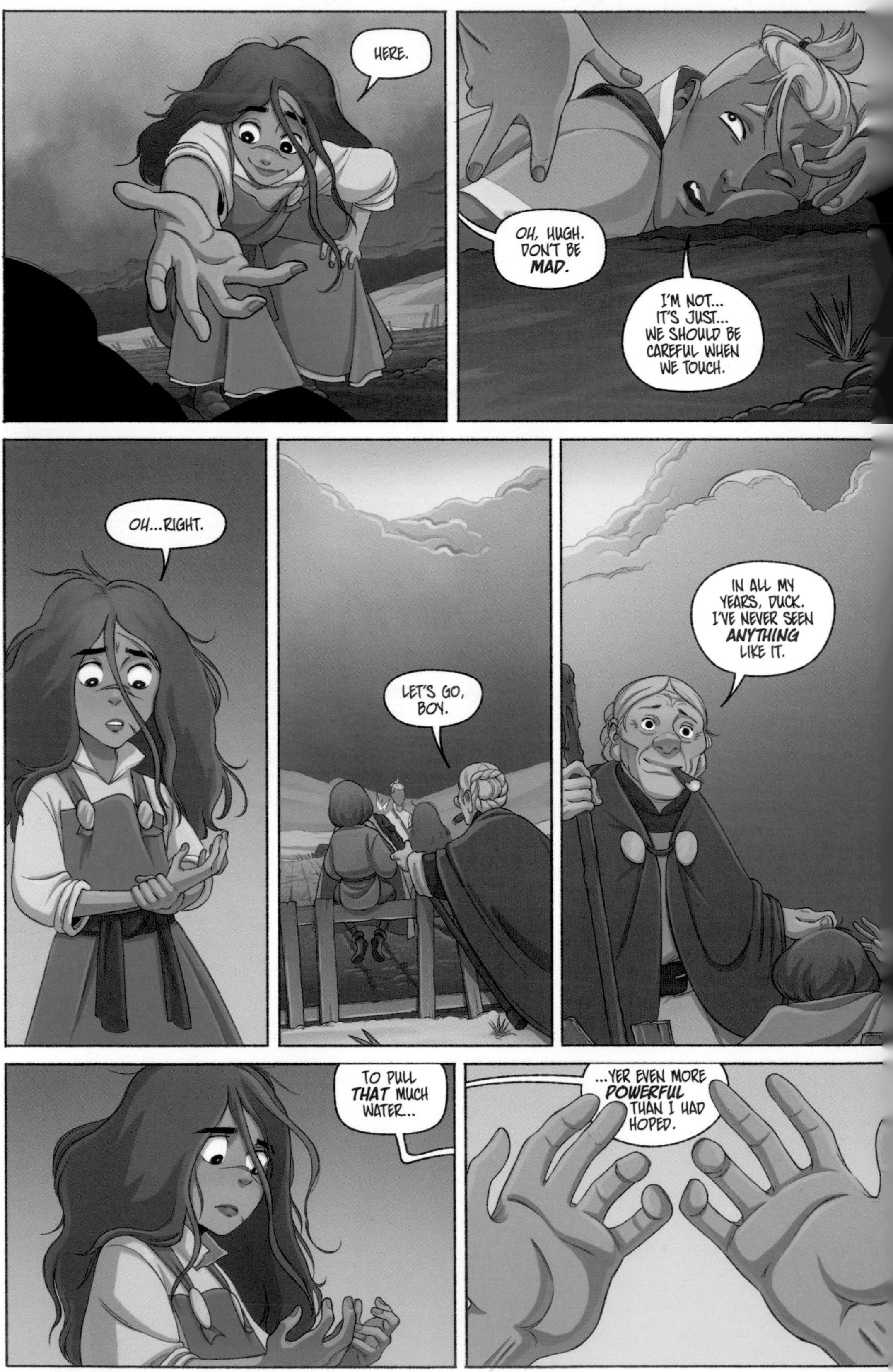
HERE.
OH, HUGH. DON'T BE MAD.
I'M NOT... IT'S JUST... WE SHOULD BE CAREFUL WHEN WE TOUCH.
OH...RIGHT.
LET'S GO, BOY.
IN ALL MY YEARS, DUCK. I'VE NEVER SEEN ANYTHING LIKE IT.
TO PULL THAT MUCH WATER...
...YER EVEN MORE POWERFUL THAN I HAD HOPED.

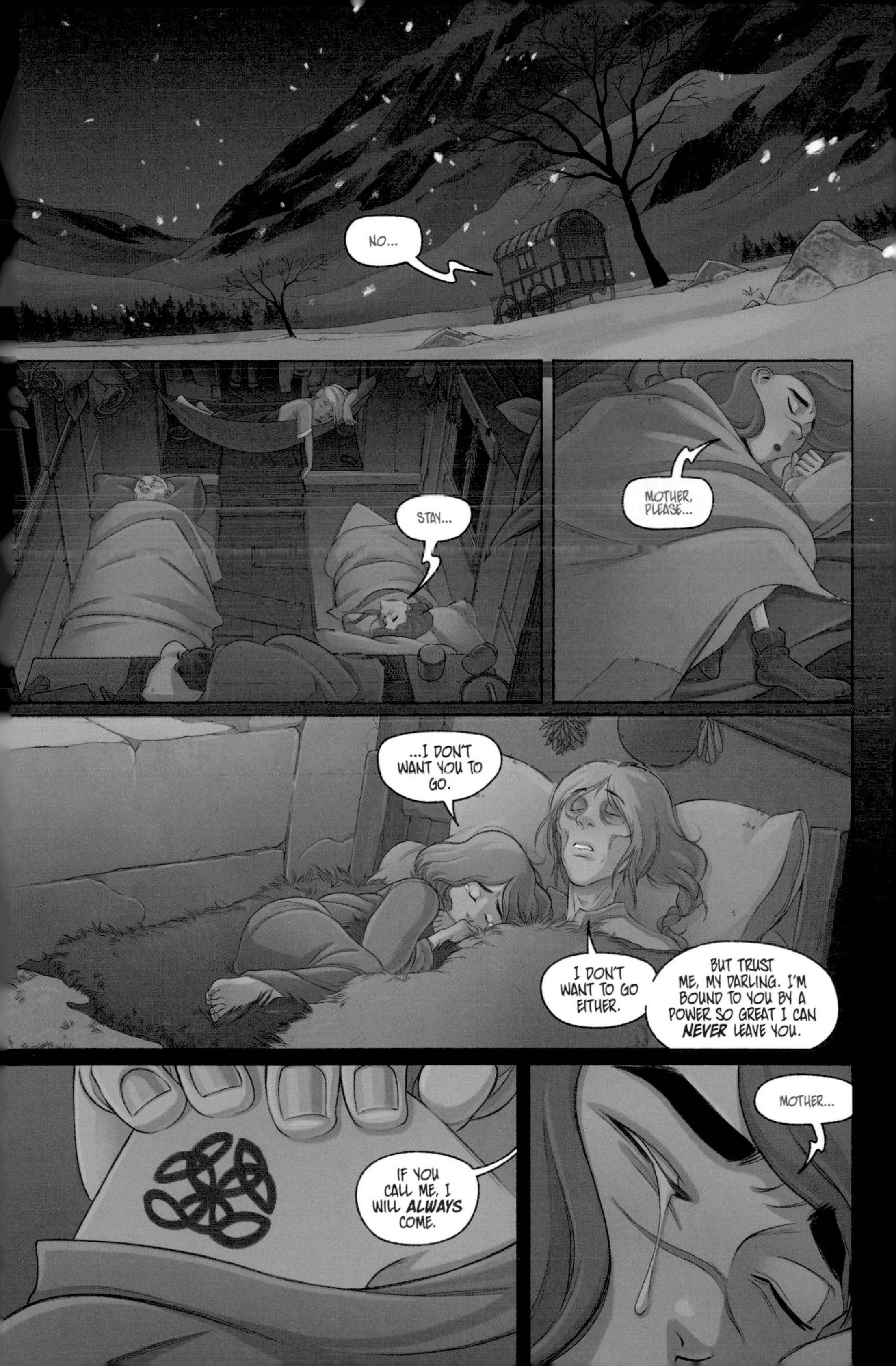
NO...
STAY...
MOTHER, PLEASE...
...I DON'T WANT YOU TO GO.
I DON'T WANT TO GO EITHER.
BUT TRUST ME, MY DARLING. I'M BOUND TO YOU BY A POWER SO GREAT I CAN NEVER LEAVE YOU.
IF YOU CALL ME, I WILL ALWAYS COME.
MOTHER...

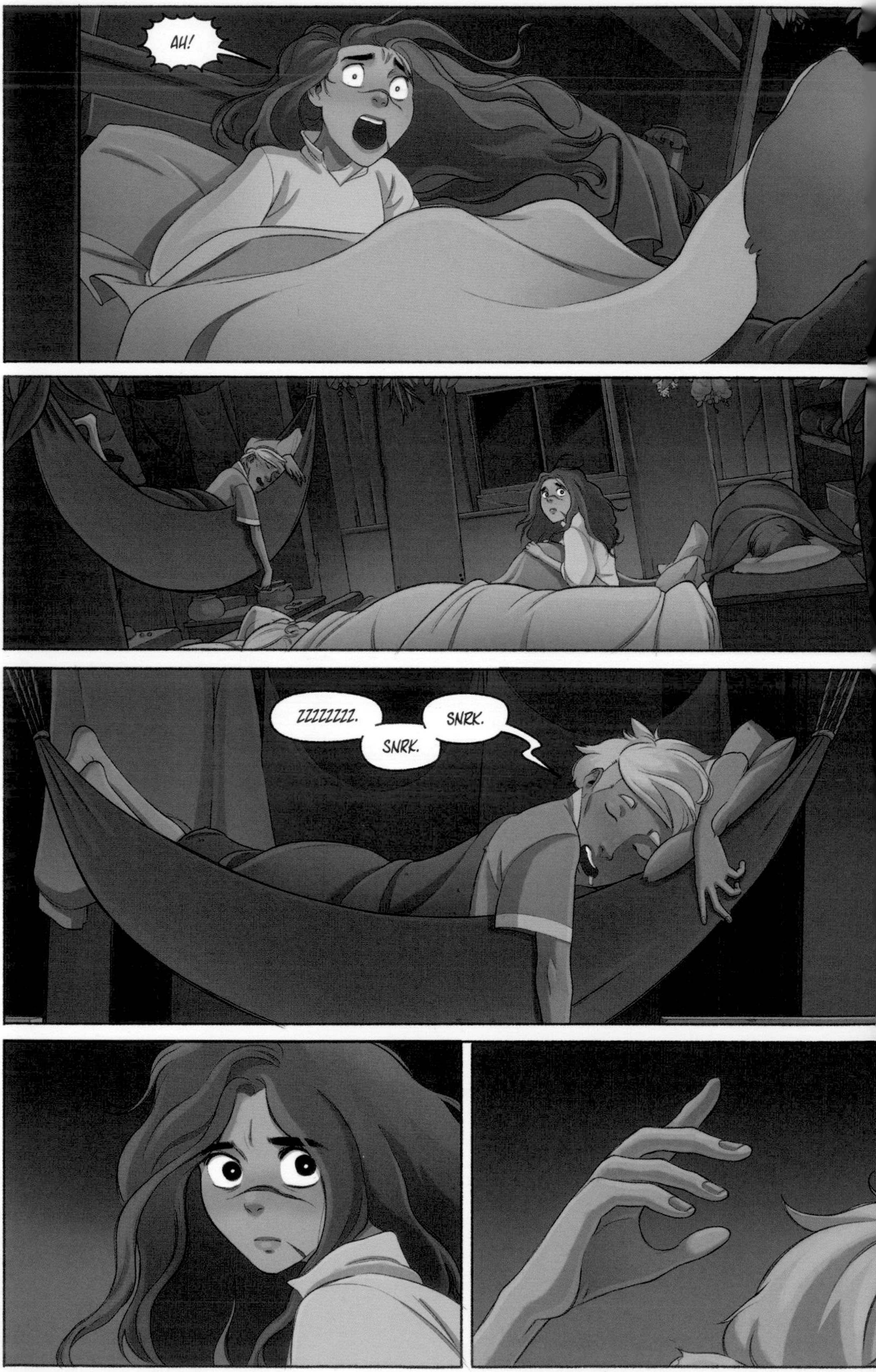
AH!
ZZZZZZZZ.
SNRK.
SNRK.

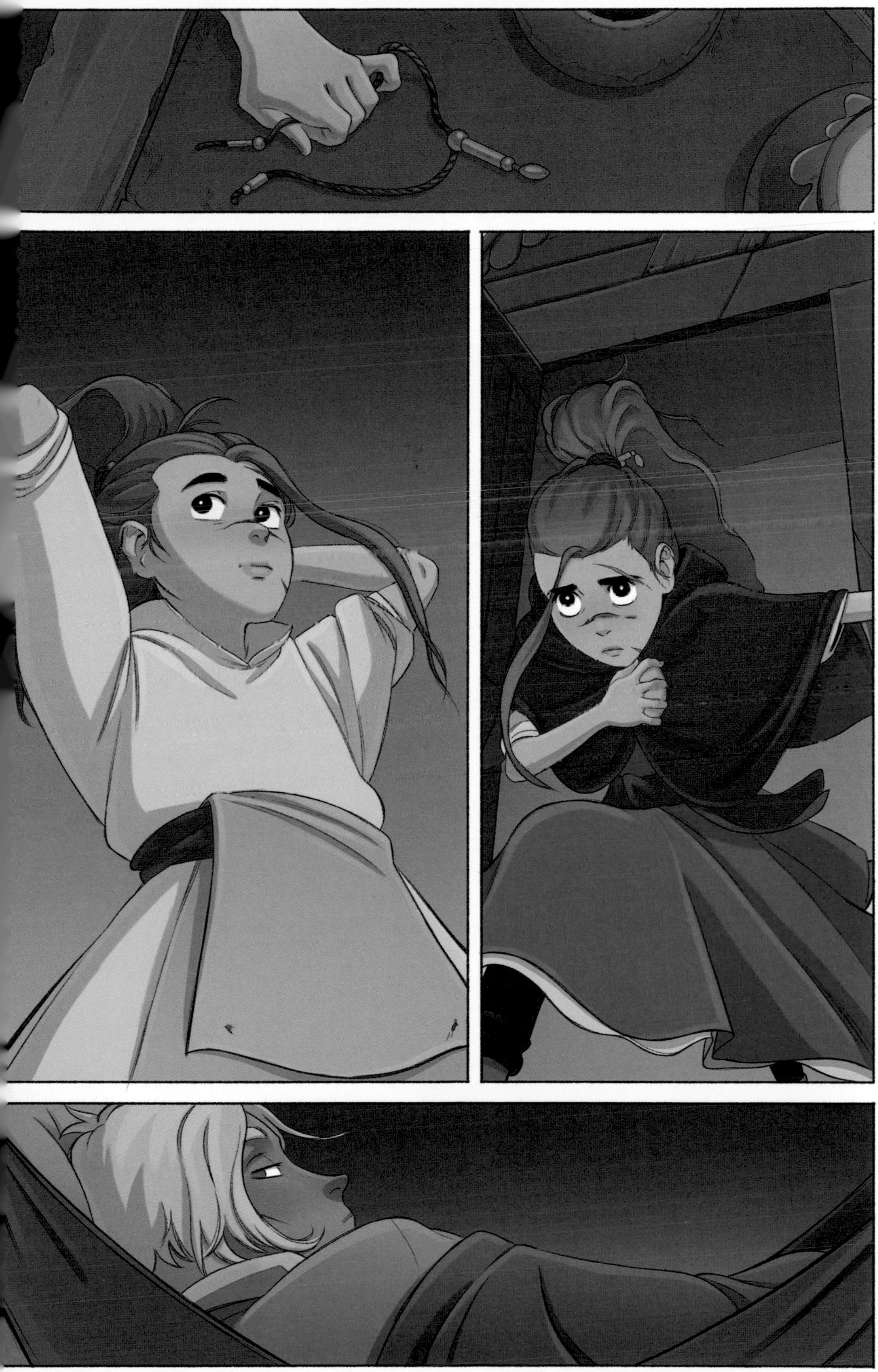

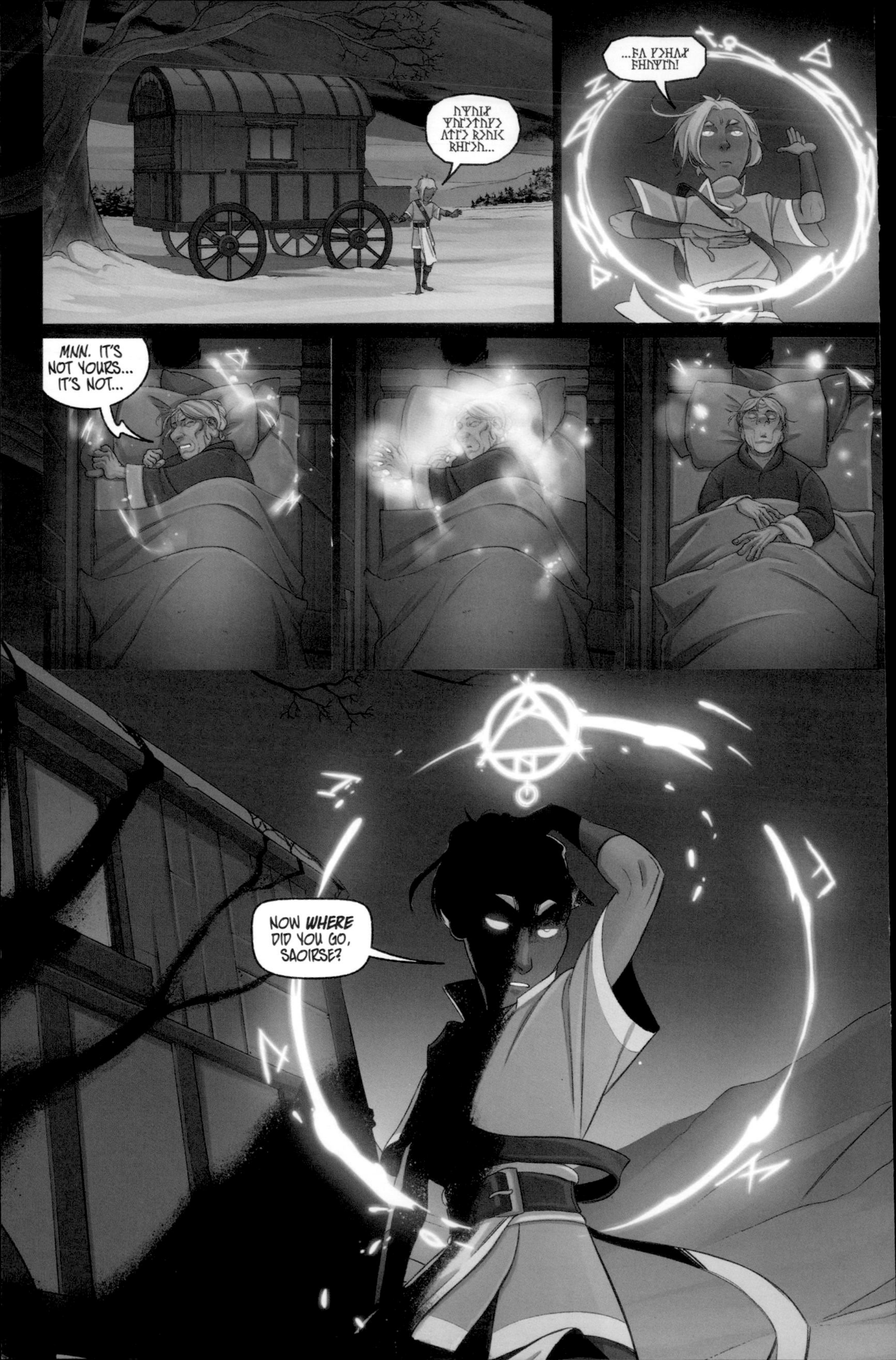

MNN. IT'S NOT YOURS... IT'S NOT...
NOW WHERE DID YOU GO, SAOIRSE?

CHAPTER **FIVE**

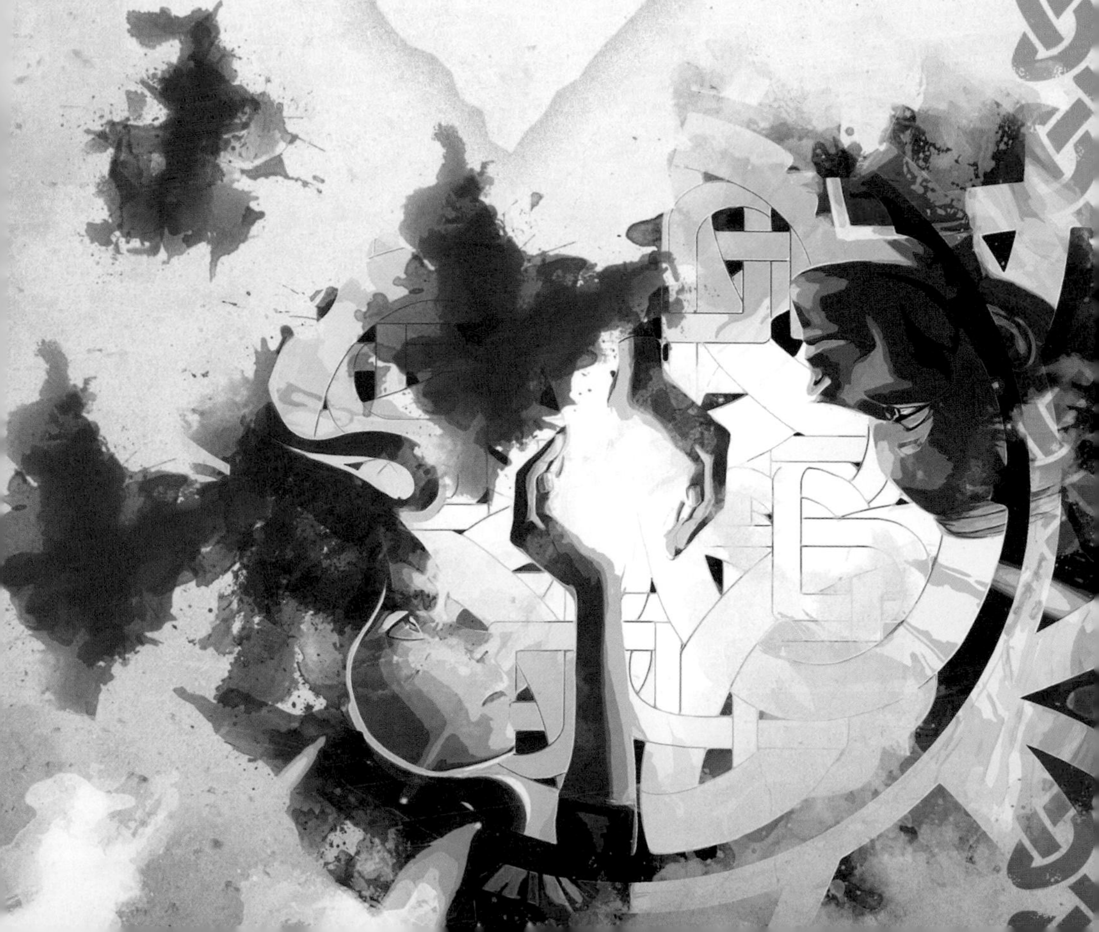

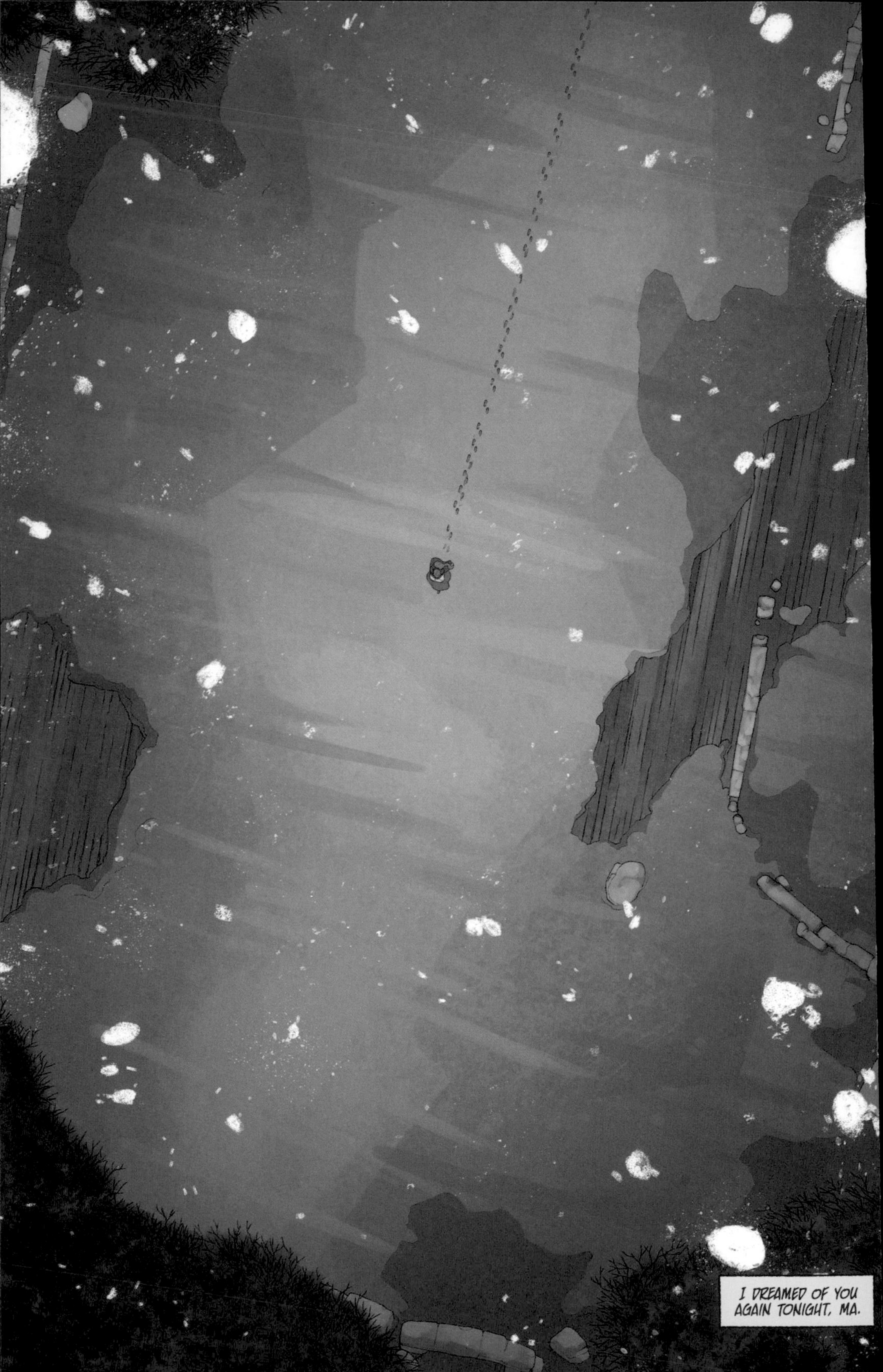
I DREAMED OF YOU AGAIN TONIGHT, MA.

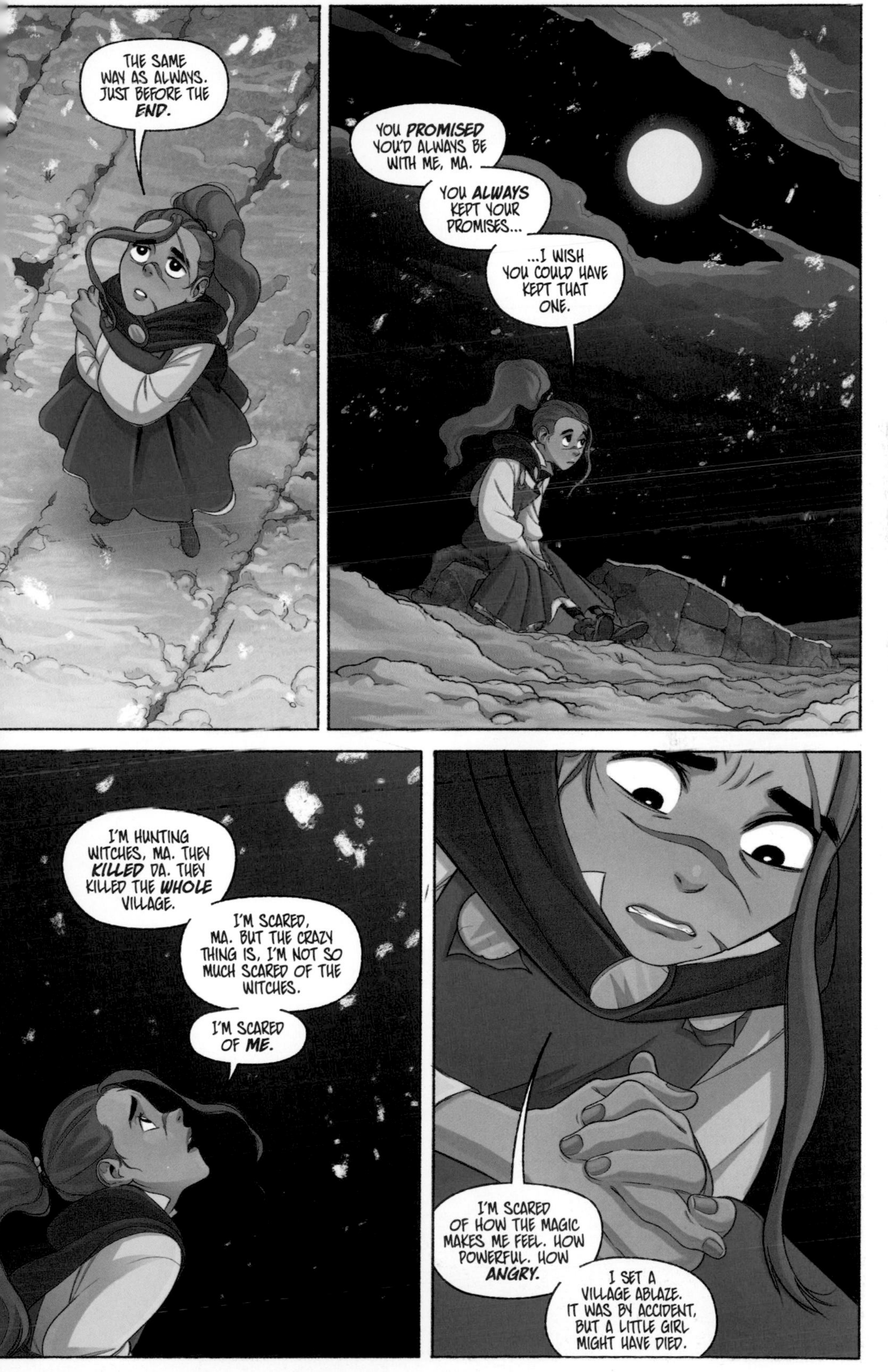
THE SAME WAY AS ALWAYS. JUST BEFORE THE END.
YOU PROMISED YOU'D ALWAYS BE WITH ME, MA.
YOU ALWAYS KEPT YOUR PROMISES...
...I WISH YOU COULD HAVE KEPT THAT ONE.
I'M HUNTING WITCHES, MA. THEY KILLED DA. THEY KILLED THE WHOLE VILLAGE.
I'M SCARED, MA. BUT THE CRAZY THING IS, I'M NOT SO MUCH SCARED OF THE WITCHES.
I'M SCARED OF ME.
I'M SCARED OF HOW THE MAGIC MAKES ME FEEL. HOW POWERFUL. HOW ANGRY.
I SET A VILLAGE ABLAZE. IT WAS BY ACCIDENT, BUT A LITTLE GIRL MIGHT HAVE DIED.

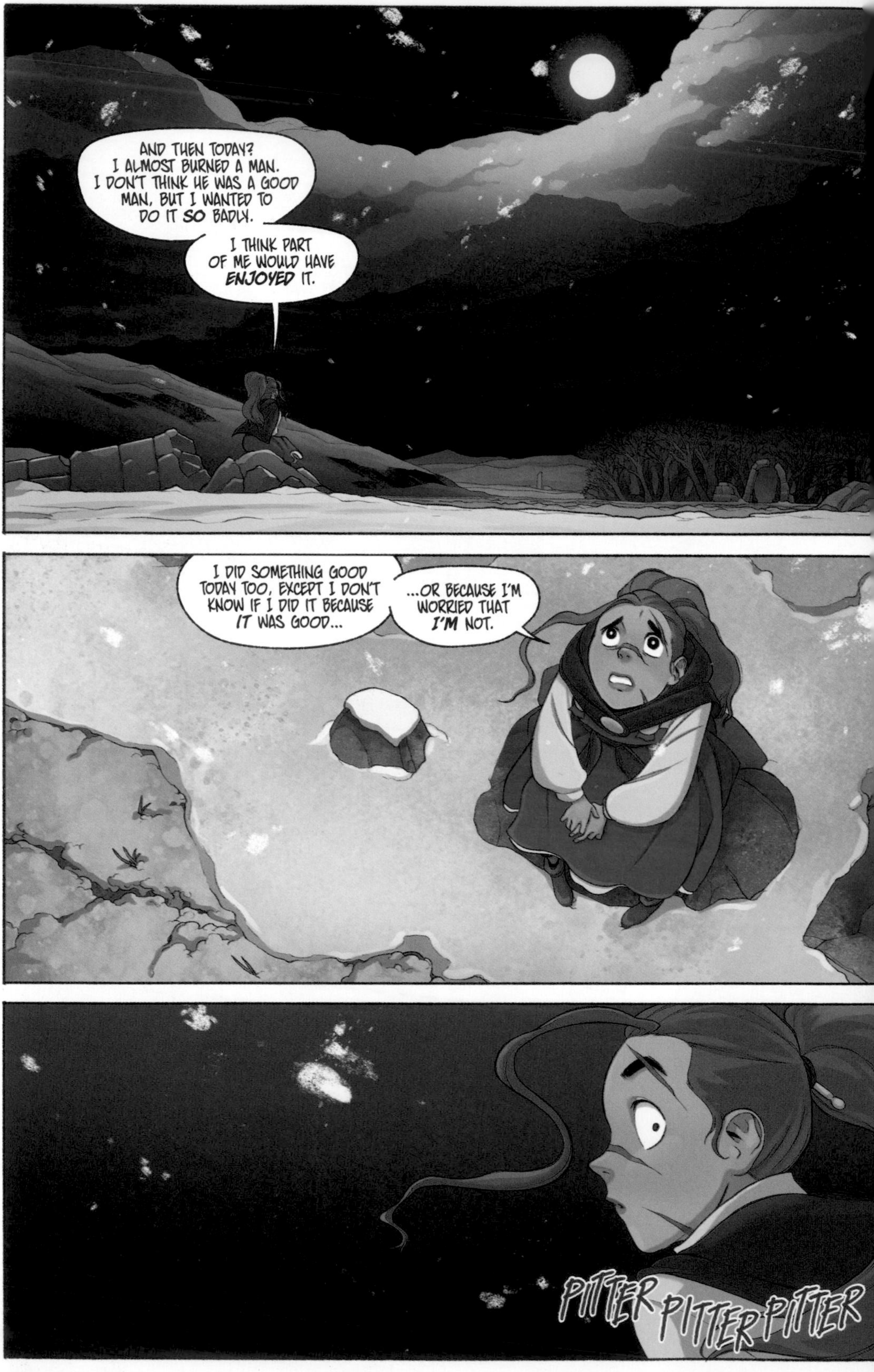
AND THEN TODAY? I ALMOST BURNED A MAN. I DON'T THINK HE WAS A GOOD MAN, BUT I WANTED TO DO IT SO BADLY.
I THINK PART OF ME WOULD HAVE ENJOYED IT.
I DID SOMETHING GOOD TODAY TOO, EXCEPT I DON'T KNOW IF I DID IT BECAUSE IT WAS GOOD...
...OR BECAUSE I'M WORRIED THAT I'M NOT.
PITTER PITTER PITTER

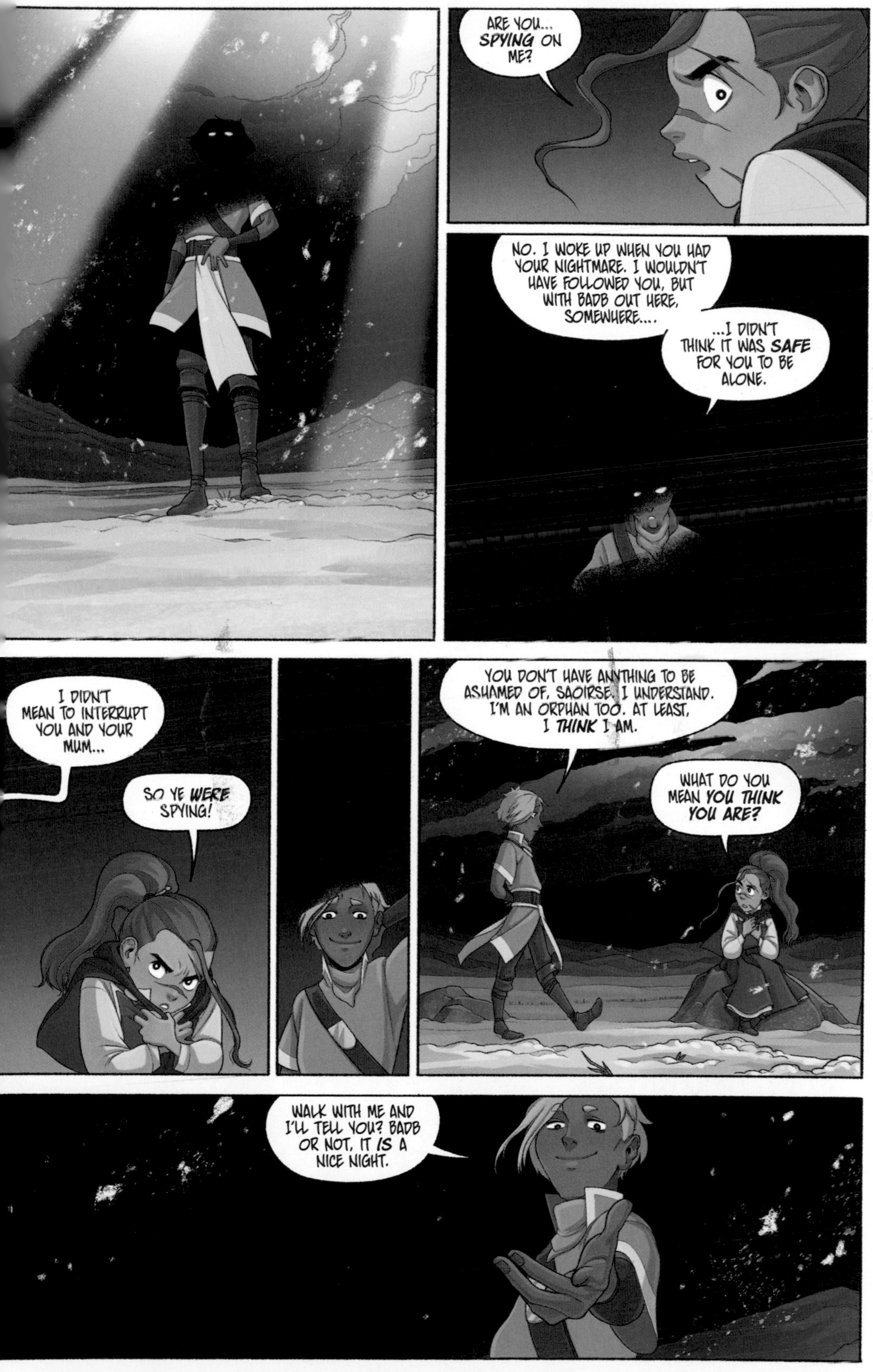
ARE YOU... SPYING ON ME?
NO. I WOKE UP WHEN YOU HAD YOUR NIGHTMARE. I WOULDN'T HAVE FOLLOWED YOU, BUT WITH BADB OUT HERE, SOMEWHERE....
...I DIDN'T THINK IT WAS SAFE FOR YOU TO BE ALONE.
I DIDN'T MEAN TO INTERRUPT YOU AND YOUR MUM...
SO YE WERE SPYING!
YOU DON'T HAVE ANYTHING TO BE ASHAMED OF, SAOIRSE. I UNDERSTAND. I'M AN ORPHAN TOO. AT LEAST, I THINK I AM.
WHAT DO YOU MEAN YOU THINK YOU ARE?
WALK WITH ME AND I'LL TELL YOU? BADB OR NOT, IT IS A NICE NIGHT.

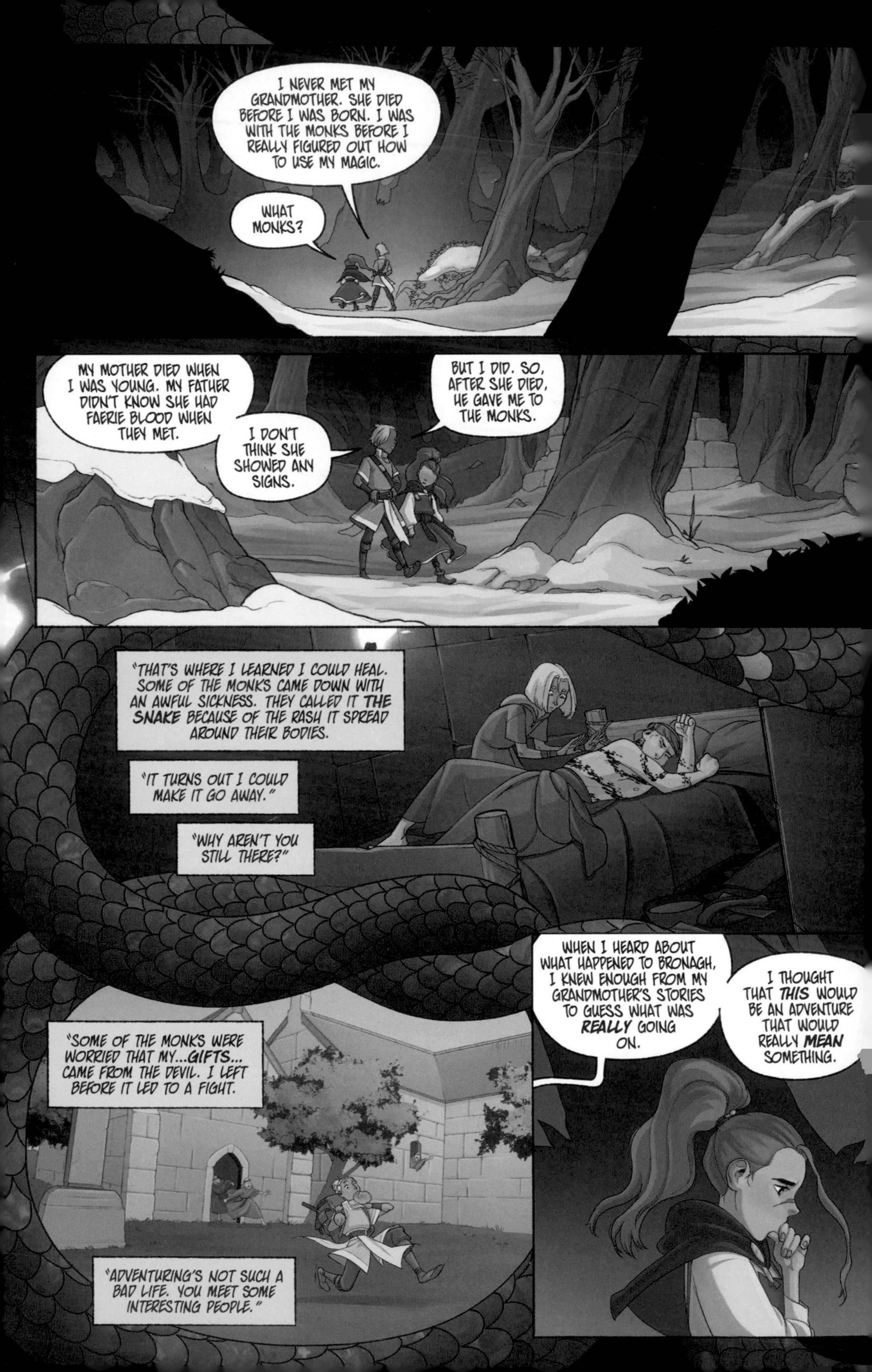
I NEVER MET MY GRANDMOTHER. SHE DIED BEFORE I WAS BORN. I WAS WITH THE MONKS BEFORE I REALLY FIGURED OUT HOW TO USE MY MAGIC.
WHAT MONKS?
MY MOTHER DIED WHEN I WAS YOUNG. MY FATHER DIDN'T KNOW SHE HAD FAERIE BLOOD WHEN THEY MET.
I DON'T THINK SHE SHOWED ANY SIGNS.
BUT I DID. SO, AFTER SHE DIED, HE GAVE ME TO THE MONKS.
"THAT'S WHERE I LEARNED I COULD HEAL. SOME OF THE MONKS CAME DOWN WITH AN AWFUL SICKNESS. THEY CALLED IT **THE SNAKE** BECAUSE OF THE RASH IT SPREAD AROUND THEIR BODIES.
"IT TURNS OUT I COULD MAKE IT GO AWAY."
"WHY AREN'T YOU STILL THERE?"
"SOME OF THE MONKS WERE WORRIED THAT MY...**GIFTS**... CAME FROM THE DEVIL. I LEFT BEFORE IT LED TO A FIGHT.
"ADVENTURING'S NOT SUCH A BAD LIFE. YOU MEET SOME INTERESTING PEOPLE."
WHEN I HEARD ABOUT WHAT HAPPENED TO BRONAGH, I KNEW ENOUGH FROM MY GRANDMOTHER'S STORIES TO GUESS WHAT WAS **REALLY** GOING ON.
I THOUGHT THAT **THIS** WOULD BE AN ADVENTURE THAT WOULD REALLY **MEAN** SOMETHING.

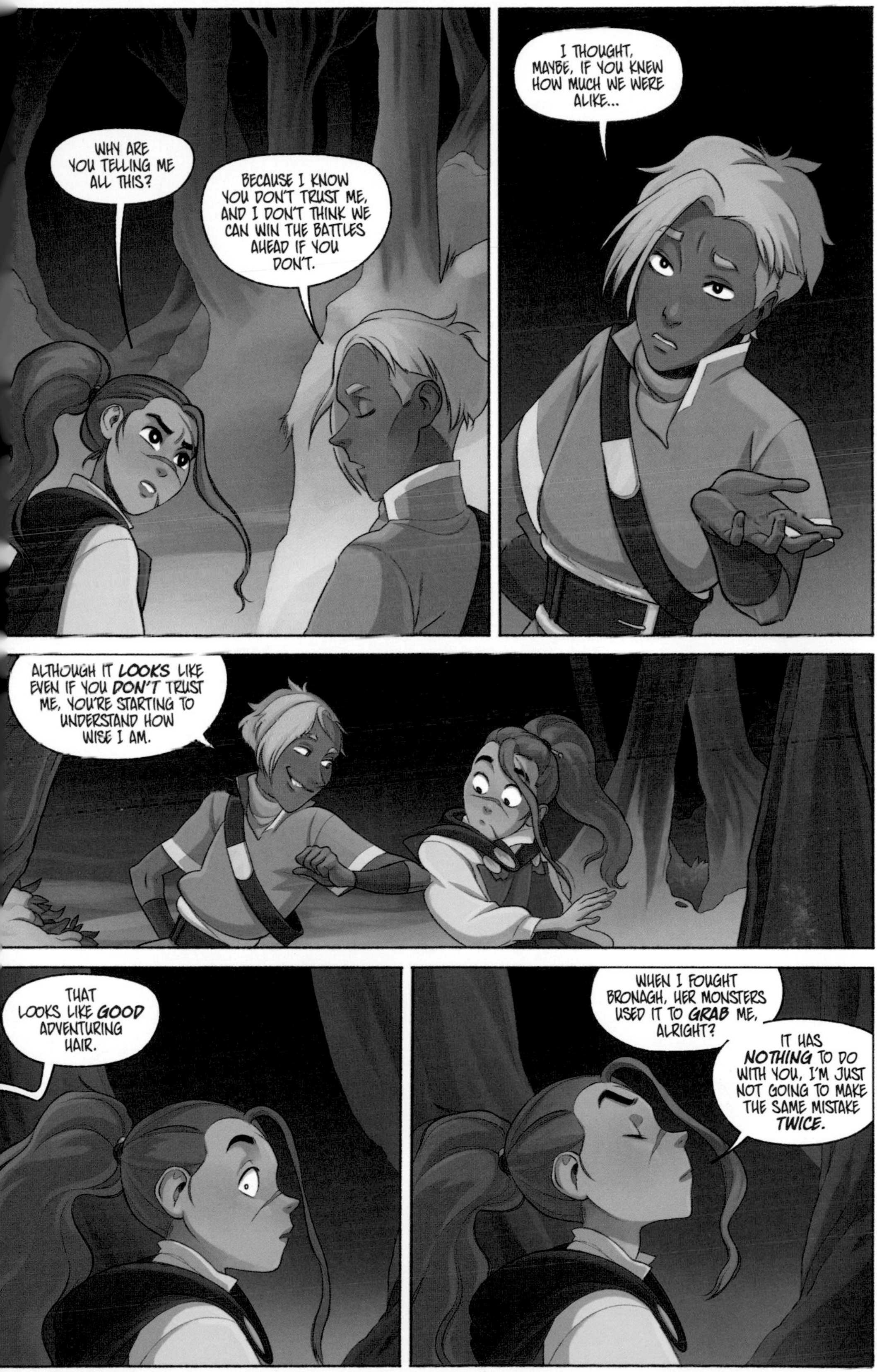
WHY ARE YOU TELLING ME ALL THIS?
BECAUSE I KNOW YOU DON'T TRUST ME, AND I DON'T THINK WE CAN WIN THE BATTLES AHEAD IF YOU DON'T.
I THOUGHT, MAYBE, IF YOU KNEW HOW MUCH WE WERE ALIKE...
ALTHOUGH IT LOOKS LIKE EVEN IF YOU DON'T TRUST ME, YOU'RE STARTING TO UNDERSTAND HOW WISE I AM.
THAT LOOKS LIKE GOOD ADVENTURING HAIR.
WHEN I FOUGHT BRONAGH, HER MONSTERS USED IT TO GRAB ME, ALRIGHT?
IT HAS NOTHING TO DO WITH YOU, I'M JUST NOT GOING TO MAKE THE SAME MISTAKE TWICE.

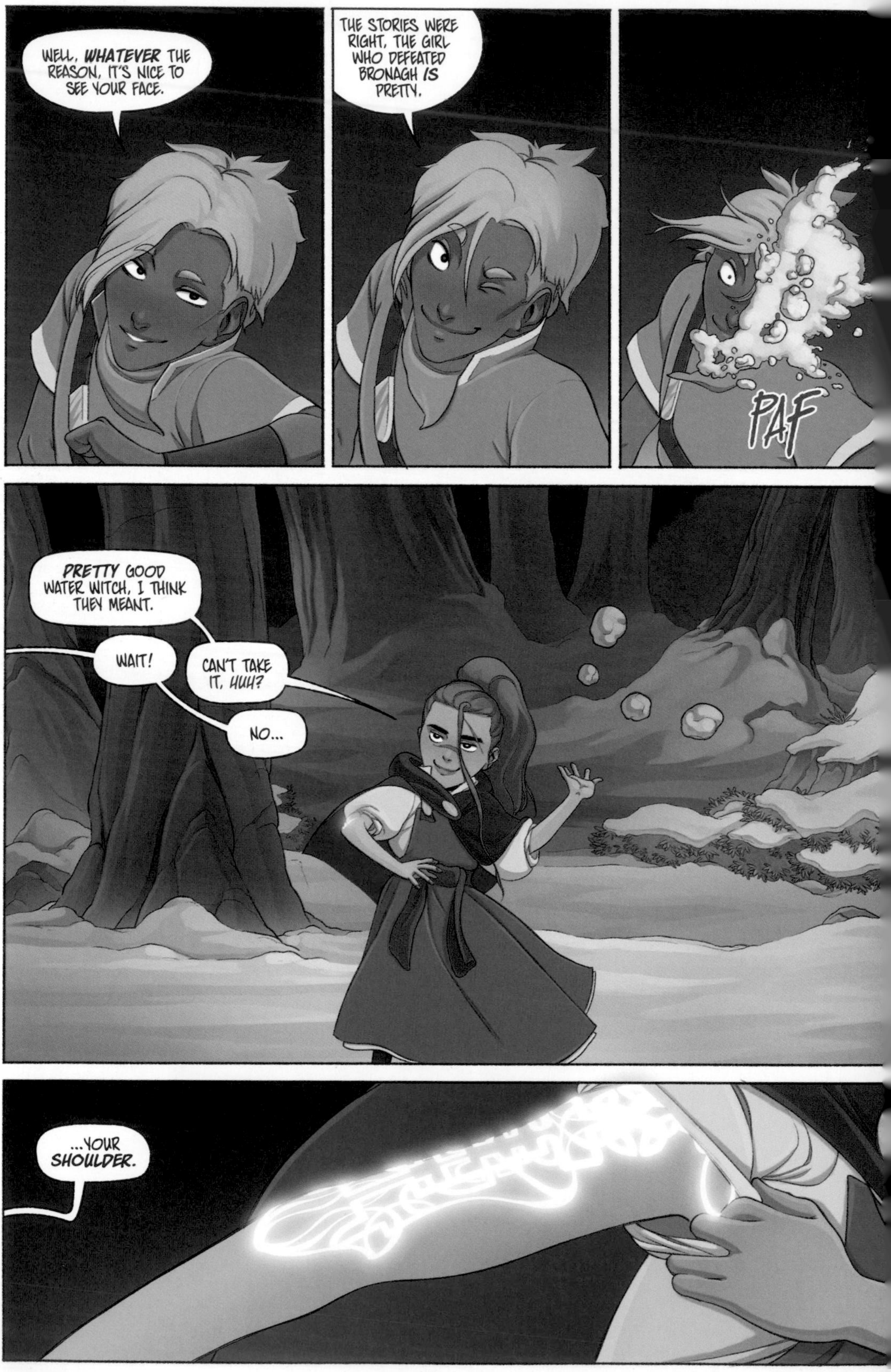
WELL, WHATEVER THE REASON, IT'S NICE TO SEE YOUR FACE.
THE STORIES WERE RIGHT, THE GIRL WHO DEFEATED BRONAGH IS PRETTY.
PAF
PRETTY GOOD WATER WITCH, I THINK THEY MEANT.
CAN'T TAKE IT, HUH?
WAIT!
NO...
...YOUR SHOULDER.

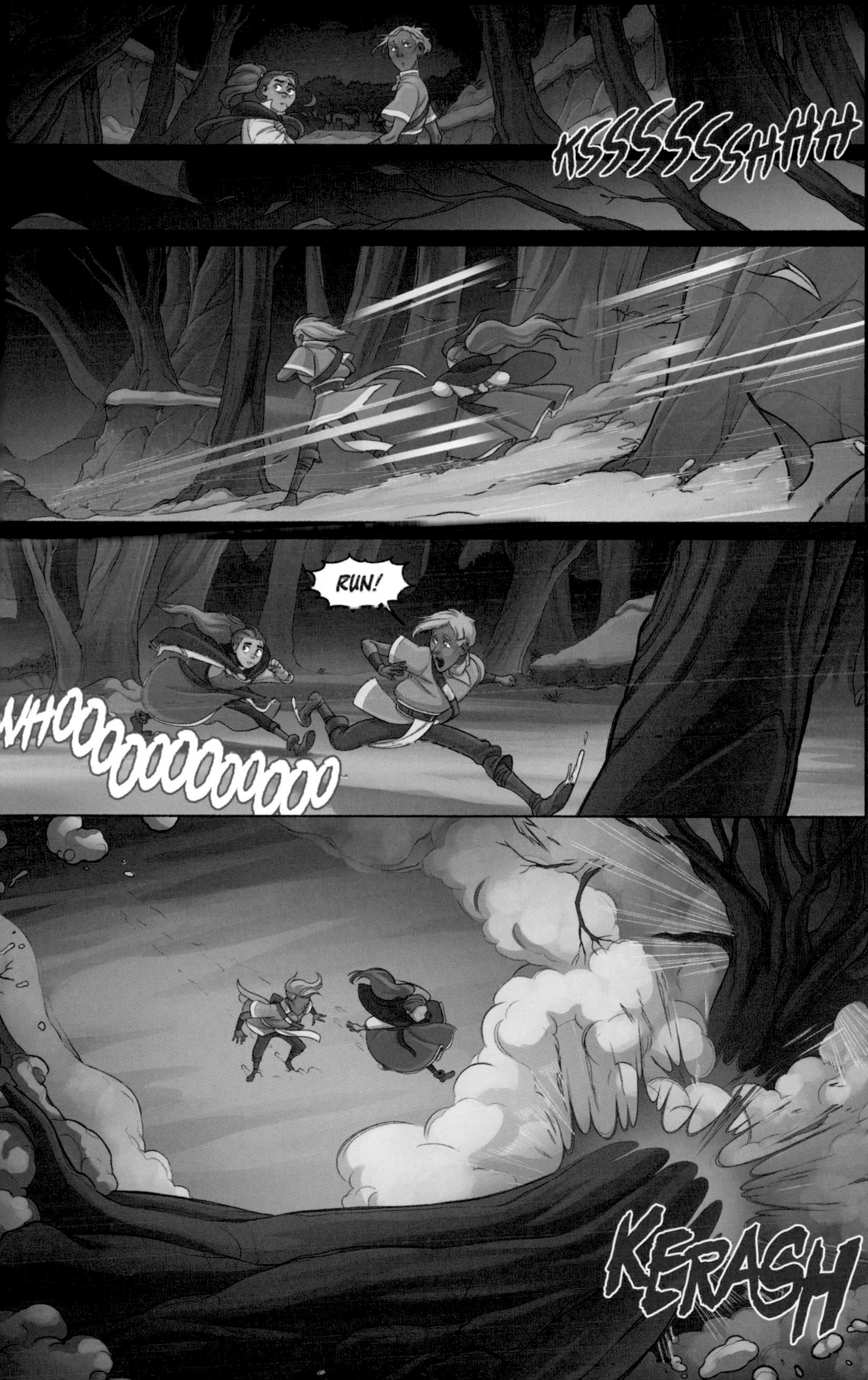
KSSSSSSHHH
RUN!
WHOOOOOOOOOOOO
KERASH

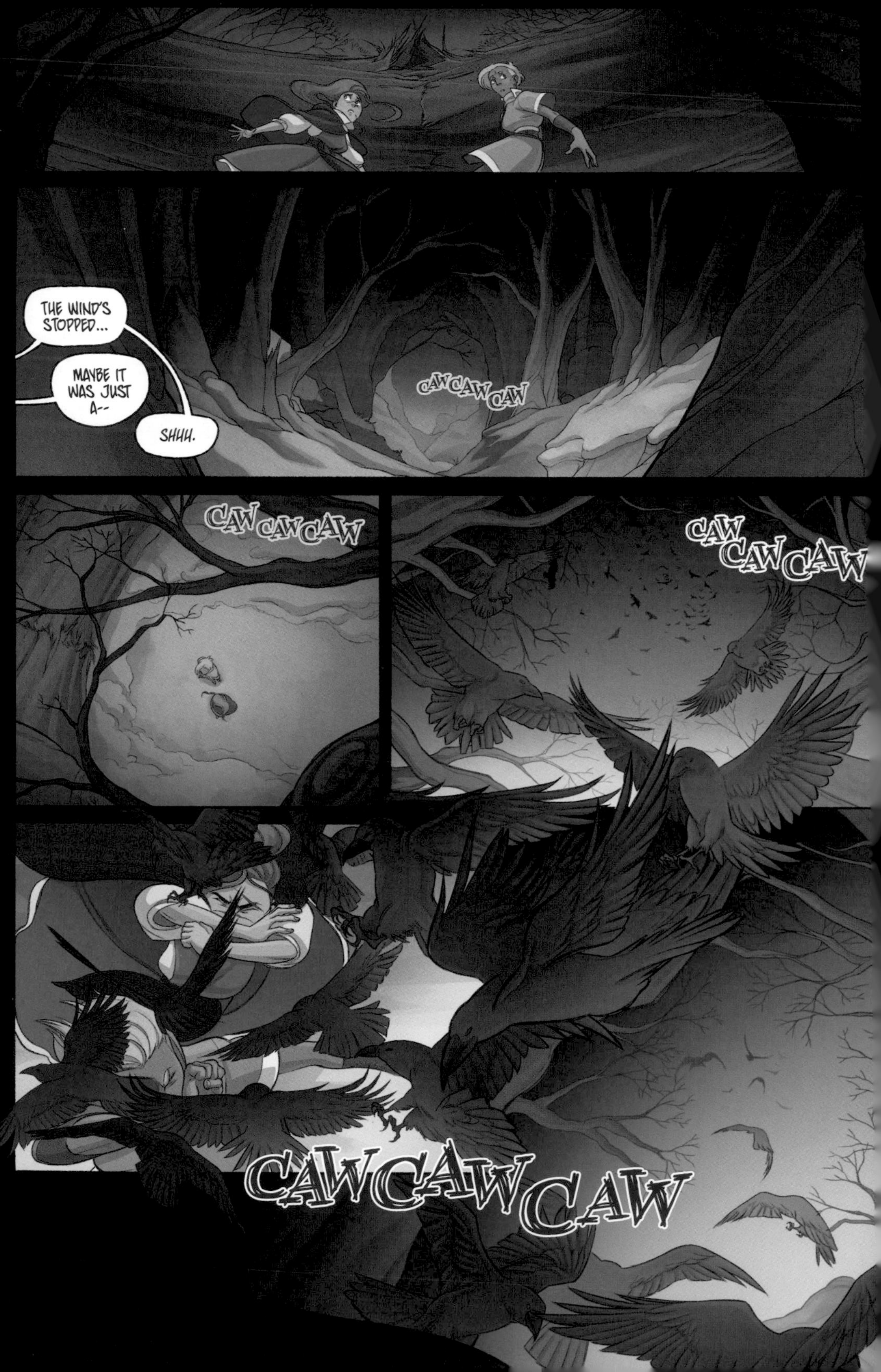

THE WIND'S STOPPED...
MAYBE IT WAS JUST A--
SHHH.
CAW CAW CAW
CAW CAW CAW
CAW CAW CAW
CAW CAW CAW

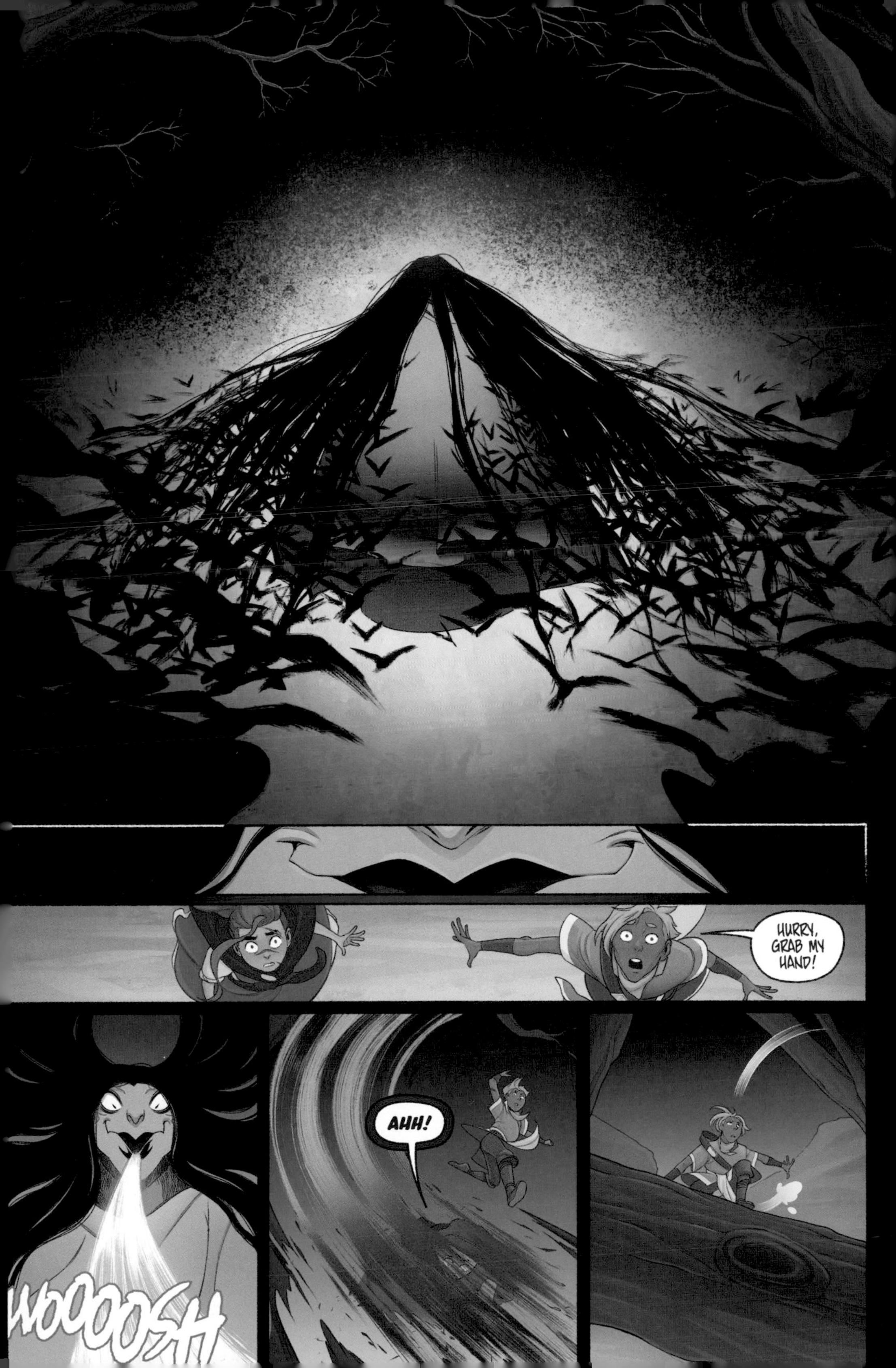
HURRY, GRAB MY HAND!
WOOOOOSH
AHH!

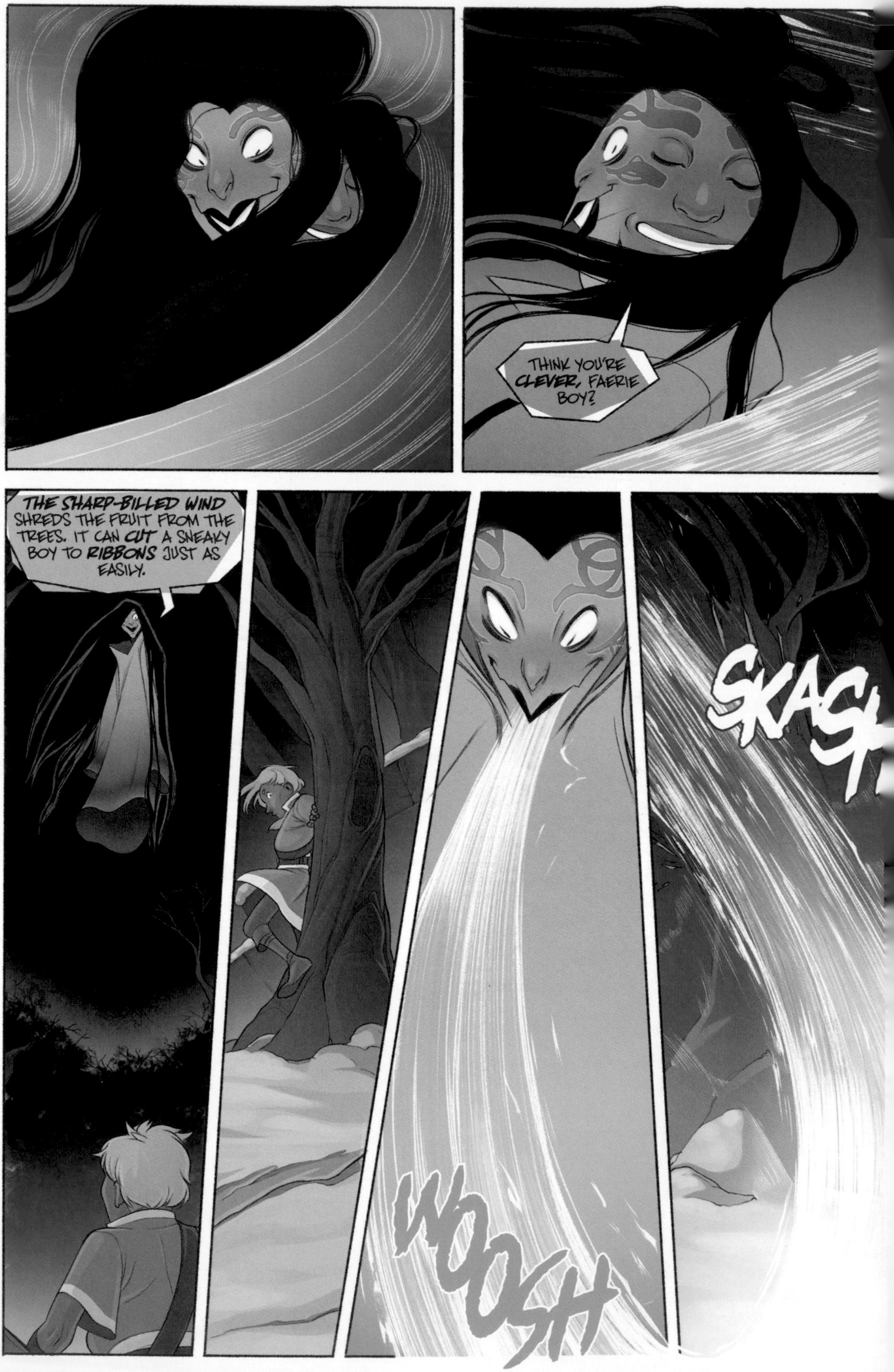
THINK YOU'RE CLEVER, FAERIE BOY?
THE SHARP-BILLED WIND SHREDS THE FRUIT FROM THE TREES. IT CAN CUT A SNEAKY BOY TO RIBBONS JUST AS EASILY.
WOOOSH
SKASH

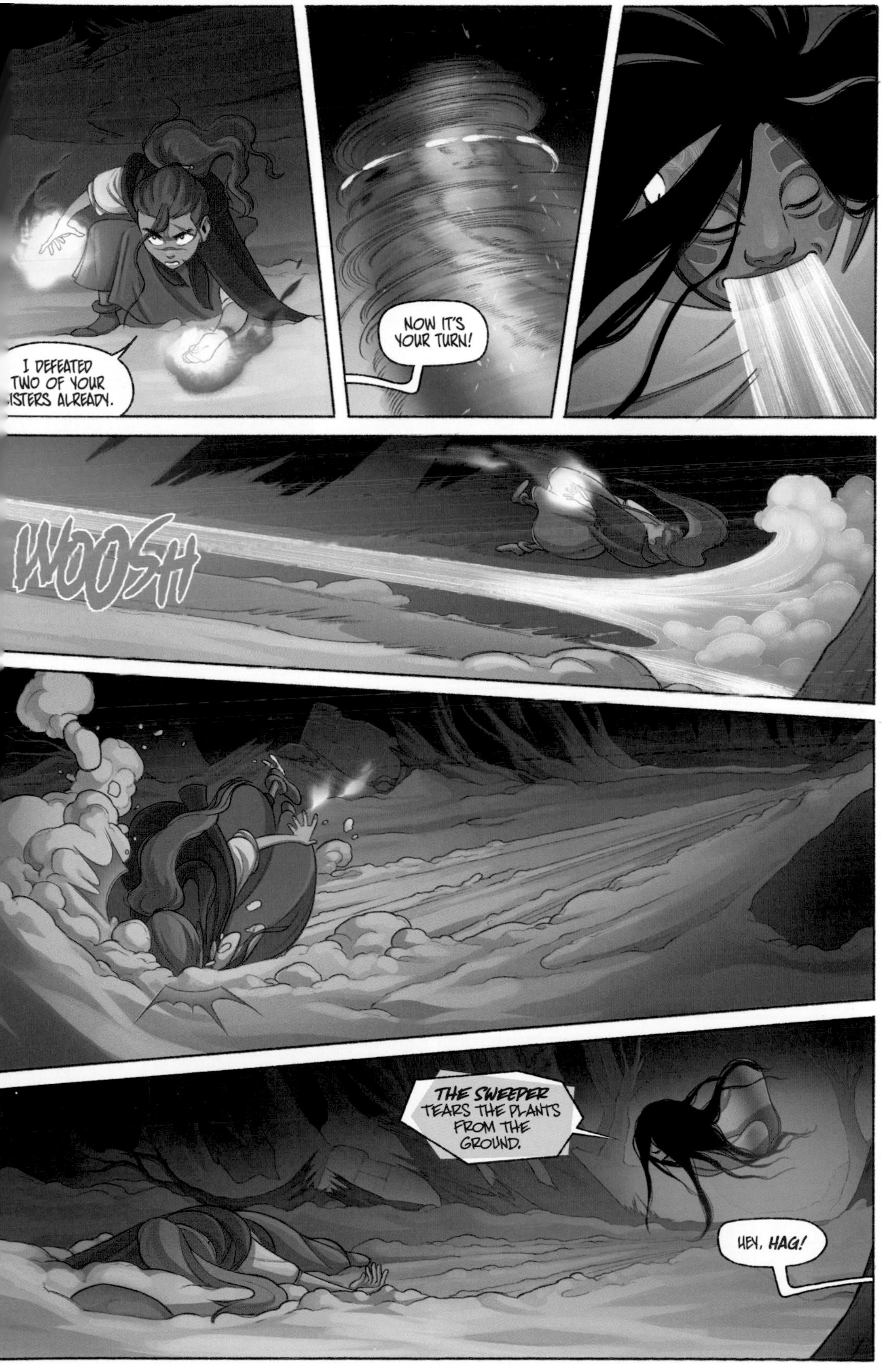
I DEFEATED TWO OF YOUR SISTERS ALREADY.
NOW IT'S YOUR TURN!
WOOSH
THE SWEEPER TEARS THE PLANTS FROM THE GROUND.
HEY, HAG!

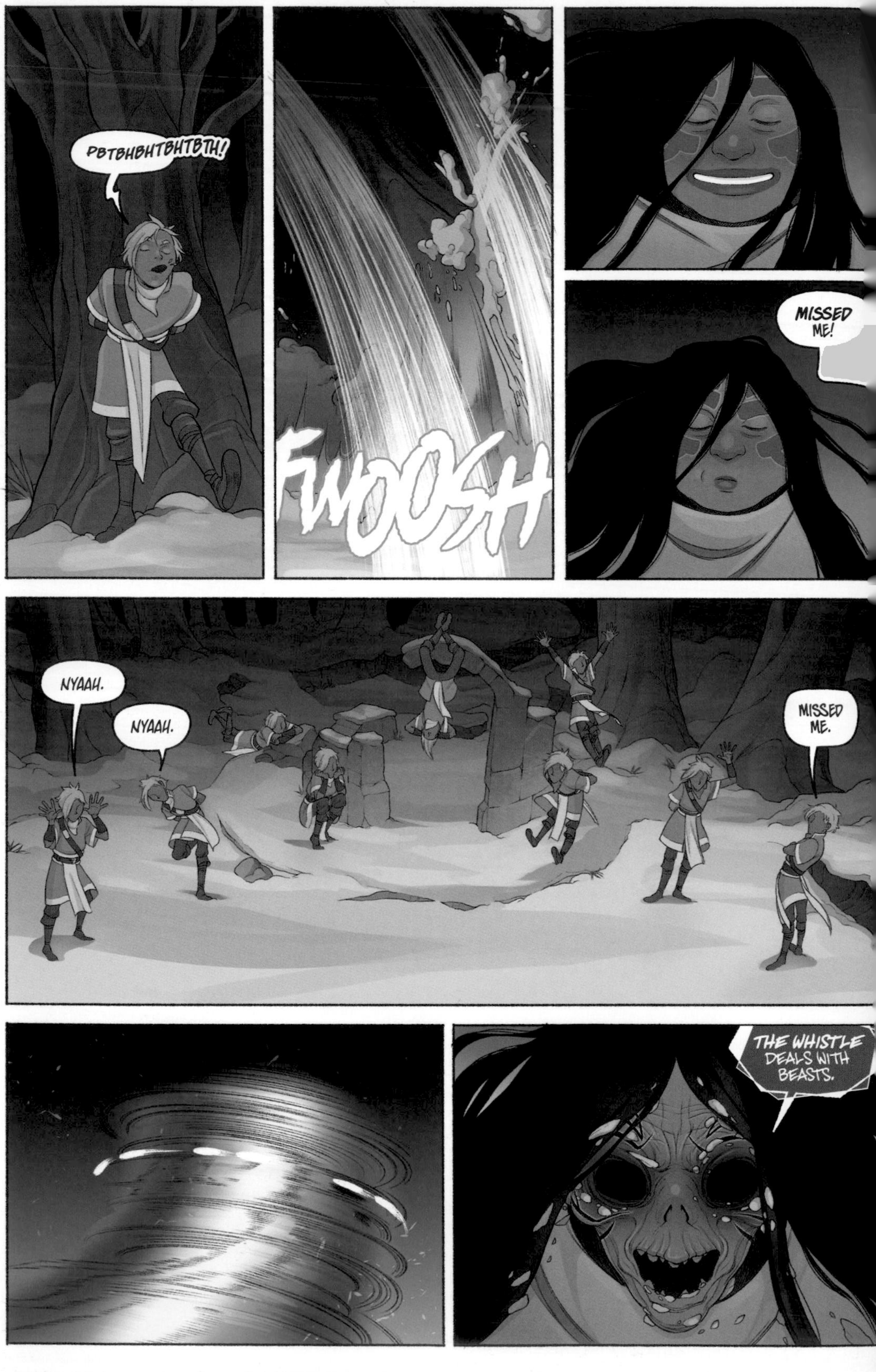
PBTBHBHTBHTBTH!
FWOOSH
MISSED ME!
NYAAH.
NYAAH.
MISSED ME.
THE WHISTLE DEALS WITH BEASTS.

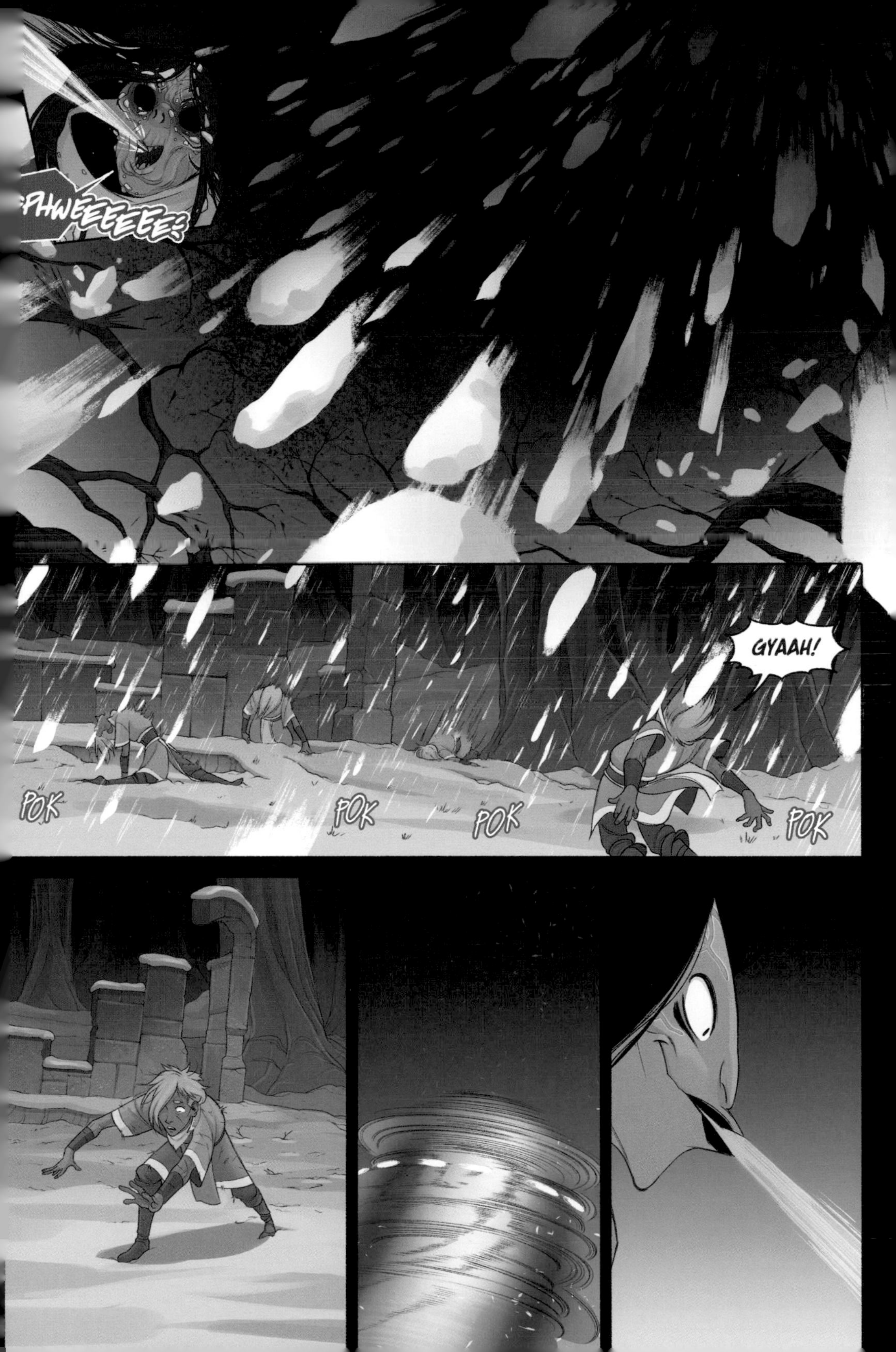
PHWEEEEEEE
GYAAH!
POK
POK
POK
POK

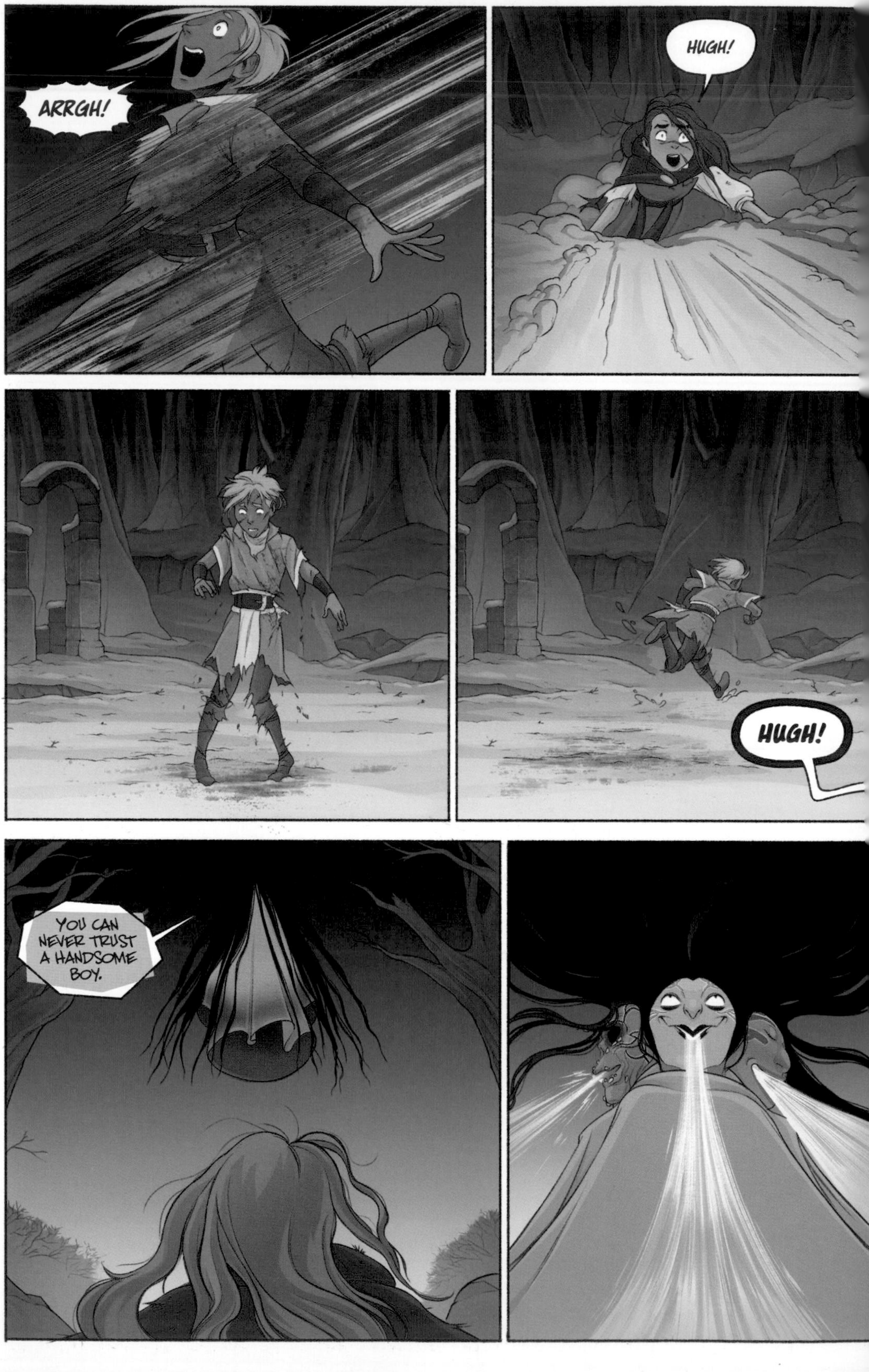
ARRGH!
HUGH!
HUGH!
YOU CAN NEVER TRUST A HANDSOME BOY.

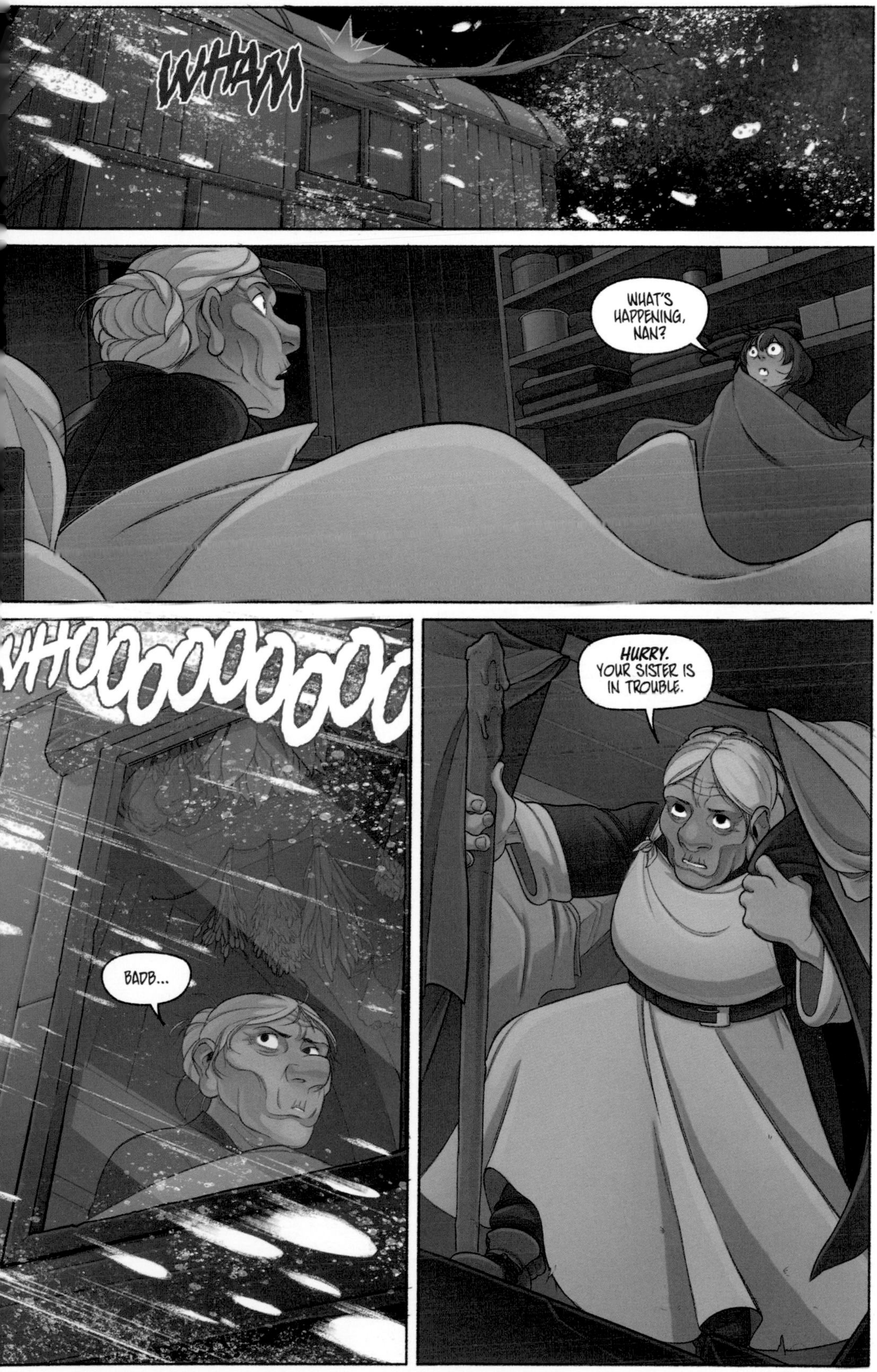
WHAM
WHAT'S HAPPENING, NAN?
WHOOOOOOOOO
BADB...
HURRY. YOUR SISTER IS IN TROUBLE.

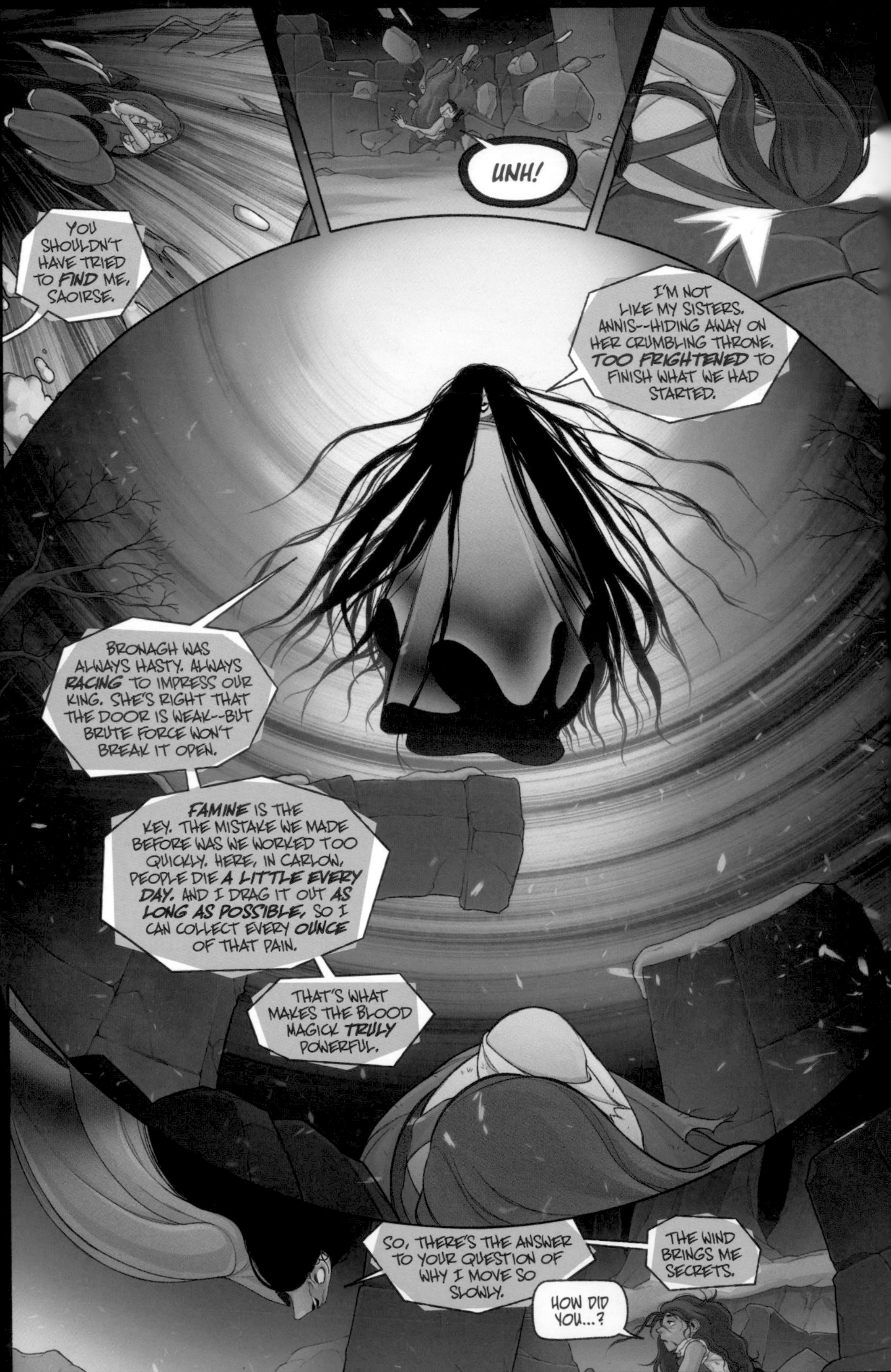

UNH!
YOU SHOULDN'T HAVE TRIED TO FIND ME, SAOIRSE.
I'M NOT LIKE MY SISTERS. ANNIS--HIDING AWAY ON HER CRUMBLING THRONE. TOO FRIGHTENED TO FINISH WHAT WE HAD STARTED.
BRONAGH WAS ALWAYS HASTY. ALWAYS RACING TO IMPRESS OUR KING. SHE'S RIGHT THAT THE DOOR IS WEAK--BUT BRUTE FORCE WON'T BREAK IT OPEN.
FAMINE IS THE KEY. THE MISTAKE WE MADE BEFORE WAS WE WORKED TOO QUICKLY. HERE, IN CARLOW, PEOPLE DIE A LITTLE EVERY DAY. AND I DRAG IT OUT AS LONG AS POSSIBLE, SO I CAN COLLECT EVERY OUNCE OF THAT PAIN.
THAT'S WHAT MAKES THE BLOOD MAGICK TRULY POWERFUL.
SO, THERE'S THE ANSWER TO YOUR QUESTION OF WHY I MOVE SO SLOWLY.
HOW DID YOU...?
THE WIND BRINGS ME SECRETS.

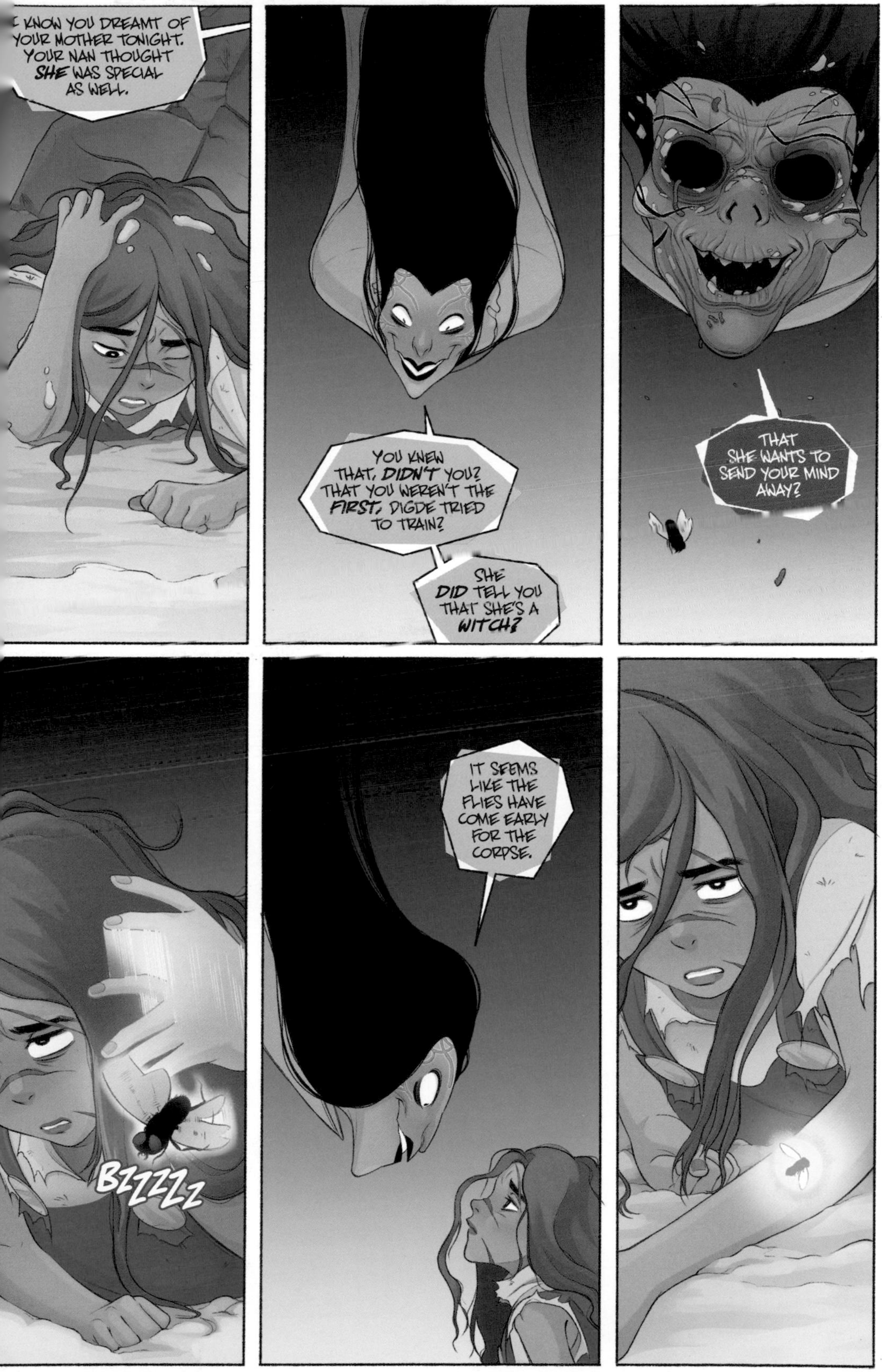

I KNOW YOU DREAMT OF YOUR MOTHER TONIGHT. YOUR NAN THOUGHT SHE WAS SPECIAL AS WELL.
YOU KNEW THAT, DIDN'T YOU? THAT YOU WEREN'T THE FIRST, DIGDE TRIED TO TRAIN?
SHE DID TELL YOU THAT SHE'S A WITCH?
THAT SHE WANTS TO SEND YOUR MIND AWAY?
BZZZZZ
IT SEEMS LIKE THE FLIES HAVE COME EARLY FOR THE CORPSE.

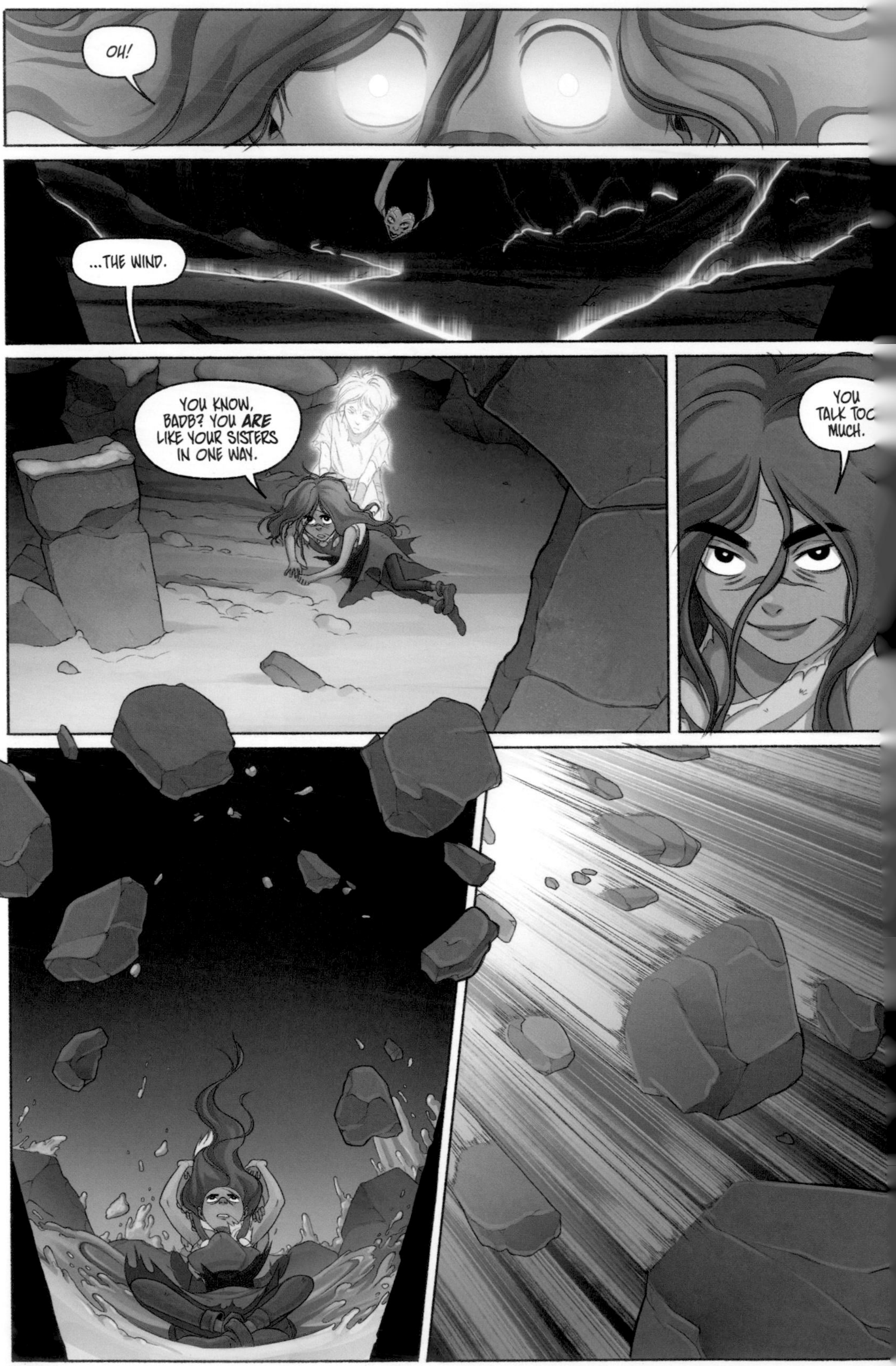
OH!
...THE WIND.
YOU KNOW, BADB? YOU ARE LIKE YOUR SISTERS IN ONE WAY.
YOU TALK TOO MUCH.

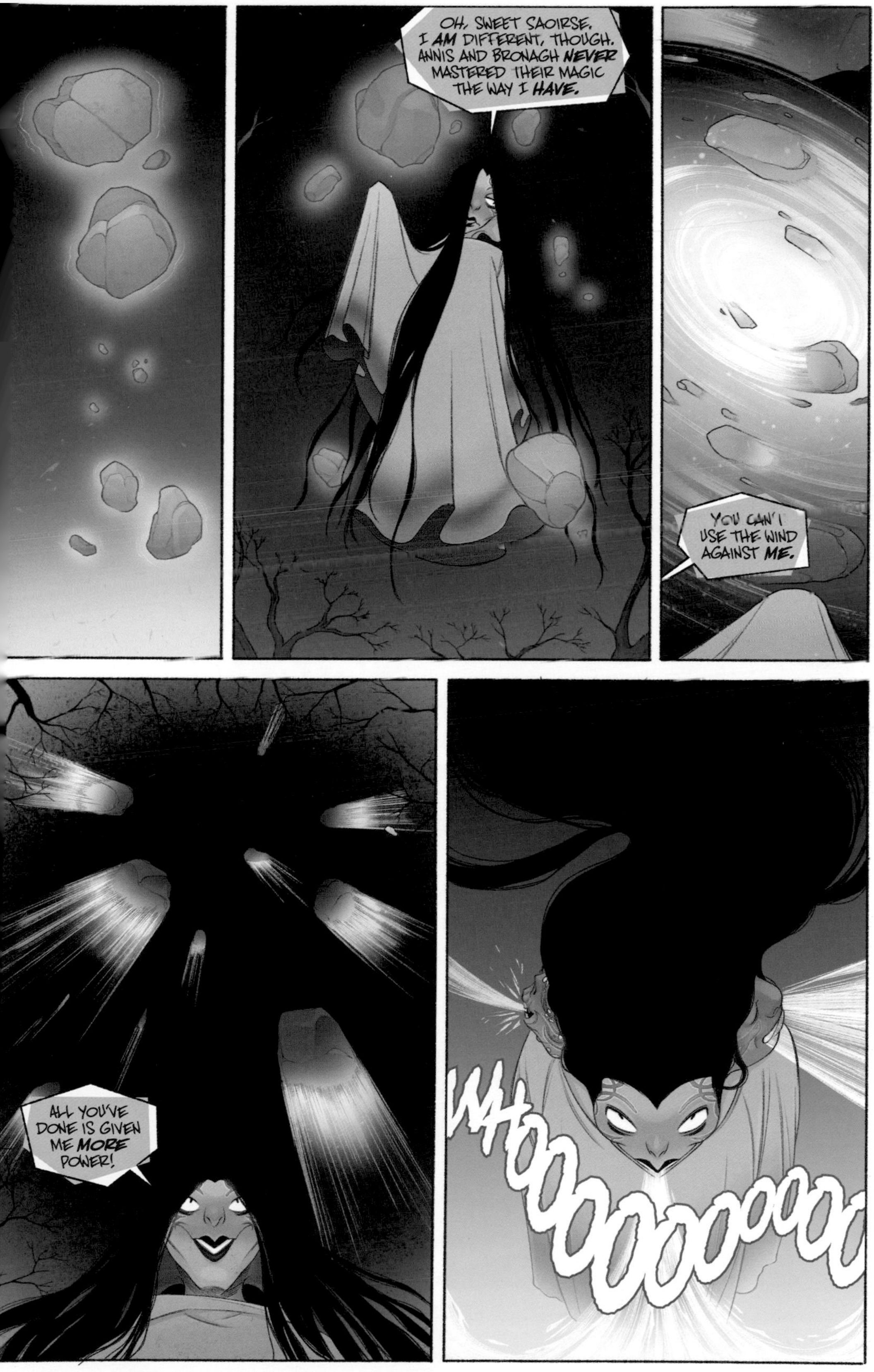
OH, SWEET SAOIRSE. I AM DIFFERENT, THOUGH. ANNIS AND BRONAGH NEVER MASTERED THEIR MAGIC THE WAY I HAVE.
YOU CAN'T USE THE WIND AGAINST ME.
ALL YOU'VE DONE IS GIVEN ME MORE POWER!
WHOOOOOOOOOOO

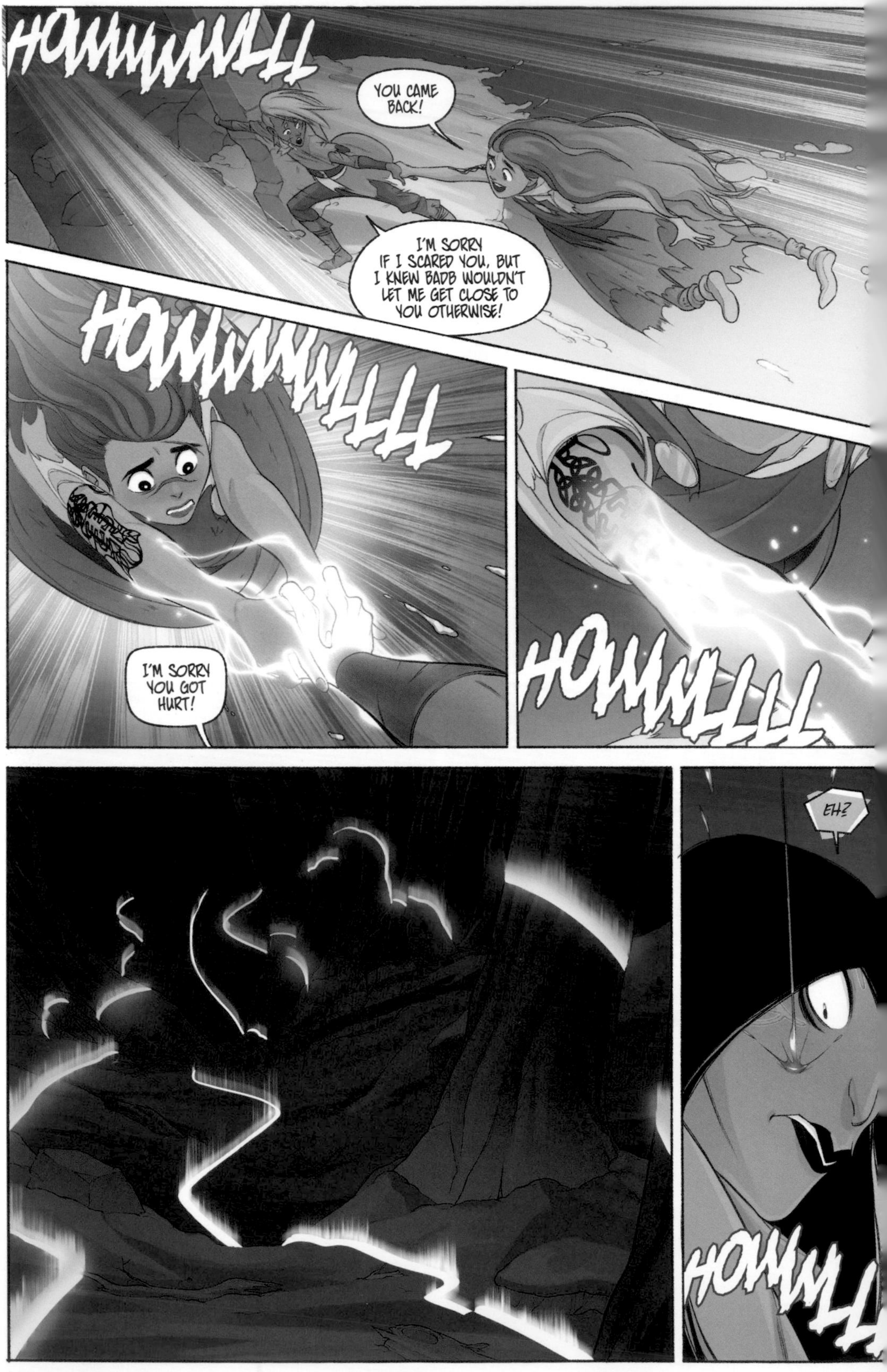
HOWWWLLL
YOU CAME BACK!
I'M SORRY IF I SCARED YOU, BUT I KNEW BADB WOULDN'T LET ME GET CLOSE TO YOU OTHERWISE!
HOWWWWLLL
I'M SORRY YOU GOT HURT!
HOWWLLL
EH?
HOWWLL

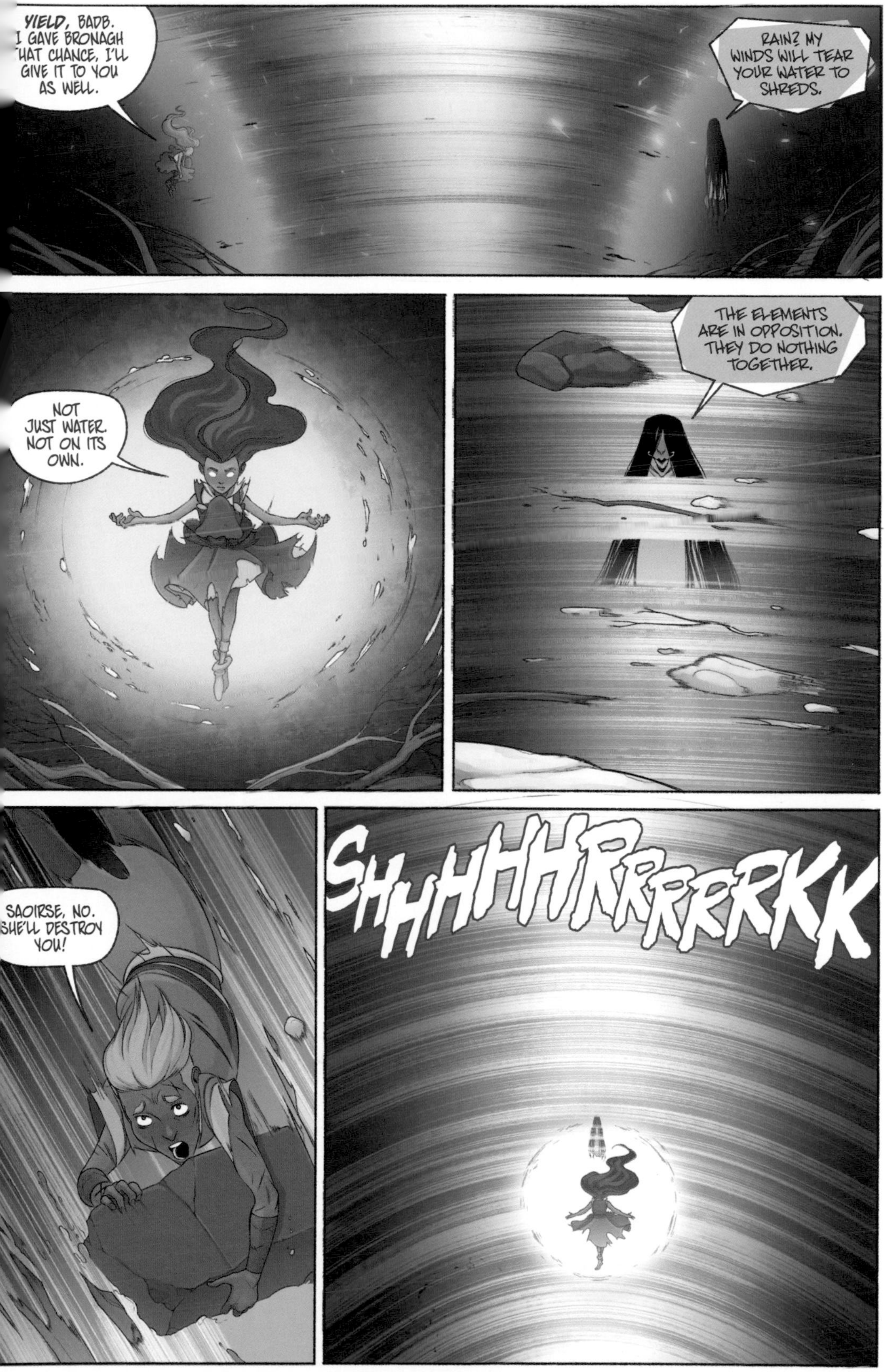
YIELD, BADB. I GAVE BRONAGH THAT CHANCE, I'LL GIVE IT TO YOU AS WELL.
RAIN? MY WINDS WILL TEAR YOUR WATER TO SHREDS.
NOT JUST WATER. NOT ON ITS OWN.
THE ELEMENTS ARE IN OPPOSITION. THEY DO NOTHING TOGETHER.
SAOIRSE, NO. SHE'LL DESTROY YOU!
SHHHHHRRRRRKK

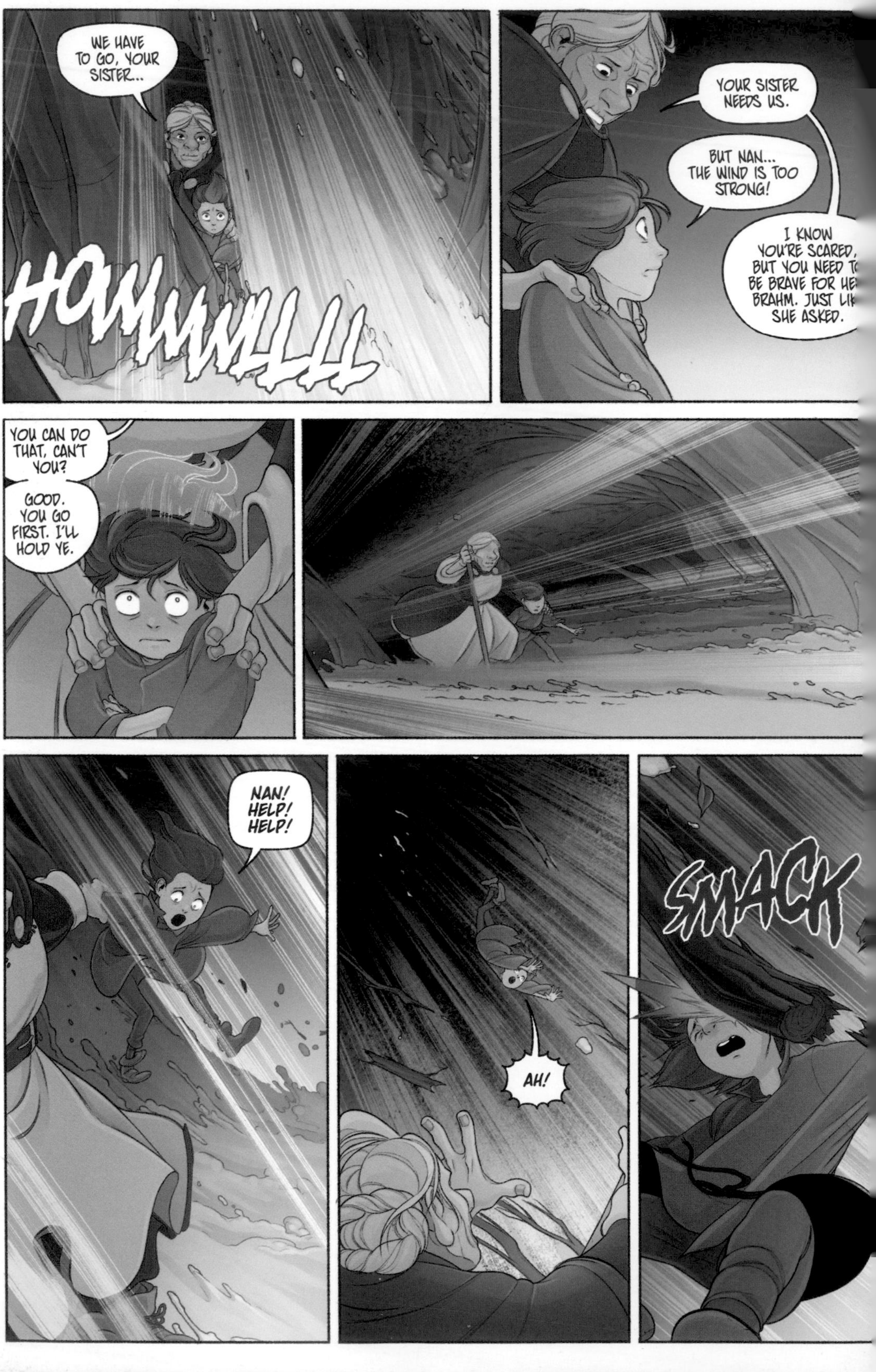
WE HAVE TO GO, YOUR SISTER...
HOWWWLLLL
YOUR SISTER NEEDS US.
BUT NAN... THE WIND IS TOO STRONG!
I KNOW YOU'RE SCARED, BUT YOU NEED T BE BRAVE FOR HE BRAHM. JUST LI SHE ASKED.
YOU CAN DO THAT, CAN'T YOU?
GOOD. YOU GO FIRST. I'LL HOLD YE.
NAN! HELP! HELP!
AH!
SMACK

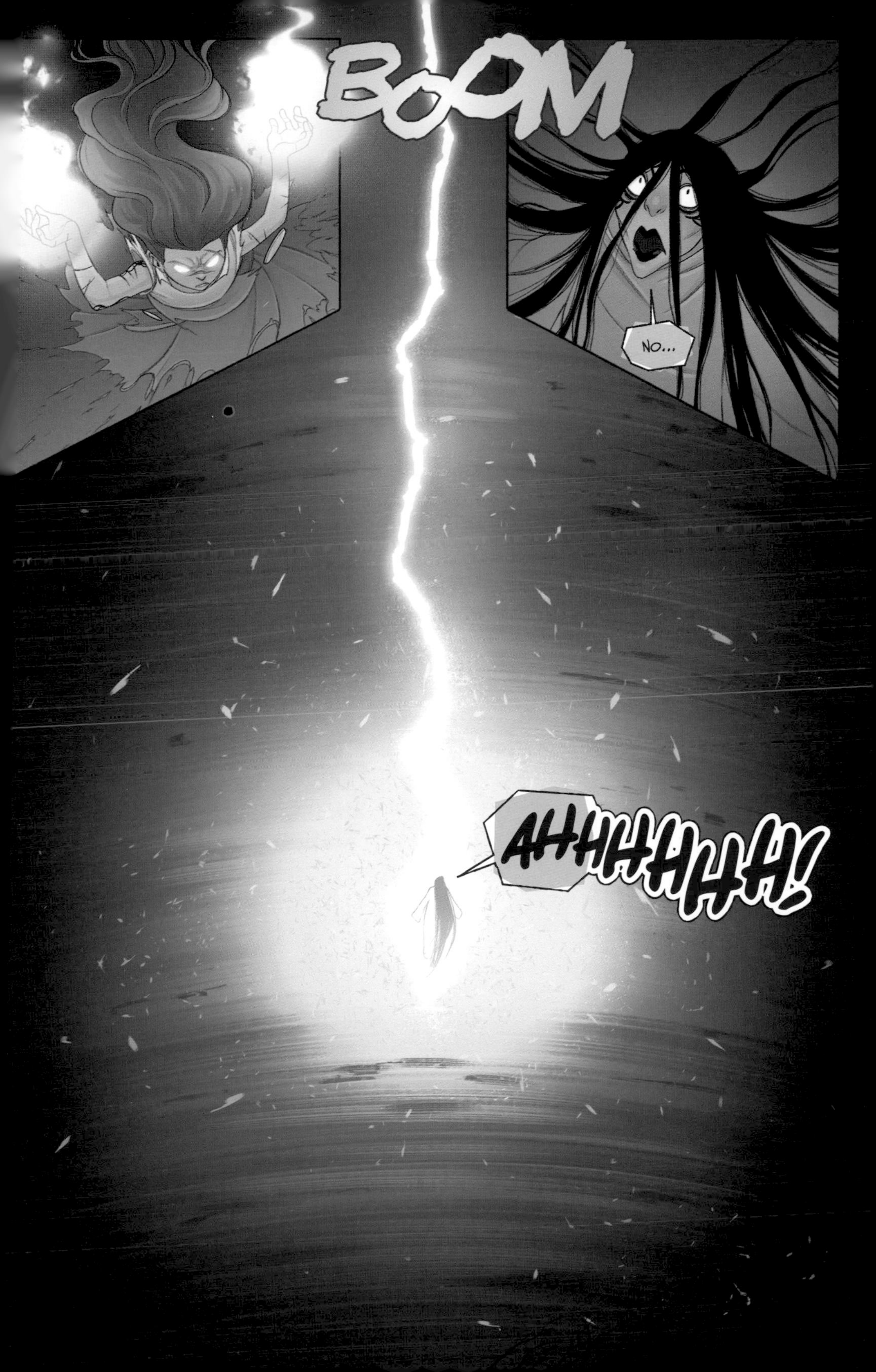
BOOM
NO...
AHHHHHHH!

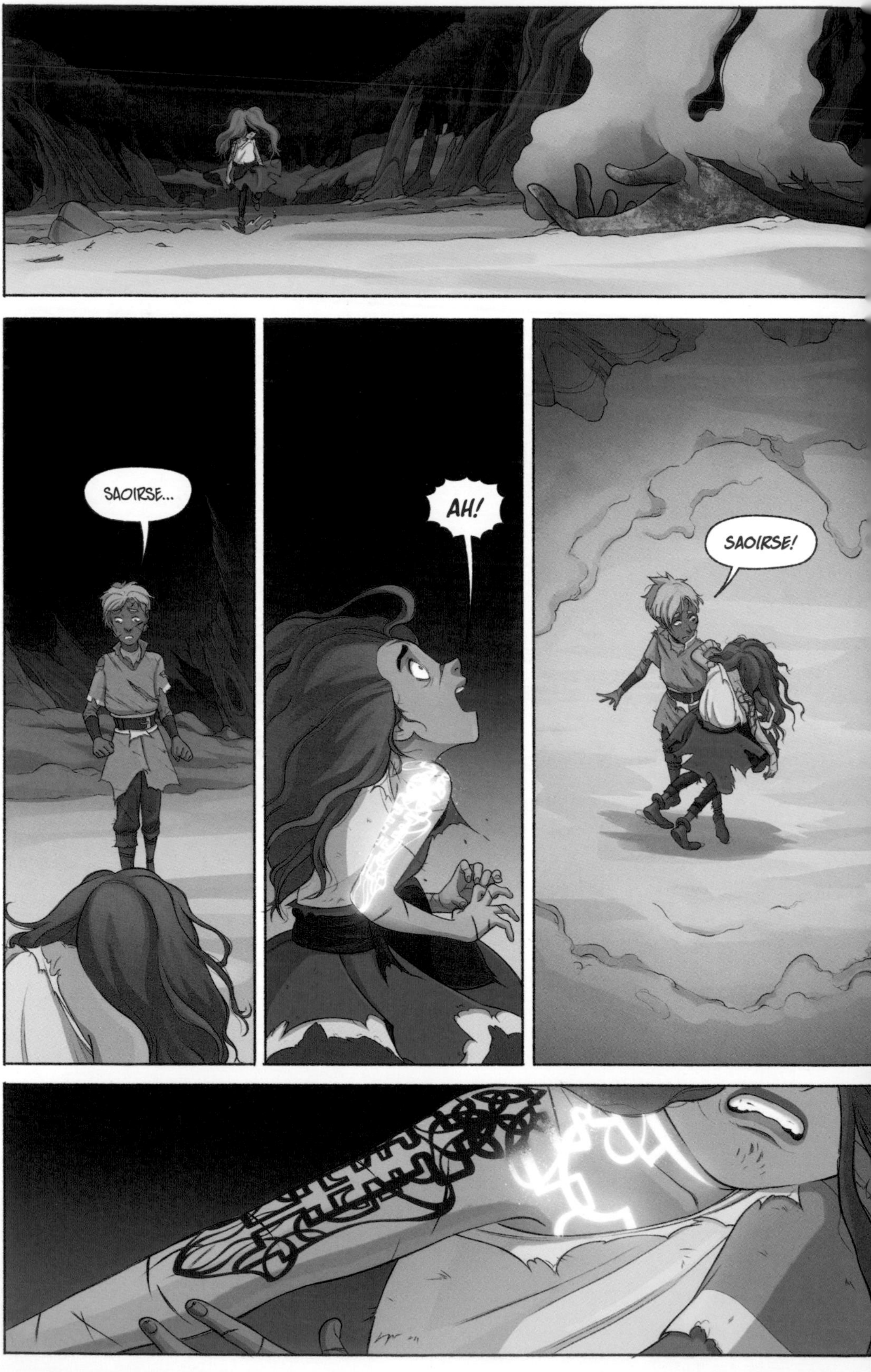
SAOIRSE...
AH!
SAOIRSE!

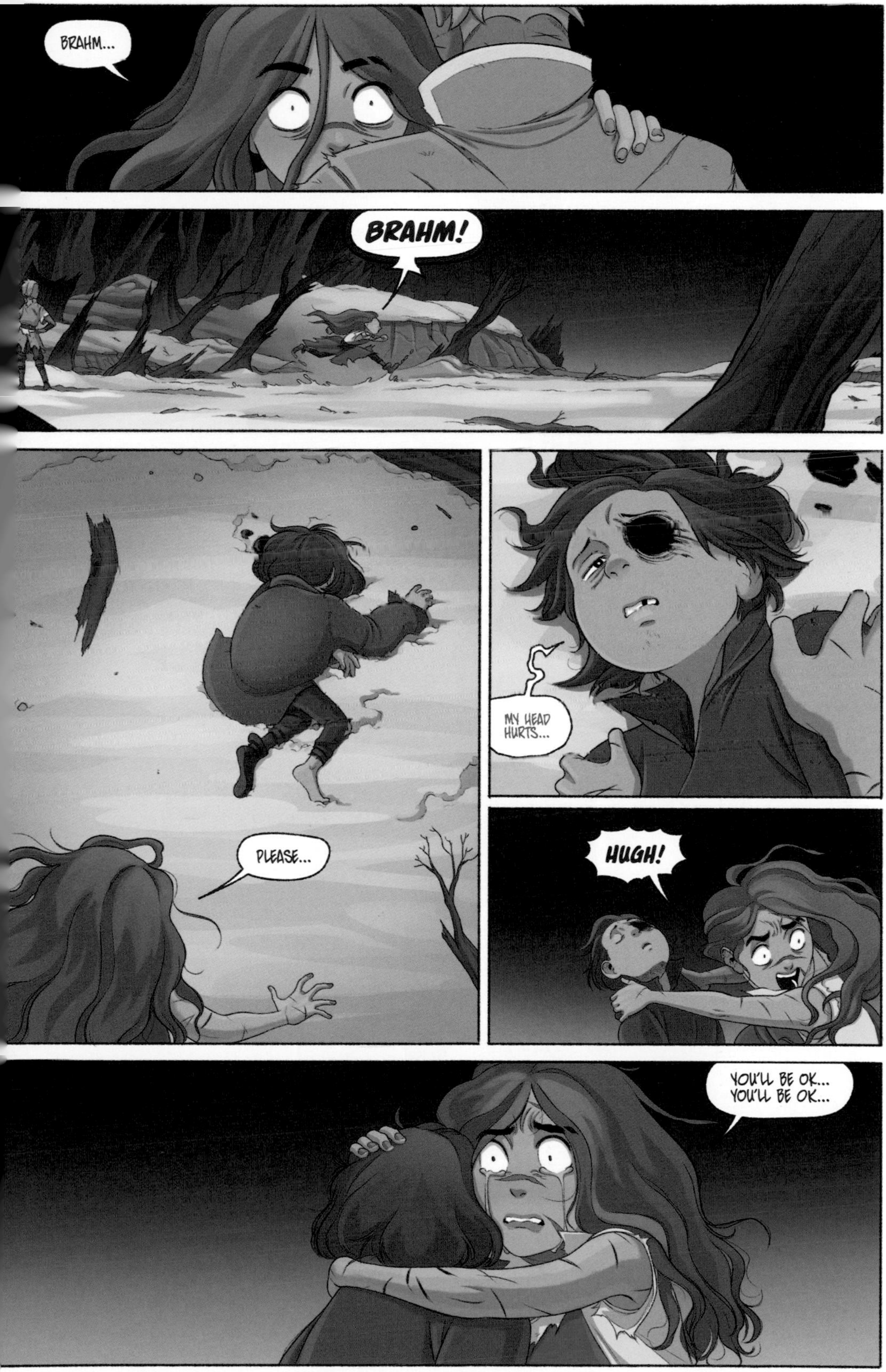
BRAHM...
BRAHM!
PLEASE...
MY HEAD HURTS...
HUGH!
YOU'LL BE OK... YOU'LL BE OK...

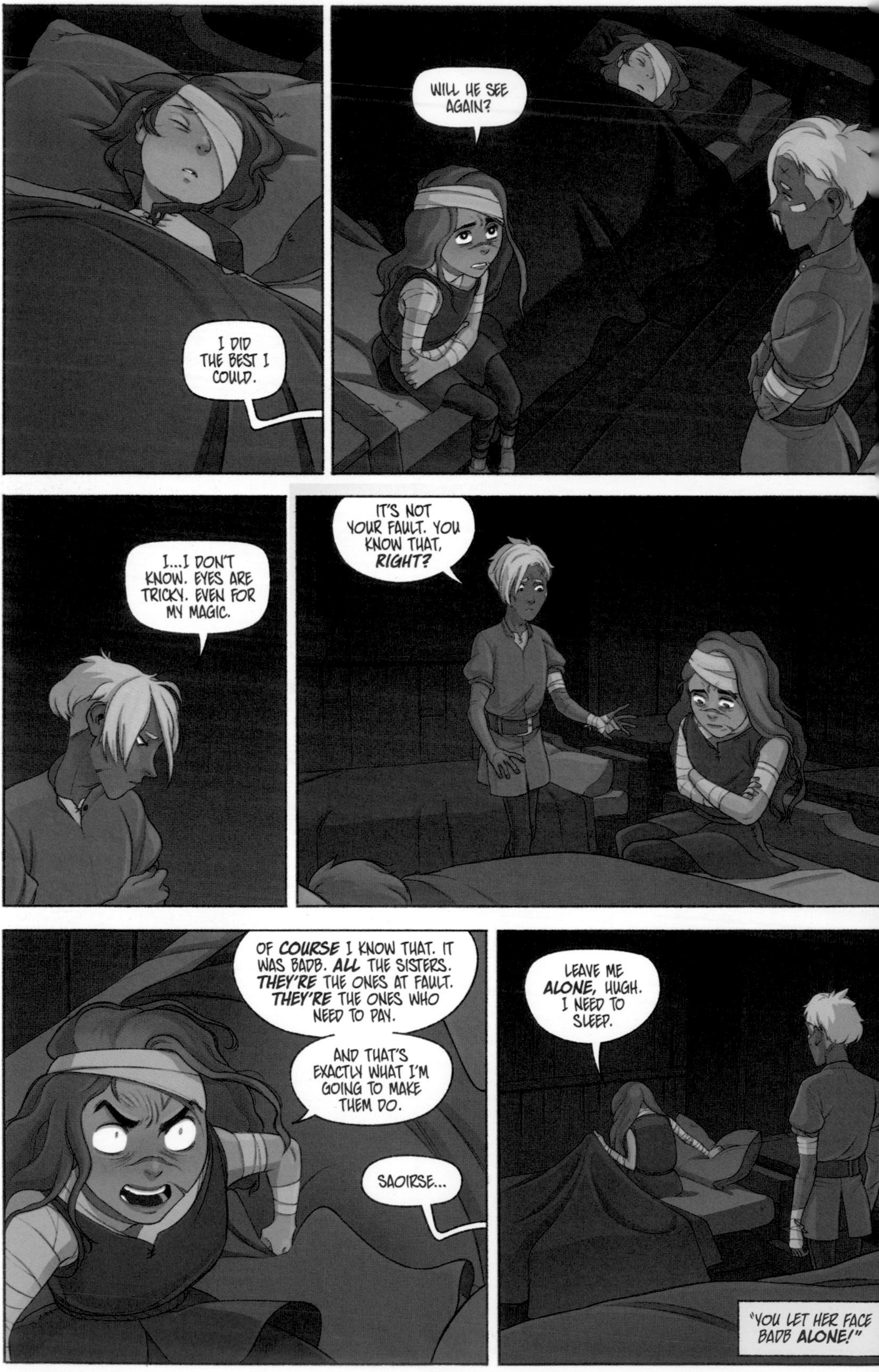
WILL HE SEE AGAIN?
I DID THE BEST I COULD.
I...I DON'T KNOW. EYES ARE TRICKY. EVEN FOR MY MAGIC.
IT'S NOT YOUR FAULT. YOU KNOW THAT, **RIGHT?**
OF **COURSE** I KNOW THAT. IT WAS BADB. **ALL** THE SISTERS. **THEY'RE** THE ONES AT FAULT. **THEY'RE** THE ONES WHO NEED TO PAY.
AND THAT'S EXACTLY WHAT I'M GOING TO MAKE THEM DO.
SAOIRSE...
LEAVE ME **ALONE,** HUGH. I NEED TO SLEEP.
"YOU LET HER FACE BADB **ALONE!**"

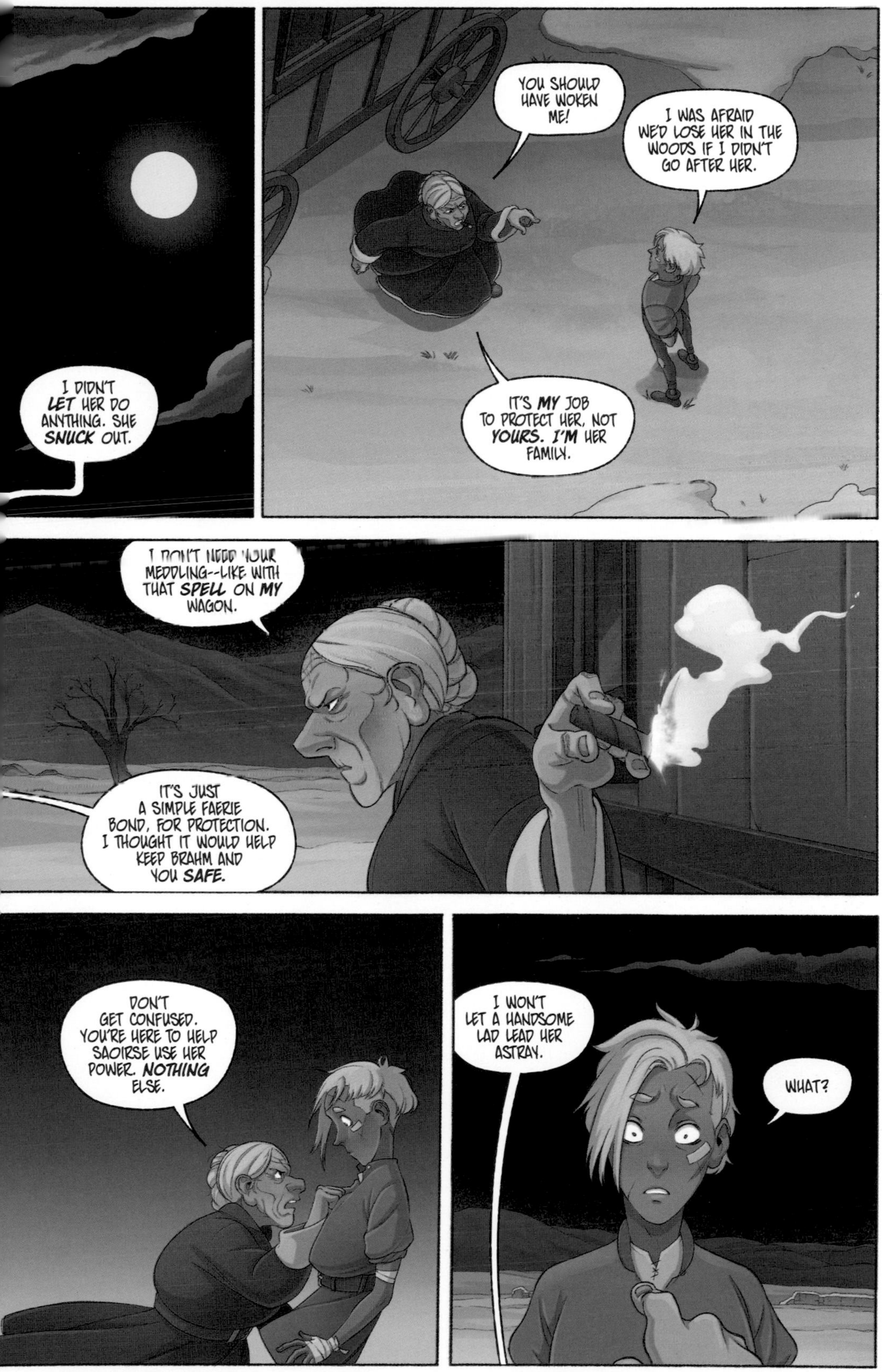
I DIDN'T LET HER DO ANYTHING. SHE SNUCK OUT.
YOU SHOULD HAVE WOKEN ME!
I WAS AFRAID WE'D LOSE HER IN THE WOODS IF I DIDN'T GO AFTER HER.
IT'S MY JOB TO PROTECT HER, NOT YOURS. I'M HER FAMILY.
I DON'T NEED YOUR MEDDLING--LIKE WITH THAT SPELL ON MY WAGON.
IT'S JUST A SIMPLE FAERIE BOND, FOR PROTECTION. I THOUGHT IT WOULD HELP KEEP BRAHM AND YOU SAFE.
DON'T GET CONFUSED. YOU'RE HERE TO HELP SAOIRSE USE HER POWER. NOTHING ELSE.
I WON'T LET A HANDSOME LAD LEAD HER ASTRAY.
WHAT?

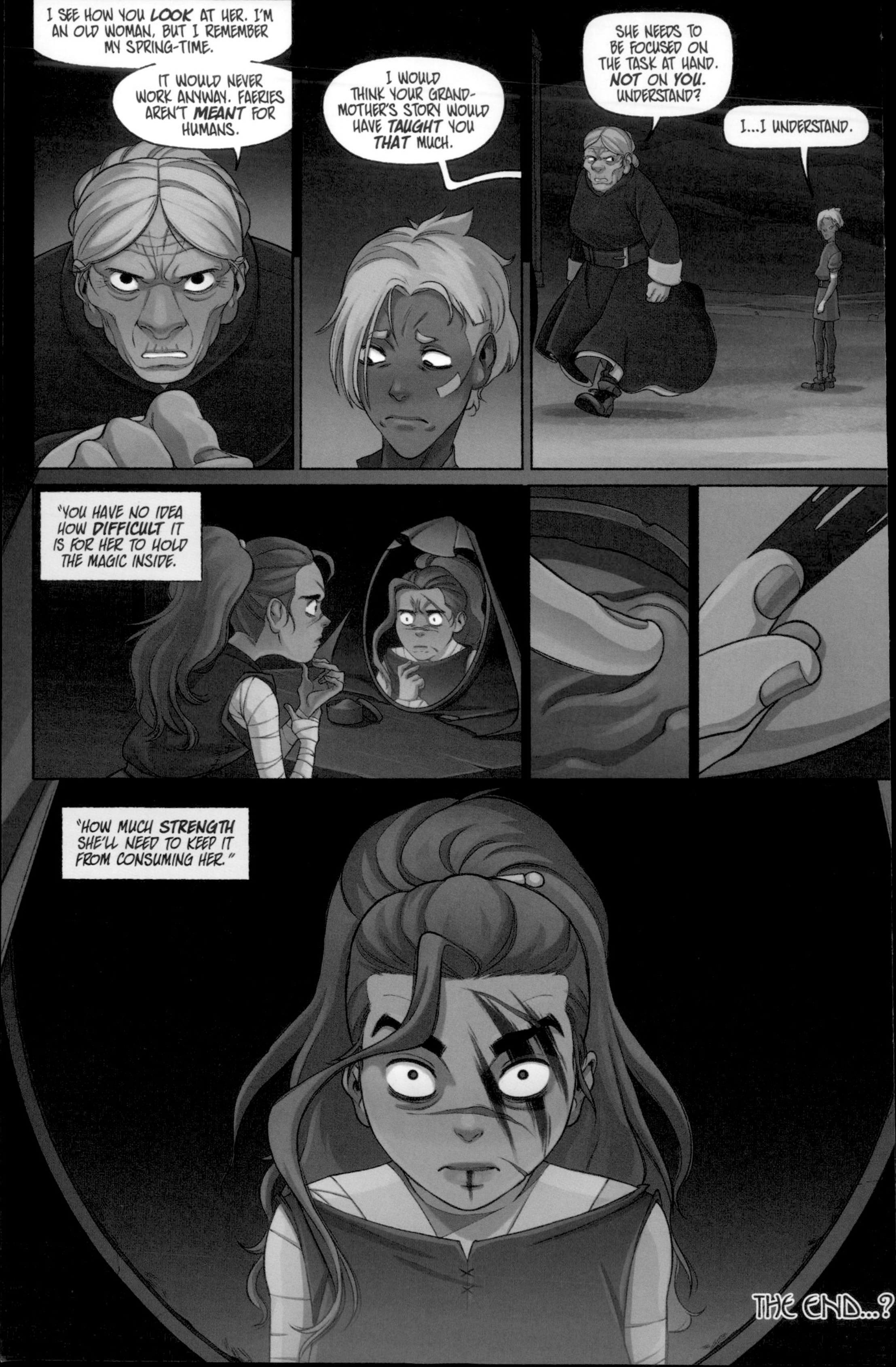
I SEE HOW YOU LOOK AT HER. I'M AN OLD WOMAN, BUT I REMEMBER MY SPRING-TIME.
IT WOULD NEVER WORK ANYWAY. FAERIES AREN'T MEANT FOR HUMANS.
I WOULD THINK YOUR GRAND-MOTHER'S STORY WOULD HAVE TAUGHT YOU THAT MUCH.
SHE NEEDS TO BE FOCUSED ON THE TASK AT HAND. NOT ON YOU. UNDERSTAND?
I...I UNDERSTAND.
"YOU HAVE NO IDEA HOW DIFFICULT IT IS FOR HER TO HOLD THE MAGIC INSIDE.
"HOW MUCH STRENGTH SHE'LL NEED TO KEEP IT FROM CONSUMING HER."
THE END...?

COVER
GALLERY

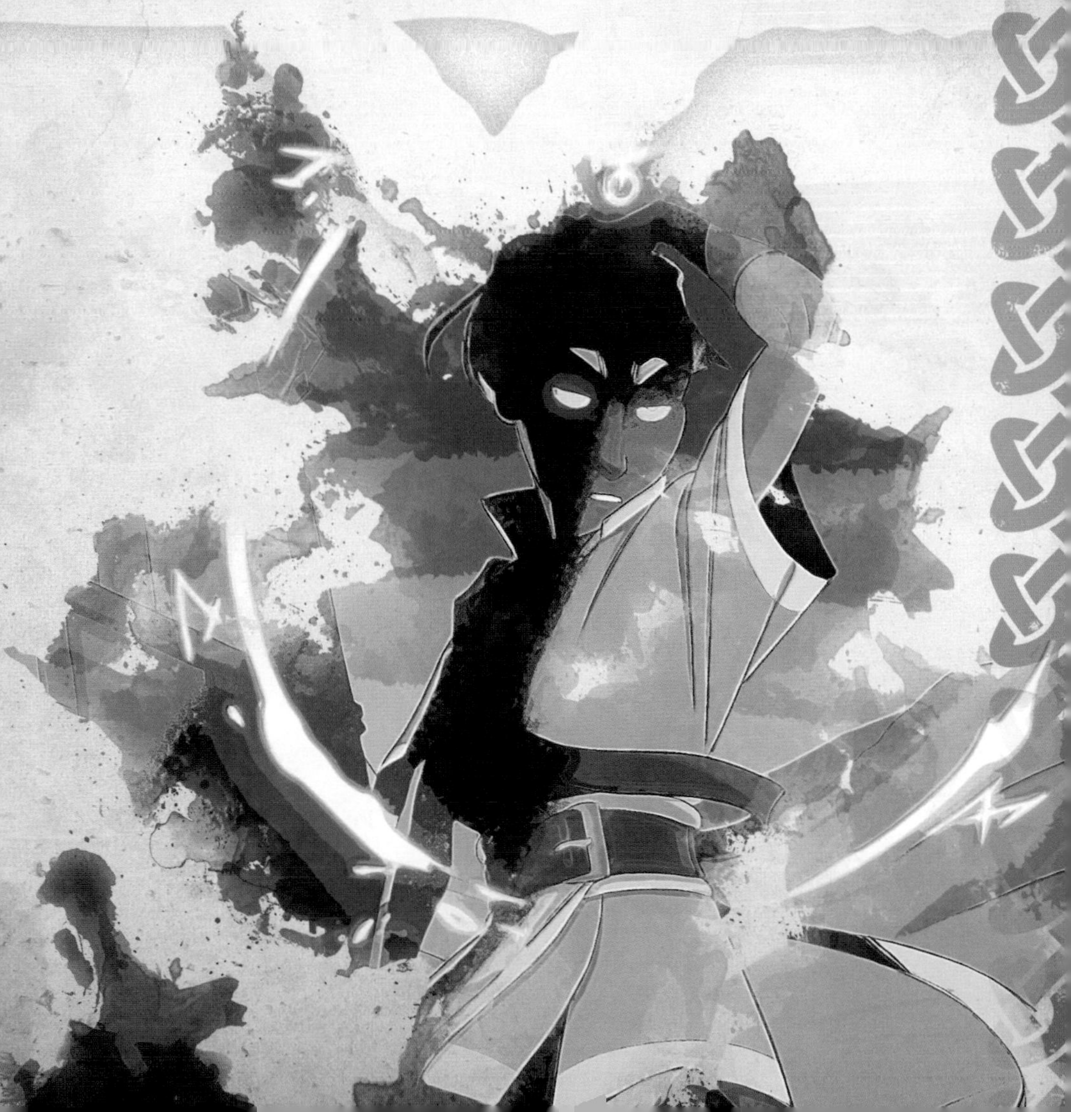

ISSUE ONE MAIN COVER

V.V. GLASS

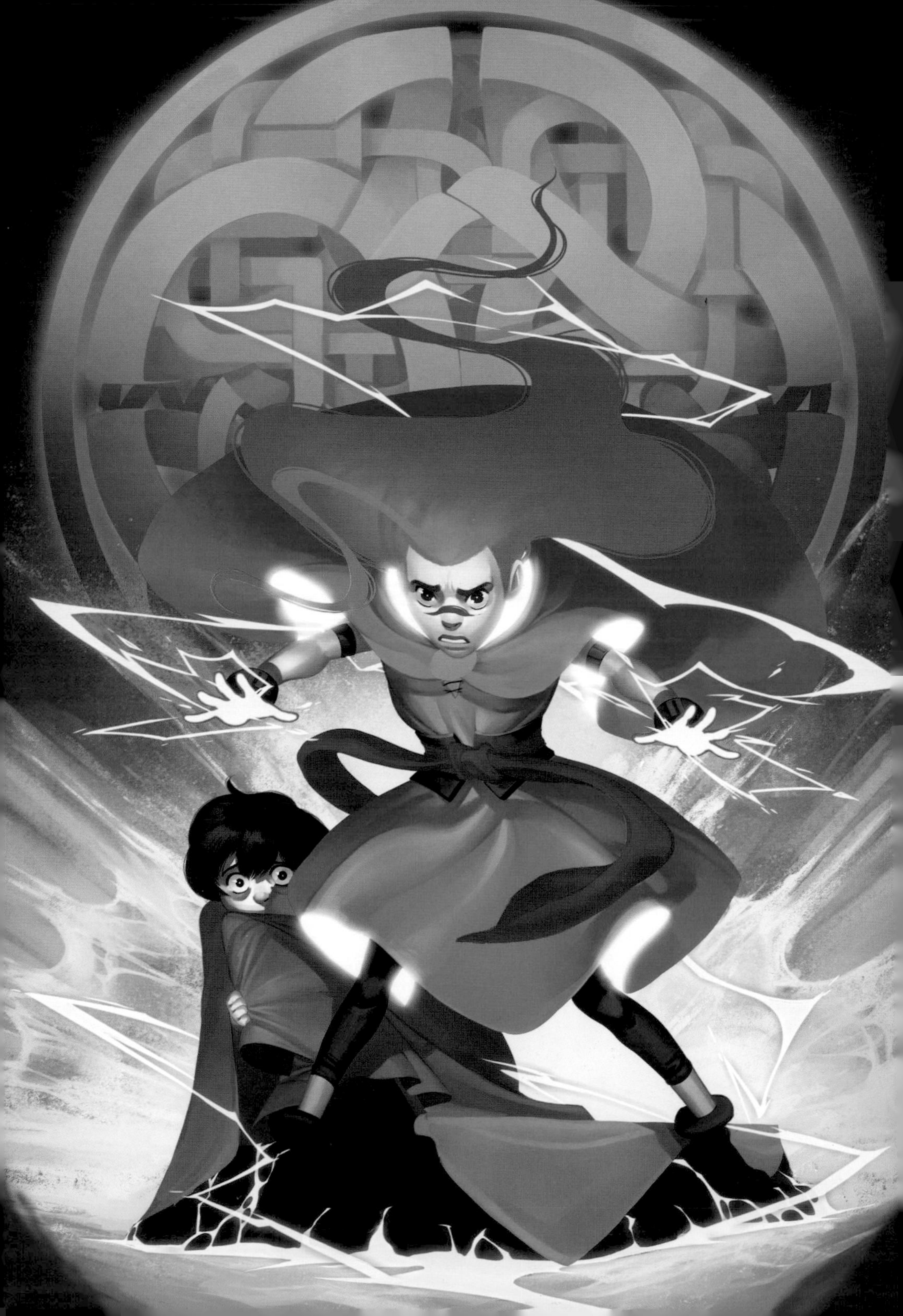

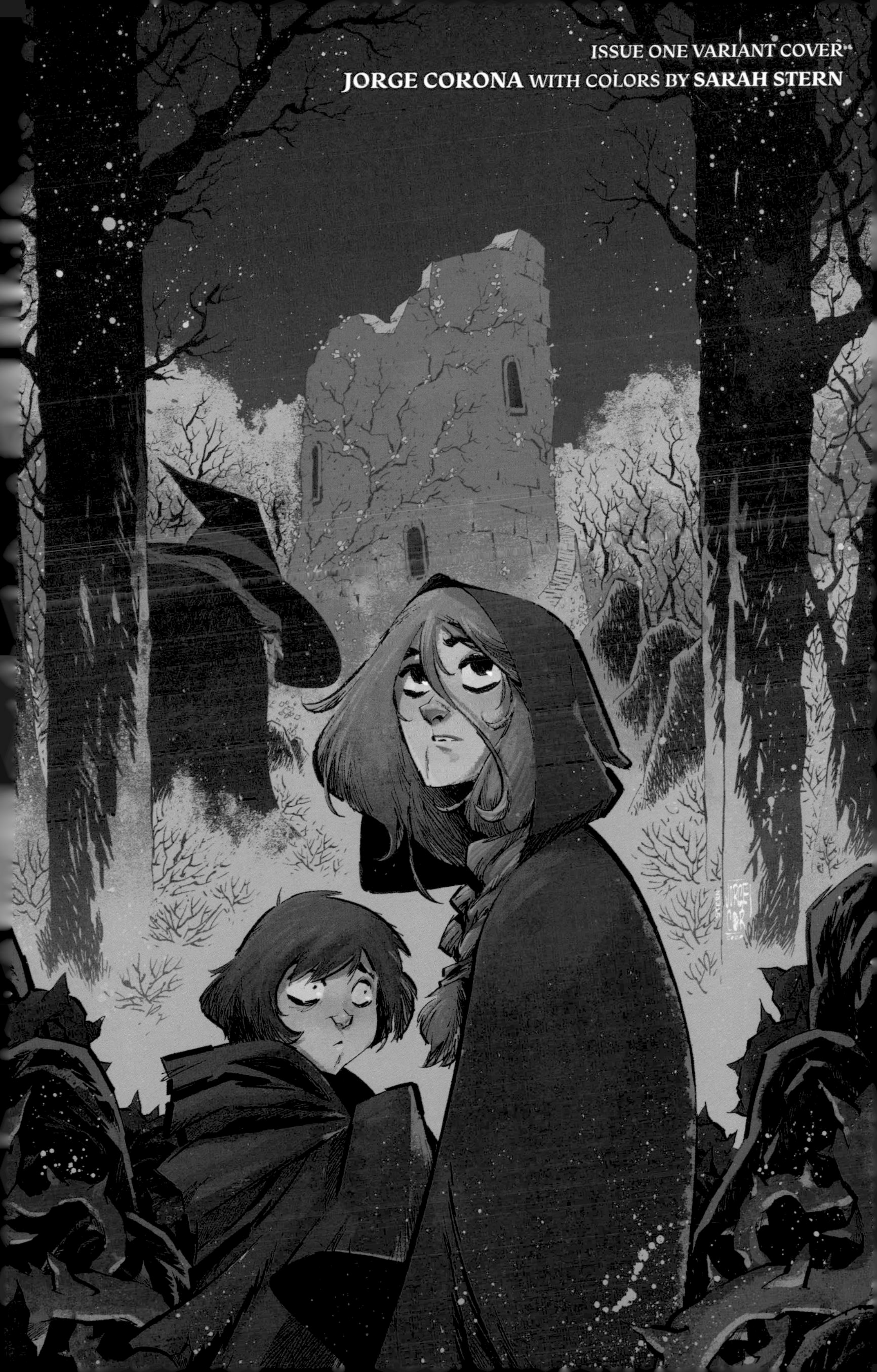

ISSUE ONE VARIANT COVER
JORGE CORONA WITH COLORS BY **SARAH STERN**

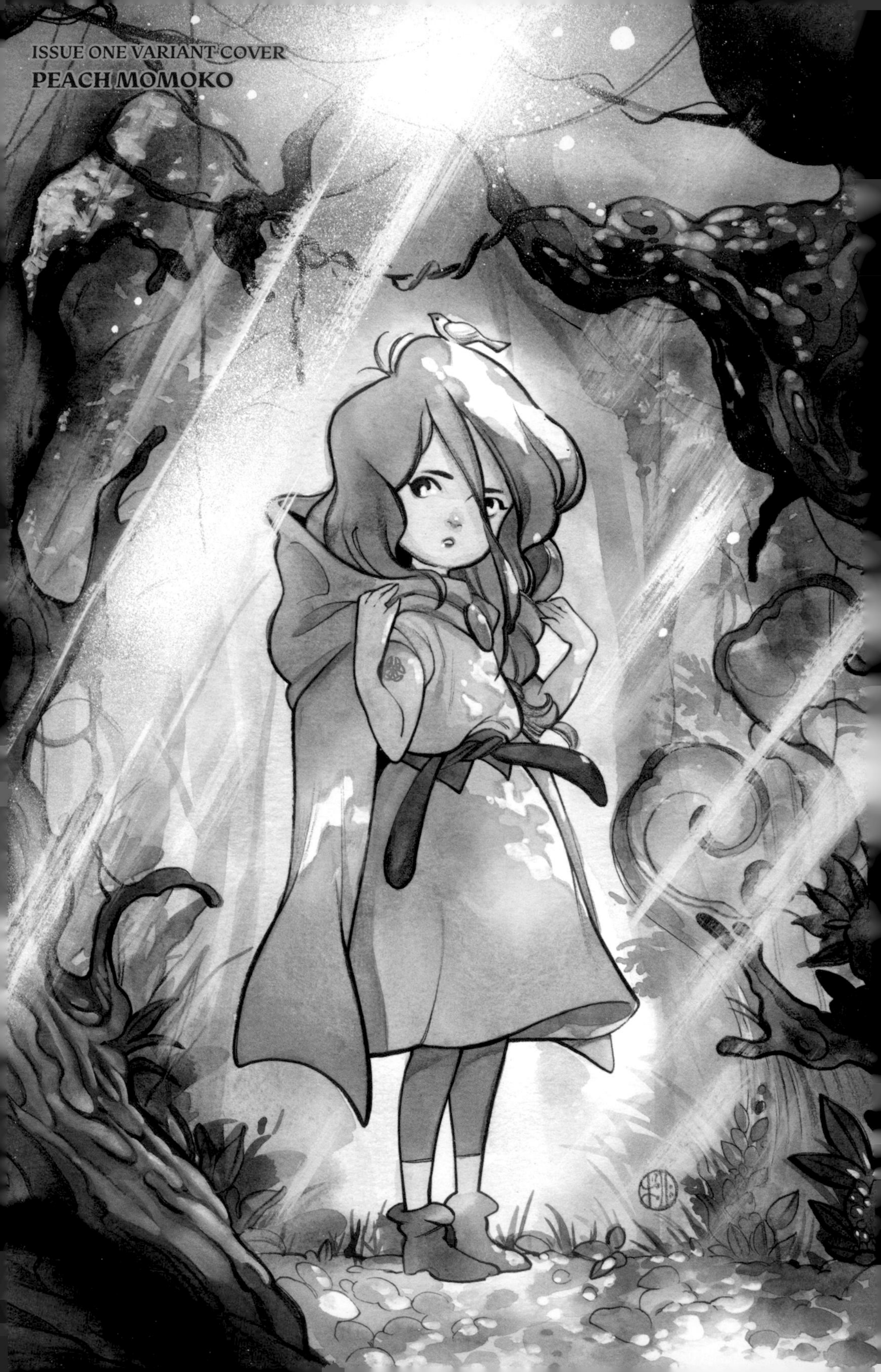

ISSUE ONE VARIANT COVER

PEACH MOMOKO

ISSUE ONE VARIANT COVER

PEACH MOMOKO

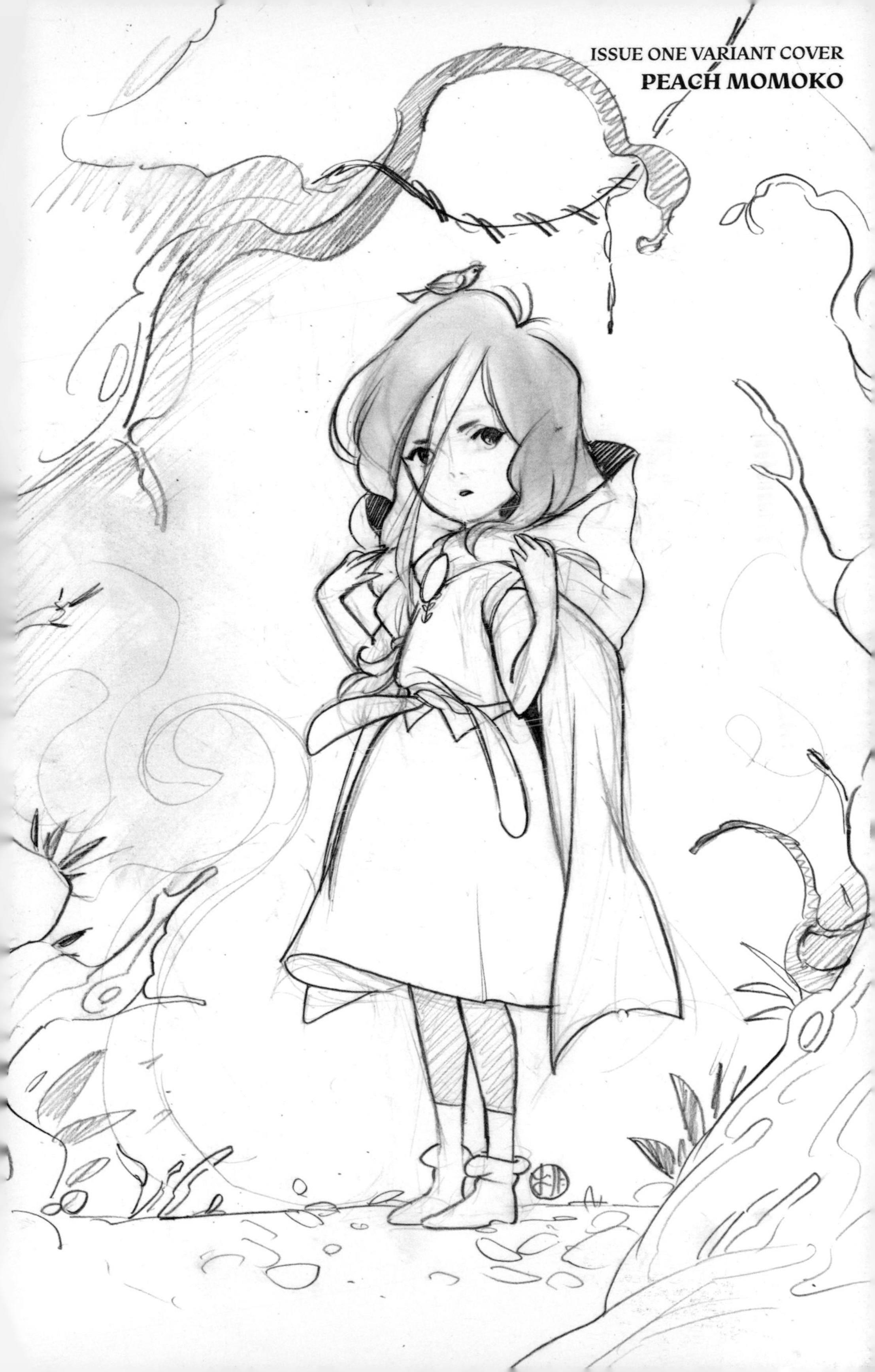

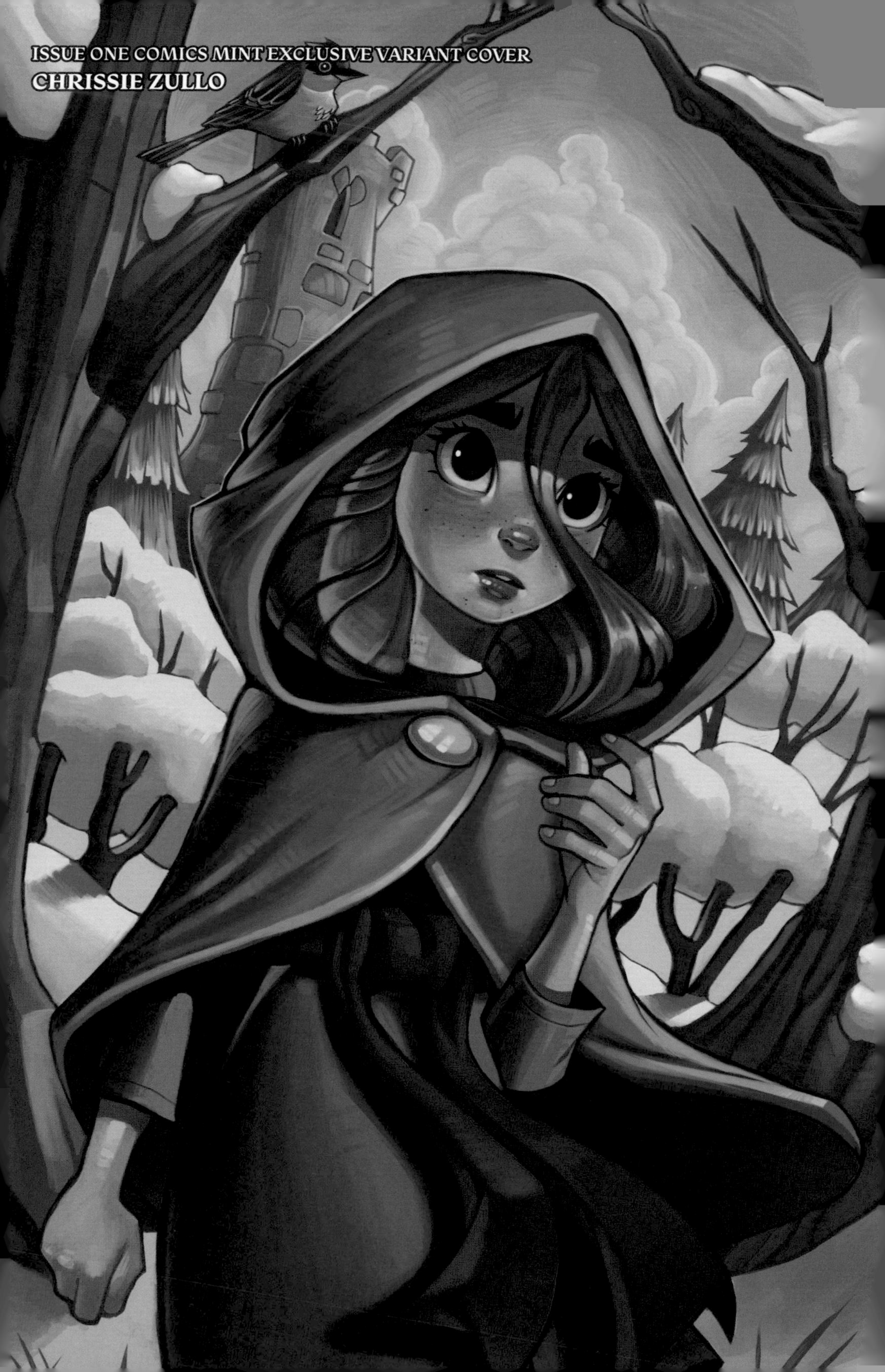
ISSUE ONE COMICS MINT EXCLUSIVE VARIANT COVER
CHRISSIE ZULLO

ISSUE ONE ARCHIE'S COMICS EXCLUSIVE VARIANT COVER

SABINE RICH

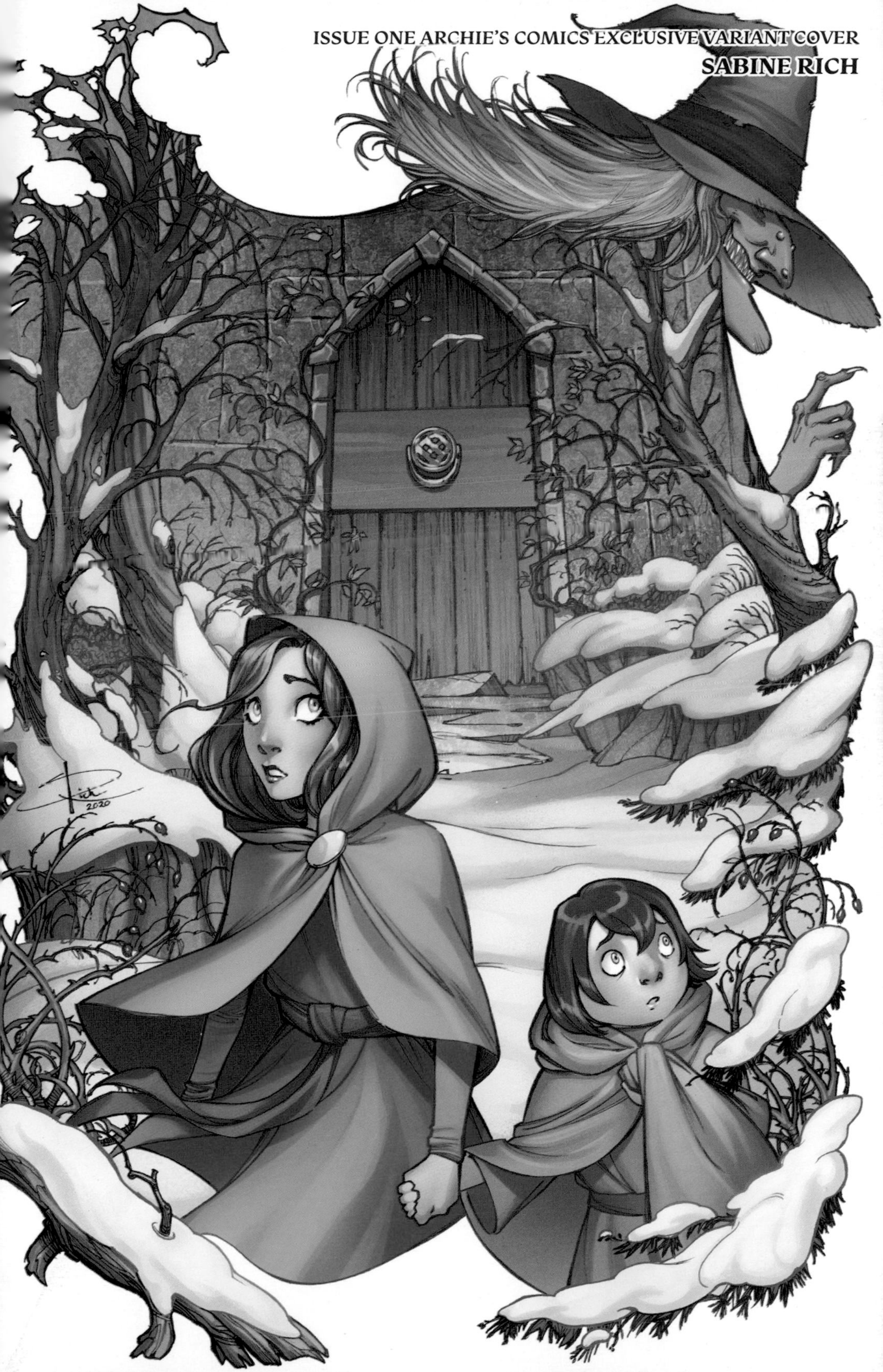

ISSUE ONE SECOND PRINTING COVER
V.V. GLASS

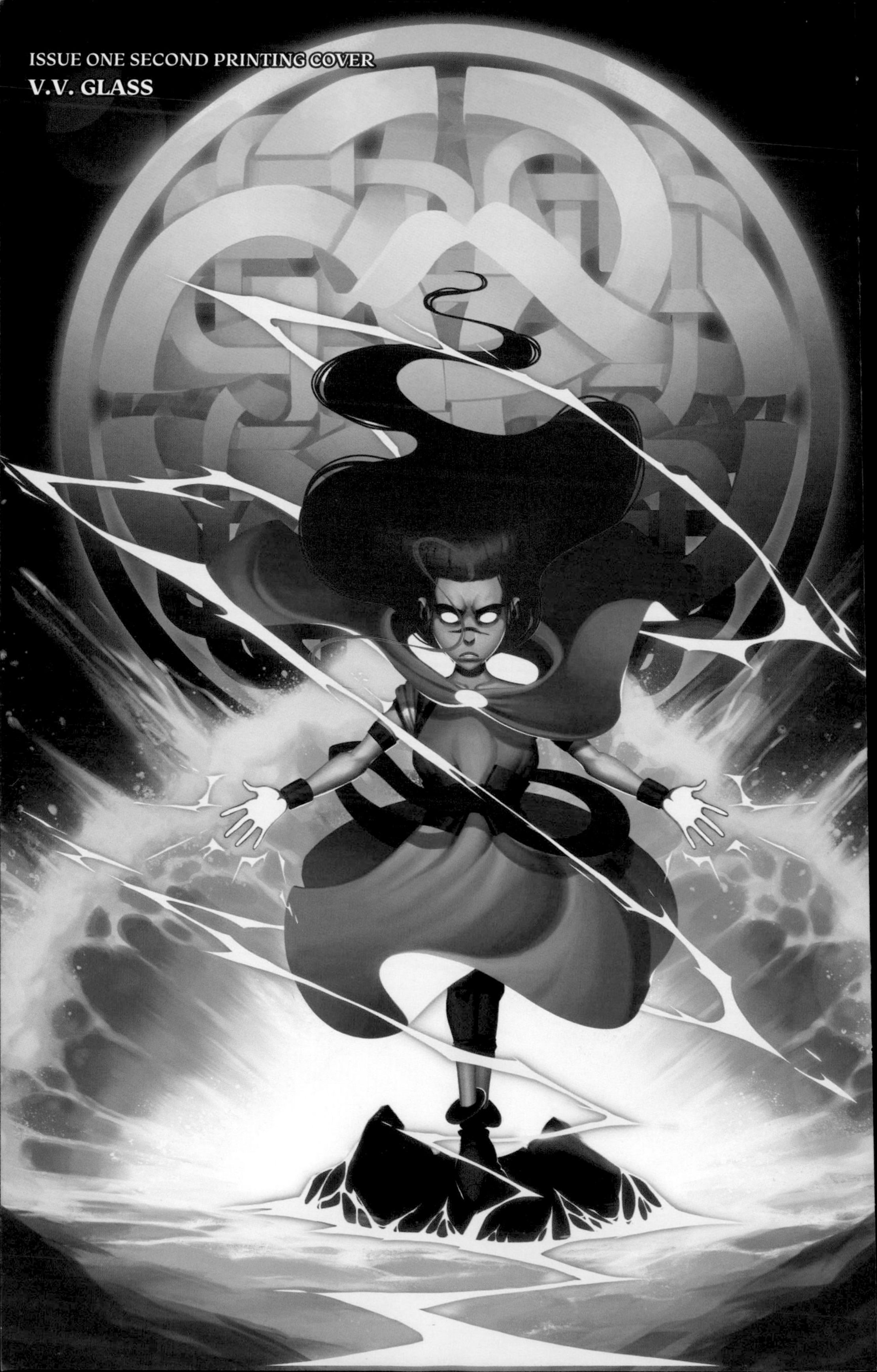

ISSUE TWO MAIN COVER
V.V. GLASS

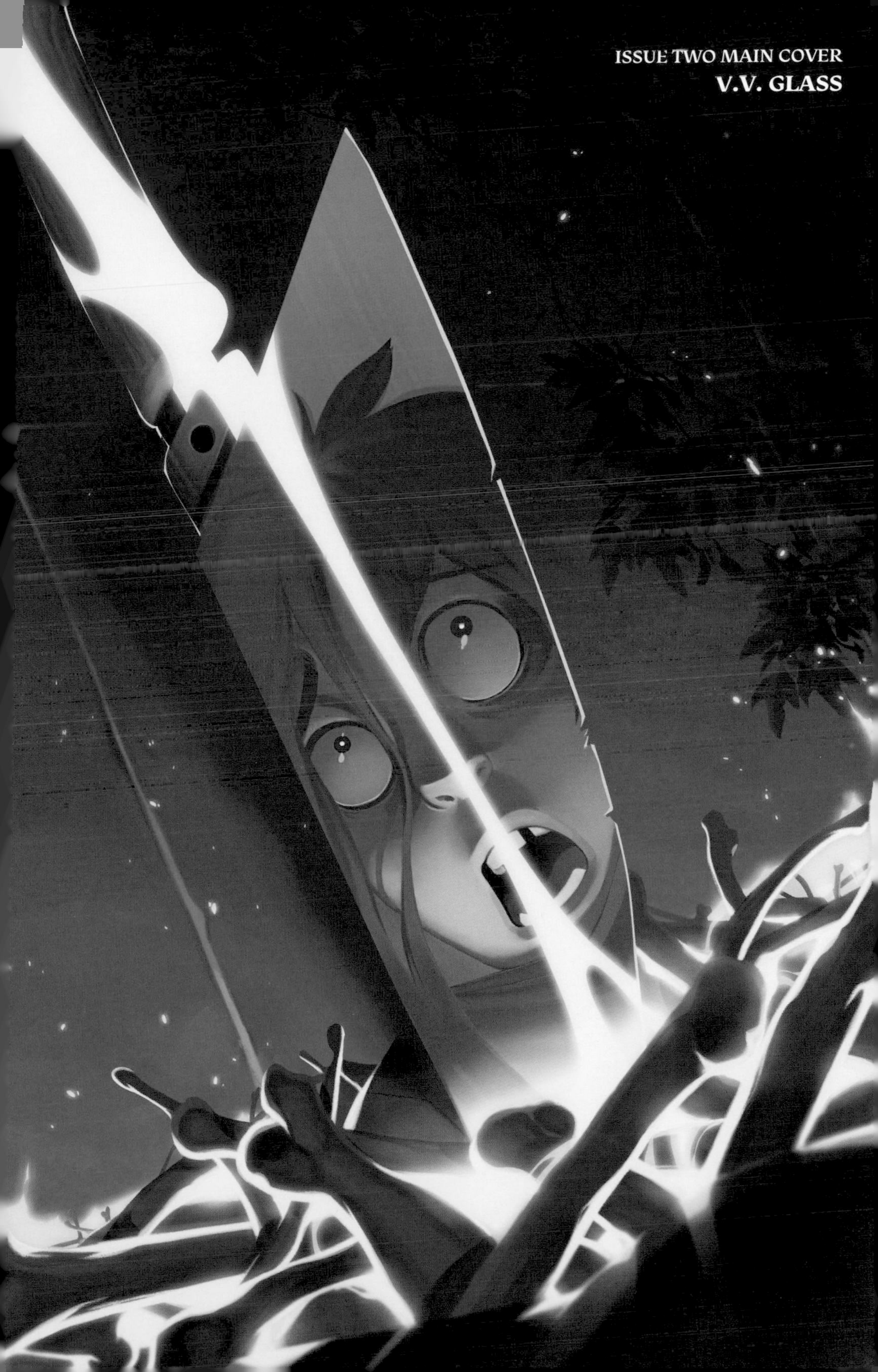

ISSUE THREE MAIN COVER
V.V. GLASS

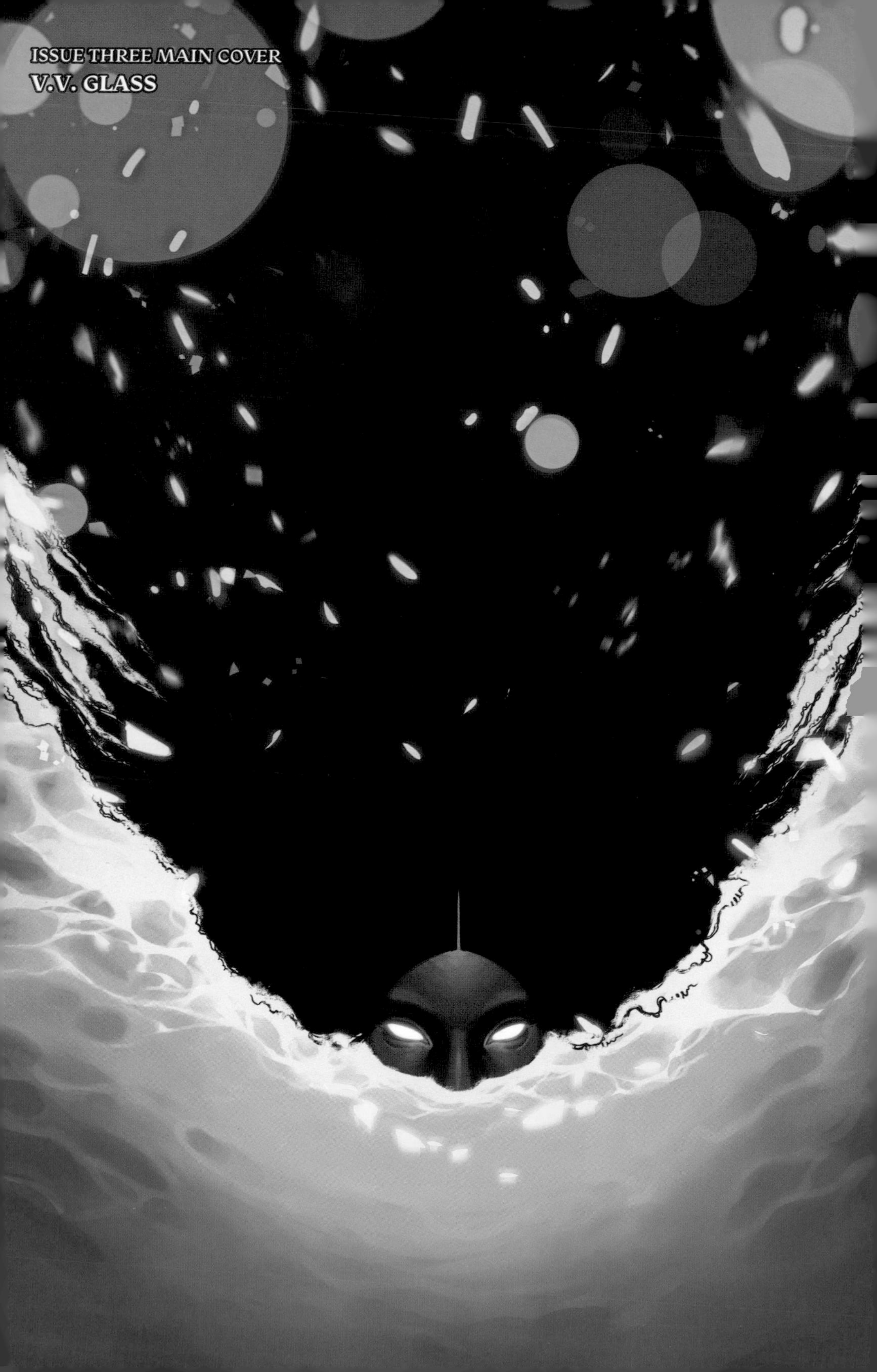

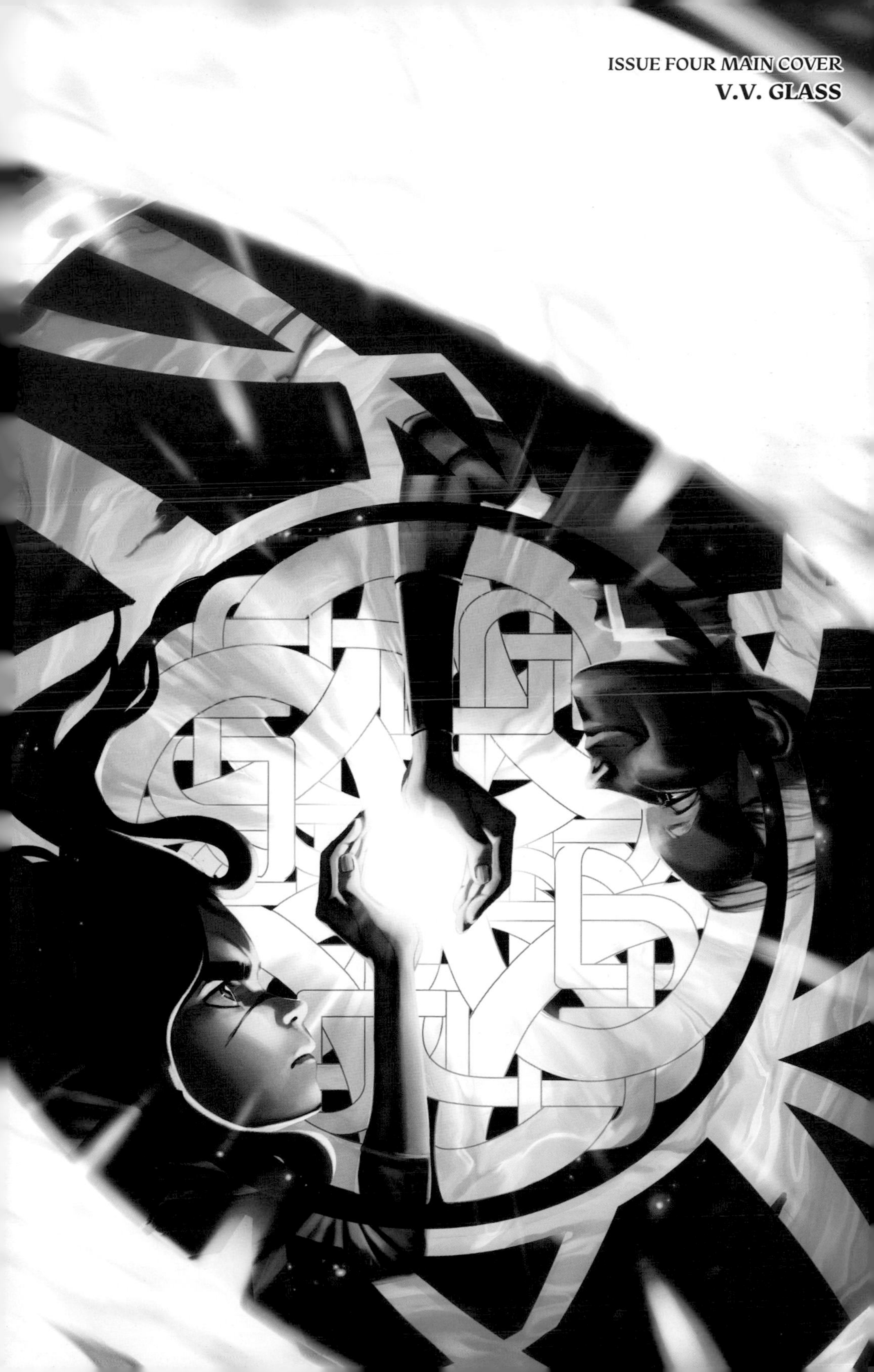

ISSUE FOUR MAIN COVER
V.V. GLASS

ISSUE FIVE MAIN COVER

V.V. GLASS

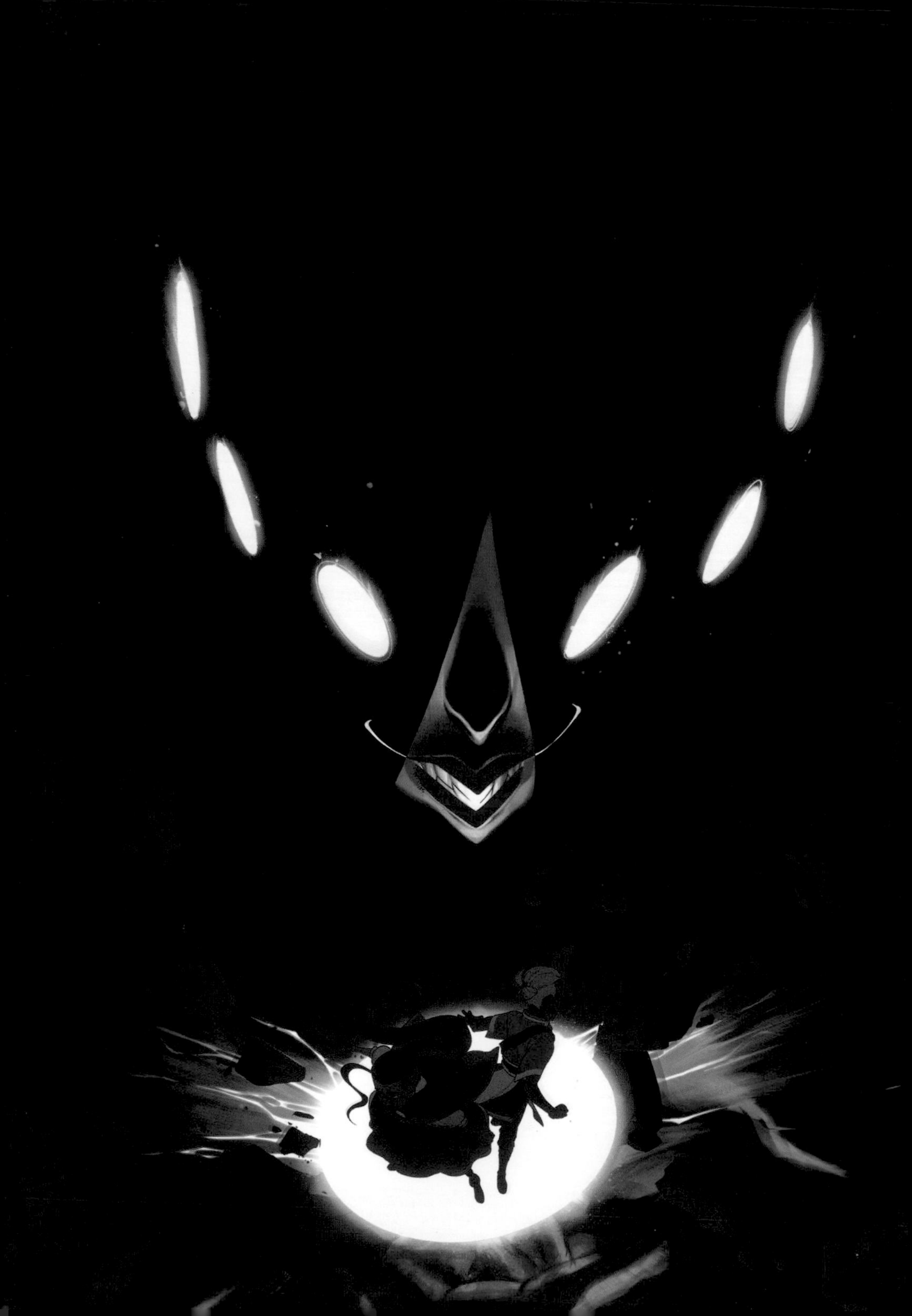

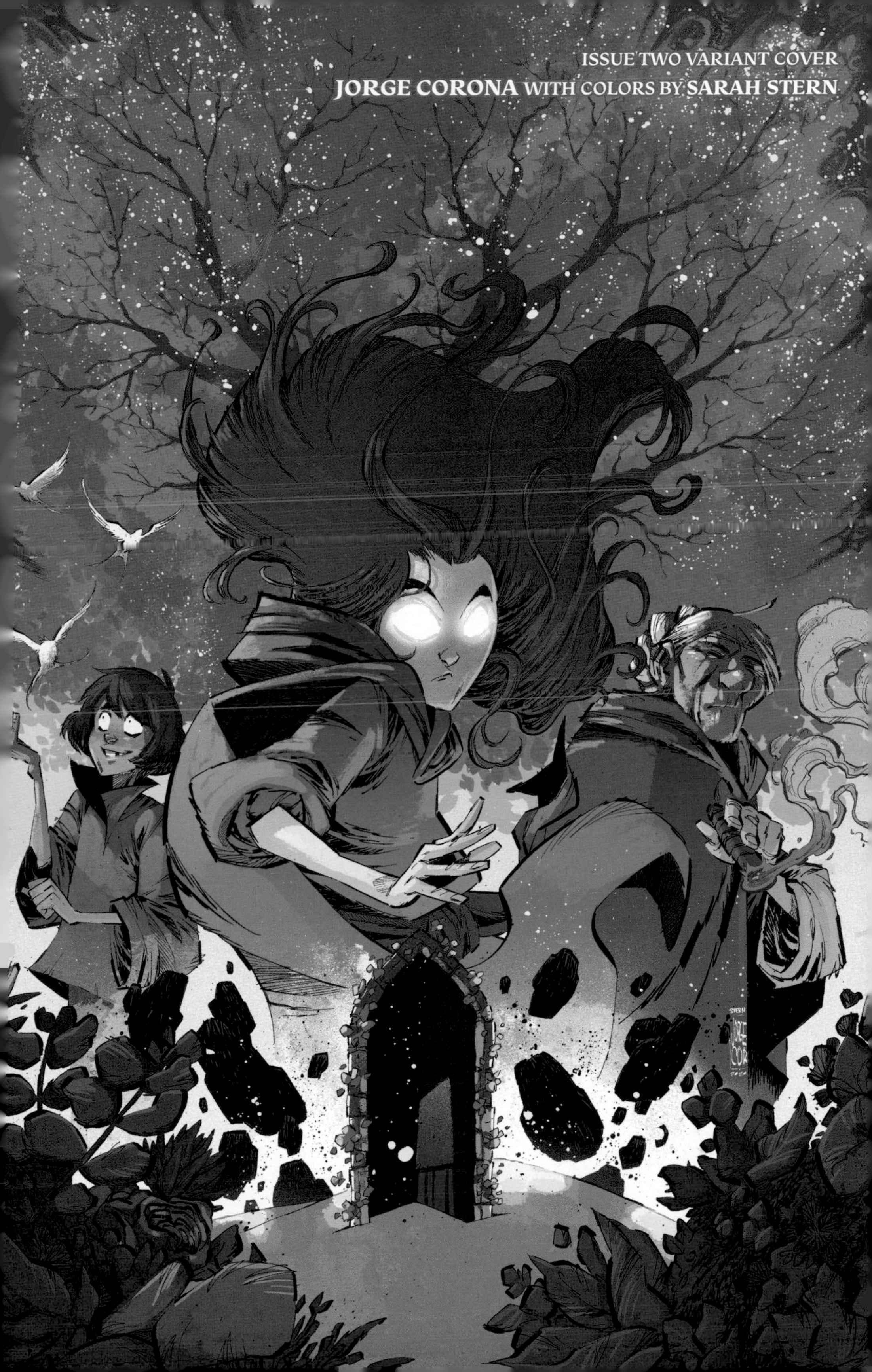
ISSUE TWO VARIANT COVER
JORGE CORONA WITH COLORS BY SARAH STERN
STERN

ISSUE THREE VARIANT COVER

JORGE CORONA WITH COLORS BY **SARAH STERN**

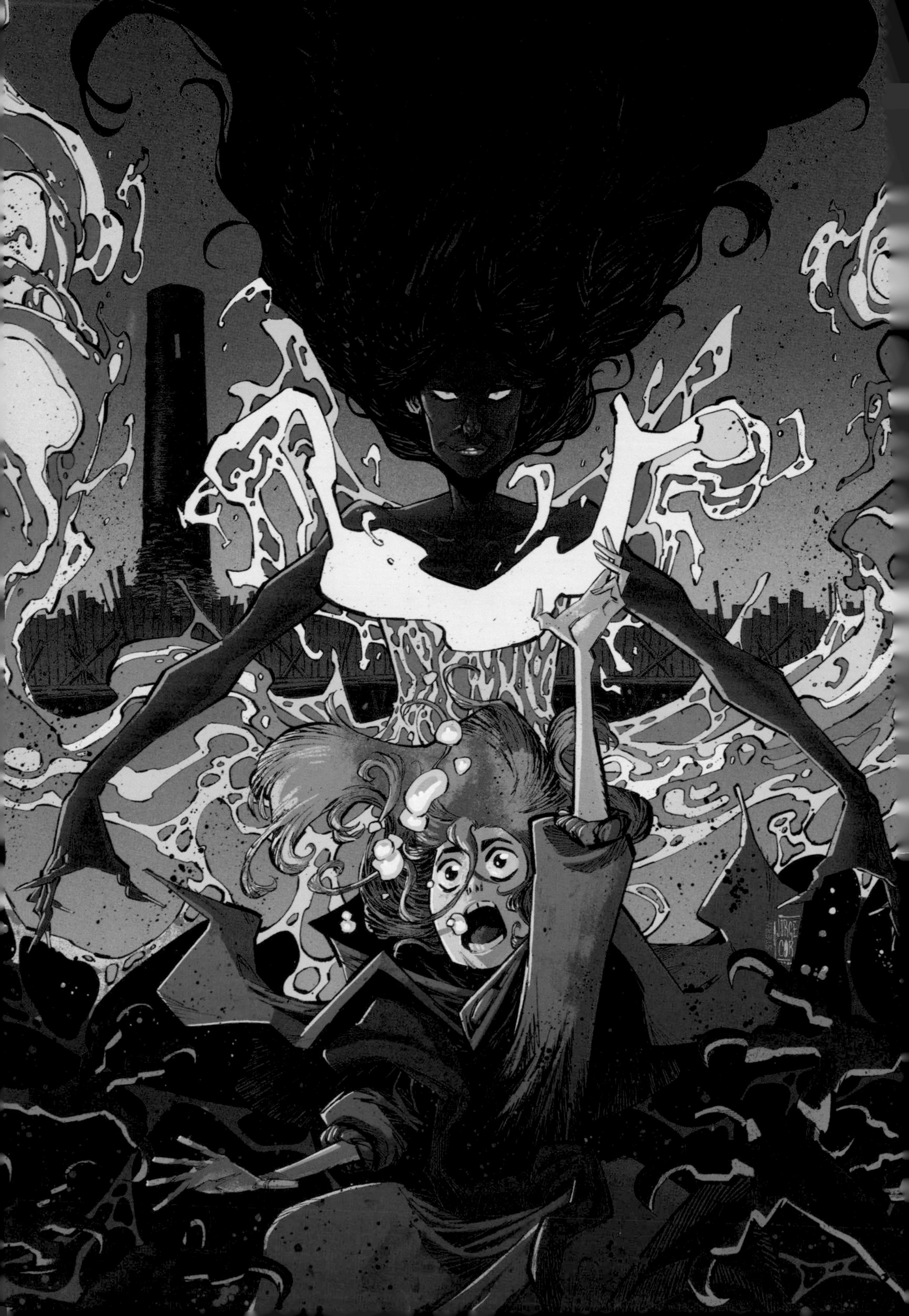

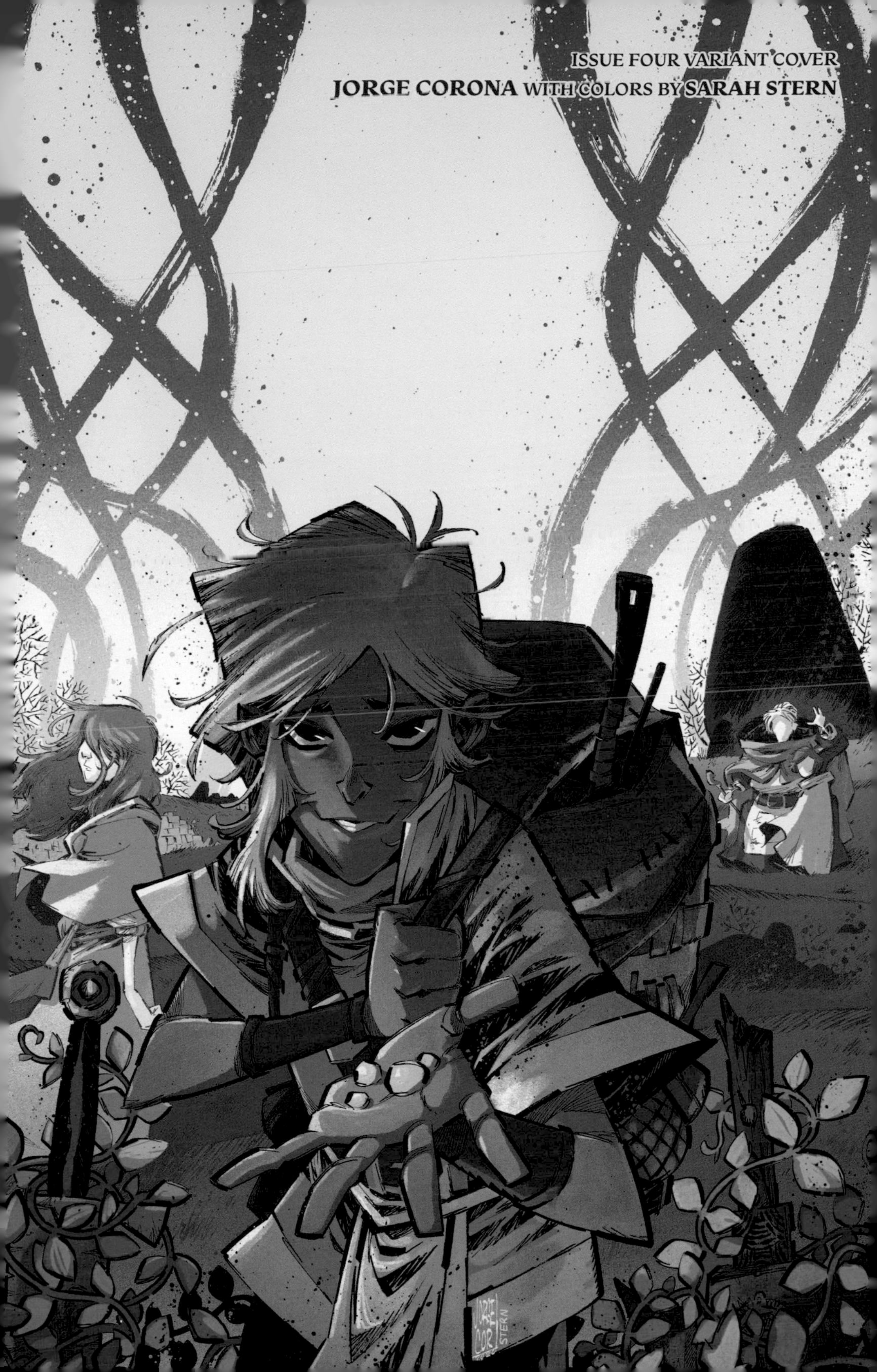

ISSUE FOUR VARIANT COVER

JORGE CORONA WITH COLORS BY **SARAH STERN**

ISSUE FIVE VARIANT COVER
JORGE CORONA WITH COLORS BY **SARAH STERN**

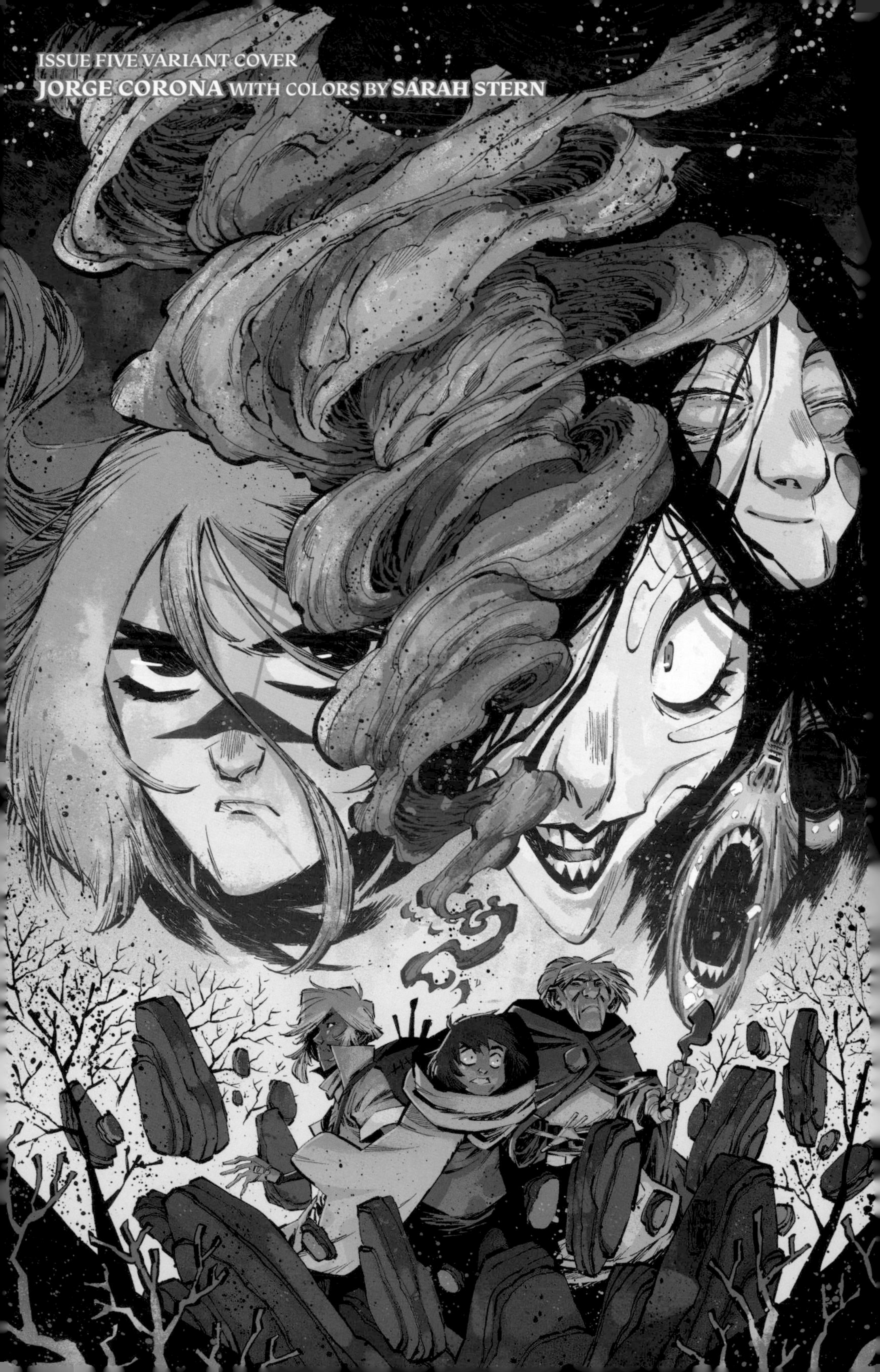